Against the glittering **____**
Adrienne Basso w**____**
mismatched co**____**
and destined for love.

P8-AQE-947

HER DESPERATE PROPOSAL

When pampered Faith Linden's father *and* her titled
fiancé, Viscount Dewhurst, die, she suddenly finds
herself in a desperately precarious position. The only
way Faith can hold on to her beloved family home is
to convince her late fiancé's younger brother, the
new Viscount Dewhurst, to marry her in his stead.
Yet when she finally encounters Lord Griffin Sainthill, she is in for a surprise: this brooding and rug-
gedly handsome adventurer is not so easily bent to
her will . . . and may be the man who can capture
her unsuspecting heart.

. . . SPARKED A STORMY PASSION

A sea captain and owner of a profitable shipping
company, Griffin Sainthill was quite happy with
his life in the American colonies. So when the
news of his inheritance finally reaches him, the
sun-bronzed seafarer is less than pleased. His
mood only darkens when he returns to England to
discover a brazen beauty intent on becoming
his bride! But when a twinge of conscience and a
stolen kiss give him pause, Griffin finds himself
embarking on the riskiest adventure of all—marriage
to a woman who will tempt him, torment him, and
turn his whole life upside down.

Books by Adrienne Basso

HIS WICKED EMBRACE

HIS NOBLE PROMISE

TO WED A VISCOUNT

Published by Zebra Books

TO WED A VISCOUNT

Adrienne Basso

ZEBRA BOOKS
KENSINGTON PUBLISHING CORP.
http://www.zebrabooks.com

To my sons, Rudy and Alex
who keep me humble
and remind me every day
what truly matters.

Prologue

Mayfair Manor
Hampshire, England
Spring, 1784

A muffled female scream from above stairs startled the two gentlemen, father and son, waiting restlessly in the drawing room. Echoing the cry of distress, the younger man leaped from his chair and started forward, but his father held him back. The son protested briefly, then rubbed his hand blearily over his face before distractedly gulping the contents of a glass of whiskey.

They settled back to wait in silence, the constant tick of the clock on the fireplace mantel the only sound breaking the quiet.

"This is madness. Whatever was I thinking, Father?" Fletcher Linden muttered with obvious self-loathing. "My wife is far too old to be going through such an exhausting ordeal. I fear her heart will break if she loses this child, and I know with certainty that mine shall shatter if Dorothea dies."

" 'Tis in God's hands," Montgomery Linden, Baron of Aston, replied, awkwardly patting his son's shoulder. "All that we can do now is pray."

Suddenly, the drawing-room doors burst open. The surgeon, ever mindful of the worried looks of Lord Aston and his son, wasted no time in making his announcement.

"I am most delighted and relieved to report that Mrs. Linden is safely delivered of her child. You may see her after her maid has removed the birthing-bed linens. Your daughter is very tiny, Mr. Linden, but appears healthy. When I left, she was squalling loud enough to hurt my ears. A good sign, I believe."

"God be praised," Fletcher mumbled. He staggered back as if his knees were too weak to support him and sank down onto a chair. The emotions overtaking him were almost painful. "Faith. My wife and I agreed if we should be so blessed to have a girl, we would call our daughter Faith."

" 'Tis fitting. Faith." Lord Aston beamed. He called for his servants and announced the birth of his granddaughter with great fanfare. The baron carried on so much that one would have thought he was the first man on earth to ever become a grandfather.

The news was greeted with shouts of good cheer and exclamations of astonishment. Feeling slightly dazed, Fletcher accepted the hearty handshakes and pats on the shoulder from several of the male servants and an emotional hug from the housekeeper, Mrs. Craig.

At long last the surgeon gave his permission and bade the anxious Fletcher to go upstairs and meet his daughter. He needed no additional urging. He bounded up the stairs two at a time and burst into the chamber just as the maid was leaving, her arms ladened with dirty linens.

Fletcher closed the door behind him. For a moment he didn't move or speak. He just stared at the woman who lay so quiet and still on the bed. Fear clutched at his heart. Surely the surgeon would have told him if there were any complications?

"Dorothea?"

Her eyelids fluttered, then opened. She smiled broadly when she saw him and roused herself from the pillows.

"Come closer my darling, and meet your daughter," Dorothea implored, drawing back the blanket from the tiny bundle nestled by her side.

"Oh, Lord." He swallowed tightly and moved forward slowly, taking small, reverent steps. "What a wonderfully clever woman you are, my love. Look at her. She is beyond perfect."

"Faith," Dorothea whispered, lifting the baby and cradling her tightly against her breast. "We have a child, Fletcher. After fifteen long years. 'Tis truly a miracle."

"I can scarcely believe it," he muttered, "even as I stare at the proof with my own eyes."

He knelt beside the bed. Joy and love and awe filled his heart to near bursting. Meeting his wife's watery eyes, Fletcher saw that she shared his wonderment and elation. With a trembling hand he stroked his finger along the baby's cheek, then bowed his head and pressed his lips lightly on her forehead.

The infant squirmed and cooed, then opened her mouth and yawned daintily. It was the most exquisite thing Fletcher had ever seen.

"It brings tears to my eyes just to look at her," Dorothea sniffed.

Fletcher smiled at his beloved wife through his own tears. He really should leave and let her rest. She was clearly exhausted and overwrought with emotion. He could hear the weariness in her speech. Yet he could not tear himself away from his wonderful, brand-new family.

"Shall we spoil her, my dearest?" Fletcher whispered. "Lavish her with attention and love, indulge her curiosities, encourage her spirit of adventure?"

Dorothea laughed. "She will become a terror."

"Nonsense." Fletcher gazed down at his child and felt a fierce stab of protection invade him. No one would dare think his child spoiled. Not as long as he was there to defend her.

He ran his finger again over the satiny smooth skin of her cheek. She blinked, then opened her eyes and stared at him fuzzily. With a small grunt she awkwardly thrust her fist into her mouth and sucked noisily. Another rush of tenderness invaded Fletcher.

Then a burst of panic invaded. What did he know about being a father? This tiny, innocent creature was now wholly dependent on him. Could he provide her with everything she needed to lead a happy, carefree life?

Fletcher felt momentarily light-headed as the enormity of what lay ahead struck fear in his heart. He wasn't a wealthy man. He and Dorothea lived comfortably, not extravagantly, here at Mayfair Manor with his father. It was a quiet, uncomplicated existence.

They were landed gentry, a lower rung on society's ladder. Respected within the rural community where they lived, yet hardly leaders of even this small society. Would this simple life be enough for his darling Faith?

He glanced down again at the baby. She had stopped sucking her fingers and fallen asleep. Her arms were held closely against her body and her face was scrunched up in a serious expression. She was so beautiful, so dear. The queer tightening in Fletcher's stomach eased.

He could not give his daughter boundless riches, high social position, or noble stature. He had neither a grand title nor an endless fortune. But he had something far more valuable to bestow so generously upon her. Love. And he vowed he would love and protect his little girl until the end of his days.

One

Captain Griffin Sainthill lay back against the soft pillows with a contented sigh and closed his eyes. The nimble lips and searching tongue of the most sought-after courtesan in all of Charleston was at this moment making a sensual journey downward over his naked body. Boldly the moist, hot strokes traveled across his bare chest, curving ribs, and flat abdomen until finally descending on the stiff erection between his legs.

Griffin groaned loudly as his body became lost in pure sensations. He and Suzanne had been indulging in all manner of bed sport for most of the day, and although darkness was beginning to fall, his appetite for this lush female remained strong.

Teasingly, she pulled her mouth off him and began nipping at the flesh of his inner thighs. He shifted his legs restlessly, but allowed her to direct their love play, confident her enthusiasm and expertise would bring them both to fulfillment.

Though not precisely a harlot, she was the type of woman he preferred—experienced and skillful in bed. She was beautiful, too. Graceful and exotic, with smooth olive-colored skin and thick, straight midnight-black hair that hung to her waist.

After nearly a month at sea he felt he was more than entitled to this day of pure decadence. Thanks to calm seas and a strong wind, the journey from the Bahamas had taken less time than usual and profits had exceeded expectations.

Griffin was well pleased with the run. It had been years since he traded along this southern route, and his latest success had him thinking it was time to include it as a regular route. Especially now that the shipping company he had put so much backbreaking work into for the past ten years was starting to show a handsome profit.

"You taste delicious," Suzanne purred. She rested her head against his flat stomach, and heat pooled in his lower body. He could feel her warm breath on his upper thighs, and a raw urgency began to climb.

He buried his hands in her dark, silky hair, guiding her downward. Understanding his need, she cupped him gently in her hands and swirled her tongue around the tip of his throbbing erection. He squeezed his eyes shut and bucked his hips. Suzanne laughed merrily. "Do you like that, my lord?"

Despite the fire she was building low in his belly, Griffin pulled back. "I've asked you not to call me that, Suzanne," he lectured gruffly.

"But why?" She lifted her head to look at him, pushing her hair back from her face. "The letter came from England before you set sail for Nassau. Everyone knows of its contents. Are you not pleased with your new circumstances? The unfortunate death of both your father and older brother have left you with a noble title. You are now Viscount Dewhurst."

"English titles are a ridiculous pretension in the

Colonies," Griffin insisted. "I shall not be using mine."

Suzanne's expression was disbelieving. Griffin sighed with frustration. He had told her numerous times he did not wish to be addressed by his newly acquired title. That was part of the life he had left back in England long ago. It had nothing to do with the man he was today.

"I think you are being exceedingly foolish," Suzanne declared. She slid her body against his, her lush breasts pressing against his side. Purring into his ear she added softly, "But I do not wish to argue."

"Nor do I." Griffin flashed her a sensual smile. Placing his large hands on her hips, he swung her around and lifted her in the air. She gave a little scream of surprise that turned to a low moan of delight as he positioned her across his lap.

Their eyes met. Without any warning, Griffin pulled her sharply downward, entering her in one swift motion. She gasped, but not in pain, for her moist body readily accepted his length. Immediately she began rising and falling upon him. He squeezed her hips and urged her to a faster, deeper rhythm, and she eagerly complied.

In the wake of their sexual delight Griffin's previous anger faded. He could not really fault Suzanne for being so impressed with his suddenly discovered nobility. She had lived all of her life here in Charleston, rising to her current occupation through cunning and skill. Though it was rumored that she slept with some of the most influential gentlemen in town, none of them were of the English aristocracy.

Griffin acknowledged it wasn't just Suzanne—everyone had been acting differently toward him since he had received the news of his inheritance. Even some members of his crew had given him strange looks as he stood at the helm and guided the ship. Yet what initially began as a nuisance was fast becoming an annoyance.

As a second son he had always known he would have to make his own way in the world. As a child it had disturbed him greatly, knowing his older brother, Neville, would one day inherit the family titles and lands, yet as he grew to manhood, Griffin learned to appreciate the freedom his birth order gave him.

Their father had expectations of a career in the military for his second son, which the independent-minded Griffin scoffed at, and he had laughed outright when his father next suggested the clergy. Viscount Dewhurst was therefore more than pleased when his younger son decided to strike out on his own, asking only for a modest stipend with which to found his shipping business.

The life had suited Griffin. He kept an infrequent correspondence with his two younger sisters, but that was the extent of his family relationships for ten years. He had felt sadness when receiving the news of his father's and brother's deaths, yet was more dismayed to realize he now had duties and responsibilities awaiting him back in England.

He had chafed at the notion of returning home, knowing once he went back, his life would forever be changed. And not necessarily for the better.

"Harder," Suzanne whispered, biting his earlobe. "Faster." Her hips lifted, and he could feel her body contracting around him. Lord, she was a lush little piece. Griffin lay back and closed his eyes. The room was now pleasantly silent, save for the erotic slapping noises their bodies made as they came together.

The sensual mood was suddenly shattered by a loud,

persistent pounding on the bedchamber door. Fearing danger, Griffin abruptly disengaged his body from Suzanne's, moving so fast he pushed her off the bed.

She shrieked with indignity as she fell, but he ignored her, reaching instead for the loaded pistol he always kept at his bedside, no matter where he slept.

"No need to shoot, Captain," a rusty voice declared. "It's just me."

The bedchamber door was slightly ajar. The brave soul who had initially opened it was now wisely hiding behind it. Yet Griffin recognized the voice of the intruder. It was Harry Dobbins, a member of his crew.

"What's wrong, Dobbins? Is there a problem with the ship? Or one of the crew?"

"Not exactly a problem, Captain," Dobbins replied. "I suppose you could say it is more of a . . . a situation. But I need to see you. Right away."

"Come in, then," Griffin commanded. When it came to matters concerning his ships there was never any question of the importance.

Suzanne shrieked again at his words. She scrambled to her feet and dove for the bedcovers. Then she picked up a pillow and threw it at his head. Griffin caught it and grinned.

Still smiling, he watched Dobbins, a tough-looking, bald-headed sailor, poke his head around the bedchamber door.

"I've got someone here I think you need to see, Captain," he explained nervously.

The seaman then opened the door completely, and in a most uncharacteristically gentle manner, ushered in a young mulatto woman and a small boy. The woman was dressed as a servant. However, the child clutching her hand was wearing clothes that were a little small and a little worn, but of costlier material.

Griffin stared at the pair for several long moments. He was fairly certain he had never before seen either of them.

"Explain yourself, Dobbins," Griffin commanded.

The seaman shuffled his feet. "I didn't know what else to do, Captain. She came to the ship and said she needed to see you right away. I knew you were here, so I brought her over."

"It could not have waited until morning?"

"I didn't think so."

"Well, young woman—" Griffin paused, as the servant's blushes and averted eyes reminded him he was reclining in bed without a stitch. With a casual air, he pulled the sheet up higher, slightly above his waist. "What precisely can I do for you?"

The girl glanced down briefly at the child by her side, then looked beseechingly at Dobbins. Astonishingly, the seaman flushed to the top of his bald head.

"She came to the ship, sir, looking for you," Dobbins repeated. "She brought the lad, along with this letter." He reached into his pocket and pulled out a folded parchment.

Griffin noted the letter was unsealed. With a grave air, he accepted the paper. "I presume you read it?"

"As best I could." Dobbins ran his hand over his bushy side-whiskers. "I never took much to reading and writing. Most of the crew's onshore, enjoying themselves. Those that are left read less than I do, so I couldn't ask anyone for help."

The sailor leaned closer and added in a gruff whisper, "Besides, what I did understand made me realize that this is your *private* business, Captain. I thought it best not to let anyone else see it. It concerns the boy."

The two men shifted their eyes to the small child

clutching the woman's hand. The boy made a small sound of distress and shrank behind her skirts.

"Are you his mother?" Griffin asked the young woman.

"I am his nursemaid. His mother is dead."

Griffin frowned. He hadn't gotten a very close look at the child, yet there was something disturbingly familiar about him.

Turning his back on the trio, Griffin swung his legs over the side of the bed and read the note. He felt Suzanne shift restlessly beside him. Griffin angled his head toward her absently, and she gave him a saucy grin only he could see, running her tongue suggestively along her front teeth.

Her playful sexuality helped to lighten his mood. But not for long. As he read the brief letter, he could feel his jaw tense. He bent forward and took a gasping breath, then reached down and scooped his breeches off the floor.

Slowly he pulled them on, detachably realizing that he had hardly absorbed the words on the page, yet they were burned in his brain.

I am sending you our son, dear Griffin, in hopes that you will find it in your heart to acknowledge and care for him. He has known little happiness in his short life and needs a father's protection, if not his love. Since I am no longer able, I beg you, take care of him.

Dressed in breeches and a hastily donned shirt, Griffin once again faced the mulatto servant. He moved closer, his lip curled in a tight, humorless smile. "You know what the letter says, do you not?"

"Y-yes." She pressed her trembling lips together.

"She asks you to care for him, because you are the boy's father."

"Who sent you?" Griffin reached out and grasped the servant's arm. "I want to talk to them. Now."

"You . . . You cannot, sir." She backed away fearfully, but Griffin tightened his grip. "The letter was written by the boy's mother, Rosemary Morton."

"You said his mother is dead."

"She is, sir. Nearly six months now." The maid's mouth twisted into a thin line as she slipped from his grasp. "The sickness came on her fast. I swear she used her last ounce of strength to write that letter. And she made me promise that if the *Defiant* ever came back to Charleston, I would take her child and this note and deliver them both to Captain Griffin Sainthill."

Rosemary Morton. Griffin racked his brain for a memory, a face to place on that vaguely familiar name. Finally the image came to mind, a tiny redhaired young woman with blue eyes, lush lips, and a ready smile.

They had met at a party he had attended hoping to further his business connections. Rosemary's father was a wealthy merchant, eager to trade goods with all the brash young sea captains.

Griffin had thought the merchant's daughter a fetching lass. There was a delicate beauty about her that appealed to him, a sultry sexiness behind the innocent facade that beckoned. She had danced with many men that night, but favored him with the most teasing and flirtatious conversation.

He had been delighted to discover she was not the sheltered virgin he had first believed. Consequently, they had shared a brief interlude of mutual satisfaction the last time he had been in Charleston. Roughly four years ago.

"How old is the boy?" Griffin asked.

"His third birthday was in August."

The timing was right. Yet Griffin was not so easily convinced. He had lived his adult life as a carefree bachelor, moving from woman to woman, seeking mutual pleasures wherever they were to be found. Yet he had deliberately chosen partners who had both skill and experience. In all of his thirty-three years there had never been a child.

"Where do you live? Who cares for the boy now that his mother is gone?" Griffin wanted to know.

"We live with the child's grandfather, Mr. Joshua Morton, out on the Sommerville Plantation." The maid stroked the boy's shoulder, and he nestled closer. "I watch over him as I have done since he was born."

Griffin frowned. Perhaps this was a mistake. "The Joshua Morton I knew was a merchant trader, not a farmer."

The servant grimaced. "Mr. Morton bought the plantation and moved my mistress out of the city when her condition became too noticeable. Once she took up residence at the plantation, she never left. The master even buried her out there, refusing to bring her body to the church graveyard in town where her mother lies."

Griffin scratched his head. He needed time to think, time to straighten this all out. "I will speak with Joshua Morton early tomorrow morning."

"No!" The servant stepped forward boldly, then glanced nervously down at the boy. She placed both arms around the child protectively. "My mistress never told her father who you were, sir. I know that he hates the man who ruined his daughter, nearly as much as he dislikes his grandson. I was only able to come here tonight because Mr. Morton is gone from the plantation. I fear greatly what he will do to me and the child if he finds out I have seen you."

A jolt of raw pain collided in Griffin's stomach. He glanced down at the boy. Even in its childish innocence, that hauntingly familiar face, black hair, and gray eyes were so very much like his own that Griffin knew he could not possibly deny the truth. *My son,* he admitted. *My flesh and blood. He has known little happiness in his short life.*

His conscience pinched him. Perhaps the first years of the boy's life might have been different if he'd known of his existence, but Griffin could not be certain.

"What is your name?" he asked softly.

The child lowered his chin and stared silently down at the toes of his shoes.

"He is shy of strangers," the servant apologized.

"But I am not a stranger, am I? I am his father." Griffin swallowed his impatience and squatted down on his haunches, so they were at eye level. "What is your name?"

The child lifted his head and regarded Griffin solemnly. "Neville," he finally whispered.

Neville! Griffin's eyes began to sting, but he fought against the emotion. His brother had been named Neville. Few people knew that fact, but he distinctly remembered that Rosemary Morton had been one of those few.

"I sail for England at the end of the month," Griffin announced gruffly. Now that he had a son, the responsibilities of his newly acquired title suddenly seemed very important. "Can you be ready?"

"You want to take the child with you? Across the ocean?"

Griffin watched as tears welled in the maid's eyes and realized she had not considered this possibility. The child, seeing her distress, stroked her hand gently.

"Perhaps it would be best not to separate him from you," Griffin said slowly. "I will make the necessary arrangements with Morton for you to accompany us. Once we arrive in England, I shall grant you your freedom," he added impulsively. "You may continue as the boy's nursemaid until he goes away to school."

The young woman took a deep, shuttering breath and lifted her chin. "I am not a slave. I'm a free woman, bound to no man or mistress. But I cannot leave my mother and sisters. I will come with you, to care for the child on the long journey, but you must promise to pay my return passage so I can come home to them."

Griffin nodded in agreement. "Passage can be arranged back to the Colonies on one of my ships." He reached out and gently ruffled the boy's hair. It was surprisingly soft and fine. "Dobbins will see you both safely to Sommerville Plantation tonight. When will Morton return?"

"Tomorrow night."

"Excellent. I shall come for you and Neville tomorrow afternoon. Once you are safely aboard my ship, I will return to speak with Joshua Morton."

The maid's eyes widened in alarm, but she didn't refute his decision. "Tomorrow afternoon," she repeated slowly. "We shall be waiting."

There was an awkward silence. Griffin slowly stood up. "Pray, in all the confusion I forgot to inquire. What is your name?"

The servant blushed prettily and managed a crooked smile. "Mary. Mary Dawson, sir."

"I thank you, Mary Dawson, for taking such fine care of Neville. And I trust you to keep him safe until he is under my protection."

"Oh, I will," Mary replied earnestly. She dropped a small curtsy, then turned to the child. "Say good-bye to the captain."

"Good-bye, sir."

The sweet, trusting, childish voice echoed through the quiet room. Griffin found he had to swallow twice before he could reply. "Good-bye, Neville. I shall see you tomorrow."

Griffin gave Dobbins a forceful glance.

"Aye, Captain, I'll keep watch out for the both of them," the sailor said.

Griffin waited till the bedchamber door shut, before walking back to the four-poster bed and sitting slowly down on the edge of the mattress. Caught up in his emotional mood, he barely noticed when Suzanne moved closer and placed a comforting hand upon his shoulder.

"He is a fine little boy," she said quietly.

Griffin nodded his head. He felt disgusted with himself for the pain the child had suffered due to his neglect. Logically he knew it wasn't his fault, for how could he have cared for the boy when he did not even know of his existence?

Still, something clenched in his gut. Injustice of any kind had always rankled Griffin, but cruelty to an innocent child was an unpardonable offense. Especially when the child was his son.

He shut his eyes for a moment to gather his strength. It certainly had been one hell of a month. In just a few short weeks he had become a viscount, and now it appeared he had also become a father.

Hawthorne Castle
Hampshire, England
Late May, 1809

"Do you think Griffin will arrive today, Harriet?"

Harriet Sainthill glanced up from the soft linen handkerchief she was carefully embroidering and smiled fleetingly at her younger sister.

"I suppose it is possible, Elizabeth. Griffin's letter arrived two days ago. When traveling from great distances, more often than not the person arrives before the missive informing one of the impending visit."

"But Griffin won't be visiting," Elizabeth insisted. "He is coming home to stay." She lifted her arms above her head and twirled around with joyful abandon. "I can hardly wait. Once he arrives, I know he shall set everything to rights." Elizabeth suddenly ceased her spinning. "Gracious, I just realized that I don't even know what Griffin looks like."

Harriet shook her head and selected a bright red piece of silk thread from her sewing basket. "You were only a child when he left, barely seven years old. I imagine he has changed significantly over the years. Most men do, even older brothers."

"It does not matter," Elizabeth insisted. She flopped gracelessly into a worn chair, then turned her head to stare out the window. "I am certain Griffin will be dashing and handsome and charming. A true gentleman. Remember the lovely Christmas gifts he sent us last year? You often remarked how that beautiful silk shawl boasted the finest embroidery you had ever seen. Clearly he has exquisite taste."

"It was Christmas two years past," Harriet replied calmly, yet she held her tongue after one glance at Elizabeth's crestfallen face.

It was obvious that the seventeen-year-old Elizabeth was firmly convinced all would be well once their brother arrived. Harriet, older by several years and wiser by cynical experience, had no illusions about the future.

Griffin's appearance could very well mean their salvation, but it could also plunge them into great despair. Harriet had learned the hard way it was best to reserve judgment when it came to the male members of the family.

"Nevertheless, it shall be wonderful to have Griffin home with us," Elizabeth insisted, but Harriet noticed her sister's hands were fidgeting nervously with the hem of her skirt.

Harriet immediately regretted both her words and attitude. The time might come quickly enough when Elizabeth's hopes would be dashed. It would only be cruel to hasten the disillusionment.

"I'm certain things will change once Griffin assumes the title," Harriet allowed with a tight smile. "I too look forward to his arrival."

It wasn't precisely a lie. At least the statement about changes. Still, Harriet was worried. She knew little about her brother, and what she had gleaned over the years through snatches of overheard conversations did not inspire great hope.

It appeared that Griffin was something of a rogue, with a penchant for the ladies and a zest for danger in both his business and personal life. Harriet could only pray that her brother wasn't a true rake, a man considered beyond redemption, lacking in even an ounce of moral fiber.

As unmarried women, both she and Elizabeth would be under his complete control, subject to his moods and whims.

"I'm hoping Griffin's past generosity will hold true once he returns home," Elizabeth said. "It would be lovely to order a fresh new wardrobe once we put away our black mourning gowns."

"Let us hope his business ventures have proven to be profitable," Harriet said, finding it impossible this time to hide the bitterness in her voice. What if her brother proved to be as miserly in his support as their father? Harriet nearly shuddered at the notion. "It will take nothing less than a fortune to clear the debts Father and Neville left behind and restore our finances."

"Is it really all that bad?" Elizabeth asked in a quiet voice, as she poked the tip of her small finger through a worn section of material on her skirt.

" 'Tis bad enough," Harriet replied, reaching for the scissors in her embroidery basket. She knotted, then snipped the end of the thread. "But that shall be Griffin's problem, not ours. Come, now, Elizabeth, no gloomy thoughts. Tell me about your visit to the village this morning."

The smile Harriet sought came easily to Elizabeth's lips. Harriet's heart softened. Her sister was in many ways still a child. Unspoiled, fresh, and trusting. She would need protection from the world that was unkind to those who made decisions with their hearts instead of their heads.

Harriet had already decided that if Griffin was unable or unwilling to provide that protection then she would assume the duty. After all, she had been looking after Elizabeth since their mother's death, which had occurred only a year after Elizabeth was born.

"There was quite a crowd at the butcher's this morning," Elizabeth said, and she began relating tales of her morning outing. "His wife has given birth to her sixth baby. Can you believe it? The child was a girl, just as all the others, but Mr. Jenkins seemed quite proud when he told me the good news. Imagine having six daughters!"

Elizabeth's grin widened before she continued. "Oh, and I saw Miss Linden in the apothecary. Her housekeeper has a nagging toothache and Miss Linden was searching for a cure. She inquired about your health and bade me to give you her regards."

Harriet's eyes narrowed. Miss Faith Linden was one name she definitely did not wish to hear.

"She also inquired about Griffin's return," Elizabeth added softly.

Harriet sat up straighter in her chair, her embroidery hastily tossed aside and forgotten. "What did she ask you about Griffin?"

Elizabeth looked surprised, and Harriet realized her urgent tone had startled her sister. But the question was too important to be withdrawn. So Harriet repeated it. "What did Miss Linden ask you?"

"She only wished to know if we had heard anything further about when Griffin might be expected home," Elizabeth replied slowly. "I thought her interest in the family showed both concern and regard for our circumstances. She seemed most disappointed to learn I had no new information."

"Oh, I can well imagine her disappointment," Harriet responded grimly. "I have no doubt that Miss Linden is hoping Griffin shall rescue her from that ridiculous will her father left. Well, she'll have to look elsewhere for salvation. With Neville's death she lost her final hold on the Dewhurst title."

"I don't understand why you dislike Miss Linden so," Elizabeth admonished. "She has always been most kind to me. And you."

"She has shown kindness only when it either suited or benefited her," Harriet insisted. "Faith Linden is spoiled, selfish, and foolish. I never understood why Father wanted Neville to marry her. Though not openly touched by scandal, her family is hardly on a social par with ours. Her father was only a baron."

"I do not believe that Father placed such a great emphasis on titles," Elizabeth said quietly.

"Well, he was wrong," Harriet retorted with a cynical grimace. "I confess to being thoroughly delighted that Neville never followed through on his promise to wed Miss Linden, for I would not have wanted her to become a part of our family."

"Harriet!" For a second Elizabeth stared at her with pure horror etched on her lovely face. "How can you be so cruel? Poor Miss Linden waited years for Neville to become her husband. I should think that given your current situation with your own fiancé you would have more sympathy."

"Our situations are nothing alike," Harriet responded hotly. She could feel the anger building inside her, that feeling of helpless frustration she'd had too often whenever she thought of her own uncertain future. "Julian is an important member of Wellington's staff. 'Tis his duty to the king that keeps him from my side.

"Army officers are a noble breed of men, with unquestionable loyalties and a tremendous sense of honor. Julian agonized over our future before he left England, but decided it would be best to wait until victory is won before we take our marriage vows. I feel honored that he holds my feelings in such high regard. 'Tis my privilege to wait for his return."

Harriet uttered the final words with almost religious fever, hoping if she repeated it enough, both in her head and out loud, she might finally come to believe it. The truth was, Elizabeth's words had struck a sensitive nerve. Harriet's greatest fear was that she would end up exactly like Faith Linden, a lonely spinster, engaged to a man who had no intention of ever marrying her.

"I imagine Miss Linden will wish to call upon Griffin when he does arrive," Elizabeth said tentatively, her voice dropping to a whisper.

Harriet drew in a sharp breath of exclamation. "If Miss Linden does have the nerve to call, we must make certain not to be at home to her."

She pulled a fresh length of embroidery thread from her basket and snapped it, then poked it through the eye of the needle. She attacked her embroidery with a vengeance, gritting her teeth against the pain that still remained strong at anything that reminded her of Faith Linden.

Gradually, Harriet's temper and passion calmed as she began working the delicate stitches of a flower. Yet her mind continued to contemplate the potential difficulties Faith Linden might cause for the family.

Harriet had long considered it a stroke of pure luck that their eldest brother Neville hadn't married the Linden chit. And Harriet fully intended to make sure that Griffin would do the same as his brother.

Two

"Is there nothing I can say that will dissuade you, Faith?" a soft, feminine voice entreated.

"Not a single thing."

Miss Faith Linden stoically repositioned the bonnet on her head and grimaced at her plain reflection. It was difficult to decide if the hat made her look older or duller or both. "To be honest, I did not think the newly entitled Viscount Dewhurst would stay more than a single night after he saw the deplorable condition of his estate. I thought he would whisk his sisters away to town at the first opportunity. Yet he has remained in residence for a full week. I dare not wait any longer."

"I still do not understand why you must confront him directly," Lady Meredith Barrington admonished, brushing a few specks of lint from Faith's shoulders. "Could you not write him a letter and ask him to call upon you at his earliest convenience?"

Faith sighed. If only it were that simple. "I have already written a letter and received no reply. If I do not somehow force my way into his house, he shall be gone and I will have missed my opportunity to plead my case."

"Do you think the viscount knows of the will?"

"He must." Faith's lips tightened. "Harrowby is a

small village that thrives on gossip. I'll wager that Father's will has been the talk around many a dinner table for months. Not to mention sweetening the conversation as the locals share a few rounds of ale at the Rose and Thistle Tavern.

"Besides, I'm certain both of the viscount's sisters know of it. How could they not? Elizabeth might not have mentioned anything to her brother, but I feel certain Harriet shall take great delight in informing him of my circumstances."

"I suppose, then, that we must conclude the viscount knows about the will," Meredith reluctantly agreed. She reached out and squeezed Faith's hand in a sympathetic gesture of support. "Perhaps he is just waiting for a proper time to broach the subject with you."

Faith made a grunting noise in her throat. *Dear Merry, ever the optimist.* In times of difficulties she could always be counted upon to offer encouragement, though in this case Faith viewed it as false hope.

Their mothers had been first cousins, but Meredith had long acted as the sister Faith had wished for as a child. They had been raised in different circumstances, far away from each other, but Meredith's annual summer visits to Mayfair Manor, which began when the girls were only four years old, had created a bond between the women that neither time nor distance could diminish.

The lessons of girlhood, the tortures of adolescence, the challenges of womanhood, were all conveyed, experienced, and shared by both girls during those long summer days and nights. They would spend hours talking, reliving each event they deemed important and significant, then next turn their attention toward dreaming and speculating about their yet to be realized futures.

The extended summer visits had ceased when the girls reached their maturity, but diligent correspondence and shorter visits throughout the years had kept their relationship strong. Faith doubted she could have survived the trials of the last few months without the sympathetic ear and steady support of Meredith. Her dearest friend had been the one constant in an otherwise frightening, desperate time.

"There, I am ready." Faith picked up her reticule and turned expectantly to Meredith. "How do I look?"

"Charming as always," Meredith replied loyally. "Although I must confess it troubles me deeply, knowing what you are about to do. A lady never visits a gentleman's home unannounced and uninvited. And you are going alone, without a proper chaperon."

"My dire circumstances demand such boldness," Faith insisted with a slight quiver. In truth, it was not the propriety of her actions but the outrageous, intimate nature of her request that had her a bundle of nerves.

Meredith frowned but did not contradict Faith's explanation. "No matter how many times I have struggled to make sense of it, I just cannot understand your father's reasoning. Whatever was he thinking when he added that ridiculous codicil to his will?"

Faith bit her lip. Oh, how many times had she asked herself that very question? "I believe Father was trying his best to protect me. When he fell ill last winter, he knew in his heart he was too sick to recover. Yet how could he die in peace with my future so unsettled?

"The old viscount had succumbed weeks before to the same illness and his son showed no inclination toward honoring the marriage contract our fathers had made so many years ago. How could I, a mere woman, possibly hope to succeed in making Neville Sainthill, who was now Viscount Dewhurst, marry me when both his father and mine had failed?"

Faith closed her eyes briefly. "By Father stipulating in his will that I must marry Viscount Dewhurst before the year of mourning ended or else I would forfeit Mayfair Manor, Father thought to give me an advantage. A means to press my claim for marriage, a way to finally bring my errant fiancé up to scratch."

Faith remembered well how upset her father was over the lack of interest and affection shown to her by her intended bridegroom. Dear loyal Father, who saw beyond her plain looks and intellectual leaning, who thought she was far more than a small, skinny woman with mud-colored hair, dull brown eyes, and a too pointy chin. He thought her worthy of a prince, but was well pleased to offer her a viscount.

Shaking off the memories, Faith continued. "Viscount Dewhurst's estate is badly in need of both the substantial income and varied resources Mayfair can offer. Father knew Neville well enough to decide he would not let that prize slip through his fingers. Neville might have found it easy to disregard me, but he would have been hard-pressed to ignore the bounty of the estate."

"I don't understand why your father insisted on Dewhurst," Meredith commented. "Neville's behavior proved he was hardly a good candidate for a husband."

"I think Father believed Neville's attitude toward me would change once we were married. Besides, as a mere baron, Father was always enamored with the notion that I should marry above my station."

Meredith's eyes narrowed. "Good intentions aside,

the results your father had hoped to achieve for you by that silly will have hardly been realized. Such a typical example of a man's pigheaded nature. They see no other possible consequences for their actions except those they desire." Meredith shook her head, her lovely face full of sympathy. "Thanks to this odious will, Neville's sudden, untimely death has left you facing a future without a husband and the prospect of losing your beloved home."

Faith forced a small laugh. "I believe I was always faced with the prospect of no future husband. Gracious, Neville and I had been engaged for seven years. He was in no hurry to rush me to the altar."

Meredith shook her head again. "I still believe your best chance lies with the courts. I have heard of wills that demand marriage by a certain age in order to claim an inheritance, but I have never heard of either the bride nor bridegroom being specifically named. Honestly, Faith, I have serious doubts that this section of the will is legal."

"Don't you understand, Merry? Naming the groom is the very point that can save me and Mayfair Manor." Faith grasped Meredith's hand eagerly. "The will does not name Neville Sainthill specifically as my future bridegroom; instead it names Viscount Dewhurst. In this instance, I believe that Neville's death doesn't null the clause, but actually strengthens it.

"Given my past experiences with my fiancé, I might have a far better chance of convincing his brother, Griffin, to honor the wishes of our fathers and unite our families in marriage. Then Mayfair Manor will be mine."

"Along with a total stranger for a husband," Meredith said dryly.

Faith cleared her throat and turned away. She could

not meet Meredith's eyes. "Griffin Sainthill is not precisely a stranger. I knew him when we were children."

"So did I, though not nearly as well as you. I mostly remember that he never wanted to include us in any of the games he and his brother devised, merely because we were girls. And I also recall receiving many letters from you complaining of Griffin's outrageous antics," Meredith exclaimed. She sat on the edge of the bed and primly folded her hands in her lap. "He was an undisciplined, unconventional, and completely wild youth. I have no doubt he has grown into a thoroughly disreputable man."

Faith bit back her smile. Oh, how dearly she hoped that were true. She could use a little wildness in her dull, staid life. "It isn't like you to be so critical of someone you do not know," Faith said gently.

"Of course. Forgive me." Meredith rubbed her hand vigorously against her temples. "I am just so worried about you, Faith. If only you would wait until my parents return from Greece. I'm sure that Papa's solicitors can help. They might even be able to declare the will illegal."

Faith straightened her spine and tried very hard to look confident. As much as she appreciated the offer, it wasn't possible to wait. Meredith's father, the earl of Stafford, was a good and honorable man, who loved his family dearly, but he was not known for his reliability.

Who else but an eccentric earl with a scholarly passion for antiquities and his devoted wife would be traipsing around Greece while the madman Napoleon lay siege to half of Europe? Faith knew it could easily be months before the earl and countess returned to England. And years before the matter of the will was settled.

"I cannot afford to wait any longer," Faith insisted. "My distant cousin Cyril was delighted to inherit Father's title, but most disappointed to discover there was little income attached to it. 'Tis he who will become the new owner if I am forced out, and I know he would like nothing better than to get his hands on Mayfair Manor. I cannot waste any more time. I must speak with the viscount today."

"I still believe you should wait for him to contact you. Yet I know you well enough to recognize that stubborn set of your chin," Meredith replied with a gentle smile.

Faith blinked rapidly, nearly blinded by the sight. That gentle smile had transformed Meredith's delicate face to breathless beauty. Though she loved Merry like a sister, a fierce pang of jealousy shot through her. Gazing at her friend's loveliness reminded her far too sharply of her own lack of beauty.

Faith believed she had long ago accepted the truth of her looks, acknowledging that she possessed little physical feminine appeal. Still, there was no denying that her chances of succeeding today with Viscount Dewhurst would be far greater if she possessed just an ounce of Meredith's stunning looks.

Ah, well, no use wishing for the moon, as her dear Papa would say. *Dearest Papa.* Faith took a deep breath and swallowed back the lump of emotion that seized her throat. How she missed him! Mother's death five years ago had been difficult, but Papa had been there to offer strength and courage. With him gone, there was no one else, save Merry.

Papa had doted on Faith as no other person ever had, nor, she sadly suspected, ever would. Special treats at dinner, a new bonnet because it was Tuesday, a pony of her very own even before she could ride.

Her mother had often remarked to her husband that he was spoiling their child, but her father merely grinned with mischief when his wife made such comments and gently kissed away the objections.

Observing the love, affection, and easy manner between her parents had fueled Faith's dreams to one day achieve such a union for herself. Those dreams were now gone, along with the parents she had loved. Her only goal now was to hold on to Mayfair Manor, the home of her childhood, the place where such love had once flourished.

"I cannot let the estate go without a fight," Faith said forcefully.

"I never thought you would." Meredith's laughter rang out. "If you are so bound and determined to embark upon this scandalous course, then you must at least allow me to accompany you. I'm only a year older, but a twenty-five-year-old unmarried chaperon is better than none at all. I can easily delay my return to town for another day."

"No!" Faith was truly horrified. Standing beside the statuesque beauty of Lady Meredith would make her look every inch the little brown wren. She was determined to at least spare herself that humiliation. "If my adventure goes awry, I do not want you touched by any hint of scandal."

"Goodness, Faith, I thought we were beyond scandal at our age."

Meredith tried valiantly to act unconcerned, but Faith could see that her carefully chosen words were having the desired effect. Meredith was toying nervously with the thin gold chain around her neck, a sure sign of nerves.

Faith felt a slight twinge of guilt. It was not her intention to distress Meredith, only to make certain that she would leave for London on schedule. And Faith knew that nothing would make her dear friend beat a hastier retreat than the threat of notoriety.

It seemed a true irony that Meredith, a young woman whose family was known for all manner of inappropriate misadventures, had a positive horror of scandal. She was constantly making excuses for her parents' erratic behavior and always rescuing her dearly loved, and decidedly wild, younger twin brothers from all manner of mischief.

"If you are absolutely certain that you do not need me, then perhaps I had best return to town." Meredith fidgeted with the catch of her necklace, then abruptly thrust her hands to her sides, as if willing herself to remain calm. "I have been gone only three days, but that is long enough for my brothers to get into Lord only knows what sort of trouble.

"When I left, Jason was keen on purchasing a matching set of bays he cannot afford for the sporty phaeton he had won in a card game, and Jasper was given to wearing his coat with the seams showing."

Faith wrinkled her brow. "Jason is putting his coat on inside out?"

"An old gambler's trick. Wearing a garment, usually a coat, reversed is supposed to turn one's luck." Meredith gave a long, suffering sigh. "I love my brothers to distraction, but they are impossible at times. I often long for the days when they were younger. Despite their constant misadventures, they were at least easier to control."

Faith knew Meredith far too well to be startled by those odd words, for it had always seemed as if Meredith was more like a mother than sister to her younger brothers. And while Faith acknowledged that there was much about Meredith to be envied—her noble position, her charm, her looks, her kind heart—the responsibility of her two mischievous brothers was hardly something to covet.

Seeing her opportunity, Faith acted swiftly. "Come along," she said, linking her arm determinedly through her friend's. "I shall walk you to your carriage."

The two women walked in comfortable silence and chatted deliberately about inconsequential things. When Meredith was settled inside her father's luxurious coach, she leaned far out the open window and grasped Faith's hand.

"Although I have grave reservations about this wild scheme of yours, I realize that you have your heart set on it. So I wish you every success." Meredith's gaze wavered. "Who knows? If you marry, you will not only keep Mayfair Manor, you will finally break the spinster's curse."

The amusement brightening Meredith's face made Faith smile. The spinster's curse had been a joke between them for many years, ever since Faith had become engaged at seventeen yet remained unmarried at age eighteen. And nineteen. And now at twenty-four still remained unwed.

Faith had developed a friendly, though not warm, relationship with her fiancé, but over the years Neville had shown little interest in solemnizing their vows. Though longing to be both a wife and mother, Faith often wondered if either would ever come to pass.

When Meredith had too remained single year after year, the spinster's curse was born. Faith had understood her own single state was due to an uninterested fiancé, yet could never come to terms with the idea that Meredith had not been swept off her feet by a handsome, dashing nobleman long ago.

She knew it hadn't been easy for her close friend.

In keeping with the eccentricities of her unconventional family, Meredith had been informed by her parents the year she made her debut into society that she would be expected to find her own husband. If he was a man of wealth and nobility, all the better, but that was not a requirement.

Yet Meredith had never really *taken* to society, and after initially beginning her search eagerly for a soul mate, was disappointed greatly with the men the beau monde offered. By and large they showed far more interest in the size of her father's fortune than her. Or even worse, they showed regard only for her beautiful face, not the mind nor the emotions beneath it.

Though they joked of it, the spinster's curse might hold a grain of truth. If they did not marry soon, they would be well and truly on the shelf.

"I shall write you the moment I return from the viscount's home," Faith promised.

She smiled and waved as Meredith's carriage pulled away. Then she turned, stiffened her back, and started walking. Around the side of the manor house, through the formal gardens, and off to the meadow on the eastern border of the estate. It was a lovely day. The sky was so bright, Faith had to squint when she looked up.

It had rained earlier, and there was still a fair bit of moisture in the air, as a warm spring mist hung over the fields and woodlands. It collected on the leaves and dripped slowly to the ground beneath, sparkling in the golden afternoon sunlight.

Even walking at a brisk pace, and taking every conceivable shortcut, it took over an hour to reach the front doors of the viscount's home. Yet as she stood staring at the tarnished brass knocker adorning the massive wooden doors, an attack of cowardice seized her. Try as she might, Faith could not remember why this had seemed like such a plausible solution an hour ago.

The need to flee came upon her swiftly, and for a moment she thought to act upon it. Yet somehow her feet remained in place. If she left now, there might not be another chance. Faith knew with certainty that both of the viscount's sisters, Elizabeth and Harriet, were away from home, taking their weekly visit with the vicar and his wife.

That was yet another reason why this was the perfect time to come calling. Above all else, she needed this meeting to be private.

Screwing up her courage, Faith lifted the knocker. Her hasty knock was answered by a stiff-necked butler she did not recognize.

"Yes, miss?"

"I've come to see the viscount. Kindly inform him that Miss Faith Linden has arrived."

Faith used her best haughty aristocratic voice. It sounded horribly pretentious to her own ears, but succeeded in wiping the look of polite disdain from the butler's pinched face.

She waited until he vanished from the hall. Then, lifting her skirts to prevent any rustling, Faith followed stealthily behind the servant, far enough away so he did not hear her, yet close enough not to lose sight of him.

When the butler opened the door to what she thought was the library, she hurried forward.

"No need to announce me," she said sweetly to the openmouthed servant, as she strode brazenly past him. "Lord Dewhurst and I are old friends."

"Miss, you cannot go in there," the butler sputtered.

But it was too late. She was already inside. Short of pulling her out by force, the butler had no recourse.

"Gregory, is that you?" an annoyed male voice inquired. "What do you want now?"

Faith's eyes anxiously scanned the large, cavernous room, searching for the owner of the voice, but she was unable to locate the source.

"Miss Linden is here to see you, my lord," the butler called out tightly. "Apparently on a most urgent matter."

"Tell her to go away. I'm busy."

The butler smirked at Faith and backed out the door without uttering another word.

Perhaps she should return at another time. She would not want to prejudice her case by broaching this most delicate subject at an inopportune time.

Coward! There is no other time.

"My lord?" Faith glanced up at the ornate ceiling and immediately noticed a large water stain marring the detailed plasterwork. The viscount's voice appeared to be coming from somewhere above her head, but she could not see him anywhere. She cleared her throat. "I apologize for my poor timing, but I must speak with you on a matter of utmost urgency. I promise to be as brief as possible."

There was no reply. It was as if the disembodied voice had vanished. Only silence filled the air. Faith shivered slightly, not knowing whether to feel hopeful or frightened.

Then suddenly he appeared from behind the floor-length draperies that concealed a tall ladder he must have been standing upon. His dark hair had a mussed appearance. He was dressed informally, wearing only tan breeches, black boots, and a white shirt. Yet despite his disheveled state, he was every inch the omnipotent male. Physically superior, with broad shoulders, long, muscular legs, and an expansive chest.

He had been a cute lad, but his adult face was more than handsome, it was also mature and strong featured. His stance was commanding, as befitted a sea captain, and Faith realized that it was a natural progression to go from a mischievous youth to a domineering man.

There was a distinct flicker of annoyance in his gray eyes, but not a hint of recognition. Even though it had been nearly eleven years since Faith had seen him, she knew Griffin Sainthill on first sight.

"Do I know you?" he barked out rudely.

"My lord." Faith dipped a low, graceful curtsy. "It has been a long time since we last met."

Maybe it was her voice. Or her curtsy. Or perhaps he had not been paying attention when his butler announced her name, because something seemed to click into place inside his brain. "Faith?" A slight smile curved the edges of his mouth. "Is it really you?"

"Yes." A rush of giddy relief swamped her. He *did* remember her. "Forgive me for intruding, but I needed to see you."

"About the will?"

Faith's mind went blank. She had played this encounter over and over in her head for days, trying to anticipate every reaction, every question, every possible objection he might have so she would be prepared with a retort. Yet she had never even considered such a blunt, cut-to-the-heart opening.

"Ye-yes. The will."

"I thought as much. I received your note, but I haven't had an opportunity to reply." His eyebrows rose fractionally. They were as elegant and finely shaped as the rest of his chiseled face. "I had not realized this was such an important matter or else I would have attended to it sooner."

Faith felt her cheeks grow hot. Caught under his glimmering gaze, the simple speech she had practiced for days promptly disappeared from her mind. She scrambled frantically for something, anything to say.

"I'm sure I shocked your butler with my boorish behavior, but I expected Chambers to answer the door. Where is he?"

"I retired him to the country. He was far too old to still be in service. Gregory is from the London house. I sold it before I came to Hampshire and brought as many of the servants here as I could afford. In hindsight, I'm not sure why I thought I needed a stiff-backed butler. He would be of far greater use to me if he could swing a hammer."

"Is that what you were doing up on the ladder? Hammering something?" Faith asked, impressed by the notion. She remembered her father supervising the workers, but she could not recall ever seeing him actually doing any of the physical labor.

He smiled faintly. "I was inspecting the ceiling. The wood and shingles are completely rotted. It will take more than my limited skills to fix it properly."

"Then I shall send a crew of workers over from Mayfair Manor tomorrow. There are many skilled men on my estate who would be pleased to help."

She suspected he was a man who would not take charity. Even from an old family friend. But he surprised her by accepting her offer with a quiet nod of thanks.

He indicated two blue-cushioned chairs set before the unlit fireplace. "Shall we sit?"

She sank down into the chair, gingerly testing the springs. It was not as uncomfortable as it looked.

Faith surveyed the rest of the room, and her confidence slowly trickled back into her. The front foyer had boasted a highly polished parquet floor, lovely vases of fresh flowers, and dust-free furniture. But back here it was a totally different matter.

Faded carpets, water-stained ceiling and walls, mountains of dust. The house reminded Faith of a beautiful piece of fruit that appears so perfect and appetizing until it is cut open to find a brown, rotten mess inside.

It was years since she had set foot inside this castle, but the rumors she had heard were apparently true. It had been badly neglected and needed major renovation. Faith smiled. She could provide both workers and funds to repair the house and would do so gladly, if she were married to the viscount.

Faith swallowed hard as she tried to envision herself married to this powerful, virile man. The very notion made her suddenly relieved she was sitting down, because her knees started quivering. Although an unmarried woman, she knew something of what happened between a man and a woman.

Neville had never been inclined to show her much affection, and she had not minded overmuch. Yet some rare feminine instinct told her that Griffin would be more forthcoming and earthy in his physical desires.

As if reading her mind, he announced suddenly, "I have shown an abominable lack of courtesy in welcoming you to my home. Pray, permit me to remedy that at once."

Then he reached for her hand, bent low, and kissed her knuckles with all the courtly aplomb of a true dandy. She had removed her gloves before knocking on the door and could feel his warm breath stirring the fine hairs on the top of her hand. Her heart seemed to miss a beat.

Raw panic seeped from a place deep inside her, but Faith conquered it. If she was bold enough to approach this man and ask him to consider marrying her, then she certainly needed to be bold enough to accept a polite kiss on the hand.

Faith took a long, shuddering breath and told herself sternly to stop acting like a silly girl. True, she might be considered intelligent for a woman, but she had grown up in the country, sheltered from the rakish antics of men like Griffin Sainthill. Yet that did not mean she was incapable of holding her own in his company.

"Tell me what you know of the will," she said breathlessly, feeling a need to steer the topic back to the purpose of her visit.

He seemed confused for a moment but recovered quickly. "I understand in situations such as yours, when an intended groom dies before the wedding, it is customary to return the betrothal ring, especially if it is a family heirloom. However, Neville's will specifically requested that you keep the ring, and I wanted to assure you that I have no objection."

"Neville's will?" Faith was shocked. She was unaware that her fiancé had even made a will. As for the ring, it was sitting at home in her jewel box, precisely where it always was, since she rarely wore it. "You misunderstand, my lord. When I spoke of a will, I was referring to my father's will."

"Your father's will? How could that possibly concern me?"

"I need a husband before the year ends or else I shall lose ownership of Mayfair Manor. I was hoping you might consider it."

The viscount stared at her for a long moment, then broke into hearty laughter. "I always did enjoy your odd sense of humor, even when we were children. I'm pleased to find that you still possess it, in abundance I might add."

Faith squirmed uncomfortably in her chair, saying nothing. Gradually his laughter died away. The room became strangely silent.

"You aren't joking, are you?" The viscount raked a hand through his dark hair. "You really must marry within the year or lose Mayfair Manor?"

Faith's nerves tightened. "Not just marry, my lord. In order to comply with the dictates of the will, I must marry Viscount Dewhurst."

His mouth quirked again. "Me? You must marry me?"

Faith struggled mightily to keep her gaze on his. "Well, you are Viscount Dewhurst."

"Surely not the one named in the will?"

"Of course not." Faith huffed and tried to ignore the growing tone of amusement in his speech and manner. How dare he think this was funny? "However, you are Viscount Dewhurst, and if we marry, Mayfair Manor shall be mine. Or, rather, ours."

"You're serious."

"Absolutely."

Her strong, steady answer wiped the grin from his face. Quickly. "Have you consulted a lawyer? Surely there must be another solution to this predicament aside from marriage?"

"I cannot afford a lengthy court battle. If I forfeit the manor I shall be given a modest income that is more than adequate for my needs. I will not be destitute." Faith tried to ignore the hollow feeling in her stomach and admonished herself to temper the look of anxious hope she felt certain was lighting her eyes.

"If you must know the entire truth, 'tis more than just losing my home, which I dearly love, that rankles me. It is my cousin's wife, Amelia. I've never cared for her. She lacks refinement, common sense, even basic kindness. She is a frightful woman and has been completely unbearable since her husband became a baron. The last time we met, she insisted that I address her as *Lady Aston*. I almost choked.

" 'Tis petty of me, I suppose, but I would do nearly anything so as not to give her the satisfaction of taking everything that is mine."

"Even marry a stranger?" Griffin remarked. His eyebrow lifted again. "She must be very frightful, indeed."

Faith blushed. Perhaps the horrid Amelia was not the only reason. Perhaps she wanted a chance at marriage, a family, maybe even children one day. She had wasted the better part of her youth waiting for Neville to make good on his promise of marriage. And now it was too late. Faith knew the harsh truth. She wasn't rich enough, pretty enough, or young enough to find a husband any other way.

"You are my last hope, my lord. My only hope."

She had said it. Spoken the words that revealed her greatest fears, her truest needs. It had been difficult but not as impossible as she'd imagined. In a strange way, Faith now felt as if a great weight had been lifted from her. No matter what happened from this point on, the knowledge that she had found the courage to do this would be a comfort.

His eyes were sparkling silver jewels, revealing nothing of his thoughts. Was he completely shocked by her revelations? Or worse, repulsed by her proposition? Faith swallowed the impulse to turn and run and instead dredged up the courage to face him.

"Tempting as your offer is, regrettably, I must refuse."

"You're saying no?" Faith whispered, hardly believing all her carefully thought out plans were beginning to crumble.

She struggled to find the right words, the ones that would force him to reconsider, to see the wisdom of her arguments. The words that would somehow miraculously make him change his mind. But they would not come.

Faith lifted her chin and searched his handsome face for a sign, a hint of his emotions. He stared back at her without expression, but his eyes were narrow and speculative. They never seemed to blink.

And then suddenly she imagined this conversation from his side. What could possibly be more pathetic than a plain, unimportant spinster begging a handsome, viral nobleman to marry her? For honor's sake? Hardly.

Faith abruptly stood up. Her heart seemed to stumble over a beat, but with effort she contained herself.

"I'm sorry to disappoint you," he said softly.

Disappoint me? Faith felt ill. His gently uttered apology was the final humiliation. She took three backward steps, praying her legs would support her.

"The fault is mine, my lord." She spoke through trembling lips. "I should never have asked you to consider honoring your brother's commitments. If I had pushed harder for marriage while Neville was alive, I would not find myself ruined today."

"Ruined?"

The puzzlement and sympathy in his face was her undoing. Never in her life had she felt so small. It suddenly became utterly impossible to stay in his company. "No need to ring for a servant to see me out," Faith murmured. She turned and headed rapidly for the door. "I'll send over a work crew tomorrow morning to help begin the roof repairs, as I promised."

Faith flushed at her choice of words. *Promised.* God help her, if she lived to be a hundred she would never again pin her hopes and dreams on the promises made to her by another.

Three

Griffin watched Faith flee the room, and his conscience pricked at him. She had been too proud, too willful to break down in front of him, but her emotions had been clearly visible in her face. Keen disappointment and total despair. Surprisingly, her stricken expression at his refusal to even consider her outrageous proposal had cut him deep. Far deeper than he'd expected.

He hadn't meant to be so blunt in his answer, so unsympathetic to her plight. But she had caught him unawares, on a decidedly bad day. Though as of late that appeared to be the only sort of day he experienced. Bad.

With a heavy sigh Griffin turned to follow after her. As he strode quickly down the hallway, he heard a slight scuffling noise up ahead in the front foyer, along with the sound of several female voices.

Perfect! His sisters had returned from their afternoon visit with the vicar. Griffin's already grim mood soured further.

Still, he lengthened his stride and arrived just in time to see the back of Faith's skirts as she scrambled out the front door. Barging rudely past his sister Elizabeth, Griffin gave chase.

"Miss Linden, wait. Miss Linden!"

She did not pause, nor turn her head. Instead, she lifted her skirts and quickened her gait, shooting forward like an arrow. A sudden gust of wind blew her bonnet askew. Griffin saw her reach up and steady it with one hand, but she did not slow her step. Griffin suspected that even if the hat had flown from her head she would not have stopped to retrieve it.

Griffin's lips curled in disgust. As much as he felt obligated to clear the air between them, he was not about to go chasing after Faith like some demented suitor. His earlier feelings of guilt dissolved into frustration. Now it appeared it would be necessary to call upon her in order to straighten out this misunderstanding.

A strong hand grabbed his arm. Griffin looked down and realized his sister stood by his side.

"What was she doing here?" Harriet demanded. She released her hold on Griffin and placed her hands on her hips. "I did not know she was planning to visit. Why did you receive her without a proper chaperon in attendance?"

Griffin turned, then paused. "I assume you are referring to Miss Linden?" he countered, glaring down to give Harriet his full measure of attention, while hoping this powerful regard might temper her hostility.

"Naturally I was referring to Miss Linden," Harriet huffed. She shifted from one foot to the other. "What did she want?"

Griffin grunted with a grudging respect. Many a hardened sailor had paled beneath a windblown tan when on the receiving end of his solid stare. But Harriet hadn't even blinked. Instead, her chin had tipped higher in the air.

"Miss Linden wanted to speak with me," Griffin said.

"About what?"

"A personal matter."

"What sort of personal matter?"

Griffin almost laughed. Harriet's tenacity was unmatched. A dimple appeared in his cheek. She wrinkled her nose at him, and Griffin broke into a chuckle. "This matter does not concern you, sister. Please, give it no further thought."

Thinking the matter closed, Griffin turned on his heel and strolled to the drawing room. The slight sound of footsteps behind him alerted Griffin to the fact that both Harriet and Elizabeth were dogging his steps.

Clearly Harriet had not been mollified by his answer. He had barely set foot inside the drawing room when his sister spoke.

"I would like to know the purpose of Miss Linden's visit and precisely what she said to you," Harriet demanded, throwing out her words like a challenge she intended to win.

For the moment, Griffin ignored her. Crossing the drawing room's faded carpet, he moved to the sideboard, his goal the large crystal whiskey decanter.

Thanks to the open windows, the air smelled clean and fresh, despite the thin layer of dust that coated nearly every surface. For an instant, Griffin felt a sharp pang of longing for the tangy freshness of the open sea. How dreadfully he missed it!

It seemed like everything in this wreck of a house was covered with dirt and mold and dust.

He poured himself a full measure of whiskey and took a long swallow before turning to face Harriet. She had taken up a position near the unlit fireplace, with Elizabeth by her side.

Griffin had trouble hiding his admiration. He had never before seen a female who could match her for sheer bravado. Except perhaps Faith. It had taken tremendous courage to come here today and lay her rash proposal before him. Once again, he chided himself for his unsympathetic response.

But it appeared he had more pressing matters that needed attention. Griffin turned his most charming smile upon his sisters. Elizabeth's eyes brightened with relief, and she responded immediately with a sweet grin. Harriet's lips never moved. She looked over at him expectantly.

"Miss Linden wished to discuss her father's will," Griffin finally admitted.

"I knew it!" Harriet exclaimed. "That little schemer. I hope the hasty departure we witnessed meant you threw her out, Griffin. I feel certain she would do or say almost anything to get her own way. She was a dreadfully spoiled little girl who has grown into a totally indulged woman. I think it was wise of you to steer clear of her."

Griffin took a moment to mull over his sister's passionate words. Harriet's dislike of Miss Linden was never in question, her earlier attitude had been very clear, yet she almost seemed repelled by her. Such strong emotion piqued his curiosity.

"Why do you dislike Miss Linden so much?"

Elizabeth gasped and turned a worried eye toward her older sister. "I think I shall speak with Cook about this evening's supper. You know how she tends to overcook the beef if not diplomatically reminded to have care. If you will excuse me."

Elizabeth was out the door like a shot.

Griffin's attention was now totally engaged, as this strange situation grew more fascinating by the minute. "Now, what do you suppose could have made our little sister so uncomfortable? Any ideas, Harriet?"

She gave a most unladylike snort. "Elizabeth is a sensitive girl who dislikes confrontation of any kind. 'Tis better she left. Now we can speak freely."

"I never intended to do otherwise," Griffin replied smoothly.

The swift lift of Harriet's right eyebrow told him she didn't believe that for an instant. But she held her tongue. Harriet moved away from the fireplace and settled herself in a dusty, oversize chair.

Griffin took the chair opposite hers and leaned forward with his elbows propped on his thighs.

"I'm listening," Harriet stated calmly.

Griffin could have sworn that Harriet's mouth curved into the faintest hint of a smile.

"And I'm still waiting for an answer to my question," Griffin explained, hoping to discover the source of his sister's bitterness. "Why do you dislike Miss Linden?"

Harriet shifted in her chair. "I don't precisely dislike Miss Linden. I do, however, mistrust her. Completely. She was engaged for many years to our brother, Neville, yet they never married.

"As far as I am concerned, Neville's death severed the relationship she had with this family. I fear that Miss Linden will now attempt to impose herself upon us, utilizing her past association. Her coming here today to speak with you only confirms my suspicions."

"Why did Neville and Miss Linden never marry?"

Harriet sighed. "I'm not quite sure. Lord knows, both Lord Aston and Father tried everything to make it happen."

"Did Neville have any specific objections to Miss Linden or do you believe he was of a mind to avoid marriage altogether?" Griffin asked.

Harriet shrugged. "I have no idea. He never actually

spoke out against her, not specifically, yet his actions certainly revealed his true feelings about the matter. If he wanted her for his wife, he would have married her. But he did not."

Griffin rubbed his chin in contemplation. "Yet Father insisted?"

Harriet's head bobbed up and down. "Oh, yes. Father insisted. Constantly and loudly. It was all they ever talked, or rather argued, about whenever Neville was home." Her expression turned sour. "If Father would have only spent a mere fraction of his time and energy on the concerns of his other children, not to mention the financial well-being of the estate, we would not be in such dire circumstances today."

"You blame Miss Linden for that?"

"I hold Miss Linden responsible for her share of this problem," Harriet stated firmly.

"I see." Griffin leaned back in his chair. In an odd way he felt relief, for her explanation told him more of what had occurred for the past few years. It shed light on the reason behind Harriet's strong dislike of Miss Linden and also assured Griffin that his original assessment of his sister was correct.

She might be stubborn, forceful, and strong willed, but it was not in her nature to be so mean-spirited without justification. She was clearly convinced of the rightness of her position concerning Miss Linden. Griffin, however, was not as certain.

Harriet cleared her throat. "You have not told me specifically what Miss Linden said to you this afternoon."

Griffin snorted. "Do I really need to say it?"

"That absurd will?"

"I take it you have also heard about the will that Miss Linden's father left?"

Harriet visibly bristled. "Naturally. Half the town has heard of that ridiculous will."

"I hadn't." Griffin leaned back in his chair. "And since it concerns me directly, I find it rather curious that I was not informed of it by my dear, sweet, loving sister."

"Elizabeth would not have known how to approach such a delicate subject with you," Harriet countered, lifting her chin and looking him straight in the eye. "Besides, the matter concerned the former viscount. Miss Linden was engaged to Neville, not you. Perhaps he has ruined her, but he is certainly not here to be held accountable.

"I know that men carry an inordinate amount of pride and arrogance and a vastly overinflated notion of honor. You might have succeeded the title from our eldest brother, but you are not responsible for his actions."

Neville ruined Faith? A vivid picture appeared in his mind, of Neville and Faith locked in a passionate embrace. It made the normally unprudish Griffin decidedly uncomfortable. "Why do you say that she is ruined?"

Harriet gave him a look that said she thought him a dense child. "No one will have her for a wife now. And that ludicrous will her father left has sealed her fate. Without the financial riches of her estate, who would want her? She is neither young, nor pretty, nor biddable. Besides, Faith Linden will forever be known in this county as Neville's unwanted fiancée. Most men are rather particular about taking the leavings of others, are they not?"

That notion startled him. Neville's leavings? Just how far had his brother gone with his fiancée? Or rather, if Harriet's interpretation of Miss Linden's shallow character was correct, how far had Faith gone in her attempt to secure her position as the future Viscountess Dewhurst? Had she foolishly allowed herself to be compromised before her wedding vows were spoken?

Griffin slowly blew out his breath. If his sister meant to discourage his interest and concern for Miss Linden, she had severely misjudged him. Harriet's words were having the opposite effect.

She cast him a sidelong glance. "Perhaps I should have warned you of the will. I apologize for my oversight. I suspected Miss Linden would attempt to contact you in an effort to gain your sympathy, but even I underestimated her audacity. Hopefully we can now put this unpleasant business behind us."

Griffin gave his sister a noncommittal smile. This conversation had only served to reinforce the notion that he needed to speak to Faith directly and honestly about her relationship with his brother. But Griffin was certainly not foolish enough to let Harriet know of his intentions.

He had learned much about his siblings since his return, especially Harriet. She was a complex woman, often too somber, too mired in duty and appearance, too involved with always doing and saying the proper thing. There were times when he honestly felt she was simply too exhausting to be around.

Yet there was another side to the elder of his sisters. Harriet was also competent and caring and unfailingly devoted to the family, himself included. She had been loving and welcoming to his young son, holding her tongue despite the speculation in her eye when he introduced the boy.

Griffin believed that Harriet suspected the true circumstance of his child's birth, but for once had kept her curiosity and questions to herself. He was grateful for her restraint and her unspoken show of support, realizing he would need all the allies he could muster when it became known that his child was indeed a bastard.

"Did Miss Linden say anything about young Neville?" Harriet inquired anxiously, as if somehow sensing his thoughts had turned to his child.

"No." A cold numbness swept through Griffin's body at the mention of his son's name. "That nasty cold has kept him confined to the nursery since we arrived, with only his nursemaid, you, me, and Elizabeth for company. Apparently the servants haven't yet had a chance to gossip to the village about him."

Harriet nodded her head eagerly. "I believe you are correct. The fact that Miss Linden never mentioned him means she doesn't know of his existence. I would not be at all surprised if she tried to appeal to your parental instincts when making her outrageous proposal and offering herself as a surrogate to your motherless son."

"Another role she is ill-equipped to fill?" Griffin teased, unable to help himself. When it wasn't directed toward him, Harriet's indignation and anger could be most amusing.

" 'Tis clearly impossible for such a self-indulgent woman to be a mother to a child born of her own body, let alone a stepchild." Harriet rose to her feet, shaking the wrinkles out of her full skirt. "Trust me, Griffin, we are well rid of Miss Linden."

The satisfactory smile on Harriet's face told Griffin his sister considered the matter closed. He dared not refute her impression, but in his heart knew that he needed to speak with Faith directly. The sooner the better.

* * *

Faith had heard Griffin call her name. Even above the gusting wind and the pounding humiliation inside her head, his voice had rung true and clear. At the sound of those deep, male tones, panic had surged through her. The need to escape was real and intense.

Her leg muscles had tightened in alarm, but Faith willed her feet to move swiftly. She bowed her head low and forged into the wind, nearly breaking into a run when she heard her name a second time.

If he pursued her, she would have little chance of escape, yet she had to try. The humiliation of facing him again was just too impossible to bear.

Forsaking the meadow, she hastened onto the main road. For once, Faith decided it had been a blessing to encounter the nasty Harriet Sainthill. At this very moment, she was most likely filling her brother's head with every unsavory detail of Faith's character and thus unwittingly delaying his pursuit.

If she was very lucky, Harriet might give her just enough time to elude him.

Her mind worked as frantically as her feet, and almost against her will, Faith relived each small detail of their encounter. The handsome set of his jaw, his initial gruffness, the ensuing friendly attitude. For an instant he had almost seemed pleased to see her. Until he learned of the reason for her visit.

Faith's cheeks grew hot. The encounter had renewed all her repressed longings—to someday be a wife, a mother, a woman who was valued, perhaps even loved. Such foolish dreams.

A clattering noise up ahead alerted Faith to the presence of an approaching carriage. Griffin? Her heart skipped a beat; then she berated herself for being so foolish. If he had a mind to chase after her, the viscount would surely be mounted on horseback.

Besides, the carriage was coming from the opposite direction. She moved to the edge of the road as it neared, but her pulse quickened when she recognized the blue-and-silver livery of the driver.

Crying out in relief, Faith surged forward. "Merry," she whispered in an unsteady voice.

The coach drew alongside and stopped. The door swung open and Meredith nearly fell out in her haste to reach her distraught friend. An outrider jumped off the back of the coach to lend his assistance.

"Help Miss Hobbins out first," Meredith instructed as the servant scurried to do her bidding. "She can ride up top next to the coachman. It's a lovely day and not too chilly. I'm sure the fresh air will feel invigorating."

Faith noticed the resentful stare and pulled expression of Miss Hobbins, Meredith's elderly maid, as she stepped down from the cozy interior of the carriage, but was feeling too miserable to give it much thought.

It would be difficult enough having to tell Meredith the results of her meeting. Best to do so without an audience.

The door shut and Meredith signaled the driver to leave. With a grateful sigh Faith leaned back against the velvet squabs. Safe. She was truly safe.

As the carriage rumbled down the country road, Faith's heart finally ceased its furious rhythm. She still felt light-headed and a bit dazed, but she was slowly regaining her equilibrium.

"Was it truly awful?" Meredith inquired in a gentle voice.

" 'Twas dreadful," Faith conceded, drawing a shuddering breath. "I acted like an imbecile, babbling on about Father's will. The viscount had no idea what I was referring to, looking at me as if I'd sprouted three heads. When he finally realized what I was asking, he rejected me."

"I'm surprised he knew nothing of the will," Meredith remarked.

"If you are surprised, can you imagine how I felt?" Faith made an attempt at laughter, but only produced a hollow, brittle sound. "I made a perfect ninny of myself and for no good reason."

"The viscount was not at all amenable to the idea of a marriage between you?" Meredith asked sympathetically.

"Amenable! He rejected me outright, in no uncertain terms." Faith took a deep breath, trying to harness her distress. Rejection was never easy, but she had felt nearly trampled by the encounter. Utterly defeated, she studied the hands in her lap. "He was my last hope, Merry. What will become of me now?"

"You will survive," Meredith stated in a firm voice. She grabbed Faith's hands and squeezed them reassuringly. "Nay, you will not only survive, you shall flourish."

Her words offered Faith little reassurance. Perhaps she would not be destitute once she lost Mayfair Manor to her odious cousin, but she would be bereft. Lacking a true home, a foundation, almost a sense of identity.

"Tell me exactly what occurred," Meredith insisted.

Haltingly Faith complied, leaving out no sordid nor embarrassing detail.

"And then I fled down the hallway," Faith explained. "At first I thought it might just be my imagination, but I clearly heard his footsteps behind me. Knowing he was in pursuit made me a bit crazed. I couldn't bear to face him again, so I ran faster. I reached the front door just as his sisters, Harriet and Elizabeth, arrived home."

Meredith let out a little squeak. "Oh, dear. What happened next?"

"I nearly bowled them over in my haste to escape." Faith grimaced. "They were provided an excellent view of my final humiliating flight, which no doubt provided Harriet with great joy. Ever since we were children she has taken a keen disliking to me."

Meredith frowned. "I fear 'tis me that Harriet dislikes more than you. We are the same age, and we had our first season together. I was certainly not a great success, but I fear that Harriet made an even more dismal impression upon society. And we can't forget about that nasty business with her fiancé, Julian Wingate. I don't believe she has ever forgiven me, nor will she anytime soon."

Faith frowned. "I had nearly forgotten about him. Didn't he propose to you, years before he and Harriet became engaged?"

"Yes." Meredith dragged in a long breath, then sighed deeply as she exhaled. "Julian was one of the more persistent suitors, swearing continually that he couldn't live without me. He must have proposed a dozen times that season. Eventually I had to stop receiving him at home. Yet still he persisted. It became an exhausting task, trying to elude him at parties, though I do confess to getting rather good at it by the end of the season."

Faith shook her head slowly, trying to imagine such an experience. "Didn't you find it utterly romantic, having a handsome young man declare undying devotion?"

"Gracious, no!" Meredith angled a glare at her friend, then blushed prettily. "Such uncontrolled passion had me breaking out in hives. How could I possibly spend the rest of my life with a man who made bright red welts and a blotchy rash break out on my skin?"

"Oh, Merry." Faith smiled, trying to picture the beautiful Meredith in such a state. "I daresay you would still look ravishingly beautiful covered in a red rash."

"But think how it would itch." Meredith tapped her fingers lightly on Faith's arm. "Surely a gentleman cannot find anything attractive about a woman who is constantly scratching at her person."

"Now, that would be a sight." This time Faith broke out into a true laugh.

Meredith joined her. "There, I've managed to chase away your gloom," she said triumphantly. "I cannot bear to see you so unhappy, Faith."

"I thank you for the distraction. And for listening to me. I'm sure by this evening I'll be back to my misery, but I do appreciate the respite."

"Nonsense. You shall come to London with me," Meredith suggested impulsively. "There is certainly no need to stay here and wallow in pity. A change of air and atmosphere will do you a world of good."

"To London?" Faith's mind began racing. It would be wonderful to get away for a few days or even a week. A true escape. There was little that could be accomplished here, now that Griffin had refused to consider her situation. Time away might give her a better perspective. Lord knows, her troubles would still be here waiting when she returned. "But I have nothing packed."

"We can make a quick stop back at the manor," Meredith improvised. "You only need to bring the barest of necessities. We shall enjoy the sights, including the lovely shops on Bond street. It shall be a grand adventure. Oh, do say you'll come to town."

"Do I dare?" Faith's eyes twinkled with excitement, but then her face darkened and she turned away. "The season has already begun. I know you have many social obligations. I would only be a burden and feel guilty about depriving you of society."

"My goodness, you of all people should know how I feel about attending society functions. They are deadly boring, every last one of them." A wicked gleam of mischief entered Meredith's blue eyes. "It would be difficult to secure invitations to the more select gatherings at this late date, yet if you have a mind, I'm sure we can devise a way to sneak you into a ball or two."

"Meredith! I couldn't."

"Why not? These events are generally such a crush no hostess is ever certain exactly who is in attendance. With my parents out of the country, Great-Aunt Agatha acts as my chaperon. She is a dear but prefers to eat heartily from the buffet and then snore quietly in a corner until it is time to leave. She would probably be pleased that I have a female companion who enjoys strolling about the ballroom."

"I suppose I could come to town," Faith said slowly. "And perhaps attend a function or two." At the sight of Merry's beaming face, Faith quickly added, "Nothing too fancy, however. I certainly don't want to meet the crème de la crème of society. Just a few of the more colorful personages will be sufficient."

Meredith agreed with a short, eager nod. "We shall sort through the invitations the moment we arrive home. With a bit of persuasion, I'm certain I can have my modiste complete a new gown for you in a few days. By then we will have determined which events hold the most interest and appeal."

Faith cleared her throat, suddenly feeling nervous. It was such a rash, impulsive act. Yet she realized this might be the only chance she would ever get to witness the ton in action. Even if they stayed on the fringes of society it would be fascinating. And given Meredith's horror of scandal, there would be little chance of anything truly disastrous happening.

"All right. I'll come."

"Splendid." Meredith smiled with approval. "We shall make a brief stop at Mayfair Manor to allow you time to pack a bag and alert the servants of your whereabouts. I have an excellent coachman. If we depart within the hour we can still reach town before nightfall."

"Wonderful," Faith replied, pressing her hand against her midsection, attempting to still the fluttering in her stomach.

"While we are in town, we shall also make an appointment with Papa's solicitor," Meredith decided. "There has got to be a way for you to keep Mayfair Manor that doesn't involve the odious Viscount Dewhurst."

Faith nodded her head mutely. She would agree to see the solicitor only to please Meredith. In her heart, she held out no hope of retaining control of her childhood home.

Yet, as much as that notion hurt, the greater distress came from knowing that despite his treatment of her, Faith had not found the current Viscount Dewhurst to be the least bit odious.

Four

"You say the most charming things, Lord Dewhurst." The sleek, elegant feminine fingers trailed suggestively up Griffin's arm, coming to rest upon his shoulder. "Though there are some who speak ill of your character. Are you truly as naughty as I've heard?"

"Guilty as charged, Lady Ashborrow." The answer sprang readily to Griffin's lips, but the usual smile did not. Then the viscount's gaze narrowed as he took a deliberate step away from the clinging woman.

He was not in a congenial mood, and his reaction to this delectable female morsel was proof of it. Lady Ashborrow had latched on to him within ten minutes of entering the ballroom by skillfully wangling an introduction from a casual mutual acquaintance, and she had not left his side in the ensuing hour.

The busty brunette was the type of woman Griffin had always preferred—mature, married, direct, experienced, and utterly lovely. Yet even her obvious interest could not dispel the gloom that clung to him this evening like a wet, misty rain.

"I can hear the musicians taking up their instruments," Lady Ashborrow hinted broadly. "I wonder if they shall open this set with a waltz?"

" 'Tis the usual choice." The corners of Griffin's mouth lifted in grim amusement. "Regretfully, a prior engagement prevents me from joining in the dancing this evening."

"If you wish to forsake the dance floor, we could take a stroll in the gardens. 'Tis a lovely evening. I noticed the moon was full." Lady Ashborrow deliberately leaned forward, displaying an ample view of her magnificent bosom. "The night flowers should be in bloom. Their fragrance can be most intoxicating."

Only mild interest stirred inside Griffin. His gaze flickered briefly over the woman by his side before becoming fixed on the opposite end of the massive ballroom. He remained silent and preoccupied while his keen eyes searched among the many guests for the one woman he feared was not in attendance.

Damn it all. Where the devil is she? Accepting defeat, Griffin turned to his companion. "I'm afraid I must take my leave of you, Lady Ashborrow. I am expected at another affair and have already stayed far longer than I intended."

Lady Ashborrow stiffened, but her artful smile remained intact. "Perhaps another time," she suggested in a calm tone.

"I shall count on it, my lady," the viscount replied smoothly. He lingered overlong as he kissed her hand, a silent apology for his inattentive behavior.

To her credit, Lady Ashborrow appeared not to hold a grudge. She gave him a final, saucy wink, snapped open her fan, and sailed majestically across the ballroom floor.

Griffin's earlier disinterest turned to regret. But he knew there was no time to be wasted on a dalliance. He had already completed his task at this ball and the night grew long. It was time to move ahead.

After a brief good-bye to his host and hostess, the viscount was once again seated inside his carriage, tapping his fingers impatiently against his knee as the coachman tried to negotiate the crowded London streets.

Griffin had been scouring London for the past five days, searching in vain for Faith, intent on settling once and for all the extent of her involvement with his brother.

That he had managed to discover that she had gone to London was a minor miracle in itself, considering how close-mouthed her servants had been when asked about her whereabouts. Even the appearance of a gold sovereign had failed to interest any of them in supplying him with their mistress's direction.

It was only through sheer luck and the blossoming romance of his undergroom with a dairymaid employed at Mayfair Manor that Griffin was able to discover Faith had flown off to London with her dear friend, Lady Meredith.

Unfortunately, the dairymaid had only been able to supply the name of Lady Meredith. Nothing more. He vaguely remembered Faith's close friend from childhood days, a long-legged blonde who enjoyed scolding him, yet he too could not recall her given name, nor her father's title.

Still, the viscount had journeyed to town anyway, naively assuming it wouldn't be difficult to find the women. Unfortunately he had been wrong. Though the members of society were a closely held group, there were quite a few of them and it was not a simple task to discover the whereabouts of two women with the limited information he possessed.

Having lived outside of England for many years left Griffin bereft of friends or even good acquaintances he could turn to for assistance in this most delicate matter. He was therefore forced to undertake the locating of Faith Linden and the mysterious Lady Meredith entirely on his own.

The selling of his London town house, which had seemed like a prudent and frugal gesture several weeks ago, added a further complication. Lacking a proper residence made it necessary to rent rooms at a fashionable and ridiculously expensive London hotel, and Griffin balked at the extra expense.

Fortunately, the viscount had ordered several new coats from a respectable tailor while in town conducting the sale of his house, so it was not necessary to waste further coin on proper clothing. Once properly housed and groomed, Griffin assumed it would be relatively easy to meet up with Faith and her friend Lady Meredith by accepting some of the society invitations that had poured in once he had discretely made his presence in London known.

However, Griffin quickly learned that he had once again misjudged the situation. Each evening there were no less than a half-dozen parties and routs held in the homes of society's chosen few. Since he had no earthly idea what sort of entertainments would interest Faith and Lady Meredith, he was forced to attend as many of these gatherings as possible.

As an unmarried viscount, Griffin was welcomed into the social whirl of the beau monde with open arms, despite his rather colorful reputation. But he quickly discovered there was a price to be paid for such blind acceptance. Speculative gleams of interest by the eager mothers in attendance dogged his every step, coupled with flirtatious giggles from their unwed daughters.

It made him decidedly uncomfortable, especially since he was not in the least bit interested in obtaining a wife. As a connoisseur and great admirer of women, he found the whole wife-hunting game a most distasteful, bloodless sport.

All too soon, Griffin began to grow weary of searching for Faith. Discouraged by his lack of success, he was fast beginning to think of this as a pointless endeavor. Yet his stubborn nature and prickling conscience bade him to continue.

Impatiently he thrust open the carriage window and called out to his driver. "Is it much farther?"

"We've only a few blocks to go, your lordship, but the street is so clogged with carriages I've nowhere to drive. Do you want me to try another route?"

"Don't bother. I'll walk the rest of the way."

With a grunt of annoyance, Griffin swung open the door and lightly jumped down from the coach, before his startled servants could offer assistance. He imagined the butler would be properly scandalized to see him arrive on foot, but he was in too much of an ornery mood to care.

On this particular starry evening he had been to no less than three different events, starting with a boring supper at Lord Anderson's, followed by an abysmal rout at the home of the earl and countess of Shrewsbury, and a crushing ball at the duke of Harrowby's.

The final stop Griffin had planned for the night was Lady Dillard's musical soiree. A gregarious opera soprano recently arrived from Italy was scheduled to perform. Of all the events of the night it was the one Griffin dreaded the most. He had never enjoyed the sweeping tones of the operatic voice, likening it to a screeching catfight, in which neither animal emerged victorious.

Still, this was the final stop of the evening. With a resigned sigh, Griffin handed his card to the dour-faced butler attending the door. The servant gave him a dubious look that Griffin quelled with a hard stare. He was immediately shown into the music room by a contrite footman.

A makeshift stage had been erected on the far side of the room and padded chairs were set before it in neat rows. A thin, white-faced young man sat at the pianoforte, and beside the instrument stood a buxom woman dressed in a gown of deep purple. Her mouth was wide open, formed into a perfectly shaped oval, from which she emitted sounds in a high range Griffin suspected only dogs could fully appreciate.

Almost against his will, his eye was drawn to the purple feather atop her head that bobbed furiously each time she swung her arm out dramatically. It was a gesture she repeated often and helped distract him from the sounds she was producing.

Forsaking a chair, Griffin hugged the wall to the left of the singer and eagerly scanned the room. Unfortunately, it was quite impossible to recognize any of the guests from this vantage point, since the primary view was of the back of everyone's head.

With a final, ear-splitting crescendo, the buxom singer flung both arms high in the air before finally snapping her mouth closed. There was a moment of blissful, utter silence. The audience then erupted into polite applause, coming to their feet while clapping. Not in appreciation, Griffin decided, but sheer relief.

It was a moment to make an opera hater's heart sing. An intermission.

Griffin smiled. Perhaps his luck was finally changing. At least he had arrived in time to miss the majority of the performance. That must be a good sign.

"I am so pleased you were able to join us this evening, Lord Dewhurst," a female voice announced. "I had so hoped you would find time to attend my musical gathering."

"You do me an honor by inviting me, Lady Dillard," Griffin replied with a charming grin. The cloying scent of gardenias enveloped him as he bowed low and took the hand of his elderly hostess. "I only regret that I arrived after the performance began."

"Never fear, my lord. Senora DeStefanis shall be singing several other selections before the evening is over."

"I hardly know what to say."

Lady Dillard giggled like a young girl, as if she suspected his true feelings on the matter. Griffin returned her smile readily. He had met her several times during this long week of social activities and actually found himself liking the old girl. If only she didn't have such appalling musical taste.

They briefly exchanged further pleasantries before Lady Dillard excused herself to attend to her other guests. With a jaundiced eye Griffin scanned the milling crowd, not really expecting to find anything of interest. More and more he was coming to believe it would be better to go back to the country and wait for Faith to return to Mayfair Manor. Nothing could be more torturous than attending these society events.

He accepted a glass of chilled champagne from a passing footman and made a final, almost halfhearted glance at the fashionable assembly. Yet as he lifted the champagne flute to his lips, his hand stilled. The cool liquid slid down his parched throat, but the taste barely registered in his brain.

For standing across the room, directly in his unobstructed line of vision, was the most exquisite female creature he had ever seen.

She turned, as if searching the room for someone

and looked straight at him. His tiredness and gloom instantly vanished. Her face was exquisite, seemingly carved of the finest pale marble and perfect in every small detail. Her silky blond hair was styled in a simple, elegant chignon, and instead of glittering jewels there were flowers artfully placed among the yellow tresses.

Dressed in azure blue, she was tall and willowy, yet utterly feminine. He found it impossible to tear his gaze away. The upsweep of her hair emphasized the slender grace of her entire torso. Even in the dim candlelight he could see that her eyes were a deep, exotic blue. They reminded Griffin of the crystal waters of the Caribbean.

She was not so bold as to smile at him, but she inclined her head slightly in his direction. He didn't even realize that he had answered her silent summons until he found himself standing in front of her.

"Lord Dewhurst."

It was not the enchanting blonde who whispered his name, but rather the tiny female standing beside her. Reluctantly, Griffin dragged his gaze away from the enchantress and found himself staring down at the very woman he had been searching for over five long days and five far more interminable nights.

Miss Faith Linden.

Griffin blinked, but she did not disappear. Then an immeasurable feeling of delight spread across his face as he witnessed Faith's reaction to his sudden appearance. She made a distinctively strangled sound in the back of her throat and turned to the beautiful blond-haired woman with a look of sheer horror etched on her face.

It was at that moment that Griffin realized this mysterious beauty must be Lady Meredith. He experienced a brief, sharp pang of regret. Pity, she would forever be beyond his reach.

The enchanting Lady Meredith must have surmised his identity from Faith's panicked expression, but she was far more circumspect in her reactions. Her body went rigid as she drew herself up to her full height and cast him a look of disdain that would have done a vicar proud.

The effect was ruined however when she dropped her fan and it bounced off the toe of her male companion, causing a mild commotion.

He recognized the man as Lord Dunstand, a pompous dandy who imagined himself an expert on all matters of propriety and refinement. Griffin dismissed him as totally insignificant, but the man could prove to be an ally if the women decided to ignore him.

Judging from their less-than-pleased reactions, Griffin had no doubt that his startled prey would have turned tail and bolted from the room. He moved quickly to prevent their escape.

"What a delightful coincidence to see you again, Miss Linden." He forced a note of calmness into his voice. "I had no idea you had journeyed to London."

Faith colored. Not a delicate, pretty blush, but a deep scarlet hue.

"Miss Linden, did you say?" Lord Dunstand bristled. He brushed off the fan he had retrieved from the floor and handed it to Lady Meredith, then turned to face Griffin. "I'm afraid you're very much mistaken, Lord Dewhurst. This is Miss Maxwell, a distant cousin of Lady Meredith's. She's visiting from the country."

"Miss Maxwell?"

"Y-yes?" Faith's hand rose to her cheek, then fluttered down to rest at her throat.

Griffin licked his lips. What sort of nonsense was this? "And your given name?"

"I say, Dewhurst, that is a rather forward request. You've only just met the woman." Lord Dunstand wrinkled his forehead. "Actually, you haven't even been *properly* introduced."

Griffin could feel the muscles in his arms tense. Apparently Dunstand hadn't heard Faith shockingly whisper his name earlier. Any fool could tell that something was amiss, but apparently Dunstand was too much of a lackwit to notice. Still, Griffin had gone to far too much trouble to let this opportunity slip away from him.

"I do beg your pardon. Dunstand, would you kindly do the honors?"

With a self-important air, Lord Dunstand did as he was bade. "May I present Lady Meredith Barrington, only daughter of the earl of Stafford and her charming cousin, *Miss Maxwell*. Ladies, Viscount Dewhurst."

There were polite murmurings and slight curtsies. Griffin itched to grab Faith's hand and bring it to his lips for a startling kiss, but wasn't sure how she would react.

Instead, he deliberately moved closer to Faith, trapping her between the wall and his solid bulk. If she turned to bolt, her nose would collide directly with his chest and bury itself in his snowy white cravat. Escape was now impossible until he allowed it.

The tension steadily increased, but Griffin decided it would be wisest to hold his tongue and fully assess the situation before acting.

For some absurd reason Faith had chosen to assume an alias. Until he discovered the reason why, it would probably be best to play along.

He bowed with exaggerated aplomb. "My sincere

apologies for my earlier mistake, Miss Maxwell. You reminded me of a childhood acquaintance, but after additional consideration I see that I was gravely wrong. The woman I was referring to is far older in years than yourself."

"Oh, really?" Faith sniffed and finally met his gaze directly.

"Indeed. She is much shorter in stature also." Griffin rocked back on his heels with an exaggerated slow motion and stared pointedly at Faith. By this time the spots of color in her cheeks had darkened to an even deeper shade of red. "Most consider her a plain woman, yet 'tis not her looks but rather her volatile and unstable nature that have gained her some measure of notoriety in our small community."

"A bit unbalanced, is she?" Lord Dunstand queried with unmasked interest.

"Oh, far more than a bit," Griffin replied.

"Posh, she sounds rather frightful." Lord Dunstand smirked.

Griffin's lips twitched momentarily. "Well, one does not wish to be unkind, but she is something of a harridan. Feared by most of the children of the village, or so I've been told, and given to dressing in odd clothing and pretending to be the queen."

"The queen?" Faith echoed faintly.

"Of England, naturally." Griffin let his lips curve into a grin. "One would have to think her totally over the edge if she pretended to be the queen of France."

"There is no French queen," Faith muttered.

"Precisely."

Glaring at him, Faith ground out, "How about warts, Lord Dewhurst? Does this poor unfortunate creature also possess an abundant amount of them?"

"Now that you mention it, I do seem to recall—"

"Gracious, my throat is dry," Lady Meredith interrupted. She shot Griffin a murderous glare, then softened her features and turned to the dandy by her side. "Would you be so kind as to fetch me a glass of champagne, Lord Dunstand? I noticed the footmen were uncorking numerous bottles, but no one has ventured into our little corner. It would be a delightful refreshment to combat the warmth of the room."

"I should be honored, Lady Meredith. And I shall fetch a glass for you also, Miss Maxwell." With a sweeping bow to the ladies and a pointed smirk at Griffin, he departed.

"Well done, Lady Meredith," Griffin said in a calm, even tone. "Now that we have lost our audience, there is no need for the two of you to jump like scalded cats each time I open my mouth."

Faith fixed him with a narrow gaze. "How dare you order us about. After that disgraceful conversation I would think you would at least have the decency to leave us in peace. Good evening, my lord."

"Please, hold your recriminations for another time, my dear *Miss Maxwell*. I suspect Dunstand shall return posthaste with your champagne, and unless you would like to take him into your confidence, I would advise that you start talking. Why this ridiculous charade?"

"This is none of your concern, my lord." Faith met his gaze directly, almost challengingly. "I have already told you that we do not wish to be in your company any longer."

"I want the truth. Now." A sound that closely resembled a growl emanated from deep inside Griffin's throat. "What sort of game are you playing?"

It was truly incredible how suddenly the atmosphere had completely changed. The peaceful beauty of the evening had been shattered, the joy and amusement threatened, and all due to the sudden, most unexpected appearance of one man. Viscount Dewhurst.

Faith was certain if she thought about it long and hard she could find something worse about the evening. But it would take some doing.

Oddly enough it had been Meredith's suggestion that Faith pretend to be her distant cousin, the mythical Miss Maxwell this evening. Since Meredith had always been the soul of propriety, worrying constantly that the smallest misstep on her part would bring disgrace and scandal upon her family, Faith assumed it was an idea that had great merit.

Appearing as herself really was out of the question. Faith was in mourning for both her father and her fiancé. This harmless little lie would allow her to spend an evening among society, as she had always longed. Just one stolen evening among the glittering ton. Was it truly too much to wish for?

They chose Lady Dillard's musical evening, assuming it would be the least popular event of the night.

When it was first suggested, Faith had considered it a lark, merely a fantasy that could never become real. She had refused to go along with the idea. But Meredith had persisted, squiring Faith to the dressmaker and helping her select an appropriate new gown, regaling her with stories of the many people she might finally meet, encouraging her to take what was considered a rather slight risk.

Thus, the notion had taken hold in Faith's heart, and she found herself embracing it. The freedom of not being herself, even for just one evening, was an intoxicating notion. After all, who could it hurt?

The possibility of encountering anyone she knew was beyond remote. None of the local gentry had ventured into town, so Faith felt secure in her assumed identity—until the viscount had suddenly materialized by her side.

"I am waiting for my explanation, Miss Maxwell."

"Oh, do stop calling me that," Faith hissed. She felt as if the ground had fallen away beneath her feet and she was tumbling through the air. Where would she land? And how? On her head or her buttocks? "What are you doing here, anyway? I thought you were busy attending to matters on your estate."

A muscle twitched in Griffin's cheek and his eyes narrowed imperceptibly. "I have come to town in search of you."

"Now who is playing games, my lord?" Faith huffed, as she tore at the silk reticule she held in her hand.

His steely gray eyes burned with a flash of anger. The atmosphere became charged with increasing tension. Nervously, Faith raised her head, searching for Lord Dunstand. Drat, where was the man? How long could it possibly take to fetch two glasses of champagne?

Merry coughed behind her fan, but did not budge from Faith's side. For an instant Faith almost wished Griffin would turn his eyes away from her and once again gaze upon her beautiful friend.

In a way, it had been Merry's irresistible beauty that had led to her unmasking. Faith had not missed how Griffin's eyes had glittered when he looked at Merry from across the room. Like a magnet, an invisible force had pulled him to her side. Where he had discovered far more than he dreamed.

Faith felt a sharp stab of pain pierce her chest. Meredith and Griffin would make an extraordinary-looking couple, but contemplating the notion of the two of them belonging to each other made Faith feel ill.

This sudden distress gave Faith the courage to imitate the icy stare of disdain that Meredith had perfected when trying to disarm overbearing gentlemen.

For an instant Lord Dewhurst looked a bit self-conscious. Faith felt a surge of triumph as she witnessed his reaction, fully expecting him to finally leave them in peace.

Yet he did not move away. Instead, a wicked smile caught the edges of Griffin's mouth and traveled slowly into his eyes. "If you will not explain yourself, then I shall be forced to draw my own conclusions." He rested a sharp gaze upon Faith that made her want to flinch. "Are you trying to elude the authorities?"

"What?" Faith turned her head so quickly a piece of hair dislodged from its pins and bobbed against her bare shoulder. "That is an insufferable remark, sir. What precisely are you implying?"

Griffin gave her a smile that made her breath stop. "It has always been my experience, Miss Maxwell, that a person assuming an alias is hiding from something. Usually because they have done something illegal."

"It does not surprise me in the least to hear that you personally know individuals who have strayed from the law, Lord Dewhurst," Faith remarked dryly, in no mood to explain herself or her outrageous actions. This man was nothing to her, neither relative nor friend. She owed him no explanations.

Still, she must tread cautiously. He could easily cause a scene if he decided to challenge her identity. Faith lifted her head to show she was not afraid.

At first she was able to meet and hold his gaze, but his continued silent scrutiny started to make her nervous. His expression was deceptively amused. Faith could see that beneath his languid lids his eyes were sharp and alert. He held the power to expose her if he so chose. Would he?

She exhaled slowly. Her heart was thumping madly and her chest felt tight as a drum. Feeling herself blush beneath the intentness of his gaze, Faith self-consciously brushed the loose curl of hair behind her ear.

"We shall take a stroll in the garden," Griffin declared. "That will afford us some measure of privacy."

"I will not leave this room with you, Lord Dewhurst," Faith insisted. It was difficult, but somehow she managed not to tremble, not to react at all. The thought of walking alone in the romantic moonlight with this awe-inspiring man frightened her silly.

"I will have satisfaction in this matter," he said calmly. "If not this evening, then tomorrow afternoon. I shall call upon you at three o'clock. I expect to be received."

His words were an implied threat. A cold shiver ran down her back. Faith did not doubt his intentions, for despite his elegant aristocracy, she suspected Lord Dewhurst had hard, rough edges she couldn't even begin to comprehend.

"You will not be turned away, my lord," Meredith answered grimly. "My father's house is in Grovsnor Square. Do you know it?"

"Not yet, but no doubt I shall locate it easily. Until tomorrow, ladies."

"Good evening, my lord," Faith countered after a hesitant moment. She deliberately held herself very still as Griffin bowed, then turned and walked away.

"I'm so sorry, Faith," Meredith said the moment they were alone. "This is all my fault. If I hadn't pres-

sured you into attending the soiree this evening Lord
Dewhurst never would have found you. I hardly know
what to say."

" 'Tis no one's fault. We just had a run of incredibly
bad luck." Faith shrugged. "Griffin said that he had
come to London to find me. Do you suppose he was
telling the truth?"

Meredith raised her brow helplessly. "Why else
would he have come to town?"

"I don't know. I suspect I shall discover that tomorrow afternoon," Faith replied, trying to sound casual
and unconcerned.

Once, the notion of an impending visit from Griffin
would have filled her with giddy anticipation. Now,
she ruefully admitted, it made her distinctly uneasy.

Five

Faith lifted the heavy gold brocade drapery and peered out the window to the street below. Carriages drove by sedately, sharp-looking dandies cantered past on fine-looking steeds, tipping their hats to the fashionably dressed individuals strolling in the sunshine; a harried-looking governess raced along, fast on the heels of her wayward charges. Yet there was no sign of Lord Dewhurst.

With a sigh, Faith hoisted the fabric higher and placed her nose against the glass. She had insisted that they wait in the morning salon to greet Lord Dewhurst, and Meredith had graciously acquiesced. It was a smaller, more intimate space, furnished with light gilt furniture and priceless antiques, but more importantly, the morning salon was located on the second floor at the *front* of the house.

"I believe this situation is rather like the watched pot my dear nanny would often reference," Meredith commented. "It shall never boil if you continue to stare at it so intently."

Faith hastily dropped the curtain and whirled around to face her friend. Meredith was perched calmly on the upholstered love seat, her lovely head completely hidden behind the newspaper she was reading.

A newspaper! It was almost scandalous. Most women sat in the parlor doing embroidery or other fancy needlework, but not Meredith. Her daring both puzzled and fascinated Faith.

Meredith didn't exactly manage her own money, that would have been completely beyond the pale, but she did keep a close eye on the investments that were made with it and expressed her opinion on what she wanted done. Faith often marveled that if Meredith's two vivacious younger brothers would take merely half as much interest in their monetary affairs, their finances would not constantly be in such a dismal state.

Nor would mine, Faith thought bitterly. *Although it truly isn't my finances that are a mess, but rather my life.* In less than a month she would lose her home, and there wasn't a thing she could do to prevent it.

For a moment Faith allowed the anger at this injustice to engulf her. If she were a man, this wouldn't be happening. She would have inherited her father's title and his property whether she was married or not. A rush of pure helplessness ran through her, followed quickly by a fatalistic sense of acceptance.

She was not a man and her father's will had been meant to aid, not harm her. It was purely a case of lack of forethought that had brought her to this sorry state. Not a curse of womanhood.

At Meredith's insistence, Faith had gone to see a solicitor the day after they arrived in London. His assessment of her rather complex dilemma was not at all encouraging. Perhaps, in time, and for an outrageously sizable fee, her father's will could be successfully reversed. There were, of course, no guarantees.

Having neither the time nor the funds to enact such a procedure, Faith had thanked the man and left, feeling more and more trapped by circumstances that were not of her doing and far beyond her control.

Faith slid a hesitant glance at Meredith. Her friend was still engrossed in her newspaper. It was almost a relief not to engage in conversation, though the distraction might have been useful.

Feeling restless, Faith began to pace back and forth, her mind racing despite how many times she told herself to relax. She pulled up short and glanced down at her hands, noticing first how they trembled slightly and second the jagged edge of one of her fingernails. Absently, she brought the hand to her mouth and nibbled at the end of the broken nail.

"Now he has you chewing your nails for an afternoon snack," Meredith commented wryly. "What next, the ends of your hair?"

Faith blushed self-consciously, remembering how as a little girl she was forever putting the end of her long braid in her mouth when she felt anxious.

"How can you possibly know that I was chewing on my fingernail? Do you have a hole cut in that paper?" Faith quipped, flopping with unladylike abandon into a chair.

"I don't need a hole, the paper is quite thin." There was a rustling noise as Meredith folded it neatly in her lap. "Besides, I can practically hear your anxiety."

"Forgive me for being so nervous," Faith retorted. She shifted her position in the chair, deciding it was most uncomfortable. "I've barely slept at all since that dreadful incident last evening. Of all the people we had to encounter, why did it have to be Lord Dewhurst?"

"You said last night that it was just a run of bad luck that threw us in his path," Meredith replied sensibly. "I'm sure there is no need to be so concerned."

Faith's mouth took a grim turn. "Well, today I no longer believe in luck or fate. Besides, Lord Dewhurst mentioned that he had come to London specifically to find me."

"I'm sure he was exaggerating. Men tend to do that when they are taken unawares."

"Really?"

"Absolutely," Meredith confirmed.

Faith took a deep breath and pressed back against the chair, finding herself drawing strength from the robust determination in Meredith's voice. Merry was right. What possible harm could Lord Dewhurst intend toward her? And why would he even care about her little masquerade as Miss Maxwell? It in no way concerned him.

Yet her stomach took a steep dive when a knock came on the morning-room door. Desperately hoping the lost feelings that were engulfing her were not apparent on her face, Faith raised her head and straightened her spine.

He entered the room carrying a sizable bouquet of flowers. The sight of those lovely blooms, fresh, fragrant, and her favorite shade of pink, so startled Faith that she unconsciously rose to her feet.

"Good afternoon, ladies." He bowed politely, then smiled with casual ease.

"Good afternoon, Lord Dewhurst."

Meredith's voice was stiff, but at least she had managed to return the greeting. To her great consternation, Faith discovered she could not.

Griffin raised an eyebrow, yet thankfully made no mention of her lack of greeting. Instead, he moved forward to present her with the flowers. As he neared, Faith realized he actually carried three separate arrangements, each identically lovely.

As he presented her with the bouquet, their fingers met. A frisson of pure heat ran up Faith's arm. His touch was warm and oddly exciting. It took nearly every ounce of concentration she could muster not to sigh with giddy delight.

Griffin, naturally, was completely unaffected by the contact. He gave her a brief, curt nod and turned toward Meredith. She silently accepted a matching bouquet.

"Your chaperon?" he questioned, holding the final cluster aloft.

"Aunt Agatha is taking her midafternoon nap," Meredith replied. "She was unaware that we were expecting visitors today."

The viscount's shoulders shifted slightly as he cocked his head to one side. He glanced down at the flowers and then back at Meredith and Faith. The crux of his dilemma was clearly visible on his handsome features. Whom would he favor with the extra bouquet?

Lord Dewhurst swung his arm toward Meredith, and Faith's breath caught in her throat. Her fingers curled around the stems of the roses she held, a gift that had moments before brought her such an unexpected burst of delight. Clenching the stems tight, she barely felt the prick of a thorn. It was far more important that Griffin not see her hands tremble when he once again looked her way. *If* he once again glanced at her.

"I suppose if your aunt is given the flowers she will then learn of my visit?" Lord Dewhurst questioned.

"It is not meant to be kept a secret from her," Meredith answered truthfully.

"Splendid. Then kindly present her with these humble blossoms and convey my best regards when she awakes."

"Thank you, my lord. That is most generous." A visibly surprised Meredith accepted the flowers. "I'm sure Aunt Agatha will be delighted. It has been ages since anyone has gifted her with flowers, and roses have always been her favorite."

He acknowledged Meredith's remarks with a brief grin, then turned his head to Faith and favored her with a sly wink. She almost dropped her bouquet. Meredith, who had turned to ring for a servant to bring refreshments, did not see the gesture, making it seem all the more wicked.

Sternly ignoring the way he made her heart pound, Faith took a seat on his left and busied herself with arranging the skirt of her gown. When she felt composed enough to raise her head, she discovered Griffin and Meredith engaged in conversation. Her involvement was neither sought nor required, so Faith took a moment to more closely examine the viscount.

The elegant cut of his blue superfine coat bespoke of Weston's talents, for it fit his broad shoulders most impressively. His white cravat was tied with a simple, uncomplicated knot, but the stark whiteness showcased the healthy glow of his skin. There were black Hessian boots, polished to a glossy shine and fit inside tan breeches that clearly defined the strong muscles of his thighs.

Yet despite all this elegant civility, it was his bearing and countenance that held her so enthralled. He was a man clearly in command of himself and those around him.

He turned his head to answer a question posed by Meredith, and Faith caught a view of his profile, all sharp edges and perfectly formed lines.

"Don't you agree, Miss Linden?" a deep male voice inquired.

Startled out of her woolgathering, Faith lifted her chin. Their eyes met, and she saw the amusement dancing in those gray depths, as if he knew she hadn't a clue to what had been asked.

"No, my lord, I'm afraid I don't agree," Faith replied boldly, not wanting to give him the satisfaction of asking him to repeat his query. Besides, it was logical to assume she would take the opposite stand. There seemed to be very little that she and Griffin agreed on these days.

His eyebrow inched up in mock surprise. "How strange. I thought most women felt Prinny has been most unkind toward Princess Caroline."

"All women are not the same," Faith responded loftily, although she truly did believe the regent's treatment of his poor wife was both scandalous and unnoble.

Yet she'd sooner start nibbling on her bouquet of roses than admit to the viscount that she hadn't been paying attention to the conversation.

He stared at her for a brief moment, but let the matter drop. "If you have no objection, Lady Meredith, I would like to speak with Miss Linden alone."

Faith bit her tongue to keep her gasp of surprise from escaping.

"That is for Faith to decide, not me," Meredith responded. "Faith?"

She regarded the viscount warily. "I have no secrets from Meredith."

"So I gathered. Still, I prefer that we speak privately."

He ended his request with a smile that transformed his face from handsome to irresistible. Faith discovered it was nearly impossible to resist, though she struggled mightily.

"Perhaps it would be best," Faith replied slowly. Who knew what he was going to say? Though Faith fully intended to relate every detail to her dearest friend, it might prove less embarrassing not to have an audience.

Also, Faith had not forgotten the way Griffin had stared at Meredith last night, as if he were a starving man sitting before a ladened banquet table. The memory was vaguely disquieting. At least if they were alone Faith would have his full attention.

"Very well. If Faith wishes it, then I shall leave the two of you alone. For a time." Meredith walked toward the door, then paused to cast the viscount a cool smile. "I shall, however, stay close enough to hear any loud voices."

"She is rather protective of you," Griffin commented as the door closed. "Or is it just me she mistrusts?"

"Lady Meredith has a realistic opinion of men and is well acquainted with their limitations," Faith replied primly.

"I daresay the right man would make her change her tune. Quickly."

"Perchance, would that man be you, Lord Dewhurst?"

He gave her a long considering look that made her tremble deep inside. He seemed on the verge of saying something, thought better of it, then merely grinned. "No, I am definitely not the man for Lady Meredith."

An odd sense of relief rushed through Faith. Instinctively, she knew it would be unbearable to see Griffin pursue Meredith. With his charm, grace, and good looks, he just might be the man who finally captured her heart.

Faith assumed a thoughtful expression. "I suspect you are curious about last evening," she began, but she was interrupted by the arrival of two servants with the tea tray.

There was a great amount of fussing and shuffling as the footman and maid set up the tea service. Twice Faith found herself biting her lip in frustration. Now that the matter was at hand, she was eager to get this discussion with Griffin finished.

My heavens, would the servants never leave?

"Tea?" she offered, halfheartedly, when at last they were alone again.

"No, thank you," he replied. "Perhaps later."

Too tense to even consider pouring herself a cup of the tasty brew, Faith drew in a breath. "As I was saying—"

A sharp knock echoed through the room.

"Now what?" Faith exclaimed in annoyance, jumping up from her chair. She strode to the door and unceremoniously yanked it open. "Yes!" she snapped waspishly.

The startled young maid on the other side of the door nearly dropped the small pitcher she held.

"I f-forgot to bring the cream, miss," she stammered. "I'm so sorry."

Faith blew out a long, low breath. She took the pitcher from the maid's trembling hands. "No, I am sorry for speaking so sharply. It was not intended toward you. Thank you for bringing the cream. 'Tis exactly what we needed."

The maid gave her a grateful smile and a quick curtsy before leaving.

Faith placed the pitcher beside the silver teapot,

then glanced helplessly at Griffin. She was almost afraid to open her mouth, certain that she would once again be interrupted.

"You were speaking of last night," Griffin prompted, "although I confess after the initial surprise wore off, I did not give it serious contemplation. However, if you would care to enlighten me as to why you felt it necessary to conceal your true identity, I will gladly listen."

Faith rubbed her chin. This was certainly a far different attitude than last night, when he had practically tried to bully her into an explanation.

"Due to the unpleasantness of my father's will, I felt it might be wise to leave Mayfair Manor for a few days, so I journeyed to London with Meredith," Faith stated calmly. "Meredith thought I might find it amusing to attend Lady Dillard's musical evening, but since I am still in mourning, it was impossible for me to appear at any society function.

"Both Meredith and I felt it would harm no one by enacting the little charade of pretending to be Miss Maxwell, a distant cousin. Even Aunt Agatha saw no overt problems with the white lie, and we certainly never thought to encounter anyone who knew my true name."

"Actually, it makes perfect sense," Griffin said, his voice an odd mix of amusement and candor. "The rules of society can be rigid at times, at others they seem downright ridiculous."

"Precisely." Faith nodded her head eagerly.

"I for one am not known for my strict adherence to propriety."

Faith lowered her chin to conceal her smile. "I suspected that might be the case."

"However, there are certain rules that when broken can leave a woman in a most precarious position."

Faith's head snapped up. His voice was suddenly so somber and serious. "Whatever do you mean?"

"I am talking about indiscretion." Griffin glanced briefly at his boots. "I'm hoping that you will speak candidly to me about your circumstances, however painful they might be."

Faith wrinkled her brow. What in the world was he getting at? She searched his handsome features for guidance, but the viscount's expressionless face revealed nothing. He must have seen her confusion, for he added softly, "I am referring, of course, to your relationship with my brother, Neville."

"Oh." Color flooded Faith's cheeks. Remembering Neville and her nearly nonexistent relationship with her former fiancé forced her to confront her deepest regrets. She wasn't pretty enough, desirable enough, *womanly* enough to be a wife. His rejection of her, in front of the entire community that was her world, had ruined her, leaving her with little pride and almost no self-confidence.

"I would not use the word indiscretion to describe my relationship with your brother. It was more a case of naive stupidity." Her voice dropped to a discouraged whisper. "And while it might be true that Neville has ruined me, I realize that I must accept the fact that I shall never marry, and therefore carry on with my life to the best of my abilities."

She hadn't meant to sound like such a martyr, but it almost couldn't be helped. Speaking of Neville was always a painful reminder of her failures.

Faith caught the flicker of a smile on Griffin's handsome face. It was somewhat surprising, considering the grave nature of their conversation. Perhaps it wasn't really a smile, but rather a grimace.

Griffin breathed deeply, as the moment of reckoning was upon him. He had hoped she would refute his suspicions, deny any hint of impropriety. Yet deep in his heart, Griffin was not overly surprised. More and more he had begun to suspect that Neville might have abused his privileges as Faith's fiancé, for his brother had not been known for either his morality nor generosity of spirit.

'Tis settled, Griffin thought with grim determination. The matter that he had wondered and fretted over was now inevitable. Neville had ruined her, yet it was Griffin's responsibility to set it all to rights. Just like this bloody title. Neither sought after nor welcomed, but assumed because there is no other recourse.

Griffin eyed Faith speculatively. She did not look like a woman who would elicit unbridled passion, but he had long ago learned never to be hasty when judging a female.

His mouth tightened. If he was going to spend the rest of his life sleeping and waking beside her, he might as well make certain of one more thing.

Griffin shifted swiftly from his large chair to join her on the cozy love seat. She seemed startled, but her expression did not alter until he wrapped his arms around her waist and drew her close.

Faith's eyes widened and her lips parted with surprise just as he bent his head and kissed her. It was a full, deep kiss, filled with passion and mystery. He felt her hesitate and stiffen, yet she did not retreat.

Griffin backed off a hair's breadth, letting her make the choice. He could feel the warmth of her breath mingling with his own as she made her decision; then a smile of pure male satisfaction crossed his face as she arched up to once again meet his lips.

He kissed her again. Boldly, he caressed her lips, gliding along the tender flesh with his tongue. She opened her mouth to him and he pressed closer, tasting her fully, his questing tongue twirling seductively with hers.

It seemed like it had been a very long time since he had kissed a woman so completely. Griffin succumbed to his baser instincts and thoroughly indulged himself, repeatedly kissing Faith deeply, hungrily, until they were both nearly breathless.

She strained against him, and their kisses became more heated, more urgent. He felt his body draw up tight with pleasure. Her honest excitement stirred a restless yearning deep inside that both surprised and delighted him.

Faith's kiss held back no hesitant passion, none of the shy ignorance one would expect from a virginal maid. She did not appear overly experienced, and he surmised her skill in arousing him so quickly was due less to her carnal knowledge and more to her naturally passionate nature.

Griffin moaned low in his throat. Faith reached up with one of her hands and cupped his face, as if she feared he would pull away. Her obvious need quickened his own desire with startling intensity.

He buried his fingers in her silky scalp, disturbing the tightly coiled chignon so thoroughly that her hair fell through his fingers and spilled down her back. It felt like warm silk.

His hand slid lower, cupping her breast fully. His palm seemed to burn as his fingers traced the surprising fullness. She moaned in a soft, low voice and pushed herself closer. Her hands reached out, sliding past his lapels and twined in his hair.

Griffin thought about lowering the bodice of her gown and covering her breasts with his hands, stroking her nipples until they stiffened. He fantasized about lifting her skirts and searching out her feminine secrets, pleasuring her with deep, slow strokes, bringing her to the very edge again and again until she was nearly mindless.

He doubted she would object. She did not appear frightened or surprised by his sexual advance. Indeed, his aggressiveness seemed to fuel her own passion. Heady thoughts, indeed.

With far more regret than he ever believed possible, Griffin pulled away from Faith. He took a deep breath, then a second, drawing inward to collect himself. The band of regret that had tightened his chest when he realized he must marry her started to ease.

It seemed an odd belief for a confirmed womanizer, but Griffin believed wholeheartedly in the institution of marriage. He had always promised himself that he would not marry a woman who overtly displeased or repelled him. He would marry a woman he could someday grow to love, and who could in turn love him.

The loveless matches of society held no interest for him. He wanted a life partner, someone to share both the good and difficult times. Someone he could respect, admire, and most importantly trust.

Faith Linden was nothing at all like a wife he would have chosen for himself. She was too unsophisticated, too plain in looks, manner, and dress, too opinionated at times for a woman, and she had an independent streak that bore close watching. Still, in his honest heart, Griffin knew he could do far worse. And it certainly would be no hardship marrying a woman who could kiss as she did.

"I think, Miss Linden, that considering all the circumstances, it would be prudent for us to marry." He ran his fingers through his hair, smoothing the loose strands that Faith had mussed back into place. "In fact, we should probably marry before we return to the country. I shall see about making special arrangements this afternoon."

There was a loud gasp of shock. He turned to face her and saw a world of confusion, along with a strong glimmer of hope in the rich brown eyes that stared so steadily back at him.

"Would you be so kind as to repeat your question, Lord Dewhurst?" she whispered.

"I want you to be my wife. Marry me, Faith."

"Are you serious?" She was eyeing him with a most peculiar expression, almost as though she were hypnotized. "I do not understand. You made your feelings on the matter of a marriage between us quite clear when we spoke of this at your home. Why have you changed your mind?"

Gently catching her chin with the end of his finger, he tipped her face up to his. " 'Tis the proper thing to do, Faith. Both our fathers wanted an alliance between the families. Why not honor their wishes?"

There was a slight hesitation. Griffin felt his face turn warm, thinking she was about to refuse him. After all these years and countless women, he had finally asked one to marry him. And it suddenly appeared as though she was about to decline. How utterly humiliating.

"Yes," she finally said, her voice firm. "I shall be honored to marry you, Griffin."

Six

Faith's grin was so wide her jaw ached, but she could not seem to remove it. Married! She was to be married. To Griffin Sainthill, Viscount Dewhurst, the object of every girlhood fantasy she had ever had.

This union would not only bring her the man she had always secretly desired from afar, but their marriage would allow her to retain possession of Mayfair Manor, her girlhood home. Flustered, she grabbed a stray curl that hung on her shoulder and wound it around her fingers. Remembering how her tightly coiled hair had become loose brought a fresh smile to her swollen lips and a slight blush to her cheeks.

Griffin's kisses had heated her blood and touched her soul. He had unleashed hungers she'd never even known she possessed, awakening a sensual, womanly side of herself that she was now eager to explore.

And now she would have that chance, because they were to be married. *Dear Lord!*

Faith forced herself to take a deep breath and attempted to compose her turbulent emotions. Yet it was nearly impossible, for her blood was practically singing with excitement. Knowing that this tall, handsome, solid man was going to be hers brought her happiness to an almost giddy level. It was a miracle.

She felt as if she were flying, suspended from reality. Faith could hear her own heartbeat, loud and pounding in her ears. It was almost too much happiness to bear.

Hesitantly she looked at him. He was leaning back against the cushions of the love seat, totally at ease, his manner relaxed, almost casual. As if becoming engaged was a common, everyday occurrence. For a moment, she envied his cavalier attitude.

Or perhaps this just wasn't as important and momentous an occasion to him as it was for her.

"There is something that I need to tell you."

The solemn tone of Griffin's voice chiseled at Faith's happiness. She swallowed convulsively. "Yes?"

"I have a child. A son." Griffin looked at her keenly. "I brought him home to England with me from the Colonies."

Faith's knees turned to water. A son! Oh, dear, how could she possibly stand any more joy. In one fell swoop those secret longings she had nearly buried within herself had become a stark reality. Not only was she at long last going to become a wife, but also a mother.

Faith felt a sudden, emotional ache in her throat. She swallowed hard, struggling to speak evenly. "I did not realize that you had been married, my lord."

Something flickered briefly in Griffin's eyes. "My business affairs kept me traveling to distant ports most of the year. We did not live together."

"Only long enough to have a child?" she quipped. His head jerked up and her smile of delight widened. A son! She was going to be a mother, and there was nothing in the universe that could dim that joy. "You are very good at keeping secrets, sir. I had not heard about your child. Is he at school?"

"No, he is too young to be sent away to school. He

is nearly four years old." Griffin's expression grew thoughtful, and the frown between his brow eased. "Would you prefer that I have him sent away?"

"Goodness, no!" Faith exclaimed in horror. "I was merely applauding your powers of discretion. Harrowby is a small village. I've never had any success in keeping my affairs from becoming the object of town gossip, yet you have managed to keep both your former marriage and heir a private matter." Faith leaned forward eagerly. "Tell me more about your little boy."

Griffin smiled with obvious relief. "He is a sturdy lad, quick of mind, with a natural curiosity, yet he is oddly self-contained for one so young. He managed the crossing well, barely having any seasickness."

"Ah, a natural sailor, just like his father." The pride in Griffin's voice pleased Faith mightily. It was clear he held his child in great affection. She took that as a sign that bode well for her own future offspring, if they should be so blessed.

"Coming to England has been a difficult adjustment for him, however." Griffin sighed. "His nursemaid returned to the Colonies soon after we arrived. She was more like a surrogate mother to him, since his own died nearly a year ago. At this point, I'm afraid I am more of a stranger than father to him."

"Poor lad. It must all be so frightening and confusing for him. Have you engaged a new nurse?"

"I did, but the girl was not suitable. My sister Harriet has since interviewed several young women for the post, but had not settled upon one when I left to come to London."

Faith nodded her head vigorously. "That shall be my first duty when we return home. After all, it is a mother's responsibility to see to the welfare of her children, not an aunt's." She dipped her head shyly.

"Do you think he will be pleased to have me as his new mother?"

"I have a feeling that young Neville will be delighted."

"Neville?" Faith echoed weakly. "The boy's name is Neville?"

The customary amusement faded from Griffin's handsome features. "I was away at sea when he was born. His mother thought to honor my family by naming him after my brother."

"Oh, dear." Faith flushed deeply and looked away. Who would ever have believed such rotten luck? Of all the names in Christendom, why did the woman have to select that one? Could she not have named the child after his father? Or grandfather?

It seemed as though Faith was destined to remain tied to the past. Now, through this innocent child, she would forever be reminded, most likely each day, of someone she had longed to forget.

"Faith?"

She lifted her head automatically. They stared at each other for a few long, tense moments.

"It really is an awful name, isn't it?" she ventured softly.

The corners of Griffin's mouth began to slowly crack, and then he burst out laughing. " 'Tis dreadful. Hardly an appropriate name for a little boy. I remember my brother never liked it, either. Perhaps we shall give our young Neville a nickname."

"That's a splendid idea. I'm sure if we put our heads together we can come up with a name that is agreeable to all of us."

"We shall make that our first task when we return home," Griffin decided. "A new name for our son."

"Yes," Faith said softly, as a tempest of emotions

swirled through her. She liked how he had referred to the child as *our* son, and was even more pleased with the notion of being included in selecting a nickname for the boy. It made it seem as if they were already becoming a family.

"Since you are of age, I assume there is no one I need to ask permission for your hand in marriage?" Griffin inquired.

"There is no one," Faith responded shyly. A fleeting memory of her father and how delighted he would have been with this sudden turn of events tugged at her heart. "However, I would like to consult with Meredith's solicitor again, to make certain that I will be able to retain ownership of Mayfair Manor once we are wed."

"An excellent suggestion." Griffin rose to his feet. "I shall accompany you."

He had not phrased his words in the form of a question, yet the ensuing silence told Faith that Griffin would at least listen to her objections if she decided he should not be at the meeting with the lawyer. Since she had none, she remained quiet.

"I prefer not to wait long to formalize our vows," Griffin continued. "Would you mind very much if we forgo all the fuss of a formal wedding and marry quietly? I can easily and quickly obtain a special license."

Return to Harrowby a married woman! Faith could think of nothing she would like better. "A quiet ceremony will do very nicely. My only request is that Meredith, her two brothers, and Aunt Agatha are in attendance."

"That can easily be arranged." Griffin extracted a gold timepiece from the pocket of his waistcoat and consulted it. "There is ample time to begin organizing things this afternoon. Will Thursday morning suit?"

"Yes." Faith closed her eyes briefly. Thursday was a

mere three days away. "I feel like I should pinch myself, to make certain this isn't all a dream." She gave him an impish grin. "Or perhaps I should pinch you, instead?"

"Do so at your own peril, my dear," Griffin countered, as a roguish smile surfaced.

Faith shivered. That grin reminded her of all the things she found nearly irresistible about the man—the easy charm, the masculine vitality, the sensual strength. Their eyes locked, and something strange and intimate seemed to pass between them.

Griffin lifted her hand to his lips and pressed a soft, delicate kiss on the top of her wrist. At his warm touch, the hunger and longing inside her once more sprang to life.

Faith involuntarily shivered again, and she wondered how on earth she was going to wait until Thursday.

"I still don't understand why we must attend Lady Dillard's ball," Faith declared grimly, as her shoulder pressed sharply against Meredith's.

The carriage rattled down the cobbled road, swaying and jostling the four passengers inside. Faith tried glaring at Griffin, who was seated directly opposite her, but the approaching darkness lessened the effect of demonstrating her ire. "Could we not have written Lady Dillard a note, explaining the situation? Or called upon her in private?"

"No," Griffin replied firmly. "Since you made your initial appearance at her home as Miss Maxwell, 'tis only fitting you should now reveal the truth at her ball. Besides, it is logical to assume that many of the same guests who attended the musical evening will be in attendance tonight. It will be much simpler and far more efficient to let everyone else know the truth also."

Faith crossed her arms beneath her breast and huffed loudly. "I shall be changing my name the moment we are married. Who will even remember that I was, for a most brief time, Miss Maxwell?"

"Probably someone you don't wish to," Griffin replied philosophically. "You must trust me on this, Faith. It is far better to take the matter in hand now."

"His lordship is right," Aunt Agatha agreed with an enthusiastic bobbing of her head. "Best to get this silly mess settled."

Faith huffed out another breath and tried glaring at Meredith's elderly aunt. Ever since she had agreed to marry him, only two days ago, Griffin had become a constant visitor to the household.

He took meals at Meredith's home, engaged an elegant hired coach for carriage rides to the park at the fashionable afternoon hour, and even accompanied the three women to the shops on Bond street. And in that short time he had managed to somehow completely charm the older woman.

It was a pattern that Faith could not avoid noticing. It seemed that nearly any female Griffin came in contact with, be it nobility or gentry or common maid, seemed to fall instantly under his spell.

Even Merry was starting to thaw toward him.

"I still think we could have written Lady Dillard a note," Faith persisted peevishly.

She frowned at Griffin in the dimly lit carriage, then clamped hard on her jaw. Even though Faith knew she had already lost this battle, she could not seem to let the matter drop. Partly because she was very nervous about facing all these exalted people with her former lie and partly because she chafed at taking or-ders from Griffin. It was one aspect of their engagement she hadn't fully anticipated.

If her fiancé was disturbed by her negativity, he gave no indication, replying calmly, "After we are married, I don't plan on spending a great amount of time in town; however, I would certainly be remiss in my duty if I allowed this charade to go uncorrected.

"I realize you wish to let the matter go unaddressed, but honestly Faith, would you really prefer that I throw my cloak over your head and hide you from view each time we encounter someone who knew you as Miss Maxwell?"

"Perhaps I could learn to press myself behind architectural columns or perfect leaping into shrubbery to conceal myself," Faith suggested, summoning up her brightest smile. "Then we wouldn't have to be so concerned about you needing to toss your garments over my head."

Griffin's gaze found hers in the murky darkness of the coach. "I shall want to show you off when you are my wife, not hide you."

It was a gallant, flattering sentiment, but Faith was too distraught to fully appreciate it. "I don't understand why it should matter so much," she grumbled.

"Society can be most unforgiving," Meredith said. "They are quick to criticize and even quicker to condemn. If you reveal the truth now, there will be a minor ripple, but if you attempt to conceal it, a great wave of scandal might someday wash over the entire family. When you least expect it."

"How dire," Faith mumbled under her breath, feeling a sting of betrayal at Merry's agreement with Griffin. Was there no one at all who would take up her side in this discussion?

Griffin reached across the small space that separated them and took Faith's hand. He had removed his gloves for the short carriage ride to Lady Dillard's home. Faith could feel the strength and power in his fists and a slight roughness in his palms. Yet the bones of his hands were long and elegant.

"I'm nervous," Faith blurted out.

"I realize that," Griffin replied, cocking his head to one side. "I promise to stay unfashionably glued to your side throughout the evening. And Lady Meredith and Aunt Agatha are here to lend support. You are not alone, Faith."

She felt the heat flare in her cheeks. They were all trying to be supportive of her and she was acting like a spoiled child. The course had been set; she had no choice but to follow it. The least she could do was approach it with determination and dignity.

Resolutely, Faith buried her doubts and launched into a nonsensical discussion about the weather. This lighthearted conversation continued for the remainder of the journey and seemed to place everyone at ease.

Still, the nerves that had settled during the carriage ride quickly began churning inside Faith the moment they started climbing the long circular stairway that led to Lady Dillard's ballroom. Faith kept her chin raised at an almost ridiculously high angle, determined to show no fear.

It was, however, impossible to keep her breathing even as the footman announced in a bored monotone, "Viscount Dewhurst, Lady Agatha Hastings, Lady Meredith Barrington, and Miss Faith Linden."

Faith had expected hushed whispers and stares, perhaps a finger or two pointed accusingly in her direction. Yet it seemed that no one in the elegantly crowded ballroom was the least bit interested in their party's arrival, aside from a few lush-looking females.

And their gazes were rather blatantly directed at Viscount Dewhurst.

As the four approached the receiving line, Faith was relieved to note they were alone with their hosts. She managed a wobbly curtsy for Lord and Lady Dillard and braced herself for trouble, all the while praying she might yet escape a completely embarrassing explanation.

Then Lady Dillard cast a quizzical gaze at her that sent Faith's hopes plummeting.

"What? What did that dolt of a servant say? I apologize for my footman, Miss Maxwell. He's gotten your name wrong, the fool." Lady Dillard turned and tapped her fan insistently on the sleeve of the elderly gentleman at her side. "I think the servants have been getting into the wine again, Lord Dillard. They are getting the guests' names muddled. Summon the butler at once, so he may give the man the severe dressing-down he deserves."

"Can it not wait until after the party?" Lord Dillard inquired wearily.

"It most assuredly cannot!" Lady Dillard stomped her foot. "I will not have my guests insulted by foolish servants."

Griffin raised a forestalling hand. "Please, Lady Dillard, there is no need to speak with your servant. He did not make a mistake. This charming young woman is indeed Miss Faith Linden, very soon to be the Viscountess Dewhurst."

Lady Dillard's eyes narrowed. "I thought her name was Maxwell."

"I'm afraid you must lay the blame for that at my feet," Griffin said. He leaned closer and whispered in the older woman's ear. "We had a silly argument, and she thought to avoid me by hiding out in London.

Fortunately, I was able to track her down and smooth her ruffled feathers. I so hope you will offer your felicitations. We are to be married tomorrow."

Lady Dillard glanced again at Faith, but this time her eyes were alive with speculation. "Well, if you have chosen her, Lord Dewhurst, then she must be worthy in ways that are not so immediately apparent."

"You have no idea," Griffin replied. "Faith has taught me that in matters of the heart a mortal man has no recourse but to follow his emotions."

It was precisely the right thing to say. Griffin's words expertly and cannily tapped into Lady Dillard's romantic side. She smiled her approval at the couple.

"I'm so pleased you were able to attend my ball," Lady Dillard replied. "I hope you enjoy yourselves this evening."

With a start, Faith realized the interview was over. She gave Lord and Lady Dillard a quick curtsy and clutched tightly on to Griffin's arm as he led her away. It was not until she reached the crowded ballroom floor that Faith realized she had not uttered a word directly to Lady Dillard. Griffin had done all of the talking and charming. Perhaps it wouldn't be so horrible to on occasion allow him to control a situation.

"Shall we dance?" Griffin suggested, holding out his hand.

"I do not have permission to waltz," Faith cried out, as he pulled her onto the floor. "The last thing we need to do is create a scandal. I thought the purpose of our coming here this evening was to avoid one."

"Ah, but this time we shall create a scandal together." He favored her with a smile so wickedly handsome it made her heart leap. "That makes it all the more exciting."

Faith rolled her eyes at his male logic. Yet she made

no protest as he swept her into his arms and whirled her onto the dance floor.

Though she very much enjoyed dancing, Faith had done little of it in public. And never a waltz. But the excellent dance instructor her father had insisted on hiring had done his job well. She was able to follow Griffin's lead without treading on his toes.

They completed the circuit of the large dance floor twice before she was able to glance at the other couples. Faith immediately noticed that the other women were not being held as intimately by their partners. Griffin's hand was firmly pressed into the small of her back, and mere inches separated their upper bodies.

"I think you are holding me improperly close, my lord," Faith whispered.

"Do you object?"

She tilted up her head and gazed into his eyes. "Quite the contrary. I prefer it."

He answered her saucy quip by pulling her even closer. Faith relaxed a little and smiled, enjoying thoroughly the feel of the muscled arms that held her, the view of the broad chest displayed before her, the freshly washed scent of his snowy white cravat.

"How are your nerves?" Griffin asked.

"Better, but not yet conquered. I'm hoping we won't have to stay long this evening."

"If I know Lady Dillard as well as I think I do, the gossip about our impending marriage and your little prank to avoid me should be spreading through the ballroom like wildfire. It shall make our task far easier."

"Good."

"Ah, there is Lord Dunstand," Griffin commented. "The man's an insufferable boor, but it would probably be wise to speak with him next, as soon as our dance concludes."

Faith stumbled, but Griffin caught her, making a deft turn away from the gentleman in question. Faith sighed with relief. The easy victory with Lady Dillard had been accomplished by sheer male charm. Faith strongly doubted that tact would work with a gentleman such as Lord Dunstand.

All too soon the dance ended. Faith glanced longingly at the terraced doors on the opposite side of the ballroom, but made no move toward them. As if sensing her indecisiveness, Griffin leaned down and whispered in her ear. "After we speak with Dunstand, you shall dance with me again."

Heat filtered through her and a fluttery feeling rose in her chest. She was about to comment that any more than two dances in one evening would be considered most improper, but the smirk on Griffin's face stopped her. It was almost as if he was daring her to protest.

"I shall look forward to our next dance with great anticipation, my lord," she said, wondering suddenly if he would kiss her this evening. Perhaps later, when he said good night.

He had done no more than briefly brush her hand with his warm lips since the afternoon he had proposed, and she admitted to herself that she missed those melting kisses that seemed to ignite every nerve in her body.

She was so distracted by those memories, she didn't realize they were facing Lord Dunstand until his nagging voice broke into her fanciful thoughts.

"Ah, Miss Linden. Good evening. It is Miss Linden, is it not? Or have you decided to once again change your name?"

"I would have thought you had heard by now," Griffin said casually. "Come tomorrow, she will be Viscountess Dewhurst."

Dunstand raised one eyebrow and shifted his gaze to Faith. "Is that true?"

Faith managed a wan smile. "Yes. We had a small quarrel. Griffin followed me to London and quickly located me, despite my efforts to hide from him."

"A small quarrel sent you fleeing from your intended? How very peculiar." Lord Dunstand's superior sniff soon had Faith gritting her teeth.

"I felt certain a man possessing such wit as yourself would find Miss Linden's little prank most amusing," Griffin added. "Only those individuals with superior breeding and intelligence can truly appreciate the irony." He leveled a hard stare in Lord Dunstand's direction, a look that was filled with such dire warning, it left Dunstand with no choice.

He cocked his head rather sharply and said tersely, "I wish you both every happiness in your marriage. You seem a most well-matched pair."

A great sigh escaped Faith's lips as she watched Lord Dunstand turn and stalk away. She was beginning to feel better. With considerably calmer nerves, she took Griffin's arm and set about to greet another gathering of guests.

After conquering Lady Dillard and Lord Dunstand, facing the rest of the noble assemblage was an easy task. Faith merely followed Griffin's lead, smiling at the appropriate moments, making only the minimal comments necessary. She was certain that people would think her a vapid creature, but for once Faith didn't care.

This was an alien world to her, and although Griffin had been away for many years, he fit easily into it.

This was the society in which he had been raised, and as her father was fond of saying, noble blood will tell.

True to his word, Griffin stayed at her side for most of the evening. He spoke to anyone they encountered that knew her as Miss Maxwell, and before long had even Faith believing that they were a couple caught up in an emotional whirl, separated briefly by a silly misunderstanding.

The ballroom was a maddening crush, and despite her enjoyment of the evening, Faith was more than pleased to take a walk in the garden when Griffin suggested it.

They spoke quietly of inconsequential matters as they slipped farther into the fragrant depths of the garden, beyond the elegant shrubs and blossoming bushes. The warm night air was heavy with the scent of flowers and the promise of the forbidden.

Finally they stopped in a secluded corner, where it was dark and quiet. The gentle silence of the night was broken by the sounds of rushing water from the ornamental fountain behind them, the melodic warbling of the night birds, and the strong, erratic beat of Faith's heart.

Griffin turned and faced her. She could just make out the steely gray of his eyes in the moonlight. They moved with undisguised heat over her body, making her feel womanly. Powerful.

The faint sounds of laughter drifted out to them, reminding Faith of the risk they were taking. Even though they were to be married tomorrow, it would be most unwise if they were caught out here. Alone. Oddly, the thought made Faith even more excited.

Yet her nerves soon got the better of her, and she began to chatter aimlessly, as she always did when her anxiety rose. "Did you meet Lord and Lady Martin this evening? They are a most fascinating couple. He is a member of the House of Lords and most active—"

Griffin cut off her words in midsentence with a fierce, possessive kiss. For an instant Faith stiffened, but she soon began to melt as he gentled his invasions.

Griffin's lips softened and molded themselves to hers. His tongue darted out for a swift, warm caress, sending a flash of heat to her stomach.

"I've been wanting to do that all evening," he whispered.

"Truly?" she asked breathlessly, unable to believe that she could incite such desire in him.

"All evening," he reiterated. His hand gently cupped the back of her neck, teasing the tender flesh with the warm tips of his fingers, stroking shivers up and down her spine. With his hand firmly planted in the center of her back, he drew her forward to start another, deeper kiss.

She melted into the embrace, tasting the warm inside of his mouth. Her knees felt weak, and she could no longer hear the sounds of the night above the thundering of her heart. Her entire being quickened with sweet anticipation. Faith could feel her breasts start to swell, the nipples straining against the silk bodice of her gown.

As if sensing her desire, Griffin's hands moved down to her chest, slipping inside the top of her low-cut gown to cup her roundness. Lightly, insistently, his fingers teased her nipples into tight, hard buds, the heat of his fingers inflaming her already aroused senses.

Faith's hands moved restlessly to the hard, muscular plane of his chest, then crept slowly around his shoulders. He buried his face in the nape of her neck, and she could feel his breath hot and eager against her sensitive skin.

Faith breathed deeply, filling her nostrils with his dark, musky, masculine scent.

"We should probably return to the ball," she suggested weakly. "Merry and Aunt Agatha will wonder what has become of us."

"Soon," he whispered, nuzzling her temple.

She lifted her head to speak again, but he silenced her with another tender kiss. The faint shreds of protest fled quickly and Faith joyfully gave herself over to the passion, the excitement.

Griffin's teeth nipped at the lobe of her ear; then his moist lips began a slow, languid journey down her throat. A faint moan escaped her swollen lips as the liquid heat ran swiftly through her body.

He paused when he reached the tops of her breasts; then with a deep groan he lowered his head and pulled a nipple into his mouth. Faith gasped loudly at the tingling she felt, the sudden moisture that rushed between her legs.

Was that normal? Embarrassment made her face grow warm, but she soon forgot her distress as Griffin's questing mouth moved to her other breast. He rimmed the edge of her nipple with his tongue, then sucked hard on the bud until it tightened.

"My stars," Faith whispered breathlessly. "My legs feel like rubber. I'm very much afraid I'm going to keel over."

"Don't worry, sweet Faith. I won't let you fall."

The tight bands of muscles in his arms told her he spoke the truth. Faith smiled. He would prevent her from collapsing, even though he was the cause of her weakness, with kisses and caresses that drove her senses to the very brink.

She let her mind and body drift, knowing by the timbre of sincerity in his voice that she could trust him to take care of her. It brought an oddly unfamiliar sense of comfort to her heart.

Yet Faith almost did fall at the feel of his large hands stroking over her hips. She started trembling when she felt his fingers reach under her skirts. Expertly he brushed aside her undergarment. Faith gasped, and she gazed frantically up at the night sky, as if searching among the heavens for the means to control her confused emotions.

She knew he would stop if she asked him. But the words stuck in her throat. It was too delicious, too enthralling to end now. Besides, they were to be married tomorrow. Did it really matter if they anticipated their wedding night by a mere twenty-four hours?

His hands grew bolder, caressing her upper thighs with light, teasing fingers, until she felt the moisture gathering and the pleasure becoming nearly unbearable.

"Griffin?" Her voice was a softly whispered plea.

She pushed herself forward, almost mindlessly, seeking relief from the restless tension he had created deep, deep inside her. Faith felt his body tighten, heard him curse softly under his breath.

"My God, you make me forget my very name," he growled roughly in her ear as he abruptly pulled away his hands.

"Please, Griffin, you cannot mean to stop," she cried. Her hands reached out blindly for his.

"A true gentleman would never leave such a lovely lady in distress," he whispered sensually. His lips grazed the vulnerable skin beneath her ear. "Yet this is a matter of some delicacy. A woman's passion."

A woman's passion. Those hoarsely spoken words

set her blood raging and her heart soaring. Finally, after years of curiosity and secret longing she was experiencing passion.

His hands moved behind her knees, and without warning he swung her into his arms. Faith closed her eyes and leaned into his solid, warm strength, sighing softly when he settled them on a garden bench tucked beneath a towering tree.

He positioned her awkwardly across his lap, but Faith barely noticed. She struggled to draw breath as she felt his hand slide downward, toward the very center of her longing. His fingers probed gently, parting the slick fold of her sex, kneading her overheated flesh in precisely the right spot. Warm shivers raced across her skin, and she shuddered each time he stroked her.

She lifted her face to his, and he answered her silent plea with a rough, hard kiss. Her lips clung to his as the rhythm of his strokes increased. Restlessly she moved her hands down to his, clasping the strong wrists. The hair on his arm felt crisp and springy, the muscles of his forearms were tense and strong.

It was such an intimate, unfamiliar act, yet she felt totally at ease with it, suffering no twinges of virginal horror.

"Let yourself relax," he whispered roughly against her face, before sinking his teeth into the fleshy lobe of her ear. "Trust me."

How could she not? Sprawled half naked in a moonlit garden while the musicians played at Lady Dillard's ball and the cream of society mingled and danced and flirted, Faith realized she had already placed all her trust in this man. And a goodly piece of her heart.

The rhythm and pressure of his hand increased. Small sobs of delight escaped from her lips as she

rose with him, wantonly opening herself to his shame-
less caress.

The spasms of pleasure broke without warning. Her
wits scattered, Faith could do nothing but cling tightly
to Griffin and let the sensual delight wash over her.
She cried out in surprise and wonderment, and he
caught her lips with his own to capture her ecstasy.

Her body convulsed, and she could almost feel the
blood rushing past her ears. For an instant she felt
more alive, more attuned with her body and emotions
than ever before.

Faith drifted slowly down to earth, finally becoming
aware once more of her surroundings. The warm kiss
of the gentle night breeze against her still-heated skin,
the fragrant scent of garden flowers now mixed with
the pungent scent of fulfilled desire.

Yet despite the great pleasure Faith had just enjoyed,
she felt a yearning within herself for something that
was just beyond her reach. Something that only Griffin could give her.

"But there is more. I know there is more." She wiggled in his lap and found the hard proof of her words
poking insistently against the soft cheeks of her bottom. "Why must we stop? Oh, Griffin, we are to be
married tomorrow. Does it really matter?"

"Good Lord, you would lead angels down a sinful
path and they would follow joyously." He clenched
and unclenched his fingers repeatedly, then rubbed his
forehead vigorously as if he were in great pain. "We
shall wait because it is the proper and civilized thing
to do. I vow, I will show more respect than my brother
did, Faith. So no matter how much you tempt me, I
shall not make you mine until we are legally wed."

Seven

Heaving a disgruntled sigh, Griffin gingerly shifted the womanly bundle in his lap. Faith protested and wrapped her arms tightly around his neck. Biting back a curse, the viscount gently disengaged her entwined fingers and attempted to set her on her feet.

The erection straining against his breeches was painful, and each wiggle of her luscious backside was like a knife probing an open wound.

"Come, let me help you fasten your gown," he said gruffly. "I loosened a few of the buttons earlier."

His words had the desired effect of freezing her movements, and Griffin swiftly took advantage of the situation. He set Faith on her feet and stepped behind her. When he was finished fastening the buttons on the back of her gown, he turned her to face him.

"You are a man of infinite talent, my lord," she said quietly. "Adept at not only divesting a lady of her garments but also dressing her."

"It seemed prudent to learn both tasks," Griffin quipped, but the charming grin on his face faded at the sight of Faith's somber countenance.

What an idiotic thing to say! Boasting of his previous experience to his future wife. He was sure she was now wondering how many other women he had performed this intimate service for, and while the num-

ber was rather large, the frown on Faith's face told him
the number she was imagining was far greater.

"After tomorrow, you shall have the exclusive right
to my services as a lady's maid," Griffin declared sincerely.

"You do me a great honor, sir." Faith plucked a
small leaf off a nearby bush and crumpled it between
her fingers. "I hope that shall not prove to be too
great a hardship for you."

He reached for her hand. "I shall not take my marriage vows lightly, Faith. And I expect the same fi-
delity from you."

Her face brightened considerably at his declaration
of intended faithfulness and Griffin's heart swelled. It
was puzzling, but for whatever reason, her approval
was something he inadvertently sought.

He felt confident that if he set himself to charm
her, he would succeed. Faith was unlike most of the
women he had known. On the surface she seemed simpler, less complicated, but he was not foolish enough
to underestimate her intelligence. No, the main difference between Faith and the women of his past was
that Faith needed him.

Griffin wondered suddenly what it would be like to
lie beside this woman and watch her sleep at night.
He eyed her with speculation, and she returned that
gaze with a steady one of her own. He usually thought
it uncomfortable to stare at a woman without speaking, yet with Faith he did not experience that awkward
feeling.

"I'm glad we took a w-walk in the moonlight," she
said softly. Her hand strayed to his chest, and she
played absently with the silver buttons on his waistcoat. "Lady Dillard's ball is a lovely party, but it is
quite magical out here in her luscious garden."

" 'Tis you who bring the magic to the evening, Faith."

Her eyes flashed with genuine pleasure at his outrageous flattery. Griffin's insides tightened. He shifted from foot to foot, disturbed to discover the restless yearning he felt was not entirely due to sexual frustration.

She was to be his wife, his lifelong responsibility, yet he realized suddenly that he was looking to her to fill not only a physical but an emotional need inside him. A void he had never before acknowledged.

He had known many women in his lifetime. Yet his heart and head had not made a decision about the sentiment of love. Was it truly an emotion that could be achieved and sustained for a long period of time? A lifetime, perhaps?

He had no answers for those questions. All he could acknowledge was that his pulse was quickening with a primitive sensation that was caused specifically by this one particular woman who stood beside him.

He could feel her looking at him, watching with luminous brown eyes, seeming to hang on his every word as if what he said was the most important thing she had to hear. It was a heady responsibility. He felt exceptionally gentle toward her and the keen pressure to make certain his words were creating sweet memories in her mind.

"I'm afraid our magical time has come to an end for this evening. We had best return to the ball before our long absence is noticed," he said. "Tongues will start wagging."

She nodded in agreement, but he could see her expression was solemn, almost wistful. He touched her hair and she lifted her face.

"So now we are concerned about the gossipmongers, my lord?" Faith queried, rubbing her arms briskly. "Earlier we did not care. Or so you said when we began our waltz. However, before that it was of paramount importance to avoid gossip and scandal at all costs. Why, 'tis the very reason we attended this ball."

Her eyes narrowed. "Gracious, I feel as though I need to write all this down in the margin of my dance card, since it is impossible to follow your constantly changing opinion on the matter."

"I promise my moods shall not be so mercurial in the future."

"Do not make promises lightly," Faith said. "For I shall hold you to your word."

"I never doubted that you would." He bent his head and gave her a brief, soft kiss.

A rueful smile appeared on her face. "Now you seek to distract me."

"A distraction? Is that how you view my kisses?" A roguish smile surfaced. "I must be losing my touch."

She laughed. "I don't believe that is possible."

He gave her a sheepish grin, then raised her ungloved hand and brushed her knuckles with warm lips. Griffin heard Faith suck in her breath. The air was once again taut with tension and awareness of each other.

It was clear that something had altered between them. Exactly what, Griffin was not certain. He heaved a slight sigh. What strange, maddening spell had she woven around him?

He focused on her face, studying her intently in the glimmering moonlight. With the blush of color in her cheeks, she almost looked pretty. The dress she wore had a plunging round neckline that bared her shoulders. The excellent cut and fit of the garment did much to showcase her limited female assets.

It made her appear taller, more buxom, more womanly. The simple lines and lack of lace, bows, and other fripperies allowed the deep green of the fabric to offset what Griffin decreed as her best asset. Her lovely, soft, pale, creamy complexion.

Her expression was open, her gaze steady. She lacked experience in artifice or teasing, and her flirtatious inclinations seemed natural and genuine. Griffin appreciated knowing she was a woman he could trust and around whom he could relax. It would be unbearably exhausting to have to keep one's guard up around a spouse.

She had followed his dictates by coming to the ball this evening, even though she had not fully appreciated the need. Griffin was more pleased than he could say that she had bowed to his demands.

Bowed, but not crushed, which gave him even greater delight. Her face was in the shadows, but Griffin imagined he could see the firm set of her chin. She was spirited and opinionated and not adverse to showing either trait. He had been amused to observe her earlier nervousness and admiring of how quickly she managed to conquer it.

Griffin acknowledged that he was anticipating their marriage bed with more enthusiasm than he believed possible. This little garden escape had merely hinted at the depths of her sensuality. She had come into his arms with an eagerness many women would have feared showing.

There would be no messy virginity to bother about on their wedding night, no ignorant fears and maidenly modesty. That thought pleased him, too.

The odious Lord Dunstand was far more correct than he realized. They were a matched pair.

Griffin had always considered himself a practical man. As a second son he knew his future had to be earned, and he had taken the task of establishing himself with single-minded determination. Now that he had inherited the title, he would apply that same determination toward all of his newly acquired responsibilities—and that included his marriage.

He might not know her all that well, but what he did know of Faith pleased him. The possibility for a solid union and a happy future loomed like a lighted beacon flashing through the darkness.

They walked quickly along the moonlit garden path with only the sound of their footsteps and the faint strains of music and conversation coming from the house to break the silence. There was still a lingering trace of tension and awareness between them that seemed to heighten the excitement.

"How shall we enter the ballroom without being seen?" Faith whispered as they reached the terraced patio.

"Very carefully," Griffin replied with a ready grin.

Faith giggled and squeezed his arm. She retained her tight grip as he slowly opened a narrow French door. With an economically lithe movement, he slipped inside Lady Dillard's ballroom, pulling Faith along with him.

Once successfully inside, Griffin shut the door firmly and assumed a casual, bored air. His eyes wandered lazily over the many guests filling the room, none of whom were paying them any attention.

The viscount turned and exchanged a conspiratorial smile with Faith. She held her finger to her lips, to silence his gloating. The moment the next dance began, Griffin pulled her into his arms and once again twirled her about the dance floor, feeling strangely pleased with himself.

The dawn brought gray skies and showers, but by late morning the sun had managed to peek through the clouds. Faith fidgeted and fussed for most of the morning, trying desperately to focus her mind and calm her emotions. When that failed, she set herself to doing small, inconsequential tasks, but they did not hold her attention.

Her wedding was scheduled for 3:00 P.M. and it was barely noon. Faith wondered how she was going to pass the next few hours without losing her mind when a loud knock sounded on her bedchamber door.

"Come in," she called out in an almost desperate tone.

The door opened slowly and Meredith appeared on the threshold. "Am I intruding?"

"Heavens, no." Faith reached out and practically pulled her friend into the room. "I'm going batty in here all by myself. I've supervised all the packing, taken my bath, had my hair arranged and rearranged three times. 'Tis too early to start dressing, and I cannot concentrate on either my book or my needlework."

"All brides are nervous on their wedding day," Meredith said. "Grooms, too, I suspect."

Faith laughed, trying to imagine Griffin nervous about anything. "Perhaps some grooms. Not mine."

Meredith smiled briefly. "Actually, I came here for another purpose. I was wondering if there was anything you wished to discuss. Do you have any questions you'd like to ask?"

"Questions? About the wedding ceremony?"

"No, about the wedding night."

Faith looked at her friend in disbelief. Then, with a quick motion she pulled out a chair. "Sit," she commanded.

Meredith sat, and Faith took the chair opposite hers. She said nothing further, just looked at Merry with open curiosity.

Meredith took a deep breath. "Since you don't have a mother who can tell you these things, I thought I might be able to help. Aunt Agatha volunteered to speak with you, but she looked so nervous I doubted she would be able to string two coherent thoughts together."

Faith's eyes grew large and round. "Are you saying that you have *personal* experience to convey to me? Exactly when did this happen? And with whom? Oh, why have you never told me this before, Merry?"

A delicate brow arched up. "Don't be a goose, Faith. I do not have any real experience in these intimate matters. I do, however, have knowledge." Meredith picked up Faith's hairbrush by its silver handle and twirled it anxiously between her fingers. "You know that my mother is very committed to progressive thinking and has always seized every opportunity to display that attitude."

Faith bobbed her head up and down eagerly in response.

"Well, on the night of my eighteenth birthday she came to my bedchamber, much the same as I have now done with you, and initiated a rather frank conversation about marital relations. She told me that her own mother had come to her on the eve of her wedding and told her half truths in such a vague manner that she was totally confused. And extremely terrified, even though she held my father in great affection.

"Determined that such a fate would not befall me, my mother explained, in most graphic detail, the intimacies of the marriage bed."

"Meredith, you're blushing," Faith declared in an astonished voice.

"I'm embarrassed," Meredith admitted. She fumbled with the hairbrush in her hands, then dropped it to the carpet.

"We have been friends forever," Faith insisted, bending down to pick up her brush and return it to its rightful place on the dresser. "We have discussed everything under the sun with each other."

"This is quite a bit different from our usual conversations."

"Does this mean we are finally growing up?"

"It means we are getting old." Meredith chuckled softly. "And this conversation is aging me faster by the minute."

Faith smiled. "Your mother only had your best interests uppermost in her mind. I think you should feel grateful for her openness."

"Why? I doubt I shall ever marry. In my case, this is useless information."

"Knowledge is never useless," Faith insisted.

Meredith made a noncommittal grunt. "I shall gladly share mine with you, where it will have an opportunity to be tested."

Faith glanced down and rubbed the tip of her slipper into the carpet. She wanted to feel terribly sophisticated discussing these matters, but in truth she was having difficulty refraining from bursting into nervous giggles. Still, it seemed foolish to waste this golden opportunity to ask just one question.

"I've grown up in the country, around animals my entire life," Faith said. "I certainly understand the . . .

ahem . . . basic mechanics involved. But I was wondering, is it usually done in darkness? And what about nightclothes? Are they worn or removed?"

"I'm sure there are no specific rules or protocol about clothing," Meredith said after a few very long seconds. "Mother did mention that as much as a husband will admire you in a lovely gown, he much prefers a wife to be out of it. Apparently it increases the enjoyment. As does having sufficient light. And a variety of locations. And positions."

"Positions? Egad!"

Meredith's stoic expression crumbled slightly. "All right. I admit I didn't understand what she meant about the positions, either. At the time, I was thinking too much about being naked in a well-lit room to ask." Her expression grew thoughtful. "The location comment I believe refers to making love in a place other than a bedchamber. Or on a bed."

"Like in a moonlit garden?"

Meredith looked a little surprised. "Yes, I suppose that is quite possible."

"Oh, I feel certain it is," Faith said with a sly smile, remembering the previous night.

Once she had feared that Griffin might find her unappealing and unattractive, but last night in Lady Dillard's garden he had proven his desire for her.

She remembered with pleasure the spiral of heat that had slid through her entire being at the touch of his lips, the way she had trembled at his gentle touch, pushing herself boldly forward to experience each marvelous new sensation. It had been heavenly.

The sound of his deep silken voice, telling her that he would wait until they were wed before claiming her as his own. He would show more respect than his brother and wait until they were wed. Unlike his brother. Not until they were wed.

"Oh, my dear Lord," Faith whispered in horror, as the true meaning of his words sank into her brain. *He would wait!* Because his brother had not waited. His brother had compromised her, *ruined* her.

It cannot be true! Yet as she repeated Griffin's words of last evening over and over in her head, Faith knew she was not mistaking his meaning. Overwhelmed by passion, excited by his kisses and sensuous caresses, she had not been coherent enough last night for the words to have effect. Here in the cold, stark reality of daytime, the meaning became horribly clear.

The only reason Viscount Dewhurst agreed to marry her was because he thought she had been ruined by his brother and it was now his duty to set this wrong to rights.

"Oh, my dear Lord," Faith repeated. How utterly depressing.

Meredith reached out and patted Faith's fingers awkwardly. "I really don't think there is any reason to become distressed over these intimate aspects of marriage. Mother assured me that physical relations between a man and woman can be extremely pleasurable and improve greatly over time."

"Improve?" Faith squeaked.

"Oh, yes." Meredith blushed. "Lord Dewhurst does look at you with such smoldering passion at times. He is certainly intrigued by you. If you pardon my saying so, he strikes me as a man who knows his way around a boudoir. Whatever you don't know, I'm sure he would be pleased to teach you."

He thinks I am a fallen woman!

Faith nearly shouted her thoughts aloud, but they

were simply too embarrassing to voice. Just imagining that Neville, who had been sparing in his attention, let alone in his affections toward her, attempting a seduction was ludicrous. That he would have succeeded was pure fiction.

"Do you have any other questions?"

"What?" Faith rubbed her eyes with the heels of her palms. Questions? "No, no more questions, Merry. I thank you for your candor this day. I know it wasn't easy."

Meredith stood up. Her face revealed deep relief. "I shall have Cook prepare a light respite for you. I heard you barely ate any breakfast this morning. Ignore your nerves and eat a hearty meal. You must keep up your strength. We certainly can't have the bride fainting at the altar."

Faith managed a wobbly smile. "A fainting bride. That would be a most disastrous turn of events, would it not?"

The elegant carriage carrying the bride, Meredith, and Aunt Agatha arrived a few minutes early at the stone steps of the old church.

"I'm glad the rain has held off," Meredith commented.

"Yes, that is a stroke of good luck," Aunt Agatha agreed.

Faith made no effort at even a polite comment. She had spent the entire carriage ride trying to establish a firm grip on her nerves. Her mind was in turmoil. For the past hour she had paced the floor of her room, the train of her lovely gown sweeping the carpet clean, as she tried to convince herself that there was a simple, easy solution to this dilemma.

If only she could think of the appropriate words, the precise phrasing that would reveal this newly discovered truth to Griffin in such a manner that it would make no difference in his decision to become her husband.

Yet she feared greatly that once he knew it was not necessary to marry her for honor's sake, he would wish her well and walk out the church doors. Without her.

The notion brought on anxiety of almost hysterical proportions. She was so close, so close to achieving her dream of marriage and motherhood. 'Twas almost too cruel to have been given this glimpse of paradise before it was so unceremoniously snatched away.

You could wait, a nagging voice inside her head whispered. *You could wait until after the ceremony.*

"Oh, shut up," Faith muttered under her breath, mortified at this shameful aspect of her character that had been dominating her thoughts.

"Is something wrong, Faith?" Meredith inquired.

"I'm just a bit nervous," she answered.

"It's to be expected," Aunt Agatha said. "Most brides—Oh, gracious!"

With a decidedly lackluster display of interest, Faith turned to see what had caused Aunt Agatha's midsentence outburst. She cast only a cursory glance out the window and was treated to the sight of a large coffin, carried by several stout pallbearers descending the church steps.

Absently, Faith noted the presence of the hearse, solemnly awaiting its burden, and the horses, wearing long black plumes upon their heads, prancing impatiently. They seemed rather high-spirited and unsuitable for the task ahead.

As the church bells began the somber peal for each year of the deceased's life, Meredith tapped urgently on the roof of the carriage. Her coachman instantly understood her meaning, and the carriage lurched forward. Faith caught only a fleeting glimpse as they drove away of the black-clothed mourners, some no doubt professionals hired to lend dignity and importance to the event.

"What a horribly bad omen." Aunt Agatha huffed with agitation and reached for her reticule, no doubt in search of her smelling salts.

"It means nothing except that we arrived early at the church," Meredith insisted impatiently. "We shall circle the block, slowly. I'm certain by the time we return there will be no other carriages."

Meredith's prediction proved correct. When they returned, the hearse and all signs of the funeral had gone. And a light drizzle had begun.

" 'Tis raining!" Aunt Agatha exclaimed. "Now that truly is a bad—"

"Nonsense." Meredith gave her aunt a frigid stare. "This is a joyous day. Hurry inside before you get wet, Aunt Agatha. I'll assist the bride."

Faith kept a fixed smile on her face as she descended from the carriage. A few drops of rain sprinkled on her face, but she barely noticed them. The heavy weight that had settled on her chest had blocked out all feeling.

She knew the moment she stepped into the church she would have to summon Griffin so she could inform him that she was aware of the true reason for the marriage. And she must then tell him that he was completely mistaken in his assumptions.

She had not been compromised by his brother, or any other man. The misery ran so deep in her spirit, Faith was even unable to summon any indignation over Griffin's poor opinion of her morals and character.

She tried again to formulate the words in her mind, wondering fearfully how she was ever going to find the courage to speak to him. She was barely aware of Meredith fussing with the skirt of her gown, placing her mother's prayer book in her trembling fingers, and giving her a sisterly hug of affection.

"Merry, you must ask Lord Dewhurst to come out to the vestibule. I have a most urgent matter to discuss with him."

Utter silence greeted her request. With a start, Faith realized she was talking to herself. Fear of losing Griffin had made her hesitate, and that hesitation had cost her the chance to get him alone without causing a major fuss.

Cautiously, Faith peered down the long aisle. She could see that Meredith and Aunt Agatha had already taken up a position at the front of the church. Her eyes searched among the three male figures also there, and she easily distinguished Griffin from Meredith's twin brothers, though they all stood together.

Her face hot, Faith stepped out of the vestibule. The urge to turn and run was strong, but she conquered it. She could see the beads of rainwater outside sliding down the lovely stained-glass windows. Candles had been lit on the altar, and their gentle flickering cast an inviting, intimate glow.

All eyes had turned toward her. Everyone was waiting. Faith curled her hands into fists around her mother's prayer book, and with a pounding heart and a head filled with doubts and misgivings, she began the endless walk down the aisle. By the time she reached the altar, her heart was thundering so loudly she was certain that everyone, including the kindly vicar, could hear it.

I shall whisper in Griffin's ear the moment I get close enough that I need to speak to him.

Yet as Faith gained his side, she couldn't control the skip of her heartbeat at the sight of him. She had forgotten how beautiful he was—not attractive, not handsome, but beautiful. And disturbingly virile. Dressed in his wedding finery, he cut an elegant figure in his tailored blue frock coat and buff knee breeches. His white cravat was tied in a more elaborate knot than usual, and there were gold buttons adorning his finely embroidered waistcoat.

She gazed at his profile, taking in the high set of his noble brow, the fine, straight line of his nose, the square cut of his jaw. Faith swayed on unsteady limbs as she caught a whiff of the scents she had now come to associate with him—the clean smell of soap, the starch of his linen, the tang of leather and masculinity.

Oh, how could she so willingly give him up?

She was minutes away from becoming his wife, his companion, his mate throughout this lifetime. Yet if she opened her mouth, that all might change in an instant. He could easily refuse to marry her, and then all would be lost. Her dreams of being his wife, mother to his little boy and perhaps children of her own one day. Mayfair Manor would also be gone, lost to a popinjay cousin and his odious wife.

"Are you cold?" Griffin whispered.

"What?"

"You are trembling. Are you cold?"

"No, I'm not cold." She stared off into the distance, her eyes unfocused as she tried to formulate the words in her mind that would stop this madness, tried to find the courage deep in her soul to call a halt to the ceremony so she could explain.

"Faith?"

"Yes?" Startled, she turned to face Griffin again.

" 'Tis your part in the ceremony. You must answer. Will you be my wife?"

For an instant he appeared vulnerable, almost as if he were uncertain of her answer. Then his expression changed to reveal his warm, roguish charm and Faith was lost.

She melted at the gaze of those warm silvery eyes that stared directly into hers. How truly foolish she had been, to so completely underestimate her feelings.

He was more, so much more, than someone she found attractive, engaging, charming. She was in love with this man. And more than anything in the world, she wanted him to be her husband, her companion, her one and only lover.

To her surprise, Faith realized that she was fully prepared to do just about anything to make that happen.

Her conscience warned her loud and clear that she was making a grave mistake, yet her wayward heart simply could not allow this one, slight chance at happiness to slip away unchallenged.

Drawing in a fortifying breath, she whispered, "Yes."

Tendrils of guilt curled around her heart the moment the word was spoken. She wanted to call it back, to halt the ceremony, to explain herself, but it was too late.

In a matter of minutes the service ended. Dazed, Faith lifted her face toward Griffin. He gave her a warm smile that made her feel like an utter toad, and then his lips descended on hers in a proper, chaste kiss.

Meredith rushed forward, tears in her eyes, and soon the rest of the family surrounded the newly married couple, offering congratulations.

Heart thundering with fear and confusion, Faith accepted a hug from Aunt Agatha. *Wait! Stop. I must explain!* Glancing over the older woman's shoulder, Faith caught Griffin's eye. His roguish smile of delight sent yet another tremor of guilt through her entire body.

She shut her eyes in dismay. *Dear Lord, what have I just done?*

Eight

By the time the guests were seated around the dining room table, the rain had stopped. Griffin glanced at the various elaborate dishes spread before them, wondering idly how they would possibly make any noticeable progress in eating all this food. It seemed as though Lady Meredith had instructed the staff to prepare dishes for sixty guests, instead of the six that were in attendance.

Clearly no expense had been spared, evidence of Lady Meredith's deep affection for the bride. The finest silver, crystal, and china graced the table, along with whispery lace-edged tablecloths, napkins, and beeswax candles.

Servants, formally dressed in powdered wigs and gold-trimmed dark blue livery, moved soundlessly about the room, anticipating each guest's needs. The scent of fresh flowers blended with the succulent aromas of the tantalizing food, and the flickering candlelight provided an almost fairy-tale atmosphere.

Though the wedding feast was worthy of the regent, Griffin noticed his bride had allowed very little food to be placed on her plate. She picked at the tender medallions of veal in cream sauce and fresh asparagus, pushing the items around with her fork whenever anyone happened to glance her way.

"Are you not hungry?" Griffin asked.

"Not especially." Pursing her lips, Faith lowered her wine goblet to the table. "Have you a minute to spare for your bride, my lord? There is something I need to discuss with you."

Griffin's eyes met hers across the rim of his own wineglass. "Only a minute? Less than three hours ago I pledged you a lifetime, dearest."

Faith looked oddly dubious at that remark. "All I require is a few minutes," she responded.

Griffin regarded his brand-new wife. She had sat by his side throughout the small supper party, uncharacteristically fidgeting in her chair, almost as if she were too nervous to sit still. It was a wonder that the fabric of her pale blue silk gown hadn't been crushed into a mass of wrinkles, since she had arranged and rearranged the skirt so many times.

Despite the very small number of guests, it had been a lively meal, with much laughter and telling of childhood stories. Faith had initiated no conversation, joining in only when she was directly asked a question or expected to comment. To Griffin, her merriment had seemed forced at times, her laughter overbright.

He had imagined that she would be happy on this, her wedding day, yet she had smiled only briefly throughout the day, and the joy had not quite reached her eyes.

Griffin attributed her attitude to excitement and nerves and viewed her with an unusual sense of pride. He had never seen her look more lovely. The blue gown showcased her fine, creamy skin, and the halo of white flowers crowning her dark brown hair gave her an innocent, fresh look that made him feel both protective and aroused.

The nervous tapping of Faith's fingernail on the

stem of her crystal goblet drew his attention to her hand and the simple gold and ruby ring she wore. His wife. 'Twas almost too impossible to believe.

"Can our little discussion not wait until after the meal is concluded?" he asked, leaning close so as not to be overheard. "Lady Meredith's staff has gone to such great pains to produce this lovely feast. It would be rude to abandon it so soon."

"We need not be gone more than a few minutes," Faith replied. "I fear I have already waited too long." Her voice trailed off to a dull murmur.

Griffin's gut clenched. What the devil did she mean? Such clandestine mystery was not part of Faith's nature. Or was it? How much did he really know about his new bride? True, they had grown up together, but those childhood memories were no indication of her current character.

Striving to lighten the seriousness of her mood, he said, "Come, madame, there cannot be anything of such grave importance that would tear us away from our wedding feast. We are to leave in another hour. Can you not wait to reveal your secrets until then?"

"Secrets long held can often be the most dire," she whispered.

The amusement fled from his face. "I was merely jesting. Your tone and attitude suggest that you are not."

"It was not my intention to alarm you," Faith said quickly. She lifted her goblet and took a healthy swallow of wine. "Perhaps this discussion is best saved for later."

"Are you certain?"

"Yes." A hint of red crept into her cheeks. "I'm being foolish. Forgive me."

Relief flooded him, followed by a spurt of devilish teasing. "Now you have aroused my curiosity. Shall I try to guess? Will you tell me that you have a penchant for drinking large quantities of Madeira in the early afternoon? A difficult, but not impossible habit to overcome."

"Griffin," she said, with an undercurrent of warning in her tone.

He stroked his chin thoughtfully. "You have already buried four husbands, all of whom died under suspicious circumstances?"

"Good heavens!" Faith rolled her eyes heavenward, but the slight upward curve of her lips spurred him on.

"I know. You snore. Abominably loud."

"Griffin!"

Meredith raised her head to stare at them. Griffin flashed her his most charming grin, then turned his attention back to his wife. "It seems as though all I have done since I inherited this bloody title is have serious discussions. I'm relieved to be spared that on our wedding day."

There was a wealth of sympathy in her soulful brown eyes. "It will keep," she said quietly.

"I'm most pleased to discover you are not a woman who must always have the final word in a discussion or argument," Griffin commented with an easy smile. "It bodes well for our future."

"Really?" She drew a measured breath.

"Yes." He bent his head low and brushed her temple in a tender, chaste kiss. "For I am a man who cannot let a discussion rest unless *I* have had the last word."

Faith smiled, as Griffin had intended, and this time the delight of amusement did reach her eyes.

The newlyweds left as soon as the meal concluded, after another round of hugs and well wishes. Since he no longer had a London town house, Griffin had planned to cover only a few short miles on the journey home to the country, intending to stop for the night at a fancy posting inn that boasted superior accommodations.

He thought it a charming place and hoped his bride would be as pleased with the choice for their wedding night. The matter that seemed so urgent to discuss during their nuptial feast was not brought up during the carriage ride, and Griffin decided his assumption had been correct. Nerves and excitement had made an inconsequential matter seem far more important in Faith's mind.

Upon their arrival at the Sign of the Dove Inn, the viscount and his bride were met by the innkeeper, who offered hearty congratulations and escorted them personally to their rooms.

"There is only a single bedchamber, as his lordship requested," the innkeeper explained. "Though it has a sizable sitting room and dressing area."

He threw open the connecting door to demonstrate, and they dutifully peered inside. Griffin watched Faith curiously as she digested this information about their sleeping arrangements. Her already white face grew even paler, but she managed a rather polite tone as she remarked, " 'Tis a lovely room. I'm certain it shall do nicely."

The innkeeper beamed under that faint praise, and after assurances from his guests that nothing further was needed, he departed.

At last they were alone.

Faith flitted about the room, making a great show of untying her bonnet and removing her gloves. Griffin took a step closer, and when he was near enough, he slid his arm around her waist and pulled her against his hip. He tried to make the movement appear casual, but the tilt of her chin told him he hadn't fooled her for an instant.

That sweet, knowing look in her eye just made him want to kiss her even more. Odd, how nearly everything she had done in the six hours since becoming his wife made him want to kiss her.

So he did. With one swift motion, he dipped his head and claimed her mouth. Her lips parted almost immediately, and he quickly took advantage of her sensual invitation. He could taste the champagne she had drunk at their nuptial dinner on her tongue, and that special, sweet warmth that he had come to appreciate as only hers.

Faith grasped the lapels of his coat and leaned into him, heaving a little sigh of excitement. Her eagerness made the need inside him build and coil low in his gut. She began pressing soft, feathery kisses along his cheek and jaw, punctuating each kiss with a low murmuring sound, and he felt a fresh stirring of desire blended with a rush of tenderness.

Griffin caught Faith's chin between his fingers and raised her face up for a tender, delicate kiss. He could feel the fine sheen of sweat that had broken out on his forehead and knew if he didn't slow down he would have her on her back, with her skirts raised within minutes.

He couldn't remember a time when he had felt greater anticipation for a woman. With her plain looks and slender form, Faith had somehow effortlessly roused a hunger in him that sent his blood surging thick and hot through his entire being.

"Your maid is waiting outside to help you prepare for bed," he whispered against her mouth. "I fear if we do not stop kissing this very instant, the poor girl will fall asleep in the hallway still awaiting your summons."

Faith pulled back and stared into his eyes. Her fingers slowly traced the contours of his face as if she were memorizing every line. The expression on her face was so tender that Griffin felt a sharp, brazen, almost primal need to claim her as his own—before she slipped away from him.

Shaking off those fanciful thoughts, he turned away. His arms felt empty, so he filled his hands with a goblet and poured himself a glass of port that he had no intention of drinking.

His sudden withdrawal seemed to trigger Faith's nerves. When he turned to face her again, Griffin noted that her hands were twisting together so fiercely he feared she would dislocate one of her fingers.

"Are you hungry?" Faith inquired. "Should I ring for a tray of food to be brought?"

Griffin caught her by the shoulders as she paced near him. Briefly he shut his eyes to master his overwhelming desire.

This was her wedding night and their first time together. Griffin wanted everything to be as nearly perfect as possible. He would take his time to explore her body; he would learn the secrets of her passion so that their ultimate joining would be wildly pleasurable for both of them.

"I will adjourn to the sitting room so that your maid may assist you." His gaze swept over her slowly. "Don't keep me waiting too long, dearest, for I fear I shall burst."

Griffin backed toward the door, never once taking his eyes off her. Then, with a final smile of encouragement, he shut the door.

At the sound of the latch closing the door, Faith shivered and hugged her arms tightly about her waist. Though she tried to look anywhere else, her gaze was fixed on the large bed in the center of the room, with its elaborate, old-fashioned tapestry hangings. It was a massive piece of carved mahogany furniture that sat so high off the floor, a footstool was provided for guests to climb upon to reach the mattress.

The rich blue silk coverlet had been pulled back to reveal linens and pillows that looked fresh and clean, and so utterly inviting. Yet Faith dared not even sit on the edge of the bed.

The silence of the room grated on her already frayed nerves. She ran both hands back through her hair in frustration, heedless of the pins that fell to the floor.

The moment of reckoning was nearly upon her. She had tried, albeit not very hard, to tell Griffin the truth before they had left Merry's home, during the wedding supper. But he had been in no mood to discuss anything of a serious nature, so she had allowed herself to be charmed out of making her declaration.

The carriage ride had been surprisingly brief. Faith initially thought the enforced intimacy of the closed carriage would provide the perfect setting for this serious discussion, but she sensed the moment the coach lurched down the street that Griffin preferred to ride in silence.

Deciding to comply with his unspoken request, she had spent the majority of the journey staring at her husband's profile, studying the subtle waves in his thick, dark hair, and marveling at how that noble face could so easily set her heart fluttering. By the time Faith had determined there had been enough quiet and gathered her courage, they were pulling into the court-yard of the posting inn.

The arrangement of sharing a single bedchamber had definitely surprised her, but Faith felt she had succeeded in disguising her shock. She thought all married couples had separate bedchambers. Even her own dear parents, who had been very much in love throughout their entire married life, slept in separate rooms.

Apparently her new husband had other notions. Faith glanced once again at the bed, shuddered, and looked away. A subtle knock at the door signaled the arrival of her maid, and Faith welcomed the distraction.

The young woman was actually a servant in Merry's household, loaned to the new viscountess for the journey home. She would return to London within the week and a local girl would be given the honor of serving Faith.

Provided she still was the Viscountess Dewhurst at the end of the week.

Faith pinched the bridge of her nose with her thumb and forefinger. Having no other choice, she shoved aside that horrifying fear. It was useless to speculate on Griffin's reaction when he discovered the truth.

Faith shivered again and moved closer to the fire. The efficient maid followed her, silently unhooking the tiny row of pearl buttons down the back of her gown. Faith was grateful she needed to give the servant no directions, for she found she could not keep her mind focused on anything but the upcoming event. Her wedding night.

Faith dutifully raised her arms and allowed a soft white nightgown, made of the finest sheer muslin, to be shimmed down her body. Next, the maid removed the few remaining pins from her hair and brushed the brown strands with long, rhythmic strokes until it rippled down her back.

"You have very pretty hair, my lady," the maid said. "Shall I braid it or leave it loose?"

"Leave it loose," a male voice quietly instructed. "I should like to see it spread on the pillow beside me."

Faith spun around in her chair and met the pair of heavy-lidded gray eyes calmly watching her every move.

"As your lordship wishes," the maid said, giving Faith's hair a final stroke. Then, with a quick curtsy and a shy smile, the servant hurried from the room.

Faith fumbled for the matching silk wrapper the maid had left draped across the foot of the bed. Griffin moved forward to assist her, the merest hint of a smile gathered at his lips.

All at once Faith felt hot. Her hand fluttered to her throat and she prayed the dim candlelight hid her red cheeks.

Griffin was wearing a midnight blue silk dressing gown. The fragile covering made his shoulders seem enormously broad. The garment was loosely belted at the waist, and he had rolled up the sleeves, displaying strong forearms covered with silky-looking dark hair.

At this close proximity she was fairly certain he was naked beneath the garment. Just thinking about that fired both her blood and her imagination. She quickly wrapped the belt of her robe around her waist and pulled it tightly closed.

Griffin gently placed his knuckle beneath her jaw, lifting up her chin. Faith stood very still.

"Nervous?"

"Terrified," she whispered.

"So am I." One corner of his mouth turned up in a faint smile.

Faith's eyes flitted away. Never before had she been so aware of her feminine shortcomings. Her lack of height. Her small bosom. Her plain features.

Her virginity.

"You mock me, Griffin," she said.

"Never, dearest." His fingers brushed her brow, pushing back tendrils of hair that curled around her face. "Tease you, perhaps, but never mock."

Faith shifted uncomfortably in her bare feet. His gentle sweetness would be her complete undoing.

Then she made the mistake of touching him. Softly, almost casually, on the chest. She could feel the heat of his body through the silk of his dressing gown and the hard strength of the muscle beneath.

"Come along." Griffin held out his hand. " 'Tis past time we were in bed, my dear."

Faith stared down at those strong, masculine fingers as the uncertainty rippled through her heart. If she was going to tell him the truth, she certainly needed to speak now. This instant. For she knew in her heart that once her back was pressed against that soft mattress, with Griffin looming above her, there would be no time for words.

Yet if she told him the truth he could simply walk away from her. Have the marriage annulled, since it would not be consummated. Could she bear it?

"Faith?"

Startled, she looked up. Her heart began its wild thundering again. The candlelight turned his hair to near blackness, his eyes to a silvery glow. She found herself drowning in their intense reflection. His closeness, his near nakedness made her aware of him over every inch of her flesh.

Tell him! But the words lodged in her throat and the silence stretched on for an eternity. Fingers trembling, Faith raised her hand and touched his chin, stroking the rough stubble of his beard.

"You are right. 'Tis getting late, my lord. I heard the clock strike ten just before you arrived." Faith reached deep down and summoned up a smile. "Perhaps we had best go to bed."

"Your wish is my command, my lady wife," he replied huskily, proffering his arm courteously.

At that moment, Faith didn't know which emotion warring inside her was greatest, fear or anticipation. With a shaky breath and a wavering smile, she placed her hand on top of Griffin's and followed him toward the large bed.

Griffin smiled as Faith made no move to douse the candles, oddly pleased he wasn't married to a shy, inexperienced young virgin who would require hours of patient coaxing. One who would merely submit to him in silence, tensing at his slightest caress, lying rigid underneath him in outrageous shock as he tried to consummate their union. A woman who would feel compelled to try and hide her dislike of marital relations, gritting her teeth as he labored over her. Who would tense up and feel pain, because she expected pain. Who would find no joy in their mating.

Yes, he was indeed fortunate with his choice of bride.

Griffin placed his hands about her waist and lifted her onto the high bed. She gave a little gasp of surprise and gripped his shoulders tightly to steady herself.

Her eyes were wide as she gazed at him. He leaned closer and placed a tender kiss at the corner of her mouth. Reaching up, his fingers traced the delicate spot at the back of her skull, then traveled leisurely to the shell-shaped curve of her ear and the sweet line of her jaw.

Lightly, he caressed the softness of her cheek, moving downward to the slim column of her throat, and then finally, possessively to the delicate curve of her breast. Gently, he thumbed the peak of her nipple until it budded and tightened.

He heard the catch of Faith's breath. She wiggled her shoulders but did not pull away. Griffin traced her lips with his tongue, then kissed her deeply. His hands roamed freely over her body. She was warm, soft, and shapely. Griffin's erection grew painfully harder as he anxiously awaited the moment he could lose himself inside her sleek warmth.

She made no protest, indeed no sound at all as he gently, yet forcefully, pressed against her shoulder until she lay flat on her back. Her eyes remained pinned to his. The silence that bound them was fraught with tense desire, heavy with the promised anticipation of great fulfillment.

Griffin captured those silent lips and kissed her again, sucking ravenously on the tongue she eagerly offered to him. The pace of urgency suddenly heightened. His arousal become more rigid and enlarged, aching for release, and he prayed his bride would be quick to rise to passion, since he doubted he could last long.

" 'Tis a lovely night ensemble, but completely unnecessary, do you not think?" Griffin said smoothly as he pulled off Faith's wrapper and lifted the nightgown above her head.

He quickly shrugged out of his own robe and eagerly joined her on the bed. He stretched out fully beside her and gathered her close, savoring the feel of her warm flesh.

" 'Tis very warm in here," she said.

"Aye, and will get even hotter, dearest," he replied, nuzzling her neck. He cupped her full breast with his hand, then bent his head and pulled the nipple into his mouth.

Faith closed her eyes and let out a soft groan as he sucked deeply. He felt her fingers run up and down his spine in restless excitement, felt her legs shift anxiously beneath him.

He was fleetingly aware of the tension building within her, for it seemed to rival his own. A world of sensations rippled through him as he caressed her delicate flesh. She was soft and yielding in his arms, pulsating with heat and passion.

Boldy, Griffin moved his hand to her belly, stroking and kneading the soft flesh. His other hand strayed to her breast and tugged gently on the turgid nipple that was still moist from his earlier ministrations.

Slowly, he parted her thighs. Her eyes remained locked on his, round with excitement and wonder. She gasped as he stroked the dewy softness, quivering in his arms, her breathing swift and shallow.

He quickened the pace, circling the swollen nub of her womanhood. Her nostrils flared, and she pushed herself against his hand, her fingers biting into his shoulders. The slick wetness told him she was more than ready, yet he hesitated, struggling to gain control of his own rampant desire.

"Griffin, please."

Her whimpering cries of urgency proved to be his breaking point.

"I had wanted to go slowly and savor each moment, but you have pushed me beyond my control, dearest.

Perhaps it would be best to take the edge off first, so we may enjoy ourselves at leisure."

He lifted her legs and pushed them wide, then buried his face between her wantonly splayed thighs. Greedily, his tongue sifted through the dark curly hair until he found her core. Faith clung to his neck, sobbing, panting, her body trembling and tightening.

"Shh, relax, dearest. Let it happen," he whispered wickedly.

He placed a gentle hand on her flanks to calm her, lightly stroking her fevered flesh. Then he once again settled his mouth against her intimately, laving her tenderly, yet relentlessly, with his tongue.

Within minutes, Faith arched and cried out, digging her heels into the soft mattress as she lifted herself up. Then Griffin felt the spasms break over her. He held her tightly as she shuddered with the strength of fulfillment.

"I didn't know," she whispered brokenly, as he continued to stroke her lightly with the tip of his finger. "I didn't know."

"Ah, but there is more, my sweet wife. So much more," Griffin said hoarsely.

Bracing on his elbows, Griffin pulled himself above her. Her neck and chest were flushed and fevered, her nipples red and swollen. She had that languid, contented look of a sated woman, and it made him hunger to possess her, to drive himself deep and long inside her. To become part of her.

Griffin seized Faith's hips in his grasp, overcome with an urgent need to take her with a wildness he had never before felt with any other woman. Desire raging beyond sanity, he arched his back and thrust hard into the tight, silky sheath.

Faith gasped and tightened beneath him. The feel

of his body joined with her was incredible, and he hungered for more. Withdrawing slightly, he thrust deeper inside her.

"Oh, my!"

Her softly whispered cry of pain distracted him momentarily. With effort, he stilled inside her.

"You feel very tight. Am I hurting you?"

"No, I, ah, no." She smiled at him sweetly.

He bent his head and nuzzled her neck, tasting her with soft kisses while trying to regain control of himself. But it was impossible. She was too wet, too warm, too utterly delightful. How could he not lose himself in the magic of her body?

With a groan, Griffin eased his hips back, then surged forward, thrusting harder and deeper until suddenly he felt the unmistakable barrier inside her break. *A maidenhead?* Astonished at this discovery, Griffin pulled back. But Faith's inner muscles contracted around him and instead of disengaging himself completely from her body, he thrust back, more forcefully this time.

His passion had been raised to such a fevered pitch it took no more than a few deep thrusts before the waves of sensation crashed around him. Shuddering, he bellowed a hoarse cry and spilled his seed deep inside her.

Gradually, reality returned, yet Griffin felt paralyzed, aware only of the mad thumping of his heart and the residual pulsating of his cock. It wasn't possible. Yet it was unmistakable. She was a virgin. A damn virgin!

"Griffin?" Faith's voice was a worried whisper in the darkness of his heart.

Their eyes met and hers darted away. In guilt. His gut twisted. Never in his life had he had a naked woman beneath him who looked so completely uncomfortable.

"It seems you have some explaining to do, madame," he whispered dangerously. Still breathing hard, he disengaged himself and sat back on his haunches. "What the bloody hell is going on?"

Thankfully she didn't even pretend to misunderstand his meaning. "I tried to tell you. At the church, before the ceremony. Then later, at the wedding supper. You would not listen."

"Are you saying this is *my* fault?"

"No, of course not." She swallowed hard.

"Then what exactly are you saying, madame?"

"I had meant to tell you, the moment I realized that you believed I had given myself to Neville and was no longer a virgin." She hesitated, looking steadily back at him, her eyes wide and face pale. "But I could not."

"How convenient." He cast her an intense, calculated stare.

Faith's chin lifted defiantly. "Are not most husbands pleased to discover their bride's untouched state? I thought you would be happy to discover that I was in truth a virgin."

He studied her through half-lowered lids. "You know very well that the reason I married you was because I thought my brother had compromised you. Had I realized it was your intent to exchange your virginity for your integrity I would have withdrawn my offer."

She flinched, and a blush stung her cheeks. It moved him not a whit. He wondered fleetingly what else she had kept from him, what else she had lied about.

Griffin felt betrayed, furious, shaken. To have been deceived so callously, so completely by her. And to think he had earlier held such high hopes for this marriage. Had silently congratulated himself on his choice of bride. Now, he felt a fool. A surge of bitterness rushed through him.

He crossed the room and yanked open the sitting room door. He quickly found his garments, hastily discarded in blissful ignorance earlier. Jamming himself into his breeches, Griffin gathered up his shirt and boots.

"Where are you going? What are you going to do?"

He whirled at the sound of Faith's voice. She stood trembling in the doorway, in a disheveled dressing gown, looking deliciously warm, with swollen lips and ruffled hair. Her brown eyes brimmed with tears, but for once the sight did not move him.

"Where are you going?" she repeated.

"Out," he muttered in breathless agitation.

"Out? Where? 'Tis the middle of the night."

"I don't know. I need time to think, time to decide." He cast her a look of pure disgust. "I need time alone, away from you."

After delivering those scathing words, Griffin made for the door, turned the handle, and vanished into the night.

Nine

Faith spent the remainder of the night in total misery. Tears seemed a useless commodity, though she shed them copiously, until it felt as if there were none left within her soul. The coming dawn brought little comfort. She lay alone in the massive bed, cold and heart sore, her ears straining in the half-light of morning.

There were no sounds emanating from the connecting sitting room, and her heart ached with misery, wondering where Griffin had spent the remainder of the night.

Finally, as the late-morning sunshine flooded the room, Faith's maid appeared.

"Good morning, my lady." The maid came close to the bed and dipped a small curtsy. "I've brought hot water, scented soap, and fresh towels. Are you ready to begin your morning toilet?"

The servant's cheerful voice implied that she found nothing amiss, but Faith knew she was an intelligent woman. Surely she had to be wondering why the bridegroom had so completely disappeared. Or perhaps the servant had already seen him downstairs in the taproom?

The thought made Faith shiver, but at least offered the hope that he had not left the inn and returned either to London or gone home. Without her.

Gingerly Faith sat up in bed. Pushing aside her embarrassment she asked softly, "Have you spoken with Lord Dewhurst this morning?"

The maid looked confused. "No, my lady. I have not seen him, nor his valet. Do you want a message delivered to his lordship?"

"N-no, thank you." Feeling more foolish than ever, Faith sank back down among the pillows. In truth, she wished she could curl into a tiny ball, bury herself beneath the thick coverlet, and simply disappear.

"They don't have a proper bathing tub or else I would have insisted on a hot bath," the maid informed her. "I hope this warm sponge bath will do."

" 'Tis fine," Faith said with a grimace. With difficulty, she managed to drag herself out of bed, deciding it was probably better not to have a steaming tub filled with water awaiting her. She might be tempted to drown herself.

Faith allowed the maid to sponge her from head to toe with a wet cloth, then dry her briskly. Normally she would be embarrassed to have such a personal task performed by a servant, but considering the great mess that her life had suddenly become, this event ranked very low on the list of concerns.

"Would you like to wear the same traveling ensemble from yesterday or shall I press a fresh gown from your trunk?"

"It doesn't matter," Faith said. She heaved a listless sigh. "You decide."

The maid nodded. She brushed the gown Faith had worn the previous day, gathered clean undergarments from the trunk, and helped her dress.

"Shall I have your breakfast brought into the sitting room, my lady?" the maid inquired, as she caught the thick mass of hair at the nape of Faith's neck, lifted it, and twisted it into a knot.

The thought of food made her stomach turn. Who could possibly eat at a time like this? Faith glanced in the mirror, watching solemnly as the maid set the knot of hair in the middle of her head and added pins to the handiwork to keep it from tumbling down.

She sighed again, remembering how Griffin had specifically asked that her hair be left unbraided last night. It seemed to please him, and he had stroked the silky tresses lovingly, repeatedly running the strands through his fingers like they were grains of sand.

"Breakfast?" the maid asked again.

"The sitting room will do nicely for breakfast," Faith replied.

She doubted she would be able to swallow a bite, but at least it would get her out of the bedchamber. The bedchamber that held so many intense memories. Of unfounded joy and ecstasy. And helpless fear and regret.

All too soon, Faith found herself seated at the cozy sitting-room table, with a veritable feast spread before her. Insisting she could serve herself, she dismissed the innkeeper's minions. Needing something to occupy her hands, she poured a steaming cup of hot chocolate and let it sit untouched in the cup until it grew tepid.

Where is he? Idly, Faith twisted the fine gold and ruby-studded band she now wore around and around her finger. *Is he ever coming back? Or does he just plan to leave me here? Alone?*

Mentally Faith began to calculate the amount of coin on her person. She had no idea of the cost of these fine accommodations and worried that the meager sum she carried would not be enough. Of course, Griffin might have already settled the bill. Even without that burden to contend with, Faith knew she did not have enough funds to hire a carriage to return her to Mayfair Manor.

There might be enough to pay for passage on the mail coach, but the notion of spending hours cramped inside a stuffy vehicle with strangers left Faith feeling queasy. She supposed as a last resort word could be sent to Merry for help, for London was not a great distance away.

Yet Faith resisted that final, ultimate admission of failure. For now.

The sound of a creaking door interrupted her gloomy musings. It swung open abruptly, and Faith froze at the sight of an elegant, polished boot crossing the threshold.

Griffin Sainthill, Viscount Dewhurst swaggered into the room as if he owned it. He was freshly shaven and wore an immaculate ensemble of clothing, complete with a costly morning coat of deep blue that Faith had never seen.

From the delicate loop of his white cravat to the gleaming shine of his Hessian boots, Griffin presented a picture of polished elegance. Yet this fashionable demeanor was very much at odds with the raw virility emanating from his every step.

Faith's breath caught in her lungs. *He has returned!* Perhaps only briefly, perhaps just to tell her that he was leaving her permanently, yet the practical side of Faith's nature was relieved to see him. At least now she would not be left to wonder and worry and speculate. She would finally know her fate.

Faith drew a breath. There was so much to say, so much to explain. But where to begin? She licked her lips and gathered her courage, yet one quick glance at her husband's closed expression left her caught in a strangling sense of panic.

The silence between them lengthened, becoming so complete it was terrifying. Griffin crossed the room to stand beside the table. Faith tilted her neck up to stare at him and tried valiantly to swallow the lump in her throat.

"I see that breakfast has been served." He flashed a wide smile, then snatched a piece of crispy bacon from the platter resting in the center of the table and popped it into his mouth. "I hope you have saved some of the choice dishes for me. Or have you greedily consumed them all?"

Faith smiled wanly, not knowing what to make of his strange mood. He was teasing her, with that wicked grin and flirting banter, but there was no merriment in his eyes, no mischief on his handsome face.

After chomping down on his bacon, Griffin took the seat opposite hers. He filled a plate and proceeded to consume a hearty breakfast. For perhaps the first time in her life, Faith felt stricken to silence. The awful quiet ensued, though Griffin gave no outward indication that it concerned him.

She noted with some degree of envy that he took seconds of several dishes. When the viscount finally ceased eating, he exhaled with blatant satisfaction and sat back in his chair.

"Shall I ring for more food?" Faith asked. "I'm sure the innkeeper would be flattered to see the justice you have done to the meal."

"Justice?" Griffin raised an eyebrow. "Ah, so now you are concerned about justice. How interesting."

Immediately Faith realized her mistake. She felt the remnants of her slight smile fade away. She had been deluding herself, assuming because he had no difficulty eating he was in a congenial frame of mind. In her nervousness, she had completely underestimated the degree of his anger.

Even with the barrier of a solid wood table between them, she could now sense the tightly coiled impatience inside him. Nervously, Faith lifted her cup, but the pungent odor of chocolate made her stomach heave. She returned it to the table without taking even a small sip.

"Is there something you wish to say to me, Griffin?" she finally asked, breaking the tension she could no longer tolerate.

"There is much I have to say, my lady wife." His smoky eyes were suddenly ablaze. "Yet first, I believe that you have some explaining to do."

Faith felt the tremor snake through her body. The brilliant sunshine that heated the room brought her no ease. She felt horribly cold, chilled to the very bone, for this cold came from deep inside her.

She stared at him. For a moment she was too afraid to think, let alone speak. She noticed, for the first time, the icy coldness behind his silvery eyes, the harsh set of his mouth, the steel in his voice.

She closed her eyes tightly, briefly, then looked directly at him. "I had meant to tell you the truth once I realized that you believed Neville had compromised me."

"Oh, really?"

The scorn in his voice nearly caused her to flinch. Griffin's handsome, hard features blurred before her eyes. Faith felt the sting of emotion as tears threatened, but she would not let them fall. She knew how much he despised a woman's tears. The very least she owed him was to spare him that unsavory sight.

"I did try to tell you," she blurted out loudly. His brow raised at her outburst. Faith took another breath.

"I only realized a few hours before the ceremony why you had decided to marry me. I was shocked and confused, uncertain of what to do. Eventually I decided it would be best to have a private word with you the moment I arrived at the church."

"Apparently you changed your mind," he said dryly. "Why?"

Faith hung her head. "I lost my nerve, and by the time I regained it, the ceremony had begun. I found myself in a haze, lost in a strange dream. Before I knew fully what was happening, we had spoken our vows. I had pledged myself to you. The deed was done. You were smiling at me, seeming so pleased. Everyone was hugging and congratulating us, and then later at the wedding supper there was so much laughter and merriment. I suppose I could not bear to see it all end."

"You did mention at supper that you needed to speak with me," Griffin admitted grudgingly. He stroked his chin thoughtfully. "Concerning this matter?"

"Yes." Faith knew she had been utterly mad to give in to the temptation of waiting to say anything. But she had wanted this marriage so badly. "I also attempted to tell you in the coach on the way to the inn last night. But once again I could not find my voice."

His eyes narrowed. "Are you saying that you did not plan this from the first? You did not intentionally deceive me when I came to London in search of you?"

"Is that what you think?"

"How could I not?" He shrugged his shoulders expressively. "Your need was great. Without me for a husband you would lose your beloved Mayfair Manor. I cannot fault you for falling to temptation to make a fool of me when the opportunity arose, as much as I despise your treacherous methods."

Faith crossed her arms protectively over her chest. True, she had been at fault. And she was willing to accept responsibility for her actions and face the consequences. But to be conceived as a thoroughly corrupt woman was a harsh accusation. And wholly unfair.

"I did not set out to trap you, nor deliberately deceive you."

"I beg to differ, madame."

"You are wrong."

"No, madame, I was *wronged*," he said with difficulty through nearly clenched teeth.

Faith's heart sank. Things were far worse than she had imagined. The look in his eyes was dark and unforgiving. She lifted her cup and took a sip of her now cold chocolate. It rolled around her tongue, leaving a bitter taste.

"What will you do?" she finally dared to ask.

He stared over the top of her head, gazing out the window for the longest moment. "I have few options. We can hardly annul the marriage after the bedsport we shared last night."

Faith drew in a sharp breath. It took a moment to find her voice, for there was a heavy weight pressing on her chest that made speech nearly impossible.

"Then I suppose it must be a divorce," she said slowly. "Will you petition or shall I?"

"Divorce!" His head spun around wildly.

"I see no other solution. I do not think I can live with a person who holds me in such contempt."

"The hurt is raw, and I am angry, Faith." Griffin passed a hand over his mouth. "Given time I should be able to forgive you."

"And if you cannot? Then shall I find myself swiftly and firmly cast off?"

He drummed his fingers impatiently on the table.

"I can make no promises nor predictions concerning my future feelings toward you."

"That is not the sort of marriage I want."

"Well, you should have thought about that before you deceived me." Griffin's gray eyes flashed with anger.

"I am willing to take the lion's share of the blame, but 'tis not entirely my fault," Faith responded. "If you had not mistakenly held my character in such low esteem, then you would not have proposed marriage in the first place."

Griffin sat up and leaned over the table. "I asked you point-blank if my brother had ruined you, madame. And you replied that he had."

"I spoke the truth. I was ruined, unfit for marriage in the eyes of nearly everyone I knew." A grim, lopsided smile twisted on her face. "After being engaged for so many years without becoming a wife, there were many who wondered at my shortcomings, which surely must be vast and unbearable. When Neville died, I knew in my bones there would never be another opportunity for me to be married.

"I have few illusions about myself as a woman, Griffin. I could never have attracted the attentions of an eligible suitor."

He faced her fully, and she could see the stubborn set of his jaw. "What utter nonsense. I might have proposed to you out of a sense of duty, but I find you desirable. Surely other men feel the same."

"You find me desirable?" Excitement lit her eyes. The serious issues of the discussion paled at this unexpected admission. "Truly?"

"That is hardly significant." Griffin cast her a superior male glance. "And completely irrelevant."

Faith anxiously crumbled a piece of toast, then brushed the crumbs off her fingers. Griffin began to speak, but his words no longer had the power to distress her. He found her desirable! All her life she had craved that kind of male attention. 'Twas almost unbelievable to hear that from the man she had fallen so deeply in love with, the man who was her husband. At present.

In Faith's mind, that single admission changed everything. Now there was hope, a real chance for their marriage to continue. Griffin said he could probably forgive her in time. Still another reason to hope. The memories in her head of the night they shared started churning, making her suddenly breathless and overwarm. Faith remembered sharply the intimacy they had shared, the way she had so wantonly craved his touch, had so completely shattered in his arms.

No man could be so gentle, so loving, if he did not care, at least a little, about the woman in his arms. A third reason to hope.

"Faith? Faith? Are you listening to me?"

She felt his hands on her shoulders. With renewed determination she lifted her chin and stared at him.

"I have tried to explain myself, Griffin. I have apologized, several times, for my actions. I know not what else I can do. You have indicated that perhaps in time you will learn to forgive me. That is generous of you, yet I know that I cannot spend the rest of my life trying to atone for this mistake." She grasped the table edge and stood on her feet. Her legs felt like thin spindles that could hardly support her weight.

Faith knew this was a calculated risk, but was determined to brazen it out. If there was any chance at all for a successful life together, she had to regain her pride and self-respect, or else Griffin would never be able to see her as anything other than a liar and a cheat. "As soon as I can hire a coach, I shall return to Mayfair Manor. If you wish to continue the marriage we have contracted, you may find me there."

He stared at her in disbelief. "You expect me to simply say no more about this matter?"

"Yes." She turned from him and walked to the door. "I will not stay where I am not wanted, nor will I go begging constantly for your forgiveness. I want to be your wife, Griffin, not your whipping boy."

It was the longest five steps she had ever taken, but somehow Faith managed to open the door and walk inside the bedchamber. Utter silence followed her.

The quiet was complete. Griffin stared at the closed door in amazement, still marveling that Faith had calmly delivered her ultimatum and then walked through it. He waited for the anger to boil over, the rage to engulf him, but it did not come. Perhaps the anger had all burned off last night, when he had left the bedchamber and his bride, to find himself walking about the barn and stables of the posting inn for several hours.

In the wee hours of the morning Griffin had summoned the innkeeper, giving him a cock-and-bull story about needing a larger chamber for his valet. Fortunately there had been an unoccupied room prepared, but instead of his servant, Griffin had spent the remainder of the night in these accommodations, tossing fretfully on the bed, trying to sort out his feelings, and wrestling with the problem of his wife.

Would she never cease to surprise him? He, who had long believed he understood the workings of a female mind, who had enjoyed many different types of relationships with women throughout the years.

Griffin had always prided himself on the ease in which he conducted these many liaisons. The lack of fuss, overwrought emotions, demanding restrictions that other men complained of when speaking about their wives or even their mistresses and lovers, were never a difficulty he had to face.

Yet now he was saddled with a wife he barely understood, who seemed to enjoy high drama. This was very quickly making his life far more complicated than he had ever believed possible.

Yet, in truth, the problem ran far deeper than his lack of understanding his bride. It was difficult for Griffin to fully acknowledge that he had been hurt by her duplicity, wounded by her deception, for that would mean that he cared for this vibrant woman with his heart and not his head.

Griffin had always thought himself invincible to the pain that women could inflict. It was an unpleasant and unwelcome discovery to realize that he was wrong. And he blamed Faith for forcing him to make that rather distressing realization.

Griffin let out a long breath of air and rubbed his hand across his stomach. The full breakfast he had consumed in order to show Faith that he could calmly cope with this situation now sat heavy in his stomach. He suddenly wished his pride had not demanded such a blatant demonstration.

But, now, what would he do? Calmly continue with this marriage or try to decide if there was a dignified way of extricating himself from his newly spoken vows?

Perhaps the fault was not entirely Faith's. Perhaps he had begun this marriage with false expectations, thinking it would be a quiet, unemotional, dignified relationship, much like the one his parents had shared.

In his ignorance, Griffin had merely assumed he and Faith would eventually settle into a life that included mutual respect, shared values, and warm, yet restrained, companionship.

Now he knew better. He realized the moment he had truly claimed her as his own last night that would be impossible. Not because she was a virgin, which had shocked the hell out of him, but because her passionate and heated response had fired his blood beyond rational thought.

Griffin had felt so strongly the need for physical distance between them last night partly because of that response. In all the years, he had never been deliberately cruel to a woman. It went against his nature to be harsh with those who were weaker and more vulnerable.

Last night he had clearly seen the look of pain and the shimmer of tears in Faith's eyes. He had heard her statements of genuine regret. Yet he had stormed from the bedchamber, unable to forget that he had been duped into this marriage.

Did not every man have the right to expect honesty from his wife?

Drumming his fingers slowly on the table, Griffin pondered this question and was forced to admit that he had not been completely honest with Faith on the matter of his son. She believed the boy was the product of an earlier marriage, and he had not bothered to correct that mistaken assumption because it had been far easier than trying to explain the truth.

Was his sin not as great as his wife's? Griffin slapped his palm on the table and quickly suppressed the thought. *His* actions were not in question at the moment.

Maybe in time they could learn to work things out between them satisfactorily. Griffin wasn't entirely convinced, but he was certainly astute enough to realize it couldn't be accomplished if they were apart.

His mind made up, Griffin stalked to the connecting bedchamber and yanked open the door. Faith, in the act of donning her traveling cloak, turned with a startled gasp. She dismissed her maid with a nervous nod, then straightened to face him.

"The Viscountess of Dewhurst does not ride in a hired coach," he announced in his best aristocratic voice. "I will leave my carriage and driver at your disposal."

"How will you return home?" A worried frown creased her brow. "Or do you intend to stay in town?"

"I will return to the country. 'Tis a fine day, perfect for a good, long ride on horseback." He couldn't help the self-deprecating grin that settled on his face. "I find that my stomach often objects if I travel too long in an enclosed vehicle."

The first real smile of the morning flashed across Faith's face. Griffin was surprised to realize how glad he was to see it.

"You were captain of a sailing vessel for many years," she said, "yet you suffer an upset stomach from the motion of a vehicle?"

"A ship is a far different conveyance than a poorly sprung coach," he replied gruffly.

"Yes, of course." He saw the wide smile she tried to hide behind her hand. "I thank you for your generosity, my lord."

"I'm not being generous. I'm being practical."

"Of course, my lord." The smile instantly vanished. Faith frowned and flushed deeply, casting her eyes down to her hands.

"I do however have one favor to ask of you."

"Yes?" She looked up into his eyes and he could see she was very confused.

"I cannot abide being 'my lorded' by you."

"I see. I'm sorry."

She sounded almost meek, not at all like the woman he knew.

"In the future, would you please address me by my name, not my rank."

"If you wish"—she hesitated, then smiled slightly— "Griffin."

He nodded with approval. "I have given you the protection of my name, the dignity of my rank, and the security of my fortune." He smiled at that last bit, knowing he would also be putting Faith's funds to use in restoring his family's property.

"I am not unaware of the advantages of our marriage. Nor am I ungrateful." She gave a particularly tight tug on the strings of her cloak as she tied a large bow at her throat to secure the garment, then picked up her gloves and reticule. "I thank you for the use of your carriage. I shall make certain it is returned the moment after I reach Mayfair Manor."

"I think not."

His stern voice halted her progress toward the door. "You wish me to keep the carriage at the manor?"

"No."

She looked uncertainly at him for a moment. "What shall I instruct the servants to do with it?"

"Nothing. You will be returning to my home so the coach can be properly placed in the carriage house where it belongs." Griffin set his jaw in a hard line. "No matter what our differences are, I do not intend to live apart from my wife."

With his message faithfully delivered, it was now Griffin's turn to pivot on his heel and calmly walk out the door, leaving behind a very bewildered Faith.

Ten

It was not the triumphant homecoming Faith had always envisioned. Instead of familiar servants lining the drive poised to wish her well, their faces beaming with happy, expectant grins, there was complete silence as the coach rattled down the long drive. Instead of an eager husband clutching her hand in support as she approached her new home, Faith sat alone in the carriage, with only her nerves for company.

Griffin had ridden on horseback the entire way home, refusing to abandon his mount even when a light drizzle had started. At first she was glad to be spared his tight stares and accusing glances, but as the miles ticked away Faith began to feel sad and lonely without him.

She remembered fondly the days before their wedding, when Griffin would come to Merry's house intent on amusing them both. His boyish charm and wicked sense of humor brightened every afternoon. Would she ever see that side of him again?

The carriage halted. Faith fleetingly hoped it would be Griffin's hand that reached in to assist her from the vehicle, but instead it was a white-gloved footman's. Telling herself she was expecting far too much, too soon, of her newly acquired husband, the Viscountess Dewhurst emerged from her cocoon.

She was relieved to note that Griffin had not been so completely lacking in manners. He waited, with a purely unreadable expression on his face, for her to join him at the closed front door. It took more courage than she'd imagined it would to lift her chin and walk toward him with at least a semblance of dignity.

"I take it you had a pleasant journey," Griffin said rigidly when she reached his side.

"The ride was surprisingly gentle," Faith replied, wishing he would offer her his arm. Her knees were feeling stiff and weak. "I'm pleased to report I did not give up my breakfast, even when we hit an occasional rut in the road."

"I envy your strong stomach," he remarked with a slight grin. " 'Tis a stroke of good fortune to be blessed with such an iron constitution."

"To match my hard-as-iron head?" Faith quipped.

Griffin's grin flashed again briefly, and a delightful warmth rippled through Faith, softening the doubt and apprehension. If she could summon the courage to tease him, perhaps there was hope for the future.

Still, it was difficult for Faith to contain a groan when the front door swung open to reveal the butler she had previously tricked to gain entrance to the house. He was a tall, bone-thin man with a streak of gray running through the middle of his limp, dark hair. Faith saw the amused glint appear in his eye momentarily when she entered the house, yet it quickly disappeared when he discovered her sudden change in status.

"On behalf of myself and the entire household, may I offer my sincerest congratulations on your marriage," the butler choked out.

"Thank you," Faith replied graciously. "I look forward to meeting the entire staff and becoming acquainted with each and every one of them."

It clearly was the wrong thing to suggest. The butler looked properly scandalized for a split second before his face slipped back to a formal mask. "As your ladyship wishes."

"Are my sisters at home?" Griffin inquired as he handed his hat and gloves to a waiting footman.

"Yes, my lord," the butler replied, seeming relieved to have a more familiar question. "They are in the music room, attempting to give young master Neville a musical lesson on the pianoforte."

"Kindly inform them that I have returned from London, and instruct them to join us in the drawing room. I have important news that I wish to tell them personally."

"I understand," the butler said with a polite bow. "Shall I have refreshments sent?"

"Just tea."

Faith's brow wrinkled at Griffin's answer. So this was not to be a celebratory meeting. No champagne to toast the bride and groom and wish them every happiness. A part of her applauded Griffin's lack of artifice, yet deep down she was disappointed.

They walked side by side to the drawing room without touching, thanks to the wide foyer. Faith paused at the entrance, her heart pounding uncomfortably, worry causing the sweat to bead on her upper lip.

Faith was not anticipating a warm reception from Griffin's sisters. Harriet had never liked her, and young Elizabeth usually followed her strong-willed sister's lead. Faith told herself their opinions did not matter overmuch; it was Griffin's son she must win over.

Yet there was no denying that life would be far

more congenial if her new sisters by marriage would accept her into the household willingly. With a worried frown, Faith settled herself in a chair near the corner while Griffin paced in front of the fireplace. They spoke not a word to each other.

When the drawing-room door opened, only two women walked into the room. Apparently the child had been sent back to the nursery.

"Griffin! You've come back!"

Young Elizabeth launched herself at her older brother, and he caught her in a warm embrace. He kissed her on the forehead, then leaned over and did the same with Harriet. Faith noted the older woman's stony countenance cracked slightly at this gesture of brotherly affection. Neither of the women had noticed Faith sitting quietly in shadows.

"Look who I've brought home with me."

Griffin gestured with his hand, and three pairs of eyes turned in her direction. Faith's heart constricted as she gave her new family a wan smile. They stood together on the opposite side of the room, a united wall.

The space separating her from them was only a few yards, but it felt vast and overwhelming and terribly lonely.

"How lovely of you to bring a visitor," Elizabeth proclaimed in a cheerful voice. " 'Tis so nice to see you again, Miss Linden."

"She is no longer Miss Linden," Griffin announced in an unemotional tone. "Faith is now the Viscountess Dewhurst. We were married yesterday."

Harriet noticeably pulled away from her brother's side. "Have you gone completely mad?" she hissed, her color fading. "Married. To her? If this is a joke, I find it to be in very poor taste."

"I see that your sisters are well acquainted with your sense of humor," Faith spoke up. Clutching her hands together firmly in her lap, she tried desperately to rid her voice of the fluttery, weak tone. " 'Tis no joke, Harriet. Griffin and I exchanged vows in a London church yesterday afternoon. We are well and truly man and wife."

Harriet gasped loudly at the indelicate reference, while Elizabeth merely looked puzzled. Faith felt her face go hot with embarrassment at her faux pas.

"Must I remind you there is a young lady present?" Harriet sniffed. She pulled a finely embroidered handkerchief from the pocket of her gown and pressed it beneath her nose. "I do not know how you conducted yourself while living at Mayfair Manor, but in this home we do not speak so openly of such personal matters."

A shot of anger speared through Faith. Her remarks had been unintentional, due to nerves, but Harriet's comments seemed definite and cruel. Faith tried to work up the nerve to reply to this taunt, but could think of nothing sufficiently scathing to say.

"That is enough, Harriet." There was a wealth of warning in Griffin's tone, but his sister seemed far too upset to heed it.

"What could have possibly possessed you to consent to such a match?" Harriet questioned, turning once more to face her brother. "And why such haste? You only left for London two weeks ago. Could you not have waited a decent interval before wedding?"

"I understand that you are surprised and shocked by this sudden news, but have care, Harriet. You are speaking of my wife and your new sister."

Though Griffin's words were spoken calmly, Faith detected the faint tension in his jaw.

Harriet cast a deliberate glance at Faith. "This is not shock; 'tis a nightmare," she muttered.

"Enough! You overstep yourself, sister. Now apologize to my wife." Griffin's face grew harder, the taut expression cutting off any further protests from Harriet.

"That isn't necessary—" Faith began.

"Be quiet, Faith," Griffin commanded, his hard gaze boring into her.

For a moment Harriet merely stood silently, her jaw clamped shut. Elizabeth moved closer and clutched her sister's hand in support. Harriet released a tight sigh and made a curt nod of her head toward Faith. "My apologies." She said nothing more, but the fury in her eyes bespoke of her true feelings.

Tea arrived. Harriet made a move to excuse herself, but one stern glance of warning from her brother effectively prevented her departure. With obvious reluctance, she settled herself on the edge of a delicate upholstered chair, directly opposite Faith.

There was complete silence as the servants set out the tea tray.

"Cook sends her apologies for such a simple tea, my lady," the young footman said hesitantly. "She hopes to provide you with a far more worthy dinner, to properly welcome you to your new home."

"Everything looks lovely," Faith insisted. "She has done wonders on such short notice. Please convey my sincere thanks to Cook for her efforts on my behalf."

The servant smiled, then bowed and left. Faith and Harriet reached simultaneously for the silver pot, their hands colliding. The pot tipped precariously for an instant, but set itself to rights.

"Sorry," Faith mumbled, snatching away her hand. Harriet gave her a long, searching look. "I have once again forgotten myself. Forgive me. 'Tis your place now as mistress to pour the tea."

"But this is a *family* afternoon," Faith replied. "It is perfectly proper if you do the honors."

"I wouldn't dream of overstepping my place," Harriet said stiffly, folding her hands primly in her lap.

"I insist."

"Oh, I couldn't."

"Griffin?" Faith turned beseechingly to her husband for support.

"Just pour the damn tea and be done with it, Faith." The viscount glowered at both women, then threw himself into a chair.

Faith struggled against the despair that threatened to choke her. Though Griffin had earlier defended her, he now sided with his sister against her. That hurt. As did realizing that winning Harriet over was going to be a nearly impossible task, if every small conciliatory gesture Faith offered was met with such open hostility.

Faith wheezed slightly as she tried to draw a breath, telling herself firmly that it did not matter. Harriet's blatant disapproval was the very least of her problems at the moment.

Yet the tears still gathered in her eyes, as much as she tried to prevent them. Faith tilted her head a bit, so no one could see her expression fully, and poured the tea.

"I take mine with just sugar," Elizabeth offered helpfully. Wariness flickered in her eyes as she glanced at her older sister. "So does Harriet."

The single snort of disapproval from Harriet was her only acknowledgment of the comment. Silently Faith dropped a large lump of sugar into the cup and handed it to a very sullen-faced Harriet. The other woman accepted it with a curt nod, then placed it untouched on the table.

"I think I'll have a whiskey instead," Griffin replied, when Faith held out a cup in his direction.

Faith wished she had the nerve to ask him to pour her one also. Though she had never tasted anything stronger than wine, the supposed bliss of strong spirits held great allure at the moment.

Instead, she took a small sip of the tea she did not want and waited. No one said a word.

"Was the journey pleasant from London?" Elizabeth finally asked.

" 'Twas fine," Griffin answered.

"Any rain?"

"A bit."

"Oh." Elizabeth took a sip of tea. She looked uncertainly at her brother. "Did the roads get muddy? From the rain?"

"Naturally."

"How tiresome."

Faith sighed. While she certainly appreciated Elizabeth's efforts to engage in conversation, Faith felt too stiff and ill at ease to lend support. Besides, the subject matter of this riveting discussion was fast putting her to sleep.

Harriet seemed to be of a similar opinion. In the fading candlelight, Faith could see the other woman's eyes glaze over. Though never considered beautiful, Faith was surprised to realize what an attractive woman Harriet was, when there were no scowls marring her charming features.

"You have not asked about your son," Harriet said suddenly, abruptly changing the subject. "I hope your preoccupation with your sudden wedding has not driven him from your heart."

Griffin paused in the act of pouring himself a second draught of whiskey to glare at his sister. "I suggest that you do not test my rather limited patience any further."

Harriet raised her chin. "The child missed you. He asked us each day when you would return."

Griffin's expression softened. "I heard you and Elizabeth were trying to give him a lesson on the pianoforte. Is he at all musically inclined?"

"I'm not certain," Harriet replied. "It is far too soon to tell. After all, this was only his second lesson."

Elizabeth giggled. "He certainly likes banging on the keys."

Harriet also smiled, indulgently. "He is a boisterous lad and when confined indoors tends to be more exuberant than usual."

"I look forward to meeting him," Faith interjected eagerly, hungering to mother this spirited child. Perhaps with him she could finally achieve what she truly sought, the companionship of a real family.

"He is in the nursery eating his supper and cannot be disturbed," Harriet insisted. "He does not take well to strangers. I believe tomorrow will be soon enough for introductions."

"I had hoped to see him today."

"Tomorrow," Harriet stated firmly, rising to her feet. "And now you must excuse me. There is much that needs my attention. I will see you at dinner. 'Tis served promptly at seven. We keep country hours, you know. Come along, Elizabeth."

Elizabeth stiffened, then slowly returned the half-eaten pastry she was munching to her dish. With an apologetic shrug toward Faith, the young girl brushed the crumbs from her fingers and followed her sister out of the room.

Faith's mind spun. She wanted to roar with frustration. Instead she turned to her husband for support. Griffin raked his hair back with his hand and took a long swallow of his drink. His weary expression proclaimed he was not in the mood to oversee another battle between his wife and his sister.

Faith took a deep breath. She despised the knot of disappointment and emotion churning in her stomach, despised the weakness and vulnerability she felt.

She had expected a less than welcoming reaction from Griffin's family, knowing that Harriet had little fondness for her. Yet this open hostility was almost more than she could bear. There had been a gleam of outrage in Harriet's eyes that could not possibly be mistaken.

Suddenly, Faith wished she was once again on the road, traveling alone in the carriage. But instead of bringing her to her new home, it was taking her far away from this place of tension and discord.

"I shall wear the green silk this evening," Faith informed the maid that had been assigned to assist her. "Please make certain it is pressed in time for me to dress for dinner."

"Yes, my lady." The older woman carefully extracted the gown from the cumbersome traveling trunk. " 'Tis a beautiful dress. What jewels do you wish to wear?"

"None. This is only a simple family dinner. It would be vulgar to offer an opulent display."

Faith felt her cheeks grow warm at the lie. There was in fact no jewelry to match the magnificent dress. She owned only the few simple pieces that had once belonged to her mother, nothing that was even moderately appropriate for this formal gown.

The maid eyed her slyly. She was an older woman, with many years of service in the household. "I know where the family jewels are kept. I could ask his lordship's valet for the key to the safe. There's a lovely diamond necklace that belonged to his lordship's mother that would be a perfect match for the gown."

For an instant Faith was tempted. It might be worth suffering Griffin's wrath just to see the expression of horror on Harriet's face if she entered the dining room wearing their mother's necklace. That subtle reminder of Faith's place in the household would surely put a bee in Harriet's bonnet.

"All I require is the gown," Faith said, reluctantly deciding to let the opportunity pass. Tweaking Harriet's nose was not the way to secure her position in the household. Like it or not, she was going to have to find a way to peacefully coexist with her new sister-in-law or else everyone would suffer.

'Twas really enough of a statement to wear the new, expensive fashionable gown to dinner. Faith could not help but notice the condition of both Elizabeth's and Harriet's clothing. Well-worn and several years out of fashion.

Yet it was not for Harriet's benefit that Faith had chosen this particular garment. She needed that dress for courage. She had worn it to Lady Dillard's ball the night she and Griffin had been wildly indiscreet in the garden. Perhaps the sight of her in the dress would spark a more pleasant, or even scintillating memory in her husband's mind.

With a quick curtsy and a look of disappointment, the maid left. The minute she was alone, Faith turned to her open trunk. Kneeling, she carefully pushed aside the layers of petticoats and frilly undergarments until she located a large, misshapen parcel wrapped in brown paper.

Extracting her prize gingerly, she held it aloft and carefully examined it to make certain it had not been damaged in transport. Finally satisfied with the condition of the package, Faith tucked it under her arm, rose to her feet, and headed for the door.

She poked her head out and surveyed the hall. No one was about. Clutching the package firmly in one hand, Faith quietly slipped out of her bedchamber.

She froze when she heard the sound of footsteps approaching, but they turned away before reaching the corridor. Releasing her pent-up breath, Faith glanced at the longcase clock that stood in the hall and confirmed that she had nearly an hour before the maid would return.

Relying on her memory, Faith climbed the stairs to the third level. As a child she had on occasion been a visitor to the nursery, and she assumed it would now serve as the room for Griffin's son.

A young woman, dressed in a loose gown and clean apron, rose to her feet the moment Faith entered the large, airy room.

"I am the new Viscountess Dewhurst," Faith announced haughtily. "I have come to visit my stepson."

The young woman hesitated. Faith was certain the news of her sudden marriage and arrival had spread through the servants' quarters, but so apparently had Harriet's disapproval. Yet having come so far, Faith was not about to be denied. Summoning her strength, she stared down at the servant in a superior manner. And prayed the girl would be properly intimidated.

"The young master has just finished his supper," the servant said finally, stepping aside.

Faith looked beyond her and saw a small boy quietly playing with a set of blocks near a closed window. The servant made a move to call the child, but Faith motioned for her to be still.

Cautiously, Faith approached the boy. He must have heard her drawing near, for he turned suddenly and looked directly at her.

Faith's heart leaped, and she nearly dropped the parcel she was carrying. He looked so much like Griffin! Somehow, with the confusion of his name she expected the boy to look like her former fiancé. But there was no denying that this child was Griffin's son.

"Hello, Neville," Faith said softly.

The child's expression altered. He was not frightened, but definitely wary.

Faith held out the large, wrapped package. "This is for you. I hope you like it."

"What is it?" the child asked as he took the package and held it tightly in both hands.

Faith smiled. "Why don't you open it and find out?"

Hesitantly, the little boy looked down at the parcel, then back up at Faith. She nodded encouragingly, and he carefully began peeling away the paper.

Faith was amazed at his control. Most children, nay most adults, would have torn into the wrapping in seconds. But Griffin's son meticulously pulled back the strips until the gift beneath was revealed.

"It's a ship," the boy exclaimed in wonder. He held it up for his nurse to admire. "Just like Papa's."

"Does it resemble Papa's ship?" Faith asked eagerly, moving closer to the child. "I've never seen your father's vessel, but the man in the shop who sold the boat to me said it was a fine example of a trading schooner."

"Will it float?" the boy asked, running the tip of his finger along the edge of the main sail.

"I'm not certain." Faith bit her bottom lip, hardly believing she had been foolish enough not to inquire if it was seaworthy before purchasing the toy. "Perhaps we can test it tomorrow. There is a large pond on the edge of the south woods that would make a perfect spot for sailing ships. Would you like me to take you there in the morning, Neville?"

The child wrinkled his nose. "I don't like being called Neville."

"Really? I didn't know. What should I call you?"

"Georgie."

The servant quickly intervened. "The young master's middle name is George. Just this week he has asked to be called Georgie. Miss Harriet and Miss Elizabeth have indulged him, but if you prefer, my lady, we shall call him Master Neville."

"Oh, no." Faith smiled broadly. "Georgie is a splendid name. I could not have chosen a finer one myself."

She knelt down and drew closer to the boy. The urge to reach out and give him a hug was strong, but Faith controlled the impulse. He did not appear to be the type of child that would encourage affection from a stranger, and this relationship was far too important to Faith to hurry.

"So, shall we try to sail your new boat tomorrow, Georgie?" Faith asked.

The child propped the boat in his lap, seeming to consider the question carefully. Then with a sunny smile replied, "Yes, please."

Faith answered that grin with one of her own. "Splendid. I will see you in the morning, young man."

She stood on her feet, reluctant to leave, yet not wanting to push the situation too far.

The little boy's gaze drifted to her face, and he gave her a puzzled frown. "Who are you?" he asked, with the forthright manner of an inquisitive child.

"My name is Faith," she said softly. "I am your new mama."

"Does Papa know about you?"

"Yes."

The child nibbled the edge of his fingernail thoughtfully. "Then I guess it is all right."

Unable to resist, Faith leaned over and gave him a quick kiss on the cheek. He suffered the attention with good spirits and waved a friendly good-bye as she left. Faith practically floated away from the nursery. Things had gone far better than she had dared to hope.

The successful encounter with young Georgie bolstered Faith's sagging spirits. She sailed into the dining room dressed in her lovely green gown, feeling confident and renewed. Neither Griffin's silence nor Harriet's thinly veiled jibes during the meal had much effect on Faith's good mood.

Young Elizabeth made a considerable effort to be friendly, a feat that earned her scowls of disapproval from her older sister. But Faith would not be defeated by Harriet's attitude. She encouraged Elizabeth's conversation and was rewarded with an occasional remark from her husband.

But once they adjourned to the drawing room, the tension subtly began to grow. Faith became distracted as she began to wonder where her husband was going to be spending the night. In his bedchamber or in hers?

"The hour grows late," Griffin announced suddenly, crossing the room to stand beside his wife. " 'Tis time we were abed."

Griffin held out his hand. Faith rose gracefully to her feet. While she was definitely nervous about being alone with Griffin, it was certainly preferable to staying and being tortured by his sister.

After a solemn good night to Harriet and Elizabeth, Faith took Griffin's offered hand and allowed herself to be led from the room.

They turned at the top of the steps, following along a corridor that ran the length of the house. The hall was lit by candles in brass sconces that were badly in need of polishing. Faith absently noted that the thick rug beneath her feet could use a thorough cleaning, too.

Finally they arrived at her bedchamber door. Faith turned to face Griffin, and her knees suddenly felt shaky. Would he join her? More importantly, did she want him to?

Yawning, Griffin rubbed his face with his hands. "It has been a rather long, emotional day. I imagine we both need a good night's sleep."

"Yes." She replied automatically, for in truth the last thing Faith wanted was to go into that vast bedchamber alone and try to sleep. She wished she had the courage to reach out and touch him, to tell him what she really needed: to be held tightly in his arms while she slept, sated and exhausted by their lovemaking.

Instead she stared down at the pattern in the carpet as they lapsed into tense silence.

"Good night."

Faith lifted her head and saw Griffin's hand reach for the door handle of his bedchamber. Not wanting to be left alone in the hallway, she also gingerly reached for the door to her chamber, holding it tightly for balance.

"Good night, my lord," she whispered, unable to hide the slight edge of bitterness in her voice. "I hope you sleep well."

The click of a door latch was his only response.

Eleven

It had been there, clearly in her eyes. Desire. Yet Griffin had turned away from it. He could hardly believe himself. Griffin Sainthill rejecting such a blatantly sexual invitation. From the woman who was his wife, the one female in the world with whom intimate relations were sanctified by man and God.

Clearly the world had gone mad. Nothing about the evening, or the day for that matter, had turned out the way Griffin had planned.

He had expected Harriet's disapproval of his marriage, for he was well aware of her dislike of Faith. But he had not been prepared for the depth and magnitude of his sister's anger and resentment.

The attack had stunned Faith, too, yet she had managed to hold up her end and strike back. Once again he had misjudged his bride. She had looked to him for support and he had given it, but only once. Left to her own devices, Faith had stood her ground.

This hidden depth of strength had served Faith in good stead and made him more curious about her. Yet it also made him even more wary. Experience had taught him that surprises from his wife were not always pleasant.

"Is there a problem, my lord?"

Startled, Griffin glanced up and saw his valet hovering near the doorway. He had been so lost in thought he had not even heard the servant enter the room.

"A problem? No. Why do you ask?"

"Forgive me, but you were scowling so fiercely I thought that something was terribly wrong."

Feeling somewhat self-conscious, Griffin stared at the servant without saying a word. Apparently, his passionate thoughts about Faith were not as easy to conceal as he'd believed. Even when she was away from him, he was unable to get her out of his mind.

Griffin tried schooling his features into a more neutral expression, then decided to hell with it. The servants would gossip no matter what he did.

A thoughtful frown creased the valet's forehead. "Did you require my assistance in preparing for bed, my lord?"

"No."

The servant nodded, then moved to the large bed. He removed the coverlet and drew back the sheet. "Shall I prepare a warming pan for the bed linens? It was a warm day, but there is a chill in the night air."

Griffin grimaced. His valet was trying to be subtle. Naturally the staff would be taking a keen interest in the newly married couple—and their sleeping arrangements.

"A warming pan is unnecessary," Griffin declared.

The valet nodded again and began to busy himself brushing the traveling coat Griffin had worn earlier in the day. Griffin stared hard at the man until he raised his head. With a flick of the wrist, the viscount signaled he wished to be left alone.

The valet hesitated a moment, then bowed politely and took his leave.

Griffin moved to stand by the window, the one located farthest away from the door that connected to

Faith's chambers. He sighed and shoved back the heavy draperies to stare out into the darkness. 'Twas a clear night, but the sight of the brilliant moon did not bolster Griffin's spirits. On this strange and unsettling eve the stars seemed cold, distant, and unfriendly.

Shaking his head at his fanciful thought, Griffin abruptly closed the curtains, then began to slowly undress. He removed his jacket, then loosened the knot of his cravat, and removed his waistcoat and shirt. Instead of neatly hanging the garments in his armoir, he tossed them over the edge of a chair, deciding that would give his valet something to occupy his time in the morning.

Straightening, Griffin drew in a breath. His bare chest swelled as he drew in another. It didn't help. He still felt restless and unnerved. On edge. He glanced briefly at the connecting door, then deliberately looked away.

Nothing but trouble waited for him on the other side of that door.

Though he had drunk a fair amount at dinner, a brandy seemed in order. Fortunately, a decanter had been left in his room; Griffin had no desire to call for his valet again and even less to be seen wandering about the house at this hour in search of alcohol.

Lips compressed, he poured himself a portion, then swirled the liquid languidly in the large goblet. Though he tried to prevent it, his mind filled with thoughts of his wife.

Was she still preparing for bed, or had she already slipped between the crisp sheets? Wearing a sheer nightrail, perhaps? Or better still, wearing nothing at all. His mind spun with heated images. It would take only a few short steps to bring him to her side. Her eyes and attitude had clearly indicated she would not turn him away. She would not deny him a place in her bed.

That might alleviate the constant ache in his groin, but it could never relieve the doubts in his mind. This was the one time in his life where Griffin was determined not to let his cock do his thinking for him.

Sleeping with Faith would cloud, not clear the issues in his mind. First and foremost they needed to spend time together or else they would never cease misunderstanding each other.

Yet he was honest enough with himself to admit he still wasn't ready to completely let go of his anger. And he did not trust her. At all.

So here he sat. Alone. What a pathetic, sorry state of affairs. Marriage, Griffin concluded as he took a large swallow of his drink, was a vastly annoying institution.

"Look how swiftly she sails," Faith cried out with excitement. She hitched up the skirt of her gown and ran along the uneven ground on the bank of the pond. "I think we've finally put those pesky sails to rights, Georgie. The boat barely tips at all. Why, at this rate she'll be across to the other side in no time."

"Hurry!" Georgie called out in delight. The little boy eagerly grabbed Faith's hand and tugged. "I want to catch the ship before it smashes into the ground."

Breathless and laughing, Faith let herself be swept along through the high grass, weeds, and muddy soil, as the two raced to beat the toy ship. The child's joy was contagious, and it did her sore heart a world of good to be carefree and relaxed for a few brief moments.

She and young Georgie had been coming to this

very place for an entire week, and it had been the one bright spot in her otherwise trying daily routine.

It had also been the secret part of her morning ritual. Only the nursemaid who cared for the boy knew of these special outings, and Faith jealously guarded this rare, private time alone with the child.

"Here it comes!" With a squeal of delight, Georgie crouched low and snatched the boat out of the shallow water.

He held it close against his chest, and rivulets of dirty pond water trailed down the front of his formerly clean shirt and knickers.

"Shall we send it across again?" Faith asked as she gently tugged the toy from the child's arm.

She pulled the lace handkerchief from her pocket and made a feeble attempt at brushing him clean. The boy tolerated her fussing with good humor, but her efforts only smeared the dirt further. With a resigned smile, Faith put away the handkerchief.

Georgie knelt in the mud and tried launching the boat. It moved a few feet away from shore, then bobbed its way back.

"Why doesn't it work? Is it broken?"

Faith pushed the hair out of her eyes and stared across the small pond. "We are trying to sail her against the wind. That's why the boat keeps coming back. We'd best walk around and launch her from the same spot."

"I'm tired of walking. Let's go in the big boat."

Faith turned to where the child was pointing and saw that an old rowboat had been pulled high on the small bank and tucked behind a clump of bushes.

"Oh, dear." Faith could instantly understand the allure of the small craft. To a young boy, it represented adventure and excitement. To her it posed only a safety hazard. "I don't think we are allowed to use the boat, Georgie. After all, it isn't ours."

But the child wasn't listening to her halfhearted protests. He bounded toward the small boat with all the enthusiasm of a puppy let loose from the kennel. By the time Faith joined him, Georgie had scrambled inside and was trying to hoist one of the solid oars.

"There are two benches. One for each of us to sit on," he announced with enthusiasm. "Look, I can do the rowing." He won his struggle with the clumsy oar and raised it triumphantly. Faith ducked quickly to one side to avoid being smacked in the head, but Georgie was too excited to notice. "Can we go for a ride. Please?"

"But it isn't ours," Faith repeated weakly. "It's wrong to take things that don't belong to us."

"Aunt Harriet says that Papa owns everything on the estate. Is this part of the estate?"

Faith was tempted to lie. It would be the easiest solution and would avoid a lengthy argument. "This area is part of Papa's land, but that means the boat belongs to Papa. Not to you. Or me."

"But Papa loves me. He says so all the time. He won't care if I use his boat." Georgie frowned thoughtfully, resting his chin on his linked hands. "Doesn't he love you, too?"

Faith was momentarily speechless. Leave it to a child to get to the heart of the matter so quickly and easily. " 'Tis not a question of love," Faith said. "We must ask permission before we use the boat. We cannot assume that your Papa would allow it."

Faith could see the boy struggling to understand her words. "I know Papa would let us," he said softly. The look of pure longing on that angelic face was almost impossible for her to resist.

Faith chewed her bottom lip. The pond was smooth as glass, completely calm. It shouldn't be difficult to row the small craft across, even with Georgie *helping*. The problem was, she couldn't swim a stroke. And she wasn't overly fond of water unless it was in her bathtub.

Perhaps they could just pretend to row. Gingerly, Faith climbed into the small craft. Georgie gave her a wide smile of delight and scooted over to make room.

He thrust the oar out the side and slammed it into a small tree. Faith laughed and positioned the oar properly. "If you are going to row us across the lake, you must practice," she declared.

At first Georgie thought that was a wonderful idea. But he had great difficulty moving the oars as they became quickly caught in the tall grass. After several minutes even Faith conceded that it wasn't much fun.

"There, I did my practicing." The child climbed out of the boat and picked up the leading rope tied at the front of the vessel. "Now we can put the big boat in the water."

Faith eyed the thick rope with speculation. She had no intention of allowing the child to row across the small pond. It was far too dangerous. They were in a secluded section of the estate, in an area seldom traveled by anyone. There would be no one near to offer assistance if they got into trouble, no one in range to hear their cries of distress.

But perhaps there was a way for Georgie to have a bit of adventure on the high seas. If she stayed on shore, holding tightly to the rope, the boat could drift out a few feet from the bank. She knew the boy would be unable to row more than a stroke or two. When he became tired, or lost an oar, she could gently pull the boat back to land.

It might not be the excitement Georgie craved, but 'twas more fun than sitting in the grass, pretending to be on the water.

Pleased with the plan, Faith climbed slowly out of the boat, nearly missing her footing as she landed.

"All set, Captain." She gave Georgie a sharp salute that he returned nattily. "Let's put the ship in the water."

Dutifully, the child stood beside her. Faith rubbed her hands together, smiling when Georgie imitated her actions. Leaning low, she pushed on the boat. Her feet slipped in the muddy ground and she nearly fell.

Georgie giggled. Faith smiled and tried again. This time she was able to move the boat a few inches. Every muscle in her back screamed with protest at the unaccustomed strain, but she had promised the child. If it took all morning, which it just might, she would get this darn boat into the water.

By the fourth push Faith had managed to dislodge the craft from its sandy bed. There was a slight downward slope that aided the motion of the craft, and the wet ground and slippery grass provided the necessary lubrication.

She was panting and sweating, but with a final shove and a loud *umph,* Faith at last succeeded in getting the boat in the water.

"Hooray!" Georgie jumped up and down with delight as the small craft bobbed drunkenly.

"Careful," Faith called out anxiously, as the child scrambled to get into the boat. "Try not to get your shoes wet."

"You sit here," Georgie decided, patting the space on the seat beside him. "I'll do the rowing."

Faith picked up the end of the rope and wound it

carefully around her arm several times. She yanked it hard, testing its security.

When she raised her head, Georgie smiled at her and again patted the seat. It touched her heart to be given such a place of honor. At least one male member of the family was anxious to have her near him.

Faith shook her head. "I'll stay here on shore while you do the rowing. Then I'll pull you back, real fast." She held up the rope to demonstrate, giving it a sharp tug. The boat obediently moved toward her.

Georgie shrieked with delight and gripped the sides of the boat. When the boat steadied, he enthusiastically picked up the oars. Face frowning with concentration, the little boy maneuvered the oars into the shallow water and tried to execute a stroke.

Faith was watching him closely, but the distant sound of thundering hooves caught her notice. She lifted her arm to shield her eyes from the sun and anxiously scanned the horizon.

In the distance, galloping along the top of the hill, were two riders. Suddenly, they made a swift turn and changed direction. Faith realized with a startled jolt that she and Georgie had been seen, for the riders were heading straight toward them.

As they drew near, Faith could see that one of the horsemen was her husband. He sat tall and commanding on a handsome black mare, slightly ahead of the other rider, who sat stiffly upright on a fine gray gelding.

The second rider was smaller in stature, and as they traversed the hill Faith noted one more important detail. This rider rode sidesaddle. Harriet. Faith's heart plummeted.

She quickly began pulling on the boat, bringing Georgie to the shore. But the child had finally mastered the art of rowing, in his own way, and worked against her efforts with jabbing, choppy strokes. The splashing water soon had the front of her gown rather damp and Georgie's hair soaked.

"What the devil are the two of you doing out here?" Griffin demanded to know, edging his mount closer.

"Enjoying the morning sunshine," Faith replied with a forced smile. " 'Tis a lovely day."

"Why is the child sitting in that rickety old boat?" Harriet asked as she joined her brother. Her eyes suddenly widened in horror. "Don't say he is going to row it across the pond?"

"Certainly not," Faith contested. She tilted her chin in hopes of looking more in control of the situation. "Georgie merely wanted to sit inside the rowboat. I saw no harm, since it is safely at the shore, and I have a firm grip on the rope."

Faith lifted her arm to give credence to her story, yet the pinched expression of dismay on Harriet's face revealed what the other woman clearly thought of the plan.

"We can all go for a ride!" Georgie exclaimed. "There is room in my boat for you, Papa, and Aunt Harriet, too."

"Perhaps another time. Please get out of the boat, son."

The little boy's crestfallen face cut straight to Faith's heart. She stepped forward to help him out of the craft and whispered, "Chin up, Georgie. We shall have another adventure out here tomorrow. I promise."

He gave her a brave, watery smile.

"Goodness, what has happened to his clothes?" Harriet asked. "They are so wet and dirty. He looks like a common village urchin."

Faith took immediate exception to her tone and

words. "He looks like a happy, healthy little boy who has been playing hard and having fun. Though I suppose that is a rather foreign notion to you, *dear sister*. Fun."

Harriet drew herself tall in the saddle and glared down at Faith. "I would expect that only a woman who has been petted, spoiled, and indulged all her life would not understand even the basic elements of responsibilities. Life, *dear sister,* is not always about having fun."

Faith didn't dignify that with a response, and Harriet continued in the same scolding tone.

"The child must learn, even at this young age, what is proper behavior for a nobleman. Unruly, ramshackle little boys grow into unmanageable, incorrigible men. It would be intolerable if such a thing happened to this child."

"He is none of those things!" Faith put her arms protectively around Georgie's shoulders. "Say what you will about me, Harriet, but I'll not have you criticizing the boy," she said in a low, forceful tone, defending the child with all the fervor of a lioness with a threatened cub.

"I am not finding fault with my nephew. The child is blameless in this incident. 'Tis the adult who is responsible, or rather irresponsible, in this matter."

Faith's back stiffened. She opened her mouth to deliver a most blistering retort, then caught a glimpse of Georgie's open face. Though not understanding the nuances of the discussion, it was obvious to the child that she and Harriet were quarreling. And Faith saw that upset him.

She put her hand to her temple to still the thumping in her head. "Papa is right. We've had enough adventuring for one day. Come along Georgie; 'tis time to go home."

"You cannot expect the child to walk back in wet clothes," Harriet bristled. "He'll catch a chill."

" 'Tis a warm day, and the sun will dry him quickly," Faith insisted, not bothering to point out that she was probably as wet, if not wetter, than the child. "The walk will be good for him."

"It will not."

Faith raised her eyes to Griffin, silently seeking his assistance, and noted that Harriet had also turned to her brother with an expectant expression. The viscount suddenly busied himself with the reins of his mount, concentrating on keeping the horse steady. Faith grimaced, realizing he was expending far more energy on this simple task than was necessary.

"Fine. He shall ride home." Faith picked up the child and moved beside Griffin's horse.

"No, he will ride with me." Harriet nudged the gray in front of her brother's horse. "Griffin has estate business to attend to. I must take Georgie to the nursery and remove his wet clothes immediately. Then a hot bath and right to bed for a rest. It will be a miracle if he doesn't have a horrible cold by nightfall."

The leather saddle groaned as Harriet adjusted her seat. "Griffin, please hoist him up here."

With a skeptical eye, the viscount dismounted, then lifted the child onto the horse. Faith kept her chin lowered to hide the growing anger in her eyes. Seeing that would only let Harriet know her actions were succeeding in upsetting Faith.

"I want to ride with Papa," Georgie declared solemnly.

"Papa has tenants to visit," Harriet replied. "He is not returning to the house immediately. I am."

"Oh." The child bowed his head low.

"You look most regal sitting upon that horse, Master Georgie," Faith said. "I think soon you will be ready for your own mount."

The boy nodded solemnly. It was far from the enthusiastic response Faith was hoping to achieve.

"I shall need help guiding my horse back to the stables." Harriet tugged on the cuff of her riding glove. "Would you like to hold the reins and assist me, Georgie?"

Georgie's chin was up like a shot. "Yes!"

"Yes, what," Harriet and Faith said simultaneously.

Georgie's eyes widened. He glanced first at Faith, then turned his head and looked at Harriet. Then he giggled. *"Yes, please."*

"We're off." Harriet touched the brim of her hat with her riding crop in a quick salute. "I'll see you both at dinner."

" 'Bye." Georgie waved merrily with his free hand. Faith wagged her fingers in reply.

"Irrational, headstrong woman," Griffin muttered under his breath as the horse galloped away.

Faith shifted her attention to her husband. "Perhaps in time Harriet might learn to control some of those more annoying tendencies," she said primly. "One can only hope."

"I was referring to you."

"Oh." Faith kicked a small stone with the toe of her slipper and walked to the pond. She bent low and retrieved Georgie's toy, gently smoothing the cloth sails.

"You were going to take him out in that rowboat, weren't you?"

Faith sighed. "I was going to allow him to sit in the boat while it rested at the very edge of the pond. He was determined to row it himself, and I knew he could never get more than a foot or two away from the shore. The rope tied to the end of the boat was new and sturdy. I wrapped it several times around my arm to secure it. There was never any danger."

"Harriet didn't seem to agree on that point."

Faith rolled her eyes expressively. "Harriet would not agree with me if I said the sky was blue and the grass green."

Griffin surprised Faith by laughing. "Yes, I believe Harriet would insist the opposite were true." He studied Faith for a long time. "I know she can be difficult, but you really must determine a way to somehow get along with her."

Faith's chin rose. "Strange, I would think that Harriet needed to devise a way to stay in my good graces. After all, this is my home."

"She is my sister," Griffin replied simply, glancing away.

"How well I know that," Faith muttered beneath her breath, needing no further reminders of where Griffin's loyalties lay. Certainly not with his wife.

The silence between them grew, pressing down upon them. The lead on Griffin's horse allowed the creature to amble forward and take a drink from the pond. The viscount followed behind the black mare and waited. Faith listened to the quiet lapping for several moments, then finally turned to face her husband.

The afternoon sunlight illuminated the left side of his face, highlighting his strong, handsome profile. As always, his male beauty took her breath away. Secretly, she longed to reach out and touch his cheek, run her fingers along the strong line of his jaw. But she did not dare.

The physical, as well as emotional distance between them was clearly defined.

"It would make life easier for everyone in the household, including yourself, if you and Harriet would get along," Griffin stated firmly. "I fear that soon this verbal sparring will reach a physical level, and I shall find myself in the unenviable position of pulling you apart like two brawling kittens."

"What a lovely picture you envision, my lord."

"Not far from the truth, I fear." He turned, and she stared at his face, noting the tightening of the muscles around his mouth. "I'm serious, Faith. You quarrel over everything to do with the boy. I cannot split the child in half."

"I know full well which end I would receive if you could." Faith glared at him. " 'Twould not be the part that I kiss good night each evening."

"Am I truly so unfair?"

"Yes." Yet even as she spoke the word, Faith knew it was not entirely true. Griffin had on the rare occasion taken her side in the argument. "If one were keeping a tally, then Harriet would have far more marks than I."

He drew in a deep breath, then released it. "Perhaps if you made this less of a competition, the final outcome would not be of such great significance."

"Harriet and I do not just disagree on the small matters when it comes to Georgie," Faith retorted. "We have a fundamental difference of opinion on how the boy should be raised. Harriet seems convinced that my ideas are a haphazard way to bring up a child. And I cannot abide the rigid routine that she insists upon.

"He is a little boy, not a soldier in Wellington's army. She has ordered his life so completely there are times when I believe she has even scheduled the times when he is to go to the privy."

Griffin laughed and shook his head. Encouraged, Faith continued. "Georgie cannot have two different women responsible for his welfare. And while I appreciate Harriet's position in the household, she is still his aunt. I, on the other hand, am his mother."

"His stepmother," Griffin corrected solemnly. "What becomes of the boy if our marriage fails? If you return to live at Mayfair Manor, who will then be the woman responsible for his welfare?"

It was a reasonable question. They had been married only a week and were holding most precariously to a relationship that was filled with hurt and mistrust.

But Faith was not about to give up. How could she possibly explain to Griffin how much this small child had come to mean to her? Georgie gave her purpose in this rambling castle that was so unwelcoming to a bride and a new mistress.

He ended the desolation she felt, filled up her barren days, challenging her to reach out to life and grab it, instead of letting it merely slip away. She would fight with every ounce of strength to hold on to this special relationship.

Faith made an effort to banish the hurt that Griffin's doubts had brought to her eyes. "I am not prepared to give up so quickly on our future life together, Griffin. Perhaps Georgie will provide the means for us to stay together."

The viscount raised his brow skeptically. " 'Tis a great burden to place on such a young child."

Faith smiled brightly, trying not to focus on how dispirited he sounded. "You are forgetting one very important fact, my lord. Georgie is no ordinary boy. He is his father's son."

Twelve

Being an early riser, Griffin usually ate his morning meal alone. He preferred to dine in the informal breakfast room, for it was one of the few rooms within the house that was in need of little repair. The cherry-wood furniture was always polished to a high gloss; the patterned wallpaper of flowers and fruit was still bright and cheerful.

There were no water stains marring the ceiling plasterwork and the sheer white draperies were neither torn nor musty smelling. Though he had few memories of his mother, Griffin distinctly remembered that this was one of her favorite rooms.

Over the course of his weeks in residence, he decided that he was glad no one had bothered to redecorate it, for it provided a fond link to his past.

He hurried in to eat his breakfast in his usual morning rush, but pulled up short when he discovered the room already occupied. Both his wife and sister were seated at the table, each silently contemplating the contents of their plates.

"Faith, Harriet, good morning."

"Good morning, Griffin," they chorused like a pair of obedient schoolgirls.

The viscount raised his brow cynically and took his seat, trying all the while to disregard the presence of the two females. He braced himself, waiting with dread for the venomous looks to begin, the veiled accusations and heated jibes to be flung between the two women.

Griffin's manner grew guarded as he tried to think of a neutral topic of conversation to introduce. And then he realized, with a good deal of amazement, that the room remained quiet, save for the clinking of silverware and the gentle rustle of linen napkins.

It was probably the first time in his four-week-old marriage that he had been in a room with his wife and sister and they were not quarreling. Or bickering. Or complaining to him about each other.

For a minute Griffin was completely mystified. He nearly opened his mouth to comment upon this rather favorable turn of events, then thought better of it. Why tug on the lion's tail when he was sleeping?

A servant appeared before he could call for one.

"Would you care for your usual breakfast this morning, my lord?"

"Yes, and bring another pot of hot coffee."

"I have more than enough to share," Faith said. She lifted the silver coffeepot set by her side and poured the hot, dark liquid into a clean cup.

"I'm having chocolate this morning," Harriet explained when Faith rose from her chair and carried the steaming cup to Griffin. "Would you care for a cup of that next?"

The viscount could only stare at his sister in astonishment. Fortunately, the footman's arrival saved him from answering. Griffin nodded approvingly as the servant lifted the lids off the silver chafing dishes, inspecting the contents as if he were amazed by what he found.

Once his plate was full, Griffin began eating, casting a subtle eye in the direction of the two women. He glanced from his wife, sitting forward and eager in her chair, to his sister, sitting straight-backed and closed.

Both women abandoned any pretense of eating and instead watched him keenly. He bit firmly into a piece of toasted bread and nearly choked on a crumb.

"Are you all right?" Faith asked with concern.

"Do you need some water?" Harriet chimed in. "Or ale?"

Through watery eyes, Griffin saw both women barreling toward him. "Stop," he whispered, coughing and gasping for air. He waved a hand at them impatiently. "I have no need of assistance."

Reluctantly, they backed away and resumed their seats. When he was recovered, Griffin eyed the pair suspiciously. They were like a set of vultures, waiting anxiously for their dying prey to take his final breath before swooping down to fight over the carcass.

What could possibly be the problem now? This obvious solicitous behavior toward him meant each woman was hoping to gain the advantage when presenting her side, and Griffin began to dread the upcoming altercation.

He acknowledged there had been a slight improvement in the relationship between the two women. They both appeared to be making an effort to get along, and were never openly hostile toward each other when there were others present, although Griffin strongly suspected they quarreled often and bitterly when he was not around to witness it.

And nothing could set the powder keg off quicker than a disagreement over young Georgie, for each woman was firmly convinced that she, and only she, had the child's best interest at heart.

In these four weeks of marriage, Griffin had come to form a pretty good notion of his wife's character, discovering she possessed one shared trait with his sister. Neither woman liked to be defeated.

"All right, out with it." Griffin pushed back his chair and scowled down the table at the anxious women. "What is the problem now? You are disturbing my digestion with all your solicitous behavior and attention this morning."

"Harriet insists upon finding a tutor for Georgie," Faith promptly replied. "I think it is ridiculous to even consider it at his young age. Perhaps in a few weeks I can begin searching for an appropriate governess who can teach him his letters and numbers."

"He already knows them." Harriet slapped her napkin on the table. "Georgie is not an ordinary little boy. He has a quick and inquisitive mind. It should be molded and challenged by a skillful teacher, not left to wither under the direction of a governess."

"He is too young for a tutor," Faith insisted. "He needs the gentle but firm guidance of a female. A governess."

"Important time is being wasted," Harriet replied. " 'Tis criminal to allow that to continue."

"He is too young for such rigid schooling," Faith repeated. "We have only just celebrated his fourth birthday."

Both female heads turned in Griffin's direction. No words were needed requesting his intervention. He returned their eager stares, deliberately keeping his expression neutral.

"I confess, I have not thought overmuch about my son's education. However, I shall think long and hard on this matter and let you know my decision once I have reached it," Griffin said, spreading his hands to emphasize that was the end of the discussion.

Miraculously, neither woman challenged his words. Harriet took a sip of her chocolate and Faith a quick bite of her toasted bread. Perhaps his forceful expression was at last making an impact on their behavior.

The viscount smiled at this fanciful notion. Both women were far too headstrong to be so easily controlled. He supposed each woman felt her position was so strong he would be easily won over to her side, so additional arguments were unnecessary.

Griffin forked in a bite of his cold eggs and suppressed a twinge of guilt. In this particular instance their difference of opinion was easy to understand. His sister knew that Georgie was a by-blow, an illegitimate child who would need every advantage his father could give him to succeed as a man in this harsh, unjust world.

Yet his wife believed the boy was his heir and would someday inherit his title and possessions. She saw no need to start him so early in education, no need to exploit his natural abilities.

"The morning post has arrived, my lady." With a deferential bow, the butler entered the room and swung a silver tray toward Faith.

She smiled with delight and lifted the packet of envelopes. Griffin noticed a slight tension begin to fill the air.

"Is there nothing for me?" Harriet inquired tensely.

"Not this morning," Faith responded cheerfully. "It appears that all three letters are for me."

Harriet let out a deep, sputtering sigh. Griffin wondered at her odd reaction. Since he had returned home there had not been any letters for his sister. Why should today be any different?

"Who is your correspondence from, Faith?" Griffin inquired. He refrained from extending his hand, even though it was well within a man's rights to read his wife's letters.

"Two are from Merry and one is a note from Lady Granville."

He noticed Harriet gaze disapprovingly at Faith. Since his sister had never in his presence spoken a word against Lady Granville, he surmised it was the mention of Lady Meredith that put her off her mood.

"Lady Granville discusses the upcoming social events among our little 'quaint local society' and hints broadly that since I am a new bride, I should be honored to host a harvest ball," Faith continued.

Griffin waited for Harriet's retort, fully expecting her to balk at the expense. But she remained silent.

The footman entered carrying another covered dish. Griffin quickly abandoned his cold meal in favor of the fresh, hot fare. Since Faith was still busy with her letters, the servant next approached Harriet.

"Do you wish more eggs and kippers?" the butler asked, a first, second, then third time.

Griffin raised his head. Harriet was gazing off in the distance, her face a study in concentration. The footman stood by her chair, extending the covered chafing dish.

The servant repeated his question, and still Harriet did not respond.

"Harriet!" Griffin shouted.

"What?" She turned her head sharply.

"Rogers has asked you several times if you wish more breakfast."

Her gaze faltered for the briefest of moments. "Sorry." She blushed sharply and put a small portion of food on her dish.

Griffin stroked his chin, examining his sister thoughtfully. "Did you sleep well last evening, Harriet?"

"Yes, I slept fine," she responded with a touch of impatience. "However, I find that I have just lost my appetite. Since I have no lengthy correspondence to read through, I shall go for a ride."

She pushed back her chair and marched from the room.

"Harriet seems upset," Griffin commented.

Faith glanced up from the letter she was diligently reading and shrugged. "I noticed no difference in her behavior." She resumed reading her correspondence.

Griffin shook his head. "Apparently, she was expecting a letter. From whom, I wonder?"

"Her fiancé, I assume," Faith replied absently. "I know of no other friends or acquaintances she corresponds with on a regular basis."

"I was unaware that she had been receiving letters from her betrothed. She rarely speaks of him."

"I suppose she doesn't have much to say." Faith wrinkled her nose. "To my knowledge, she has not received any letters this past month, although she apparently writes to him daily."

Griffin's chair was located at the head of the table, nearest the window. He glanced outside and caught a glimpse of Harriet walking slowly down the garden path. Her head was bowed, her shoulders hunched, her feet shuffling. If he didn't know better, Griffin would swear she was crying.

He saw her slip a hand up to grasp the gold locket she always wore around her neck. A gift from her neglectful fiancé? He had never inquired.

"Tell me about this man Harriet is supposed to marry. What is his name? Jonathan Winthrope?"

Faith slowly lowered her letter. "Harriet is engaged to marry *Julian Wingate*. He has no title, but is a direct descendant, on his mother's side, of the duke of Shrewsbury and part of the Dorrington family. They are, as you are no doubt aware, most highly respected and admired members of society."

"I don't care about his family," Griffin replied impatiently. "Tell me about the man."

"I've never met him," Faith said hesitantly. She brushed a stray crumb off one of her letters. "There have been all sorts of stories circulated about him, but I hardly think it fair that I repeat such gossip."

Griffin's mouth thinned. Faith showing a loyal, almost protective attitude toward Harriet?

"Is this Wingate fellow really that bad?"

Faith's eyes touched him, then glanced away. She cleared her throat. "The tales that have been repeated in my hearing paint Mr. Wingate in a most unflattering light, portraying him as something of a rake, a man given solely to his own pleasures." Faith paused, inclining her head. "Actually, his unsavory reputation is not unlike your own. That is, before you reformed your wicked ways and became a respectable married man."

"And a viscount," Griffin added with a smirk. "Let us not forget my noble title. Wingate may come from a noble background, yet he lacks a title. That could be his main problem. Becoming a viscount has made all the difference in the eyes of many in society and this community."

"It has, my lord. 'Tis also the sole reason I married you," Faith responded promptly. With a wrinkled brow and pursed lips, she lifted her china cup and took a delicate sip of the hot liquid. "To become a viscountess."

Despite her pinched expression, Faith's voice was light and humorous. Griffin had difficulty controlling his bark of laughter.

"You sold yourself short, my dear," he said with a grin. "If you had waited a bit longer, you might have landed an earl. Or even a duke."

Faith burst out laughing. "The only way I could have caught a duke for a husband is if he were a very slow runner and I possessed a very large net."

Almost against his will, Griffin found himself joining her merriment. He marveled anew at how his vast experience with women gave him no advantage when dealing with his wife. He was as puzzled by her as ever. She could laugh at herself, joking so openly with him about catching a husband, despite the wall that firmly existed between them because of her duplicity surrounding the circumstances of their own marriage.

Griffin searched for the anger that always consumed him when he allowed himself to dwell on Faith's lies, but it did not come as quickly or strongly. Was he finally starting to forgive her, in his heart as well as his mind?

He glanced at his wife. It was no surprise that these four celibate weeks of married life had not diminished her feminine appeal. More and more he found it difficult to banish her from his thoughts, whether he was awake or asleep.

Faith intrigued him, yet he deliberately kept a physical distance from her. Why? Because he feared the consequences if he succumbed. Whatever happened between them, he was determined not to become a slave to his own senses.

"Tell me more about Wingate," Griffin demanded, knowing he should be worrying about the sorry state of his own marriage, not fretting over his sister's relationship. Yet somehow it seemed far easier and more appealing to face someone else's problems. "If he marries Harriet he shall be our relative."

Faith instantly sobered. "If? Do you doubt his sincerity?"

"I question it."

A frown slowly formed in Faith's eyes. "Most of what I know of him comes from Merry. Mr. Wingate offered for her during her first season, but she turned him down flat. She told me he had a way of staring at her that made her feel singularly uncomfortable."

"I cannot fault the man for being interested in Lady Meredith. She is a stunningly beautiful woman."

Faith thrust her eyes downward, but not before he saw the flash of pain and anger. She set down her cup on the saucer so loud it rattled. "Yes, Meredith is a goddess of womanhood, beautiful and wise and worthy of worship by all men. Including you."

"Jealous?"

She opened her mouth wide, then abruptly closed it. Griffin picked up his cup and downed its remains in one gulp. Faith was still sputtering, no doubt wrestling with the perfect retort, so he used her confusion to take a closer look at his wife.

She was wearing a simple morning dress, pale yellow in color, that fit tightly across her bosom. Her hair was styled simply atop her head, and there was a most becoming flush on her cheeks. Poets would never write sonnets to her beauty; artists would not beg to immortalize her loveliness on canvas. Yet Griffin was aware of this woman, his wife, with every single fiber in his body, even though the length of the cherry-wood dining table separated them.

"Nothing to say, Faith?" Griffin teased, when she failed to reply.

"I have decided it would only inflate your already impossibly large ego to dignify your ridiculous notion of jealousy by commenting upon it," Faith said haughtily, her chin tilted at a challenging angle.

"Coward."

"Braggart."

They launched into a spirited conversation, and Griffin soon found himself feeling a flood of rising desire. He watched as well as listened to Faith as they bantered, enjoying the way she emphasized her point by moving her hands in a graceful arc high in the air.

She leaned across the table, and Griffin caught the clean, freshly washed scent of her hair. Lavender. His stomach muscles contracted sharply as he imagined removing those pins and running his fingers through the heavy silk tresses.

He closed his eyes briefly, remembering the softness of her naked flesh, the fullness of her breasts as he caressed them, cupping the roundness in his palms whilst his fingers tantalized the dark nipples into provocative hardness.

Griffin's lack of attention on their conversation brought it abruptly to a halt. Faith glanced at him with a pleasant, almost intimate smile. The viscount stood.

Breakfast was finished. He had a pile of papers awaiting him in his study, but Griffin was having great difficulty pulling himself away. He had no real reason to stay except that he wanted to see Faith, wanted to be near her.

"Business calls," Griffin announced suddenly, moving away from the table. "I hope you have a pleasant day. I will see you at dinner this evening. I shall be gone from the estate for the majority of the afternoon, so do try and avoid a hair-pulling argument with Harriet."

He bowed stiffly, then rushed from the room, in much the same manner that he had arrived. Just to prove to himself that he possessed the strength of will to do it.

Faith exited the house through the ballroom doors at the rear, deliberately going in the opposite direction as Harriet. The sun had risen higher, but the air felt moist. Glancing upward she saw a streak of low-lying clouds marring the blue sky. There would most likely be rain by the afternoon. She worried that Griffin would get wet on his errands, for she knew he would ride his horse instead of taking a carriage.

Faith paused when she reached the edge of the formal gardens and sat on a stone bench, facing the last of the summer blooms. Already the air felt cooler. Summer was nearing its end—the fall harvest would soon begin.

It gave her a sudden sense of sadness to gaze upon the withering flowers. Their beauty was wilting, turning brown and crumbling into dust. Soon they would be nothing more than compost for next year's crop of new buds.

The sun felt warm on her shoulders, and Faith closed her eyes briefly. Rising so early this morning had been difficult, and the lack of sleep was already starting to take its toll.

A high warbling sound interrupted her dozing. Curious, Faith lifted her head and noticed a small bird with a short dark beak perched on a nearby branch. It looked oddly familiar. She sat very still and it came closer, taking a short nervous hop in her direction. She smiled and fumbled in the pocket of her gown, searching for the crust of bread she had taken from the table for just this purpose.

"You must be the pretty little bird that Georgie has been feeding," she cooed, holding up the tempting treat.

Tilting its head, the small creature darted forward, blinking its tiny black eyes. Faith laughed, and the bird skipped back in fear.

"I'm sorry," she whispered. "I did not mean to frighten you. I am well acquainted with the feelings of terror and helplessness and would not wish that upon any living creature."

Faith placed a crust of bread on the edge of the stone bench, then walked carefully away, leaving the bird to enjoy its bounty in peace.

Several other birds flew around in circles above her head and swooped down to join the feast. She quietly left that section of the garden and ventured toward the ornamental fountain that Georgie enjoyed sloshing his hands in. Whenever his Aunt Harriet was not around to scold him.

It was an idyllic spot. Quiet and peaceful. The soft breeze was scented with the last of the season's roses, and she inhaled appreciatively. Faith followed the path, deliberately clearing her mind of the morning's event.

She would *not* dwell upon Griffin's unusual behavior at breakfast. For the most part he seemed to grudgingly tolerate her presence in his home. He left her mostly to her own devices, involving himself only when it was necessary to settle a dispute between her and Harriet. An event Faith had quickly learned he heartily despised.

They met at the evening meal most days and occasionally took tea together. They politely discussed the events of their day, the events of the estate, the gossip from the village. As much as Faith disliked Harriet, she was honest enough to admit that without Griffin's two sisters in the house, it would be as quiet as a tomb.

The sound of footsteps behind her slowed Faith's step. She turned and saw Griffin striding purposely toward her.

"Is something wrong?" she inquired warily as he reached her side. Her husband had left her not ten minutes ago, clearly anxious to be away from her company. "Did you forget to tell me something?"

"I did not forget; I was merely remiss," Griffin replied. "Before I departed from the breakfast room I had meant to give you this."

Without further warning, the viscount bent his head and covered her half-opened mouth with his own.

There was an instant of total shock. Then Faith's eyelids fluttered closed and her body softened. She immediately experienced that odd feeling of light-headedness, and a deafening rush of sound filled her ears, reminding her of the surf pounding on the shore.

Griffin deepened the pressure of his lips, making her own feel even more sensitive. Her mouth parted and his tongue delved inside. She could taste the slight bitterness on his tongue from the coffee he had drunk earlier. Her hand lifted to touch his face as a small sound of sensual delight purred in her throat.

Griffin drew her fully into his arms, imprisoning her most willingly. Through the flickering leaves on the trees above her, Faith could feel the warmth of the sun on her face and shoulders, but the heat it provided could not match the fire Griffin was creating inside her.

His hand reached down and cupped the fullness of her breast. One of his fingertips slipped inside the front of her bodice and began gently rolling the aching nipple.

She felt the betraying hardness of his body and boldly pushed herself closer. His hand stilled on her breast, then he broke off the kiss and pulled away. Faith could feel herself floundering, struggling to hold on to his strength.

No, please not yet. Just one more kiss.

"Griffin, I—" Words were an impossibility. Her entire body was trembling, shuddering from head to toe. She wanted desperately to be back in his arms, with his mouth pressed firmly to her lips and the hard strength of his body enveloping hers.

He pretended not to notice her agitated state. "I have decided we should host the harvest ball as Lady Granville suggested." He paused and bowed his head, in an effort to regulate his breathing. "Please make all the necessary arrangements. I'm sure that Harriet and Elizabeth will be delighted to assist you."

"A ball?" Faith croaked.

"Yes."

Stunned, Faith could only nod her head meekly. Her body was taut with unfulfilled desire and he wished to discuss a party? She was sure that somewhere there was humor in this situation, but it was impossible to discover it at this point.

"Is there anyone in particular you wish me to invite?" Faith asked faintly, not sure what else to do.

"No. I'm sure you know better than I who should be included." The viscount nodded his head curtly. "I shall leave all the details in your capable hands."

Faith sank to the edge of the fountain and breathed in deep lungfuls of air. She stared at his retreating back in dismay, her emotions in turmoil. *What just happened?*

Shaking her head in confusion, Faith took a second deep breath. She could still smell the subtle, masculine scent that was uniquely Griffin's. It clung to her skin like a potent aphrodisiac, teasing and testing her will.

For a moment she sat there, savoring the sensation of his lips pressed to hers, the feelings that engulfed her so completely when, for just an instant, she had felt desirable, protected, almost cherished.

Shutting her eyes, Faith tried to summon her common sense. She had no earthly idea what had prompted this unexpected, passionate embrace. Perhaps the reason, or reasons, were not truly significant.

The more important dilemma to be faced was determining how to again incite this romantic, passionate behavior in her noble husband. As soon as possible.

her mistress indecision, it was good news for Faith. An hour at most. When Faith and Meredith finally she prepared to travel downstairs to the harvest ball.

Thirteen

"Are you truly going to wear those gloves with that gown?" a cultured feminine voice asked in mock horror.

Faith whirled toward the outraged voice and burst out laughing. "Merry! I should have known it would be you, critiquing my new ensemble." Faith tugged self-consciously on the ends of the long gloves that extended beyond her elbows. "Don't you like them? I was told by the shopkeeper this was the latest rage in Paris."

"Then let Napoleon enjoy looking at his ladies trussed up in bandages when they attend a ball." Lady Meredith made a clucking noise with her tongue. "Those long gloves make your arms look short and squat and distract from the simple lines of your bodice. And they cover far too much of your beautiful skin."

Meredith turned to the wide-eyed maid who had been listening to the exchange with great interest. "Bring me her ladyship's glove box, so I may select a more appropriate and flattering pair."

"Yes, my lady." The maid curtsied, then rushed off to find the box.

Faith watched with growing amusement as Meredith carefully examined the entire contents before making a selection. It was good to have her friend so close at hand. When Faith had informed Griffin she intended to invite Meredith to the harvest ball, he had merely raised an eyebrow and wondered out loud if she would be interested in attending. After all, country pursuits would seem rather unsophisticated after the excitement of London.

But Faith knew that Meredith was far from impressed with the goings-on of the beau monde. Besides, she would attend this ball if only for Faith's sake. True to her nature, Meredith had arrived a few days before the party, and her efficient, supportive presence had been a soothing balm to Faith's frayed nerves.

"These shall do nicely," Meredith announced, as she extracted a soft pair of white gloves.

Uncertainly, Faith donned them. They seemed far too plain and ordinary for the elegant silk gown she was wearing. A quick glance at her maid revealed the servant's doubts, too.

"They look perfect," Meredith decided. "Much better than the others."

The hollowness in the pit of Faith's stomach eased. The strong conviction in Merry's voice left no room for doubt, and Faith was relieved to note that as usual, Meredith's fashion instincts were spot-on.

The shorter gloves were an improvement over the long, making her fingers appear long and elegant and her hands dainty and petite. Merry might claim to have no interest in the fickle dictates of fashion, but she had an innate sense of fashion that could not be denied.

The undisputed proof of that lay in the fact that no matter what the occasion, Meredith was always impeccably and flatteringly dressed.

Then again, when one had such irresistible beauty to

work with, it was easy to scoff at the current fashion. With a flash of jealous wonder, Faith admitted that her friend would no doubt look ravishing dressed in rags.

"I suppose these gloves are an improvement," Faith conceded, picking up her fan. She glanced at Meredith with uncertainty, wondering if her friend had a negative opinion about this accessory.

"You look radiant this evening, Faith," Meredith declared. "The restorative country air has done wonders for your complexion."

"I have spent nearly all of my life in the country," Faith said with a small laugh. "Did only a few short weeks in London remove the glow from my skin?"

"Of course not. However, a few months back in the country has placed an even brighter shine in your face. Or is that charming glow a result of your newly married state?"

Faith blushed. Despite the closeness she had always felt with Meredith, she was not eager to discuss her marriage. It was a jumbled, complicated mess that she didn't truly understand herself. How could she articulate her feelings of disappointment, regret, and the ever-present hope that it would all improve one day?

"I eagerly await the day when you are married," Faith said with a sly wink. "Then we can discuss the institution together and share our experiences."

Meredith's slim body tensed. "Bite your tongue, Faith. I have long believed it is not my destiny to marry. A most unpopular and unnatural attitude among women of our class, as you well know. I know that I shall need your support of my unconventional decision as the years pass, not additional pressure to do what is expected."

"I was merely jesting," Faith declared in a soft

voice. The vehemence of Meredith's declaration startled her.

"I was not," Meredith stated stubbornly.

Faith thought she had understood Meredith's position on marriage, but hearing her speak this prophecy so vehemently was disheartening. Meredith should not rule out marriage entirely. Paired with the right man, she would make a wonderful companion.

Despite everything that had gone wrong with her own marriage, Faith was very glad that she had married. And very glad that Griffin was her husband.

For an instant Faith worried that Meredith had heard or seen something between her and Griffin these past few days that caused this openly antimatrimony attitude. Faith rattled her brain for details, yet could remember no overt signs of discord.

The viscount had been a model of husbandly regard since Merry's arrival. Polite, solicitous, and interested in his wife's conversations, while properly busy with various estate businesses and other masculine pursuits that severely limited the time he spent with his wife and houseguest.

If she noticed anything odd about Griffin's behavior Meredith kept those opinions to herself.

"I must stop in the nursery before we go downstairs, so I can say a proper good night to Georgie," Faith told Meredith as they left her bedchamber. "I promised to pull the sheets extra tight and tuck him into bed exactly the way he likes. I know he won't be able to sleep until I do."

Meredith cocked her head to one side. "You really are taken with this child."

"I am." Faith grinned. "Believe it or not, Georgie keeps me sane."

Meredith raised a curved brow at that remark, but

said nothing. Griffin's son was already snuggled in bed, struggling to keep his eyelids from closing, when the women arrived. After several hugs, tickles, and kisses, he was ready for sleep. Despite protesting that he was not in the least bit sleepy, Georgie was yawning loudly, with the young nurse in charge of his care hovering near, as Faith and Meredith tiptoed out of the room.

"I wonder if any of our guests have arrived," Faith commented as they strode down the hallway. "I don't think I had one refusal for the ball. We are expecting a full house tonight."

"I'm sure it will be a great crush and a resounding success," Meredith replied. "After all, everyone is most anxious to see the new Viscountess Dewhurst."

"I have known most of these people since I was a child," Faith replied with a shake of her head. "I have not changed very much in the few months of my marriage."

Meredith's eyes filled with laughter. "Oh, there are many who would quibble with that statement, Faith. I among them."

Faith was too startled to reply. Had she really changed? For the better? she wondered. There were times when Faith felt exactly the same as she always had and yet at other moments she felt as if she had changed beyond recognition.

Faith moved along without urgency when Meredith gestured for her to go ahead, realizing her friend most likely did not know how to get to the ballroom from the third floor. This was not Mayfield Manor, where Merry knew the passageways as well as her own home. Oddly enough, Faith had forgotten that for an instant, almost as if Hawthorne Castle was now her real home.

The nerves she had managed to quell started nagging at her the moment they reached the ballroom entrance. Tonight would be her first real entrance into the local society since her marriage. She had made only the minimal amount of social calls during these first months, taking shameful advantage of her position as a new bride to avoid those duties. And avoid all the avid questions.

Tonight there would be no avoidance. Faith would be standing front and center, one of the two main characters to be scrutinized thoroughly by the local society. Griffin would be the other, and there was little doubt in her mind that her husband would be judged favorably.

Oh, how she longed to also be held in similar regard. Even from the very people who had in the past either stared rudely, completely ignored her, openly criticized her, or spoken in hushed whispers behind her back.

Faith hated feeling so vulnerable over the outcome of tonight's party, and even though it was not always a welcoming environment, she found herself reluctant to leave the protective cocoon of her new home.

Meredith made small talk as they stood at the ballroom threshold attempting, Faith realized, to ease the obvious discomfort that Faith was experiencing. But even Meredith's inconsequential chatter could not still the nerves that burst forth when they stepped inside.

None of the guests had arrived, but the sound of crunching wheels and neighing horses was quite distinct. Faith knew it would only be a matter of minutes before they began descending. Griffin, along with Harriet and Elizabeth, stood at the front of the room, forming an informal receiving line.

They were engrossed in an intense discussion, unaware of Faith and Meredith's arrival. The extra moment gave Faith a chance to collect her thoughts and make a final check of the room. Her critical eye darted about the room, mentally ticking off all the careful, meticulously thought out arrangements.

The orchestra stood at the ready, seated in the upper galley as to maximize the space for dancing. Fall flowers had been artfully arranged throughout the room to bring in an extra dash of color and lend an air of celebration. All the best beeswax candles had been lit, and they cast a romantic, inviting glow.

It was difficult to imagine that the estate had suffered from neglect and financial troubles. Tonight, the rooms that were visible to the guests glowed with fresh paint and newly repaired furniture, thanks to Griffin's frugal management and the funds from Faith's dowry and profits from Mayfair Manor.

The servants were discreetly milling about the edges of the room, awaiting the guests' arrival so they could be of service.

Faith had instructed all the footmen to be attired in simple black frocks, deciding against the more fashionable formal dress. She was therefore surprised to notice a footman stroll past her looking ridiculously formal in an old-fashioned powdered wig, silk knee breeches, and a heavily embroidered silver waist frock.

He quietly took up a position at the entrance to the ballroom and Faith realized he was poised to announce each guest, with the staid and formal fanfare that she always disliked, as they entered.

It took no effort to decide who had orchestrated this, against her specific wishes. One glance at Harriet's smug expression told Faith who was responsible.

With a feeling of inevitability, Faith advanced toward the footman, who was unfortunately standing directly beside her husband and his sisters. As she approached the group, Faith concentrated on keeping her breathing steady. *In and out, in and out.*

The black evening clothes the viscount wore made Griffin look his usual breathtakingly handsome self, and Elizabeth looked appropriately young and fresh and utterly lovely in her white muslin gown. Faith grudgingly conceded that even Harriet looked well this evening. The lavender silk gown she wore was several seasons out of date, but the high waist flattered her willowy figure and the soft color complemented her coloring.

Yet Faith knew all too well that underneath all that silk was steel. Hard, unreasonable steel.

Faith decided to give one final attempt at avoiding a direct confrontation with her meddling sister-in-law and addressed her displeasure directly to the servant.

"I am very surprised to see you positioned here, Harper," Faith said to the footman. "And wearing that outfit. My instructions for this evening were clear and concise. No formal attire and no formal announcing of the arriving guests. Precisely what part of those directions did you find difficult to comprehend?"

The footman's eyes darted uncomfortably to Harriet, and she immediately stepped forward.

"Do stop haranguing the servants, Faith. The guests are arriving." Harriet breezily slid between Faith and the footman. "Harper is here at my command. We have always announced our guests at a ball, since it is the proper and correct way to conduct any affair attended by so many of the local gentry. 'Tis expected. I assumed the omission was an oversight on your part, due to your inexperience in these matters."

"You assumed wrong. When your opinion is required, Harriet, it shall be sought. Until then, kindly keep your thoughts, ideas, and *assistance* to yourself." Faith turned to the footman, who was now regarding her with great intensity. "Go to the kitchen and see if you can help with setting up the buffet. And for heaven's sake, remove that ridiculous getup. This isn't the palace at Versailles."

"Yes, my lady." The footman bowed, a glow of new-found respect in his eye.

Harriet stiffened and drew herself up tall. "You are making a colossal blunder. It is important—"

"Be quiet, Harriet," Faith interrupted. "My decision has been made, and there is no disputing that it is *my* decision to make. The guests are arriving. If you continue on about this nonsense, all the hot air from your sputtering will fill the room, turning it uncomfortably warm, and then no one will want to dance."

Harriet's jaw dropped. With a satisfied nod, Faith turned her attention toward the arriving guests. These last days of hectic preparation had left Faith's emotions scraped raw and easily affected, but besting Harriet in an argument was precisely what she needed to regain her confidence and face the local society.

"Is everything all right, ladies?" Griffin inquired.

Harriet pursed her lips tightly and turned away.

"Faith?"

Faith lifted her chin and regarded her husband. "I have dealt with the matter, Griffin. There will be no embarrassing scenes between myself and your sister for the guests to gossip about and savor." Faith took in a full breath of air. "I daresay, the one huge benefit to my little tirade is that I have managed to startle Harriet speechless. At long last."

Her actions must have also rendered her husband speechless, for the viscount said not a word. He merely smiled at her, then took his place appropriately at her side.

Out of the corner of her eye Faith saw Meredith start to move away. She grasped her friend by the wrist and pulled her close. Thus Meredith joined the receiving line.

Faith's nerves gradually began to dwindle as each guest entered the room, their eyes filled with bright curiosity. There were murmurs of awe and approval over the decorations, compliments on the skills of the orchestra, along with an endless stream of hearty congratulations to the married couple. Some even sounded sincere.

It felt strange to be receiving so many curtsies, especially from many of the older women in attendance, but her newly achieved rank of viscountess demanded such regard.

When appropriate, Faith returned the gesture with women of greater or equal rank, surprised to realize there were very few who qualified. Lady Granville however was one such woman, and as she rose from a graceful curtsy Faith felt a strange sensation across the exposed area of her chest.

With a start, Faith glanced down and discovered her mother's necklace of pearls and diamonds had slid down her throat and come to nestle within the bodice of her dress.

"Merry," Faith hissed, the moment Lady Granville strolled away. "I need your help. Can you fasten my necklace?"

Faith turned her back and discreetly plucked the jewelry from her gown, then handed it to her friend. Meredith fumbled with the clasp, but her gloved fingers made it difficult to work the fine catch.

"Allow me," a deep male voice said.

Faith lifted her head. Griffin stood directly behind her, an unreadable expression on his face. She found herself trembling as his steady fingers fastened the necklace around her throat. His touch felt warm and familiar.

Aside from the occasional arm offered to escort her to and from a room, this was the most intimate contact she'd had with him since the afternoon he'd kissed her nearly senseless in the garden.

" 'Tis a lovely piece. Was it your mother's?" he inquired politely, when the necklace was securely around Faith's throat.

No, they were a gift from a former lover. The wicked, untrue response sprang to her lips. If only she possessed the nerve to utter it. Just once she would like to shock her husband out of his casual politeness with a truly outrageous remark.

"Papa gave them to Mother on their first wedding anniversary," Faith replied. Her hand touched the gems gingerly, making certain they were still in place. "Mother always told me they were her favorite."

"I have heard that sentiment often raises the value of a jewel in the owner's estimation." Griffin glanced again at the necklace. "But in my experience it has been the quality, number, and sparkle of the stones that elicit the most regard."

"Clearly you have been gifting the wrong women with gems, sir." Faith averted her gaze, trying to control the painful spirt of jealousy that consumed her. She had never been very interested in jewelry, but knowing that Griffin had given pieces to other women rankled.

He had never made any attempt to dispute his rakish reputation, yet his honesty did not make it easier to accept the fact that he had been intimate with other women.

And he had given them jewelry, no doubt exquisite, expensive pieces. The only item he had ever given Faith was a wedding ring. Yet, wasn't that symbolic article worth far more than a king's ransom of diamonds, emeralds, and sapphires?

Faith sighed at the thought, then averted her gaze. She hoped the orchestra would not delay much longer before striking up for the first dance and rescuing her from her gloomy musings.

The music at last began and the eager dancers scrambled for partners. Griffin opened the ball by dancing with the highest ranking female in attendance who was not his wife, Lady Granville. Faith was partnered by Lord Granville, and she smiled brilliantly as the older gentleman trod on her toes, apologizing profusely with each painful stomp.

The set mercifully ended, and Faith was released from her agony. The dance floor was crowded as couples lined up for the next set. Griffin seemed to suddenly disappear, but Merry was close at hand. She drew Faith's arm through her own and generously included her in the large group of male admirers that had formed the moment they realized Meredith was not going to immediately join in the dancing.

Meredith had willingly forgone the opening dance, and it was no surprise to Faith that her friend had succeeded in gathering such a court about her. Faith could feel and see the looks of female envy that were being cast their way, and she fought to hide her smile. None of the women would most likely believe it if they were told the truth. The lovely and vivacious Lady Meredith despised so much blatant male attention.

"May I sign your dance card, my lady?"

Faith smiled in some amusement at the young man who bowed before her. The points of his collar were so high and stiffly starched that his neck looked unusually long, and he could not move his head from side to side. With surprise, she realized this impressive dandy was none other than Squire Barton's second son, Geoffrey.

They were the same age and had attended many of the same local society functions. But this was the first time he had ever asked her to dance.

"I would be delighted to dance with you," Faith said graciously. "Though I am surprised you would sign my card when there are so many other lovely, single ladies present."

"You are the grandest lady here, Viscountess Dewhurst," Geoffrey said with sincerity. "I am honored to be your partner."

A few male heads turned speculatively in her direction. Apparently Geoffrey's interest in her spurred on his companions. Faith soon found herself passing her card to several other men, including the flame-haired eldest son of the most prosperous tenants of Mayfair Manor and the dapper Baron Harndon, a portly gentleman of haughty bearing.

There was much good-natured revelry as the men began vying for the two women's attentions. Faith could scarcely believe that some seemed as interested in her as they did in Merry.

Faith glowed under all the unexpected attention, deciding it was all harmless fun. She smiled and flirted, tapping her fan on a male shoulder, pressing her fingers on the sleeve of a gentleman's coat. She was having a wonderful time. She tried to catch Merry's eye, to share her amusement, but was unable.

Faith could, however, see Merry's foot tapping with

some impatience as she feigned interest in a story one of her admirers was recounting, and Faith was doubly grateful for her friend's support. Normally Meredith would not put up with such nonsense from such an assortment of young bucks. Faith knew Merry was only doing this for her sake, to ensure that her party, and Faith, were a success.

Mr. Huxtable elbowed his way to her side, smiled, and bowed. "My dance, I believe."

Faith consulted her card, which was nearly full. "So it is," she said, placing a hand on his sleeve.

The pattern of the dance allowed for limited conversation, but at every opportunity Mr. Huxtable flattered her outrageously. Faith responded in kind, enjoying every moment of this harmless fun.

In the midst of glittering couples, Faith saw Griffin whirl by, holding his sister Elizabeth in his arms. The young girl was smiling happily with a look of such fragile innocence and youth it made Faith's heart ache.

When the dance ended, Mr. Huxtable returned Faith to her circle of admirers, which had amazingly doubled in size. Her next partner quickly stepped up and Faith was whisked away. The dances followed in quick succession and she soon found herself breathless from the exercise.

Finally there was a set without a partner, but the circle of ever-present male admirers soon had Faith laughing and flirting, affording her little chance to relax and catch her breath.

Suddenly, a strong male voice interrupted the boisterous laughter. Faith lifted her head and saw her husband gazing with great interest at the group of men clustered about her. He took a moment to stare at each man in turn, as if sizing up their measure. Then he directed his stare at her.

Faith decided it must be a trick of the light, for the viscount glowered, looking bothered by all the attention she was receiving.

"Your dance card, madame." Griffin held out his hand expectantly.

Faith flushed and wordlessly gave him the card. She was grateful that she was standing in a candlelit area of the room so any change in the color of her cheeks would not be so noticeable.

"Why, you partnered me for three dances, my lord," Faith exclaimed when she read the returned card, noticing that he had crossed out two names and added his in their stead. "I am honored."

"Three dances," an older gentleman with gray-streaked hair groaned. "I say, Dewhurst, no fair monopolizing the most charming woman at the ball. You need to give the rest of us a chance."

Griffin's face wore a casual, even bored expression, but his eyes were penetrating and alert. "Never let it be said that I neglect my wife," he replied. "Nor that I don't honor, value, and protect what is mine."

The message was clearly understood. Several of the men backed away from her, while others turned their attention to a passing servant carrying a tray of drinks. The blush that had started earlier was now a fiery glow that spread over Faith's face and part of her neck.

Yet Faith could not help but be intrigued by the bold way she was being eyed. By Griffin. With a pounding heart she stepped eagerly into her husband's embrace.

Griffin guided her to the center of the ballroom floor, set his hand firmly at her waist, and took her hand in his. The music began, and Faith struggled to hold back a sigh.

She had danced an earlier waltz with Sir Perry, and

she could not help but compare the two men. Sir Perry danced the steps with competence but lacked the grace and style that seemed to come so naturally to her husband.

As if reading her thoughts, Griffin spun her expertly around a corner of the floor. "You appear to be enjoying yourself a great deal this evening," he remarked in a tight voice. "That was quite a collection of characters you were holding court with."

Faith stared dumbly at her husband. If she didn't know better she would say that he almost sounded jealous. But that was impossible.

"I am having a lovely time," she responded. "I cannot remember ever dancing so much at one ball. The gentlemen have been most attentive."

"Be careful, Faith. You are not experienced in these matters and would not want your actions misunderstood."

Faith waved her hand dismissively. "I have watched Meredith handle these young bucks most of my adult life. I know how to be friendly without seeming to encourage, how to appear interested without seeming to single out one particular individual."

Faith blushed, lowered her chin, then coyly lifted her lashes. "You must concede I've gotten some of it right. How else would I have managed to get the dashing Viscount Dewhurst to partner me for three dances? When the correct rule of good society is that no one can dance more than twice with the same gentleman in the same evening."

"I am your husband. The rules do not apply in my case."

"Such arrogance, sir."

" 'Tis the part of my nature that you find most appealing."

"So you would like to believe," Faith retorted, but his self-deprecating smile charmed her completely.

"There was an ulterior motive to deliberately claiming the remaining waltzes on your dance card." Griffin took a deep breath. "You might not be an overly tall woman, but at least I can waltz comfortably without looking down at you and getting a crick in my neck."

" 'Tis a comfort to know that I can provide such an important function, my lord," Faith replied with an exaggerated sigh of resignation.

"Yes, it pleases me also."

Faith jerked her head sharply, but the laughter in his eyes told her he was teasing her. She had a wicked impulse to trod on his toe, but squashed it.

Instead, Faith gave herself up to the magic of their dance, the joy of being held so intimately in Griffin's arms. The intense heat that emanated from Griffin's body produced the familiar desire to press herself closer against it.

To forget, for just a moment, that the ballroom was filled with friends and neighbors, individuals who would be thoroughly and properly shocked at her carnal thoughts and desires.

Her nearly uncontrollable lust. For her husband.

She lifted her face to his. There was a sexual awareness in the viscount's gaze that told her he felt the attraction between them.

A strange expression passed over Griffin's face. For one horrifying instant Faith worried that she had spoken her thoughts aloud.

Then she realized the music had ended, but they were still clasped in an intimate embrace. Faith heard a startled whisper, then another. Without thinking, she pulled herself out of Griffin's arms, taking a step backward to a more proper distance.

Anger flashed briefly in his eyes. Their gazes locked and held.

"I shall return to claim my other dances," Griffin promised in a deep voice. "Make certain that you are ready."

He kissed her hand gallantly, then bowed. As he walked away he took with him a small part of Faith's enjoyment of the ball.

Fourteen

It had been a lovely evening of dancing and music, complete with a true sense of community and camraderie. Faith had been most pleased to discover that the local society who had looked upon her these past ten years with a jaundiced eye now seemed more tolerant, more accepting of her.

She was no longer Baron Aston's spoiled little girl, the one that Neville Sainthill was promised to but didn't seem all that anxious to marry.

She was now the Viscountess Dewhurst, a woman whose favor was courted. The simple addition of a gold wedding band had transformed her into someone to be reckoned with, not ignored.

"You must be dead on your feet, my lady," the maid said with a sympathetic smile. "Dancing well past midnight. Why, I can't remember the last time a party went so late into the night. Or should I say early into the morning."

"It was a wonderful ball," Faith declared. She yawned slowly as the weariness suddenly seemed to overtake her. "Yet I have not felt tired all evening. Not until you mentioned the lateness of the hour."

Faith gave a laugh as the maid pulled out her hairpins with efficient fingers. Once free of the constraints, Faith shook loose her hair. The maid picked up the brush and started to run it through Faith's thick brown hair.

Faith leaned back and relaxed, but instead of closing her eyes, she regarded herself solemnly in the mirror. Her eyes were tired but still sparkling, her complexion flushed rosy with excitement from the evening's festivities.

She lifted a thick clump of hair, drawing it close to her face, and silently contemplated the plain, brown locks. There were strands of red and even gold intermixed with the brown, but the darker color was most prevalent. Faith pulled the hair forward, over her shoulders, and tilted her head.

How would she look with golden hair curling artfully about her face? she wondered. As pretty as Merry?

Faith nearly laughed out loud at the very idea. No, that was not possible. No one was as pretty as Meredith. Every male in the room had noticed her tonight. And the lucky few who had received the honor of a spoken word or a brief dance had been transformed with delight.

Griffin had danced with Lady Meredith also, and the jealousy that swamped Faith as they glided gracefully across the ballroom had made her feel small and petty. They made a stunning couple—Griffin so dark and handsome, Meredith so fair and beautiful. More than one guest had commented aloud over that fact.

It had taken a great effort to hide the sudden, sharp pangs of envy she had felt, that hollowness that settled firmly in the pit of her stomach. Yet Faith had no real cause to complain. She too had several admirers this evening.

For once she had not been a forgotten wallflower, languishing among the silver-haired chaperons. It had taken only twenty minutes for her dance card to become full. And it was not only the older, married men who had asked. The few young dandies who resided in Harrowby had also sought her attention.

But that attention all paled in comparison to the moment when Griffin had stood before her and formally bowed. For Faith, nothing else that evening had come close to the enchantment of dancing with her husband.

The waltzes she shared with Griffin had been the undisputed highlight of the night. The subtle brush of his fingers on her back had made her tremble. Being once again held in his arms had brought a shiver inside Faith that started up from her toes.

She had hoped he would kiss her. Even a quick stolen kiss after their waltz would have been welcome. Or a moonlit walk in the garden where they could recapture some of the magic that had stirred between them before they became man and wife.

Or rather, before she had tricked and deceived Griffin into marrying her.

"All finished," the maid announced cheerfully. She placed the hairbrush on the dressing table and went in search of Faith's nightgown. As soon as the viscountess was dressed in her nightclothes, the maid left.

With a sigh, Faith climbed into bed and lay quietly for several minutes, then turned on her side, plumping the pillows. After a few more restless turns Faith gave up the fight, admitting that even though she felt tired, she was too tense to sleep.

She rose from the bed, absently rubbing the back of her neck as she wandered toward the other side of her chamber, coming to rest by the windows. With a sigh, Faith perched on the low window casement, drew her knees up under her chin, and gazed out at the clear night sky.

There was a bright, full moon and myriad twinkling stars lighting the heavens. It seemed a magical night. A night of promise. A night for lovers.

Yet she had no lover. Just a disinterested husband, who most likely thought her more of a bother than she was worth. She cast an eye toward the door that connected her bedchamber to Griffin's. It was shut tight, as always.

A silent tear crept down her cheek and splashed onto her wrist. Faith brushed her cheek, then wrapped her arms tightly around her knees.

It was just a letdown from the party, she insisted to herself. It meant only that she was tired and a bit sad the evening had ended. Yet the temptation to release the tears and emotions inside remained strong. Faith fought it. No matter how depressed she was feeling, she would not sit here like a pathetic neglected wife, crying and bemoaning her fate. She would act.

Biting her lower lip, Faith looked again to the door that separated their bedchambers. She wanted to resume marital relations. Not only for the hope of the child it might bring, but to establish a connection with Griffin.

Things *had* improved between them since the disastrous morning after their wedding. At this exact moment, however, it seemed like they had made so very little progress for such a long period of time. Faith knew in her heart and mind they were miles from the point where Griffin would reach for her as a loving husband was wont to do.

She had spent more hours than she liked to admit fantasizing about that moment happening, for deep inside she knew that was what she wanted most of all. Griffin's love.

To her mind, a physical relationship between them was the first real step toward achieving that all-important goal. Except for that moment in the garden a few weeks ago, when the viscount had decided he wanted to host the harvest ball, Griffin had avoided all but the most proper and polite physical contact with her.

For the third time, Faith's eyes strayed to the closed door. Her heart contracted painfully as she contemplated all that it implied.

Distance. Separation. Exclusion.

Summoning her courage, Faith flung herself off the window seat and padded to the connecting door. She pressed her ear against the solid wood, but heard nothing. In fact, the entire house seemed unusually quiet. She thought briefly about knocking, but discarded the idea. What if he didn't answer? Would she then slink away in defeat?

Her fingertips lightly touched the door handle and slowly turned it. For a moment she panicked, worrying that it might be locked. But the door swung open quietly.

The draperies had been left open and Griffin's bedchamber was bathed in moonlight. It was dark, but the edges of the larger pieces of furniture as well as the bed were visible. The night was pleasantly cool, there was no fire in the hearth. The window was also partially open, for a slight breeze skipped across the room and swirled around her nightgown.

Tense and frightened, Faith waited to be noticed. A minute passed and all remained still. Was he sleeping? She strained to hear the steady rhythm of his breathing, but the familiar sounds of the night crept through the open window.

She took a step forward, almost wishing the floor-board would creak and garner his attention. Her heart was hammering so hard she couldn't understand how Griffin failed to hear it, and her, approaching his bed.

"Faith?"

The sound of that deep, husky voice startled her and she nearly screamed. Her mouth went dry. Answering was suddenly an impossible feat, for her tongue was twisted within her mouth. Instead, Faith heaved a heavy sigh and boldly stepped out of the shadows.

She heard the bedcovers rustle, saw Griffin slowly sit up. The linen sheet rode low on his hips, covering his body from waist to toes. His chest was bare, and there seemed every reason to assume that the rest of him was in a similar state.

Faith swallowed hard. She stared at the top of his dark head, broad shoulders, and powerful chest. The sight of his male beauty brought an unexpected tug of longing to her body, an ache of need between her thighs.

Faith moved closer to the window, deliberately placing herself in the shaft of moonlight provided by the open drapes.

"Faith?"

His voice sounded strange, as if he could not believe what his eyes were telling him. Griffin turned, and she heard the sound of a match striking tinder. He lit the candle beside his bed, and in the illumination she saw his face clearly, bathed in the golden glow of candlelight.

The stark beauty of his handsome face made her breath quicken, her heart flutter. He was all potent male—strong, virile, unvanquishable. Yet for the briefest of instants she thought she sensed in him a loneliness that was as great as her own.

Griffin's astonishment at her sudden, unexpected appearance was complete. Those silvery eyes opened wide, then narrowed. "Is something wrong?"

Faith's blush was so strong it had to be visible, even in the glittering candlelight. Her face burned as she suddenly realized how he must be seeing her, for the sheer nightrail offered little protection. She might as well have been naked.

Faith forced her chin up and stared back at him, despite her total embarrassment. Her breathing was labored and shallow. He continued to stare at her, his gaze sweeping from her flowing hair all the way to her bare feet.

Dizzily, Faith blinked but was unable to break the intensity of his burning stare. For a second she thought his eyes seemed to darken with sensual secrets. Oh, how she longed for him to share them. With her.

"Is something wrong?" he repeated.

Faith felt her skin flush. It was obvious to a blind man what she was doing there. If she had any pride at all, she would turn and walk away. Yet the emptiness inside her was so strong, the longing so deep that it gave her the courage to push herself forward. To dare to reach out to him, knowing there was a chance, a strong chance, he would slap her away.

"I'm lonely, Griffin," she whispered. "And tired of sleeping alone. May I sleep with you?"

He didn't answer, didn't respond in any manner. She stepped closer to the bed. And still he did not speak a word. Her stomach fluttered with nerves, yet Faith never faltered in her movements. Her body seemed to be oddly separated from her mind, functioning automatically, in response to some deep-seated need she could not completely comprehend.

As if someone else was orchestrating her movements, Faith's arms reached toward him, wrapping themselves around his strong shoulders. Griffin made no move to return her embrace, nor did he pull away. He just stared down at her, his silvery eyes an unfathomable pool of mystery.

Leaning forward, she pressed her lips against the rapidly beating pulse at his throat. Then she moved upward, kissing him softly on the ear, jaw, and cheek. When she reached his mouth, his lips parted in invitation. Faith nearly cried out with delight. There was no barrier to her tongue as it slid deeply into his mouth.

She linked her fingers behind Griffin's neck to steady herself. She pulled him closer. He came. She gave a little wiggle of pleasure as his naked chest brushed the tips of her breasts.

Her fingers twined through his hair, and she lovingly traced the contours of his skull, the curves of his ear. Her knees had turned to water and her heart was pounding urgently. Her nightgown hung low on her shoulders, and Faith was dimly aware of her breasts pressing almost painfully against the solid wall of his chest.

Vivid images flashed in her mind, explicit and erotic. Giving in to the temptations of her mind, she brought those images to life. Her fingers moved with boldness over his chest, her lips soon followed. She found his nipples through the whirl of crisp hair. Flicking her tongue, she laved them into hardness, then grazed them lightly with her teeth.

She heard his moan of pleasure in the still night air. Following carnal instincts she'd never known she possessed, Faith inserted her hand between their bodies. She wanted him to feel the same pleasure that she did, burn with the same erotic thrill that stirred her very soul.

Her hand skidded over his flat stomach and reached lower, to the nest of curls that covered his sex. Tentatively, her fingers closed over his pulsing erection, cradling it lovingly in her palm.

It was hot and hard and smooth. She squeezed gently, then experimentally circled the sensitive tip, massaging the moisture she discovered into the heated shaft.

Excitement flared in Griffin's eyes. Swiftly, he moved off the bed and stood beside her. His hands reached out blindly, drawing up the hem of her nightgown and then carelessly flinging it over her head. Gloriously naked, Faith twisted and turned in his arms as the heat rose to inflame her.

Griffin kissed her lips fiercely, then positioned her so that she was leaning back against him. Trembling, she fell back against his strength. His arms encircled her in a protective embrace. Lowering his head, Griffin brushed a tender kiss on her shoulder. Then he slid his hands across her breasts, down her stomach, between her thighs, and parted her legs.

"Oh, my," she gasped.

He chuckled low in his throat, and she could feel the rumble against her back. Griffin ran his other hand along her cheek and jawline, then began stroking her neck. She tipped her head back against his shoulder with each sensual caress, closing her eyes tightly when that hand moved down her neck to tease her aching breasts.

He tugged gently on the nipple, rolling it between his finger and thumb. His lips nipped at the sensitive nape of her neck, and she gasped at the sensations, pushing herself against his chest.

Her thighs opened wider, and his hand naturally fell lower. Rotating the tips of his fingers in gentle circles, Griffin teased the bud of her femininity until ripples of pure sensation shuddered through her.

"Do you really want me?" Griffin whispered in her ear.

"Oh, yes," Faith confessed with another shudder.

She expected him to roll her onto the bed, press her thighs wide, and sheath himself tightly in her welcoming heat. Instead he shifted, pushing her forward onto the bed on her stomach.

Her eyelids, which had languidly closed in passion, sprang open. Confused, Faith attempted to rise. Griffin slid one hand at her waist and the other against the nape of her neck and held her down.

"Trust me," he whispered against her ear. "I won't hurt you."

"I-I don't know what to do," she stammered, tensing when his fingers slid over the tips of her breasts and down toward the damp curls between her legs.

"Lean forward and hold on tightly to the bedpost," he commanded hoarsely.

Instead, Faith rose to her feet and turned to stare at her husband. There was just enough candlelight for her to see him clearly. The broad shoulders, tapering waist, lean, rippling muscles, that impressive chest covered with coarse, dark hair.

He was breathing heavily, and she noted his fists were tightly clenched by his side. He was so powerfully male, so extraordinarily exciting, so completely *hers*. Faith's throat constricted. He stood tall and proud, staring back intently at her as if he couldn't look away.

Then he smiled. A sexy, wicked grin that made her heart ache. Sinking her fingers into his thick, dark hair, Faith rose to the tips of her toes and kissed him fully, deeply on the mouth. Then she turned around.

Burying the last of her inhibitions and embarrassment, she did as Griffin instructed, resting her cheek against one of the tall, carved posts. She felt his hands skim lightly over her bare thighs and buttocks, and a rush of fear engulfed her.

"Don't tense up," Griffin said, bending his head to touch his lips to her ear. He grabbed the tender lobe between his front teeth and bit softly.

Faith gasped and tried to do as he requested. The crisp hair on his chest brushed against her back and she shivered. Griffin's skillful hands began once again to wander, lovingly caressing her torso, from neck to calves. The need built and coiled inside Faith, and she noticed with a sense of triumph that Griffin's breathing had become as ragged as hers.

The momentary trepidation was quickly replaced by sensations of longing and desire as Griffin slowly parted her swollen sex and thrust two fingers inside her.

"See, my love, you are ready for me," he whispered, placing the silken head of his shaft at her opening.

Faith moaned loudly as she felt him slide into her throbbing body. All the way. He held her hips firmly in place, and she arched back sensuously to receive him.

He withdrew and thrust again, stroking her masterfully. Faith pressed herself back against him, impaling herself on his hardness, instinctively seeking the exquisite gratification that only he could bring.

It was as if a dark, primal fire had ignited all of her senses. And at the center of that exquisite maelstrom was her beloved Griffin. He, and he alone, possessed the power to control this spiraling madness, to satisfy the cravings that had been tormenting her soul for weeks.

Griffin's teeth grazed the back of her neck as he pulled her hips hard against him. With a shuddering moan Faith submitted to this forbidden pleasure, feeling nearly mindless with the pleasure of it, the *rightness* of being filled so completely by him.

Within moments she began to quake as the frenzied sensation brought her to the edge of fulfillment. Spasms broke over and engulfed her entire body as he drove himself into her forcefully.

Faith's last thread of control splintered and broke. The desperate need inside her had been too long ignored, had gone too long unsatisfied. It overtook her now, a spiraling vortex of pleasure hurling her toward paradise.

It made her forget everything that had happened between them. All that mattered now was this moment, this instance of perfect intimacy. She heard Griffin shout loudly, crying out with the strength of his own climax. A single tear slid down her cheek as she felt him throb and pulse inside her, his strong body shuddering with the strength of his release.

Faith slumped forward, her body sated, her mind almost numb to sensation. Though his body had disengaged itself from hers, Griffin still held her tightly. Faith rested her head against the cool wood of the bedpost and pressed her sweat-slick back closer to Griffin's chest. His hand reached out and pulled the damp tendrils of hair off her neck, allowing the night breeze to cool her body.

Faith smiled when he buried his mouth against her now bare neck. The tips of his fingers trailed lightly down the column of her throat.

He shifted, and she felt him put a strong arm under

her knees and one under her naked back as he rolled her toward him. With grace and ease, Griffin swung her around and held her tightly against his chest.

Instinctively, she placed her arm around his neck and nuzzled close to the warmth of his solid strength. She rocked gently as he moved around to the opposite side of the massive four-poster bed.

"What are you doing? Where are we going?"

"To my bed," he whispered, kissing her softly on the forehead. "I give you fair warning, madame. I don't plan on doing much sleeping this night."

The dawn crept up stealthily, like a thief stealing away the magic of the night. From the rumpled sheets of his bed Griffin stared out the window and watched it rise, wishing all the while he could hold it back.

It had taken only one night, yet he felt as if his entire world had been turned upside down. The staid, formal marriage he had finally been able to bring himself to accept had been transformed into a sensual fantasy that would delight even the most jaded of men.

The plain, unworldly female he had been deceived into taking for a wife was a lusty, giving woman, unafraid to explore the boundaries of her sensuality. And she trusted him enough to allow him to be her tutor.

She lay in his arms, asleep, her cheek trustingly placed against his heart. Despite his exhaustion, Griffin found sleep unattainable.

Instead, he cuddled his wife. And for some odd reason, he could not seem to still his fingers. They trailed along the edge of Faith's shoulders, following the line of her arm to her elbow and wrist.

This impossible need to touch her, caress her face, rub her arms, trace languid circular patterns on her hips, was an intoxicating mystery that the viscount was not at all eager to understand.

Griffin's hand came to rest at the small of her back. As if subconsciously seeking his attention, Faith sighed and stirred, burying her face deeper into his shoulder.

Griffin felt a dangerous rush of tenderness. He fought it. A second wave hit, and he grudgingly conceded it was a useless fight. Earlier this evening he had tried to resist his beguiling wife. When she'd appeared in the ballroom, all dewy-eyed and excited, he had tried to convince himself he was not attracted to her.

She had smiled and flirted during their waltz, pressing their bodies together in a seemingly innocent manner that caused the heat to rush instantly to various parts of his anatomy. Yet still he had managed to hold on to his control. And a shred of his sanity, by telling himself he was not attracted to her.

When she had boldly entered his bedchamber Griffin had repeated those words in his mind. Initially he had wanted to look away. To ignore the magnificent gift she so freely offered him. To pretend to himself he was not interested in physical satisfaction or an emotional connection with the woman who had tricked him into marriage.

But he had been filled with longing. And hunger. A strong, powerful demanding hunger that would not go away simply because he wished it. So he had allowed himself to be seduced, enjoying every moment of the lustful encounter.

Here in the stillness of the growing dawn Griffin was now forced to admit it had been far more than just a physical joining. Somehow a bond had been forged between them tonight that had nothing to do with marriage or even sex. In a very real way they now belonged to each other.

In all honesty, Griffin did not know what to think about Faith's actions tonight. He wasn't even sure if he approved of them, which was a completely irrational and hypocritical feeling. He had benefitted handsomely from her boldness, had enjoyed most thoroughly her uninhibited response. But he would not fool himself into believing he understood all the reasons that brought her to his room this night.

Griffin could not help but wonder how their relationship would change now that she had spent the night in his bed. It was a large, comfortable bed, but he had gathered Faith against him and could not seem to relinquish his tight hold. This unexpected need startled him.

The viscount shifted slightly. Supporting his head on his propped-up elbow, he stared down at the woman in his arms. She must have sensed his scrutiny. Her eyelids fluttered, then slowly opened.

"Did I fall asleep?"

"Only for a few moments."

"Oh." She dipped her chin and adjusted the sheet, pulling it closer around their bodies. "Did you sleep also?"

"No. I could not." Unable to help himself, Griffin smoothed a lock of hair from her cheek, then pressed a quick kiss on the tip of her nose. "You were snoring too loudly for me to rest."

"You're lying." Faith stretched her neck and bestowed a lazy, contented grin upon him. "My snoring is delicate and ladylike, as befits a woman of my noble station."

"Your snoring would keep many a hardened sailor from getting more than ten minutes of sleep," he declared in a mocking tone. "I swear, if you were a member of my crew, the men would have threatened mutiny if I did not put you off the ship."

"You devil!"

Faith reached behind his head and yanked on the pillow. Griffin realized too late her intention. His elbow collapsed and his head fell to the mattress. His legs were effectively tangled with Faith's, allowing him nowhere to turn for escape. The feathery weapon hit him square on the jaw.

She scrambled away from him, took aim, and landed a second blow. Griffin dove for her, grabbing her arm just as Faith was about to land a third one.

Giggling, she fought him for possession of the pillow.

"Drop it," he commanded with a wicked grin. His words had her tugging harder. "I shall have a very difficult time trying to come up with a plausible explanation for my valet if the bed is filled with feathers."

"Then you shall have to tell him that you have found a new *ladybird*," Faith said with a saucy grin. "And she sheds."

Griffin laughed. Snaking his arm about her waist, he successfully wrestled the pillow away from her. Faith shrieked as he rolled her onto her back and pinned her to the mattress.

In the blink of an eye they were pressed belly to belly, their breaths coming in uneven pants. Faith let out a gratifying sigh and gave him a delighted smirk.

"Why did you marry me?" he asked suddenly.

Faith shut her eyes, and he felt her tense beneath him. The smile gradually faded from her lips. The silence lasted for so long Griffin thought she might have drifted back to sleep.

"I married you because I loved you," she finally

replied quietly, opening her eyes and looking at him intently.

He saw the muscles in her throat work hard as she struggled to swallow.

"Why did you marry me?" she finally managed to ask.

"Because I had no choice," he replied honestly. Her eyes shuttered closed, and he knew she had mistook his meaning. He had not married her because his honor demanded it. He had married her because a part of him had realized that she was the woman he needed to have in his life. The woman he needed to complete himself.

Griffin moved his hard, muscled thighs and pulled Faith closer, so that nearly every part of her body was touching him. She opened her eyes as he'd intended. Trying to formulate the words that expressed his feelings, he dipped his head toward her. In the predawn darkness he could just make out her soft, sweet features.

"I do not regret loving you," she declared solemnly, before he had a chance to speak.

The tempo of his breathing quickened. The words Griffin struggled to say were swallowed in her kiss. Faith wrapped her leg around his, pulling his body atop hers.

Griffin threaded his arms around her back and gave himself up to the fiery desire that overtook his senses, deciding there would be time enough to discuss these feelings.

Other, far more pressing matters had just arisen that demanded his complete and undivided attention.

Fifteen

Faith slept embarrassingly late the following morning, awakening in her own bed and having no recollection of how she arrived there. A quick survey of the room confirmed that she was alone, with only the brilliant sunshine flooding her bedchamber for company.

She drew in a deep breath and smiled faintly. The feather pillow her face was snuggled against must have been used by Griffin, for it carried his distinct, unmistakable masculine scent.

She rolled onto her back, bringing the pillow along and hugging it tightly to her chest. Sometime during the early morning hours he must have moved her to her bedchamber. Yet his lingering scent indicated he had spent several hours in this bed with her, by her side. Surely that was a good sign?

Eager to begin the day, Faith summoned her maid. As soon as she was properly dressed, she went downstairs, but found no one about. She was informed by the butler that Harriet and Elizabeth were still abed, as was Lady Meredith, and the viscount had taken his young son riding.

Faith was well contented with her own company and enjoyed a hearty meal in the smaller, more intimate morning room. She was kept busy for most of the afternoon by a variety of household tasks and did not set eyes on any of the family members, or Merry, until teatime when all the women gathered in the drawing room. Griffin had yet to make an appearance.

"I cannot begin to say what a wonderful time I had last night," Elizabeth said, her eyes sparkling with excitement. "You did a brilliant job of organizing the party, Faith. The music, the flowers, the food. Everything was perfect. It was absolutely the most magnificent ball that I have ever attended."

" 'Tis also the only ball you have ever attended," Harriet added with a rueful smile.

Faith shook her head and grinned at her two sisters-in-law. Was it possible for two women to be more dissimilar? Sometimes Faith wondered if they were truly sisters.

"It certainly was not the first ball that I have ever been to and I wholeheartedly concur with Elizabeth's opinion. I found it most enchanting," Meredith chimed in loyally. "Faith is to be commended for doing an excellent job."

"I did not do everything on my own," Faith said modestly. "I had plenty of assistance."

"Exactly," Harriet said with a smug tip of her chin.

"Faith is being far too modest," Meredith insisted. "Everyone knows that as hostess, the bulk of the responsibilities fell to her, and she rose splendidly to the occasion. 'Twas nothing less than a triumph."

"A triumph?" Harriet clucked her tongue. "You have a very interesting view of life, Lady Meredith, if you consider a simple country ball a triumph."

"Pray, what would qualify as a triumph in your humble opinion, Miss Sainthill?" Meredith asked with a frosty glare.

Faith jumped in before Harriet had an opportunity

to respond. "I'm pleased you had such a lovely time at the party, Elizabeth," Faith sputtered hastily, hoping to redirect the conversation and avoid a spirited argument between Harriet and Meredith.

It was a small source of comfort knowing that there was one person who had an even more difficult time getting along with Harriet, but the drawing room was hardly the setting to explore those differences.

Faith sent Merry a warning scowl, then lifted the delicate Spode teapot and poured a cup of the steaming brew for Elizabeth. "I could not help but notice that you never lacked for dancing partners. And you were escorted into supper by Squire Jordan. He is a fine-looking young man."

Elizabeth accepted her tea with a shy blush. "He was a most accommodating gentleman. I appreciated all his efforts to ease my nerves."

"He is an intelligent man," Meredith said. "With the good sense to recognize that you are a superior young woman, genuine in heart and spirit."

Elizabeth lowered her eyes and blushed deeper. "That is very kind of you to say, Lady Meredith."

"She is merely being truthful," Harriet interjected. Some of the tightness had left her features. "Triumphantly truthful."

"Precisely," Meredith said with a regal nod.

The teacup Faith held rattled unsteadily on its saucer. Had she just heard Harriet agree with Merry? She gazed at the two women in utter surprise.

"There was no question that Elizabeth was the prettiest young woman in attendance last evening," Faith added quickly, deciding she wanted very much for this sudden spurt of camraderie to continue. "I'm pleased that so many gentlemen took the time to notice that you were not only pleasing to the eye, but possessing of a mind."

"Not all men find intelligence in a woman a positive attribute," Harriet commented with a bitter twist of her jaw.

"Your sister is right," Meredith said. "And you must always remember to avoid those men who show fear of a woman with a mind. By and large they are imbeciles."

"Or bullies," Harriet added. She reached for a plate and heaped it generously with an assortment of sandwiches and pastries. "We all could plainly see that you garnered more than your fair share of male attention last night, Elizabeth. Yet you must not let that success swell your head. It isn't difficult to outshine some of the local girls. Mr. Renford's daughters are hardly beauties and the poor Wilding girl bears an unfortunate, though striking resemblance to a hunting hound."

"Harriet! That is a rather harsh assessment." Faith lifted the delicate teapot and filled another cup. She passed it to her sister-in-law with a grim expression. "Yet undeniably true."

Harriet's lips quirked. She finished chewing on her savory morsel, swallowed, then broke into a true smile. "Those poor girls can do nothing to compensate for their lack of looks, but what excuse can Mrs. Renford offer? Did you see her gown? How could a woman of her age and size wear such a shocking shade of red?"

"She resembled an overripened berry that looked ready to split from its skin," Meredith said with a delighted grin. She delicately bit the edge of a pear tart. "I was afraid to get too close to her, afraid that when she finally burst out of her buttons she would put out someone's eye."

There was a brief moment of silence. Elizabeth let

out a nervous giggle and everyone immediately joined in the laughter.

"My favorite was Mrs. Hormsbee," Faith said with halting laughter. "With her dark hair wound so tightly into large buns over each of her ears she looked like an old ram."

"Or a randy goat," Harriet interjected with a short laugh.

"Oh, please," Meredith huffed in a mocking tone. "I was forced to listen to the blasted woman for a full twenty minutes, expounding on how her maid's sister, who is employed by the very regal Duchess of Portsmouth, learned how to create this most fashionable hairstyle that was simply all the rage in London."

"That certainly sounds like Mrs. Hormsbee," Harriet said. "She has always been most impressed by anything that is happening in town, following the supposed fashion no matter how silly."

"Then she deserves to look like a fool," Meredith proclaimed. "Still, after seeing how ridiculous she looked last evening, one has to wonder. Does the woman even own a mirror?"

That sardonic comment brought fresh peals of laughter from all of them.

Faith looked at each of them, enjoying mightily the sounds of merriment. "We are fortunate indeed to be so perfect, are we not ladies?"

Meredith bit her bottom lip and tried to assume a somber expression. "Faith is right. 'Tis wrong of us to indulge in such merriment at the expense of others. And . . . yet . . ."

"It is so deliciously wicked," Elizabeth finished quietly, then blushed.

Harriet primly folded her hands in her lap. "Wait until you get to London and begin meeting members of true society, Elizabeth. Your tongue will never get a rest."

"Nor will your body." Meredith sighed and gave her head a tiny shake. "It is an endless whirl of activities. Dances, balls, routs, assemblies, opera parties, dinner parties, rides in the park, drives in the park, walks in the park, afternoon calls, fittings at the dressmaker for a wardrobe to match each occasion properly."

"Don't worry, Elizabeth," Faith said. "We shall make certain that you are dressed in something more flattering than Mrs. Renford."

"All those gowns," Meredith went on with a sweeping gesture of her hand. "Such a ridiculous waste of funds. Still, it cannot possibly be avoided. A fashionable woman needs an enormous wardrobe in order to keep up with the never-ending chain of social engagements. I daresay you'll discover that for yourself soon enough when you have your own coming-out. Next season?"

Elizabeth's eyes were as round as the small plate she held in her hand. "Nothing has been decided. At least that I know about. Can we afford such an elaborate season?" Elizabeth asked, turning toward her sister.

Harriet bristled and rearranged the skirt of her gown. "Do not fret over the particulars, Elizabeth. Griffin and I will make certain the proper arrangements are made. How else will you find a suitable husband?"

"I see." Elizabeth bit her lip. She did not look at all excited at the prospect that would have sent most girls into giddy rapture.

"There is the local society," Faith added hastily, not liking the expression of distress on Elizabeth's face. The younger girl looked frightened to death. "I believe last night firmly illustrated that there are many fine gentlemen living right here in Harrowby."

"Elizabeth is the daughter of a viscount," Harriet proclaimed in a waspish superior tone that grated fully on the nerves. "She can certainly do better than a local squire."

"A person of her sunny nature and delicate beauty deserves to marry for love," Faith insisted with a wistful sigh. "Be he a nobleman or a commoner."

"Marry for love?" Harriet set down her teacup and pursed her lips. "As you did?"

"Harriet!" Elizabeth shouted hastily, throwing Faith an apologetic glance. "It certainly isn't our place to speculate on the reasons for Faith and Griffin's marriage."

Faith set down her plate with a clatter. Blinking rapidly she stared directly at Harriet. "I want more for Elizabeth when she starts out her marriage than I had. As I want more for you, Harriet."

Harriet lifted her head. "That is very generous of you." Her eyes looked searchingly into Faith's. "I spoke without thinking. I did not mean to offend."

Somehow Faith managed a careless shrug. "I took no offense at your remarks," Faith said slowly. Harriet's words had cut deep, but her apology seemed sincere. "I'm sure my sudden marriage to Griffin appears strange to many people. But it is a private matter between your brother and myself that I will discuss with no one, not even family members."

For a few awkward moments there was total silence. Elizabeth shuffled the toe of her slipper and gazed at her foot, Meredith deliberately avoided Faith's eyes, and Harriet sipped unenthusiastically at her drink.

"More tea?" Faith lifted the pot and glanced briefly from one woman to the next.

It took only a moment to top off each cup that was thrust eagerly forward, since they were all nearly full.

"There is no need to fret about your first season, Elizabeth. I'm sure there is someone wonderful in London just waiting to fall in love with you." Meredith winked at the young girl. "Who knows? He might even be a duke."

"All those grand people." Elizabeth smiled hesitantly. "I fear I shall make a cake of myself."

"They are no different from any other sort of people." Meredith wrinkled her brow. "Truth be told, some are far worse than many of the good, honest folk you have known. Far too many members of the ton are all puffed up with their own sense of value and importance. It can become most tiresome."

"An astute observation, Lady Meredith," Harriet said with quiet dignity. "That sort of false pretension can be very wearing. But I'm sure Elizabeth shall be able to adjust. With the proper guidance."

Elizabeth's gown rustled as she shifted in her chair. "Considering the amount of money that the family will be forced to expend on my coming-out season, I shall feel honor bound to do my best to catch a husband."

"You must not worry about that," Faith insisted.

"Besides, not all women need to marry," Meredith said forcefully.

"Not marry? What else would I do?" Elizabeth frowned. "I cannot imagine my life as a governess or a companion to some elderly dowager. And if I cannot support myself, then I would be forced to live with my relations." She cast an apologetic eye toward Harriet and Faith. "In very short order I would become a drudge."

Faith laughed. "I cannot possibly imagine that happening."

"I am sure you will marry a fine gentleman. Yet no matter what your future, you will always have a home with me," Harriet stated magnanimously. "Though I must agree with Faith. I cannot imagine it would ever come to that."

"You will break more than your share of young and older men's hearts," Faith predicted with an encouraging smile.

"Just take care not to get your own heart bruised in the process," Harriet advised.

"We must not scare the poor girl," Meredith admonished. "There really is more to a woman's life than marriage. Or being a governess or a companion or a drudge." She smiled broadly. "I plan on someday setting up my own establishment so that I may live the way I please. Answering to no one. Neither husband nor employer."

"You will scandalize everyone in society," Harriet remarked, but there was a faint trace of admiration in her tone.

Meredith stiffened noticeably. "I can assure you that I will take great care to ensure that my behavior will continue to remain above reproach. As it always has."

Faith recognized the note of steel in her friend's voice. Suggesting that Merry was involved in a scandalous activity was still the surest way Faith knew to raise Lady Meredith's hackles.

"How will you manage without a husband to care for and guide you?" Elizabeth asked, as she rolled this utterly new and intriguing idea around her tongue. "Who will pay your bills? Your father?"

"I have an independent inheritance," Meredith said confidently. "It was a gift from my great-aunt, and I bless her memory each day for giving me this wonderful opportunity. Over the years I have taught myself the proper way to manage and invest those funds, so I need no assistance from any man. Though I am not opposed to taking sound advice from them."

Harriet sighed. "Only rich women have the interesting opportunities. I'm afraid it must be the marriage mart for you, Elizabeth. Or starvation."

"Is it really as cold-blooded as all that?" Elizabeth asked.

"Is what cold-blooded?" Griffin asked as he entered the room in time to hear the last question.

Faith's hand flew to her throat. She had not expected him to make an appearance until dinner. The viscount's clothes were slightly rumpled, but free of dust and dirt. He must have taken only a brief time to clean up after his ride.

She almost rose to her feet, feeling an intense urge to walk toward him, reach up, and put her arms around his neck. But she lacked the confidence to do so, especially since they had never embraced in front of others. It would seem rather odd if they did so now.

For a moment Faith could have sworn she had seen a blaze of warmth and delight in her husband's expression when he first entered the room. But it flickered so quickly she knew it must have been her wistful imagination.

Young Georgie stood by Griffin's side, clutching his father's hand. The boy's rosy cheeks and freshly scrubbed face attested to a quick though less than thorough cleanup. There was a clump of mud on the child's boot and a smudge of dirt on the knee of his riding jodhpurs. He smiled sunnily at Faith and her heart instantly melted.

"What is cold-blooded?" the viscount repeated.

"The marriage mart," Harriet replied dryly.

"Is that like a fair?" Georgie piped in with keen

interest. "I should like to go if it is, please. I do like seeing all the animals, especially the pigs."

The adults all laughed. "There are certainly a fair amount of swine at the marriage mart," Meredith said, her mouth curved in a wry half smile. "However, I doubt you would find them very interesting."

The child obviously didn't understand what had been said, but he forgot all about fairs and markets and pigs when he saw the impressive display of pastries. Faith had specifically instructed the cook to include Georgie's favorite cream-filled ones, intending to sneak a few upstairs to the nursery when tea with the adults was finished.

Now she would have the pleasure of watching him eat as many as he wished. As long as Harriet didn't catch her feeding them to the boy.

Faith rang for a fresh pot of tea and more cups, insisting that Georgie join them. She was fully prepared to argue this unorthodox invitation with Harriet, but the other woman made no objection.

The viscount took the seat closest to Faith while Georgie sat beside his father. To her dismay, Faith found it was difficult to control the quivering feeling of intimate warmth that overcame her at his nearness.

Wordlessly, she passed Griffin a cup brimming with tea. Sugar, no milk, just as he preferred. As he accepted the offering, the viscount's arm brushed her breast. Faith's nipple tightened at his touch, and her mind blushed with glorious memories from last night.

"May I have tea also?" Georgie interrupted. "Instead of milk."

"Certainly, dear." Faith answered, proud of the steadiness of her voice.

Faith poured only half a cup, leaving room for lots of sugar and cream. She also made certain not to fill the cup completely. An early afternoon tea shared with Georgie in the nursery had taught Faith that a little boy's hands were not the steadiest when holding a full cup of liquid.

Griffin must have also had some personal experience with Georgie's unsteady hands, for he reached out to help the child.

Again his fingers brushed against her breast. The nipple tightened further, and Faith bit her bottom lip to stifle her cry. Hastily, she pushed back in her chair and quickly crossed her arms, wondering if anyone else had noticed Griffin's actions and her reactions. A glance at the three women confirmed they had not seen anything.

Then she glanced at Griffin. He stretched out his legs, and gave her a slow, knowing grin filled with masculine sensuality. Faith gulped.

There was a gleam of wicked amusement in his eye as he asked, "Are there any more sandwiches? I find I have a great hunger this afternoon."

Unable to answer, Faith simply held out a plate. Griffin leaned closer and spoke so that only the two of them could hear. "I suppose cucumber will have to suffice. But I know it will not truly satisfy me."

"It will not?" Faith felt the blush rising in her cheeks and fought to contain it. "Shall I summon Harper and have him instruct Cook to prepare something more substantial, my lord?"

"Cook does not have what I need. What I crave."

"Indeed?" The blush was rising higher in her cheeks, but Faith didn't care. The startling sensuality in her husband's eyes held her mesmerized.

"Can I have some sandwiches, too?" Georgie piped up. "Please."

The child's interruption succeeded in shattering the

mood. Faith felt a wave of disappointment, but realized now was hardly the appropriate moment to engage in sexual teasing with her husband.

The adults spoke again of last night's ball, though the conversation was much tamer with Georgie in the room. After a time, Faith noticed the little boy's head began to droop, but she hesitated suggesting he retire for a nap. Lately, that particular suggestion had brought forth a rather spirited, rebellious response.

"I think Grace is waiting for you up in the nursery, Georgie," Harriet said pointedly. "Shall I ring for her to come and get you?"

Georgie's head immediately jerked up. "I'm not tired," he insisted.

Griffin placed his cup on the tea table and moved toward his son. The little boy gave a token resistance, then reached up his arms. Griffin stooped to pick him up. He whispered something into the little boy's ear and Georgie burst into giggles.

It made Faith's heart leap with gladness to see such closeness between father and son. It also gave her hope. Clearly Griffin possessed the capacity to love. He adored his son and was fond of his sisters. Even the prickly Harriet.

Faith picked up her cup and took a thoughtful sip. Her course seemed very clear. All she needed to do now was discover how to get the viscount to fall in love with her.

The evening meal was a quiet, congenial affair, with only the four women and Griffin. Merry made a passing joke about Griffin's harem, and he gifted her with a potent masculine grin.

Faith noted, as she tipped her wineglass to her lips

for a long swallow, that in the week Meredith had been visiting, Griffin had thoroughly charmed her. It made Faith wonder that in the right circumstances, with the right man, Meredith might abandon her fierce opposition to marriage.

They retreated to the drawing room after the meal. Elizabeth entertained them on the pianoforte while Harriet sang. Faith was surprised to discover the rich, alto voice of her prickly sister-in-law. She had never heard Harriet sing, and it was a pleasant, welcome surprise.

After the sexual tension of afternoon tea, Faith had been bracing for another assault on her senses, almost hoping that Griffin would somehow find a way to catch her alone for a few minutes. She had even spent a quarter of an hour slowly walking the garden path outside his study window, hoping to capture his attention.

Her obvious efforts had gone unrewarded. Griffin had either been unaware or uninterested in her activities. She worried briefly that her declaration of love late last night had cooled his ardor. He had been polite and attentive to all of the women during dinner, yet despite all his charm Faith thought he seemed a bit preoccupied.

She was most disappointed to no longer be receiving those sensual, heated, inappropriate glances and wondered if she had unknowingly done something to anger him.

In due time the evening came to a congenial end and everyone retreated to their respective beds. Normally Faith did not enjoy the fussing of her maid, but tonight it felt good to have someone help her remove her gown, brush her hair until her entire body felt relaxed, and make sure the fire burning in the hearth kept the chill from the room.

"Good night, my lady," the maid whispered softly as she shut the door.

Faith tried to reply, but instead gave an unladylike yawn. She snuggled under the warm covers and was slowly drifting off to sleep when the bedchamber door opened.

"Whatever the problem, I'll deal with it in the morning," Faith called out in a dreamlike state, thinking the maid had returned to ask her a question.

"I prefer that you deal with it now," came the deep male voice. "Though I confess to hoping that I am not considered a problem."

"Griffin?"

"Are there so many other men that enter your bedchamber at this hour of the night that you need to question if it is your husband?"

Faith bolted up into a seated position. The candles had been extinguished, but the fire from the hearth provided adequate light. Griffin wore a dark blue dressing robe that fell open as he walked closer to the bed. She could clearly see many interesting parts of his naked body with each step he took.

His eyes were burning with an intense desire he seemed almost proud to display.

"Alas, no man ever enters my chamber, sir. You are the first."

"A man likes knowing he is the first. And the last."

Faith inhaled sharply. What was he saying? Was this Griffin's way of telling her that he had finally truly forgiven her for the deception of their marriage?

She looked into his eyes, desperately searching for the answer. "You are the *only* man in my life. And shall remain so, until death parts us from this world."

Faith saw the flash of surprise in his face that was quickly followed by a look of pleasure.

"The memory of you coming to my bed last night has warmed me, tortured me, for the entire day. So I thought to return the favor by coming to your bed." He lowered his voice to a husky caress. "Am I welcomed?"

Her body came alive at his question, the yearning almost unbearable. Wordlessly, Faith threw back the coverlet and shifted to the edge of the bed. Creating a place, a proper place for her husband.

When he came near, she slid her arms around his neck and pulled him down beside her. They were both breathing quickly, both very much aware of each other. They came together easily, with none of the frantic urgency of last night, but with all of the heat and moisture and primal excitement.

Feeling Griffin's weight atop her brought a true sense of completion to her soul. Faith held him close as he thrust deep inside her body, the fullness no longer a strange feeling.

With a new sense of freedom, Faith joyfully put her heart and soul into their mating, lifting her body toward his as he pushed and stretched her to the limits of sensation.

A shattering, rolling release suddenly overtook her. She groaned, moving her body restlessly from side to side as it spun out of control.

"Let go." His tongue dipped to touch hers.

Faith nearly screamed as she felt the passion starting to consume her. Yet something was missing.

"You," she whispered hoarsely. "I want you to come with me." Determined, she squeezed her inner muscles around the heat of the fullness that was deep inside her. Once. Twice.

"Faith."

His voice was a strained whisper, a bid for control that was quickly lost. Faith bucked beneath him, heard him shout, felt him shudder, felt the warmth of his seed spill inside her.

Slowly, their breathing returned to normal. The weight above her shifted and moved. Faith felt Griffin gently disengage himself and settle beside her. Magnanimously, she gave him the larger of the feather pillows, then snuggled contentedly against his solid chest. Within minutes, a thoroughly delightful, sated sleep claimed her.

Sixteen

"It has been a fine harvest, my lady," Joshua Chambers, steward of Mayfair Manor said with obvious pride. He removed the gold wire-rim spectacles he wore when reading and placed them on the desk. "If the wool merchant in Bristol pays us market price for the fleece that was shorn this past spring, our profits will exceed all expectations."

"Truly?" Faith reached for the ledger eagerly and scanned the rows of neatly penned entries. "I worried mightily that I was depleting Mayfair Manor's resources this summer to supplement the flagging funds of Hawthorne Castle. I'm glad to know Mayfair can hold its own."

The steward's chest puffed out with pride. "Mayfair can outshine Hawthorne any day in both production and profit."

"I'm sure that it can." Faith squinted at the ledger page. "However, 'tis my hope that one day *both* estates can boast of similar profitable circumstances. Then we shall truly feel successful."

"In time I suppose that is possible." Mr. Chambers's pudgy jowls sagged and some of the eagerness left his face. "I know it is not my place to criticize, but Hawthorne has been mismanaged for years. The old viscount had no less than four different stewards in ten years and not one of them was a man who took great effort or pride in his position.

"Fertile fields were left unplowed while other land was seriously overplanted, depleting the soil of all its natural richness. Healthy livestock was mixed in with ailing animals, and the dairy has long been inefficiently run. That will all take time to set to rights."

"I am very aware of the various problems," Faith said quietly. "As is my husband. They shall be addressed, and solved." She stood to signal the end of the meeting and tugged on her riding gloves. "In the meantime, I must once again commend you for an outstanding job. Your efforts have not gone unnoticed, Mr. Chambers, nor shall they go unrewarded."

The delight returned to the steward's face. " 'Tis my privilege to serve you, my lady. I ask for no additional thanks or rewards."

"That only makes you all the more deserving," Faith replied truthfully. She pulled a small, fat leather pouch bulging with coins from the pocket of her cloak and pressed it into the steward's hand.

" 'Tis too much!" Mr. Chambers protested when he saw the size and felt the weight of the purse.

"You have earned every coin," Faith insisted, pleased that she was able to afford this well-deserved bonus.

Mr. Chambers had done an excellent job, and she was grateful for all his hard work. The profits from Mayfair had enabled her to provide much-needed funds for Griffin to use in restoring Hawthorne Castle. At least in that aspect of their marriage she had not played the viscount false.

Faith's father had taught her it was important to reward a man's efforts and loyalty. She took that advice firmly to heart, knowing she would need Mr. Chambers's skill and devotion if Mayfair Manor was to continue being a profitable venture, especially since she was unable to participate in the daily decision making.

In the courtyard an eager stable hand helped her mount her horse, and Faith realized how odd it felt coming to the manor as a visitor. This had been her home all of her life and she still felt a strong emotional attachment to the place and to all the people who worked there. But it was now a part of her past, not the focus of her future.

The crisp wind of the late autumn day made for an invigorating ride, but Faith took her time on the journey back, enjoying the scenery. She passed several well-tended farms, with pens filled with fat, healthy livestock and fields recently harvested of the rich crops of wheat and rye.

She saw several picturesque stone cottages with thatched roofs fronted by small flower gardens boasting a few late blooms on their vines. Wisps of smoke from the chimneys curling into the bright blue sky had Faith imagining the females of the house gathered around the warmth of the kitchen preparing the noontime meal.

It was difficult not to notice the difference in the condition of the tenant farms when she ventured from the land of Mayfair Manor to the viscount's estate. Here the dwellings were marred by worn-looking roofs, rusting gate hinges, fences tilted askew, and missing posts.

But it wasn't only the property that was run-down. Faith had heard grumblings, too, of the discontentedness of many of the tenants. Over the years they had endured inflated rents and reduced wages and felt cheated by their noble landlord.

Many had been on the verge of open rebellion when

Griffin arrived home to claim his inheritance. They waited now with a jaundiced eye to see if the new master would be like the old, reserving judgment until they were forced to voice their discord.

Faith knew this concerned Griffin greatly. He remarked more than once that he was a sailor, not a farmer. But he had put forth considerable effort to improve the conditions of his tenant farmers, reducing rents for those in greatest need, supplying tools and seeds to those who had shown real ambition.

It was a start, albeit a small one. Faith could not fail to notice that even the greetings she received from the farmers of Griffin's estate were markedly different than those of Mayfair Manor. Heads ducking, eyes shifting away, voices muttering uneasily when they spoke. It was clear they had not yet decided about her, either.

Still, Faith would not be discouraged. She smiled with warmth and encouragement at everyone she met, proud that she was able to address each person by name. She hoped soon these good people would enjoy the same comfort and security as those who toiled at the manor, and she vowed to do all she could to make that come to pass.

Her mind was so occupied with the plight of Griffin's tenants that Faith failed to notice the thick, heavy tree roots in her path until her sturdy mare stumbled over them, catching its hoof in a deep rut.

Faith slid hastily from her saddle. Leaning close, she began to rub the mare's legs, crooning soft words of comfort as she examined the injury.

She must have touched a particularly tender spot, for the animal suddenly reared. Faith clung tightly to the reins, speaking again in low tones to calm the frightened beast.

"Oh, now I've done it. You poor thing." Faith patted the mare soothingly. "I hope you are not in great pain."

With a worried sigh she led the horse slowly down the path. Turning to watch the animal's progress, Faith could immediately see the mare favoring the injured leg.

Faith sighed again. She was at least three miles from the manor, in a secluded area. She was not expected back home until later in the afternoon. It would take hours before someone realized she had not returned home and send out a party to search for her.

Knowing there was no choice, Faith tugged gently on the reins, intending to slowly lead the animal home, all the while hoping that she had caused no permanent damage to the gentle mare. Thankfully, by the time she reached the clearing, a full hour later, the horse was no longer limping. Faith's own legs were tired and she was hot and sweaty, but she would not risk riding the horse.

She crested the hill of Georgie's favorite lake. The tranquil spot looked restful and inviting. Faith decided she would relax for a few minutes by the water's edge. Suddenly, out of the corner of her eye she spied a figure racing down the slope toward the water.

"Hello. Hello," Georgie called. He lifted his arms above his head and waved them excitedly in the air.

Faith smiled and waved back. The child ran straight to her, and Faith bent down to catch him, savoring the feel of his exuberant hug. He smelled like sunshine and freshness and little boy.

"What a delightful surprise to find you here. But surely you haven't come all this way on your own, Georgie?"

"Father is with me."

Faith raised her head and caught sight of the viscount casually strolling toward them. He was dressed in a tan coat and buff breeches. Tall, black Hessian boots encased the sculpted muscles of his powerful legs. He looked relaxed and amused and utterly divine.

Faith's mouth tightened. Physical awareness of him started her heart thudding at an erratic pace. The impact of his masculine beauty struck hard at her senses. She knew it would never happen, yet she wondered longingly what it would feel like if he greeted her with the same exuberant embrace his son had.

"Why were you walking your horse?" Griffin asked as he drew nearer. "Is something wrong?"

"The mare stumbled over some thick tree roots and I feared she had badly injured herself. It seemed safer not to add the extra burden of my weight."

"You haven't been eating all that many of Cook's fine pastries," Griffin said, his teeth flashing in a grin. "Or have you been sneaking down to the kitchens late at night when the rest of the household is asleep?"

"I am in my bed each night, husband," Faith said with exaggerated innocence. "As you well know."

"It *has* been my delight to know," he added in a husky whisper. "For I greatly enjoy sharing that bed with you."

His widening grin brought a blush to Faith's cheeks and she quickly forgave him for not greeting her with an affectionate hug. "You are a fair distance from the house," she remarked. "Are you on an errand or out for a walk?"

Griffin's smile deepened. "Georgie and I are out on an adventure. We have abandoned our work for an afternoon of fishing." The viscount tapped the wooden poles he carried on his shoulder. He removed the shorter one and held it out to his son. "All you need to do is to fill your bucket with a few wiggly worms and then you will be ready to get started."

The boy reached down and scooped up the bucket he had dropped before embracing Faith. "Shall I dig some extra worms for you to use, Papa?" Georgie asked, his eyes bright.

The viscount appeared to consider the question before answering. "A good fisherman should always get his own bait, but I think in this case it would be permissible for you to do it for me."

"Hooray!" Georgie nodded his head vigorously. "Then you can take the fish from my line when I catch them."

The child leaped away in delight. Leaning closer, Griffin whispered in Faith's ear, "Georgie will never admit it, but he hates touching the fish when they are dangling helplessly from the line. I think he feels bad that they have been captured. He always tells me they are too small to eat and I should toss them back in the lake."

"He is such a sensitive little boy," Faith said softly. "Too kindhearted to bear seeing the poor creatures perish, even on his dinner plate. We shall have a difficult time of it when he realizes bacon comes from pigs. It's his favorite food."

"That certainly won't be a pleasant conversation," Griffin agreed.

The couple shifted their attention to Faith's horse. Griffin handed off the other pole to her, then bent down and carefully examined the mare's leg. Sunlight glistened in his hair, highlighting its natural shine. The sight brought on an unexplained rush of emotion, and Faith wished she possessed the confidence to lower her hand and run her fingers tenderly through his dark locks.

"Do you think she is badly injured?" Faith asked when Griffin finished his examination.

The viscount shook his head and took back his fishing pole. "It doesn't seem too serious, but I'm glad you decided not to ride her. I'll make sure Higgins takes a look at that leg the moment we return. He has a real way with animals and I trust his judgment."

Faith nodded in agreement, relieved that Griffin had found no further injuries. The viscount took up the reins and began to carefully lead the horse down the shallow hill. Faith joined him.

She put her hand on his arm when they approached the lake. "I think my poor mare needs a cool drink," Faith said. "Thanks to the dust in the road, my throat feels particularly parched, so she must be feeling the same."

The viscount brought the horse to the edge of the water and the mare immediately started lapping noisily. When the animal had drunk her fill, he led the mare to a shady area and knotted the reins around a sturdy tree trunk.

Then he turned to his wife and produced two small flasks from his coat pocket. "You are in luck today, my lady. I have brought along some refreshments. Cider for Georgie and something that packs a bit more of a punch for me." The viscount held up his bounty. "Which do you prefer?"

"Cider will be fine," Faith said. She tugged off her riding gloves and accepted the viscount's offering.

Griffin passed her the flask with an apologetic grin. "I'm afraid you'll have to swill it. Georgie insisted that would be easiest and pulled a prickly face when Cook suggested we pack a proper picnic with jugs of refreshment, plates, cups, and napkins."

"I understand. Picnics with linen napkins are for

young ladies. And glasses are far too civilized for two rugged fishermen," Faith said, removing her bonnet. She shoved a damp strand of hair out of her eye, tipped the flask to her lips, and took a long swallow.

Griffin's eyes were smiling when she returned the flask. "What is wrong?" Faith ran the back of her hand across her mouth, then glanced hastily down at her bodice and skirt. "Is cider dribbling down my chin? Have I spilled some on my habit?"

"No, Faith. I was merely observing your actions." Griffin moved closer. His masculine scent enveloped her, and the urge to embrace him heightened. "You drink with such gusto. It is quite an extraordinary sight."

"Ah, unladylike gusto." She preened shamelessly before him. "Do you find it offensive, sir?"

"Just the opposite. I find it invigorating. I like passion in my women."

Faith's heart skipped. *Is that what I am? His woman?* She looked into his hot, silvery eyes and felt herself starting to melt. Perhaps she was finally succeeding in closing the distance between them.

"Look at all the worms I've found." Georgie appeared suddenly by Faith's side, carrying his bucket in both hands. "I must have hundreds!"

With a grunt, the child lifted the bucket for their inspection. They dutifully glanced inside, their heads nearly touching in the process.

Griffin cleared his throat. "An excellent start, son."

Georgie set the bucket on the ground, crouched low, and studied the contents. "I like the big ones best." He picked up a twig and carefully nudged apart a pair of worms. "But I need more. I want to catch lots and lots of fish today." With a look of unmistakable determination the boy ran to the edge of the water to resume his digging.

Griffin smiled. "I believe that Georgie enjoys digging up the worms far more than the actual fishing."

Faith returned the smile, then turned to watch the child. "What boy wouldn't? You must stay still and quiet to catch a fish, a difficult challenge for our energetic youngster. Besides, acquiring bait is probably the only permissible excuse for mucking about in the mud and getting completely filthy."

"Judging by the condition of his clothes most days, I can see that mud possesses a certain amount of charm," Griffin commented.

He offered Faith his arm, and they strolled to a shady spot. Once there, Faith gratefully lowered herself to the grass and settled her back against the trunk of a tree. Her eyes darted constantly toward Georgie as he knelt in the mud on the banks of the lake, his small hands gleefully flinging clumps of dirt in the air.

Truthfully, she wasn't exactly certain what sort of assistance she could offer the little boy if he plunged into the water, since she was unable to swim a stroke, but her eyes never left him.

After a moment's hesitation, Griffin stretched out beside her. Though Faith's eyes never strayed from the child, all of her other senses were very much aware of the man now lying so intimately close.

"Georgie does have a talent for finding dirt, no matter where he is or what he is doing," he remarked with an indulgent trace of pride in his voice.

"A trait he shares with his illustrious father," Faith declared.

"I beg your pardon." Griffin's eyes swung back toward her.

Faith reached out and ran her hand back and forth

over the top of the grass. "Oh, come now, Griffin, you must be honest with yourself. When we were children you spent half your time in the dirt and the other half running away from your nurse to avoid your bath."

"Compared to you, I suppose I was quite a sight. You would throw a fit if you got even a speck of dirt on your clothes."

Faith's hand stopped. "Was I really such a prissy little girl?"

Griffin rolled his eyes. "You were impossible. Always demanding to be included in our games and complaining mightily if you were defeated or could not keep up. And you cried anytime your hands or face or dress became dirty."

"I was not that bad."

"You were. Thankfully, you have managed to change. A bit." His eyes lit with teasing humor. "However, you are as bossy as ever."

"Griffin!" Faith pulled up a handful of grass and flung it at him. He nimbly rolled out of the way before any landed on his person.

"See, you are as spoiled as ever and unable to take any sort of criticism. Just like when we were children."

Faith tried to school her features into an indignant expression, but instead she started giggling. "I suppose my father did on occasion indulge my girlish whims."

"On occasion? He always did as you asked." Griffin shook his head. "Neville and I often wondered what your secret was for getting your own way. I used to think it was because you were a girl, but Harriet could never get our father to even listen to her opinions, so I decided that couldn't be the reason."

"I was an only child," Faith said. "My parents had

no one else on whom to focus their love and attention. I greedily got it all."

"Your parents adored you, Faith," Griffin said quietly. "I think we all felt a bit envious of that love and devotion."

Faith drew up her knees and clasped her legs with her arms. "We were very fortunate children. All of us."

Griffin nodded. "Ah, those were carefree days. Lord, it seems like a lifetime ago." The viscount's face took on a wistful, indulgent expression that reminded Faith very much of his young son. "If I had known then that I would one day be responsible for all of this land and tenants and farms, I would have appreciated my freedom far more."

Guilt snarled at Faith. Griffin's simple words were a stark reminder of the burdens he now carried. Of the responsibilities he had never expected to assume and the wife he had never thought to have—her.

She sighed and rested one cheek on her updrawn knees. " 'Tis not so awful to be an adult, is it?"

The viscount raised his head. She felt his eyes do a slow sweep of her person, lingering on her bosom. "Oh, there are a few advantages."

Faith's spine stiffened, and she felt her shoulders straighten. She tilted her head to gaze at him. That lazy, half-lidded grin told her exactly what he had on his mind. Seduction. The desire he felt was there in his face, in the fire that smoldered in his eyes. Faith nearly shivered at the delicious thought.

Ever since the harvest ball last month he had continued to share her bed each night. Since he rarely displayed any affection during daylight hours, that nightly intimate closeness was something Faith greedily coveted.

But Faith was ever mindful that they were not alone in this secluded romantic spot. Tipping her face to the sun, she closed her eyes and pretended to relax, hoping her amorous husband would take the hint and drop the subject.

He did not. Though she kept her eyes closed, her escalating senses told her he was moving closer. Her heart gave a little jump. She could feel a blush tingle up her throat and settle in her cheeks.

Then his fingers began idly tracing patterns in the palm of her bare hand. Faith gave a small gasp at his touch as pleasure curled deep within her.

He sat up and moved closer. She still refused to look at him, yet he was impossible to ignore or dismiss. With each breath she drew, Faith inhaled the alluring, masculine scent of him, and it stirred her passions anew.

The viscount leaned in, his breath tickling her ear. "I have always wondered what it would feel like to make love outdoors, by a lovely lake, in the cool autumn air with the sunshine warming my flesh. Are you not also curious, my dear?"

Faith's breath nearly stopped. The images that overtook her were mind numbing. His hard, hot body lying directly atop hers, skin to skin, joined intimately together.

"I imagine it would be most uncomfortable," she managed to squeak out. "Lying on the hard ground, having one's shoulders pressed against the wet grass."

"Ah, love, you wound me." Griffin grasped her chin firmly and turned her head. She opened her eyes and he smiled seductively. "How dare you think me such a rough beast. I would never abuse your delicate skin in such a harsh fashion. No, it would be my back pressing against the hard earth, while you sat astride me, your legs draped across my waist.

"Or perhaps we would stand in the sunshine together, my lips caressing your neck as I snuggled closer, pressing your back against my chest. Whispering words of encouragement, I would urge you to brace your hands against the trunk of a tall oak tree and bend forward. Then slowly, gently, I would part your silken thighs and ease myself into your warmth."

Faith's cheeks grew hot. More forbidden images crowded her mind, of them joined together in the fashion of mares and stallions. Free and natural, encouraged to be totally uninhibited by the beauty of their surroundings and their trust in each other.

"You seek to corrupt me, my lord," she whispered.

"Have I succeeded?"

Yes, she wanted to shout. *You need only look at me with desire and I melt.*

Faith took a deep breath. "I fear your curiosity will not be satisfied on this day," she said haltingly. "Our son is only a few feet away. 'Tis hardly the time for such a wicked dalliance."

"Then we must return at another time. Perhaps when the moon is full?" he said in a husky whisper.

Faith shivered at the pagan thought of making love beneath the stars. "But the moonlight cannot offer the warmth of the sun."

"Is not moonlight more magical? More mysterious and forbidden?"

"I confess the cover of darkness intrigues me, my lord. Yet I fear I am too practical. Would I not be cold?"

"Not if you are with me." The viscount's hands cradled Faith's head, and he pulled her toward him, bringing his lips to hers. Their tongues met in an excited, yet controlled kiss.

When it was over, Griffin pulled back slowly, seeming to savor every moment. They stared at each other, both breathless. Faith shut her eyes briefly, unable to stop the quiver of longing that seared her.

Griffin cleared his throat. "It pains me, but I must admit that you are right, my dear. Now is not the time for our indulgences. And I promised you sunshine on your naked skin. 'Tis not fair for me to go back on my word. Yet I fear if we wait until I am finished working on these blasted accounts there will be frost on the ground. Even my boundless ardor for you will not be able to overcome those elements."

Faith smiled. "I could help you."

"Indeed?" He leered at her sexily and she blushed.

"I meant with the accounts."

"You?"

"Yes."

His brows drew together. "I have never known a female who could deal successfully with matters of business."

"Merry does it," Faith replied defensively. "Actually, she manages a fairly large fortune. Almost entirely on her own."

"How extraordinary." Griffin stroked his chin thoughtfully. "Though I suppose I really shouldn't be surprised. Lady Meredith proves time and again that she is a wholly unique woman."

His praise was like a rude jolt of reality. Faith struggled with the jealousy and resentment, eventually succeeding in conquering both. Yet she lacked the confidence to repeat her offer of assistance.

A stiff formal silence engulfed them. Faith shifted as a slight breeze ruffled a few loose strands of her hair. With a grimace she realized her chignon was coming undone, the pins no doubt loosened when Griffin had held her head and kissed her soundly.

"What's wrong, Faith?"

"Nothing." She clasped her hands tightly to her upper arms and rubbed vigorously. "Everything."

Griffin assumed a puzzled expression, but waited patiently for her to explain.

"A few weeks ago, I, along with Harriet and Meredith, spent the better part of afternoon tea spouting off to Elizabeth about how she must be sure to marry a man who values her not only for her beauty and sweet temperament, but for her intelligence. A man who is not afraid to ask her opinion in a wide variety of important matters, nor is too timid to listen to that opinion."

Griffin crossed his arms across his chest. "That is rather unorthodox advice for a young lady of society, is it not?"

"Yes," Faith replied slowly. "But 'tis good, sound advice if you are going to spend the rest of your life with someone. Don't you agree?"

"I'm not certain."

Faith blew out her breath. "Well, I am certain. Yet here I sit, feeling timid and insecure, hesitating to offer you assistance with the estate accounts. Assistance, I might add, that you seem sorely in need of."

"I thought you were jesting." Griffin's face took on a look of great interest. "You enjoy doing accounts?"

"Not really," Faith replied honestly. "But I have a rather unique talent with counting and numbers. I find that with little effort I can easily add long columns of numbers in my head. My father was most amazed by this skill, for he always found ciphering a chore."

Griffin frowned. She could see that he wasn't certain how to reply. He regarded her solemnly for a long time. To her great dismay, Faith began to feel nervous and regretful of making the bold offer.

Then suddenly the viscount broke into a wide smile. "I shall expect you to report to my study tomorrow morning, directly after breakfast. If you are only half as good with numbers as you boast, my dear, then I anticipate that we shall be able to have a private, intimate rendezvous here beneath the trees directly after luncheon."

Seventeen

Over the next fortnight Griffin found that his study was no longer a chamber of torture, a place where he needed to steel himself before entering and force himself to concentrate on the estate business he usually found so boring. He was now joined in his work by his wife, and her presence certainly livened his mornings.

To his delight, Griffin quickly learned that Faith had not been exaggerating or boasting of her talent with numbers. Her skill was indeed impressive, though she modestly insisted it was a God-given gift.

There had been a quick stab to his masculine pride when he realized what had taken him a full week to understand had taken his wife only a few hours to grasp. Yet Griffin was not a fool, and it soon became obvious that her able assistance made his life considerably easier.

In addition to her skill with figures, Faith was also able to answer Griffin's endless questions about the running of the estate. It was amazing to discover the depth of her knowledge of growing cycles, grain prices, livestock breeding, and other agricultural matters. Things that he had never had any interest in learning about, until the responsibility of the estate had been thrust upon him.

At first the viscount established a small work space

for his wife in a sunny corner of his study. This area gradually grew larger as she spent more and more time each morning poring through the vast number of bound leather account books. Before long, a dainty Queen Anne desk formerly stored in the attic made an appearance, along with other hints of a female presence.

A vase of fresh flowers, an elegant chair with gracefully curving arms, the subtle scent of lavender water wafting through the air. All these feminine distractions played havoc with Griffin's senses, making it difficult to concentrate on business.

More and more the viscount found himself fantasizing about doing a variety of stimulating and erotic acts on the smooth wooden top of his wide, flat desk. None of which had anything remotely to do with the business at hand.

More often than not, just when he would succeed in disciplining himself to ignore Faith for a few moments, she would inadvertently draw attention to herself, clucking her tongue and shaking her head in dismay as she found yet another discrepancy in their finances.

"Nearly a thousand pounds missing," Faith exclaimed in disgust, tossing down her quill. " 'Tis the largest sum I've discovered so far, yet I fear that amount will be bested before the morning ends. This particular steward was a very greedy man. His actions were a disgrace, sullying the name of all the good men who work hard and honestly in this profession."

"Which steward are you referring to, my dear?"

Faith shuffled the papers on her desk, looking for the answer. "Mr. White. He was employed here seven years ago and when he left, after working for three years, he took with him considerably more than he was entitled."

She sighed and stretched her neck. Griffin resisted the urge to reach over and massage the delicate nape, unsure if he could keep his hands from sliding lower.

"Mr. White devised a rather clever scheme of extortion by manipulating the rents," Faith continued. "I suppose when he realized that no one was paying any attention to his actions he got sloppy and entered the true amount of money he collected. He crossed it out, but did not obliterate the sum completely. All I had to do was speak with the tenant in question to discover the truth and uncover the duplicity."

"I've spoken with several of the men that run the larger farms and have gotten the same story," Griffin said. "None of them are likely to forget how unpleasant and difficult it was working for Mr. White." The viscount's dark brows drew together. "Do you think it will be possible for us to make restitution to these families?"

Faith scratched her forehead and once again consulted her papers. "That is certainly the fair and honorable course of action. However, it would probably be wisest to lower the current rents and gradually refund the difference. The farmers will certainly appreciate the extra income, and it will not leave our coffers dangerously low on funds."

The viscount nodded solemnly. "Once you have worked out all the figures, I will begin telling the farmers of their unexpected good fortune."

"That scoundrel Mr. White took great advantage of the tenants, as well as stealing from his employers," Faith said passionately. "Honestly, the man should be shot."

Griffin paused in the act of stacking several papers

on his desk. "I cannot condone the man's actions, but isn't an execution a rather bloodthirsty form of justice? Would not transportation to the Colonies satisfy your need for retribution?"

"No." Faith smiled thinly. "He stole from the estate and he stole from the tenants by inflating their rents, recording a far lower sum as payment and pocketing the difference. A most clever scheme for a man with no conscience."

"And this warrants a bullet through the heart?"

"Yes. Or a hanging." Faith steepled her hands in front of her. "Do not look so affronted, sir. I imagine there were times when you were forced to deal with less than honest individuals when running your shipping business. I cannot believe that you allowed yourself to be cheated, or that you let any sort of thievery go unpunished."

"Of course not. Anyone caught stealing was immediately forced to walk the plank."

Griffin sat back in his chair, enjoying the wide-eyed gaze his wife bestowed upon him.

"You are joking," she said after a slight hesitation.

"Are you certain?"

"Yes." A hint of rose appeared in her cheeks. "Pirates make their victims walk the plank. An honorable sea captain would never do anything so barbaric."

Griffin burst out laughing. "I've never known a pirate who would waste the time to set out a plank when he could quickly skewer his adversary with a sharp saber and then toss the poor fellow overboard."

Faith's jaw sagged. "You have known pirates? Real pirates?"

Griffin laughed again. "Faith, as a proper English noblewoman you are supposed to be shocked and horrified at the very thought of me speaking about those sorts of men, let alone knowing any."

Her brows arched up. "I do not shock easily, my lord." She shifted her attention to the papers on her desk, feigning great interest in the documents for several moments. Finally she gave up the pretense, swirled around in her chair, and leaned forward eagerly. "What sort of pirates did you know?"

Amusement flickered through Griffin. Her eager look reminded him of a curious child. Where was the staid, traditional gentlewoman he expected, the one who would be content with a life of running the household and raising the children, who would look for additional stimulation in embroidery, watercolors, and gardening?

Instead, his wife excelled at estate management and record keeping, knew more factual and practical methods of making the property successful and profitable than he did. And unconventional, dangerous men captured her imagination.

It had taken Griffin a while to understand and accept that Faith was indeed different from any gently bred woman he had ever met. And that difference was continually intriguing him.

"The men I knew were the type who would steal from their own mothers," Griffin said. "And it wasn't only the privateers. I tangled with more than one English captain who claimed a member of my crew was a deserter from the royal navy."

"Was it true?"

Griffin snorted. "Of course not. Most of my crew were of mixed nationalities and had sailed with me for years. Not that it mattered. Impressing sailors is an acceptable and abhorrent practice in the British navy."

"What did you do?"

"I learned quickly how to avoid those ships, or out-run them if we were spotted." Griffin grimaced at the memory. "If we were boarded, there were usually cases of wine or brandy that could be used to persuade the good captain to look elsewhere for crew members. If that failed, I resorted to gold coins."

Faith blinked rapidly several times. "Goodness, they sound worse than the pirates."

Griffin smiled. "There were times I had difficulty telling them apart. Yet, the sense that there is glamour or honor among pirates is a notion clearly started by someone who has never met one. While trading on routes throughout the world I came across my share of unsavory characters. Men that would make our greedy stewards like Mr. White seem like amateurs."

"Really?" Faith shivered. "Still, it must have been a grand adventure, sailing to so many different ports of call, visiting places that were unusual and exotic."

"It had its moments."

Faith's hand reached out. "Do you miss it so very much?" she asked quietly.

"At times," he replied honestly. He placed his hands over hers and began to idly stroke her long fingers. "Despite the danger, it was a good life, one I built entirely on my own. And I was successful at it."

"Unlike running the estate?" Faith said, giving voice to his unspoken thoughts.

The viscount glanced away. "I was very proud of what I accomplished with my shipping business. We gained a reputation for being honest and reliable. My crew worked hard, but they were rewarded for their efforts because we consistently made a profit."

"And so has the estate." Faith squeezed his hand. "You must not judge yourself too harshly. You stepped into a hornet's nest and have managed for the most part to come away unscathed. I think that is remarkable."

"Perhaps," he allowed. Griffin raked a hand through his hair, shoving it back from his forehead and glanced out the window.

There was a small crew of gardeners digging around an ornamental fountain, carefully preparing the beds for the coming winter. Many of the leaves from the larger trees had fallen, covering the ground in a blanket of brown. Those few that did remain on the branches looked forlorn and lonely, twisting in the wind, helpless, as they awaited their fate.

" 'Tis not only your shipping business you miss, is it, Griffin?"

He sighed heavily, pulling himself back into the conversation. A part of him rebelled at expressing his emotions, for fear they would hurt Faith. Yet deep down he knew he wanted to share this with her.

"I have always been fascinated by the sea. Even as a young boy it was my dream to go exploring, to venture beyond this quiet, simple village. 'Tis not often that the reality surpasses the dream, but, Faith, that was how I felt when I was captaining my ship.

"Alive with the excitement, the danger, the sheer beauty of open sea surrounding me. That, along with a boundless sense of freedom and a feeling of the unknown that embraced me each morning when I awoke is what I miss most of all."

He saw Faith's shoulders begin to sag as she mulled over his words. "I had no idea that you had given up such a large part of yourself to return to England. To return here."

She stared at him, her eyes huge. Griffin trailed a finger along her jaw, feeling a slight tremor pass through her.

"I came back of my own free will and have no plans to leave," he said softly. "For in truth I cannot say that I'm sorry things turned out the way they did."

There was a brief pause, and then her delicate mouth curved into a faint smile. "Neither am I, my lord."

Light rain fell, enough to cause a darkening of the soil lining the bare flower beds as it hit the ground. Griffin, positioned comfortably behind his desk, watched it through his study window, his mind drifting as he listened to the hypnotic beat of water softly tapping against the tempered glass.

Absently, he turned back to the papers piled on his desk, but they held little interest. He was working alone this afternoon on various estate and financial matters and found himself missing his wife's company.

It seemed odd that dealing with myriad estate business over the past fortnight, along with the other everyday domestic decisions that needed to be made, had bound them together more closely as man and wife. He had mistakenly believed an intimate physical relationship would accomplish that task.

In a fairly short time and without realizing it, Griffin had come to rely on Faith's advice and trust her judgment. To his surprise, he found himself wanting to discuss even the most mundane decisions with her. It puzzled him, this need he was beginning to feel. Was it a sign of weakness? Or insanity?

The simple truth was that he was starting to feel contented with this life he was so adamantly against accepting. Griffin had known from boyhood that it would be his older brother who would assume the title, along with all the family responsibilities, and he had always been glad about it.

Griffin could never remember feeling any remorse or jealousy over the fact that Neville would receive all the family's material wealth and possessions while he got a mere token. Except on his tenth birthday when Griffin had been given his brother's old pony as a gift. And Neville had received the newly purchased hunter that Griffin had long coveted.

They had scuffled over the horse, ending their verbal taunting with physical blows. Yet it had been Neville, the heir, who had received a sore rear from their father as punishment while Griffin had been given a stern lecture. Clearly, the expectations placed on the shoulders of the future viscount were far more burdensome than that of the younger son.

He had grown to manhood with a freedom of choice his brother could only dream about, and Griffin was smart enough to realize that was worth far more than a dozen prized horses.

Yet here he was, now living the life of a landed aristocrat, married to the woman chosen for his brother, struggling to make a success of the estate, and starting to find not only joy, but a sense of self in that life.

With a sigh, Griffin pushed away from his desk, stretched out his legs in front of him, and thought about how peculiar these circumstances were.

A commotion sounded in the hallway, interrupting his reflective thoughts. Griffin straightened and watched the door handle slowly turn. Since there had been no knock he knew it could not be a servant and assumed it was a family member. Probably one of his sisters.

But when the heavy door swung open it was Georgie who stood uncertainly in the doorway. The viscount smiled at the boy, who immediately began fidgeting. He knew the decidedly masculine study held great interest for the child, for Georgie had told his father more than once that he thought it was the grandest room in the house.

Apparently the boy especially liked the glass eyes of the stuffed boar's head staring down from the walls, a confession that had both startled and impressed the viscount.

Secretly he was proud of the child's bravery, for Griffin had always thought the stuffed animal heads rather intimidating when he was Georgie's age. Perhaps the child did not realize the heads had once been attached to large, living beasts.

"I was looking for you," Georgie said at last.

"Is that so? I was unaware that I was lost." Griffin grinned at his son, knowing the boy would not understand the subtlety of the humor but hoping to coax a smile.

Georgie had been told not to disturb his father when he was working and the expression on the little boy's face clearly stated that he knew he was doing something wrong.

The child did not smile. He glanced down at his foot and rubbed the tip of his shoe into the fringe of the carpet. Then he lifted his face and shot Griffin a wary look.

Puzzled, the viscount stood up and motioned for the child to come forward. With a strangled cry, Georgie eagerly raced toward him. Griffin caught the child in a hug and swung him up in the air. This action usually brought peals of laughter from the boy, but not today.

Griffin noticed a slight trembling in the small body

he held against his chest. A stab of fear shot through him as he slowly allowed Georgie to slide down to the floor.

The boy gazed up at him with wide, troubled eyes, and Griffin's suspicions were confirmed. This was not an impulsive visit, a chance to beg for a closer look at the impressive crossbow that was displayed in the glass gun cabinet or the dueling pistols locked inside a gleaming mahogany box. This was far more serious.

"You must come to the drawing room right now," Georgie announced solemnly. He placed his small hand in his father's and held on tightly. "There is a bad man and a mean lady who came for tea and they made Faith cry."

"What? I was unaware that there would be company for tea. Are you certain?"

"Yes." Georgie nodded his head emphatically. "Faith wiped her face real fast, but I saw her eyes leaking tears. She looked so sad. The bad man was talking in a loud voice that hurt my ears and waving his hands all around. Like this." Georgie flayed his arms wildly to demonstrate.

"And the mean lady said that good little boys stay in the nursery not in the drawing room with the adults and told me to leave." Georgie tilted his head. "Aren't I a good boy, Papa?"

Griffin stepped forward and took hold of Georgie's arm. "You are the best behaved little boy I know and my very favorite son."

Georgie took a deep breath. "Please make the bad people go away, Papa. I don't like them."

Griffin moved a little closer and focused on Georgie's face. He had never seen the child look so miserable, not even after his beloved nursemaid had sailed back to the Colonies. Whoever these mysterious individuals were, they had certainly made a strong impression on his son.

"By any chance, do you remember the names of this man and lady?" Griffin asked.

Georgie shrugged his shoulders helplessly.

"Is anyone else in the drawing room with Faith? Aunt Harriet or Aunt Elizabeth perhaps?" Griffin questioned.

"No." Georgie grabbed the edge of Griffin's coat with his free hand and twisted the material nervously. "Will you send them away now, Papa? Please?"

"If they are acting as you say, then they will be gone before you can say 'Napoleon is a rat' three times fast."

That final remark brought a weak smile to the boy's lips. Though the child's account of these odd events seemed sincere, Griffin could not help but think that Georgie had somehow misconstrued what he had seen and heard. Yet the boy was not prone to melodrama.

Griffin left his study and strode quickly through the hall, with Georgie on his heels. The viscount scarcely noticed the sound of hammering, scraping, and banging being created by the various workmen he passed. Though the renovations to the first floor had been completed at the end of the summer, there was much additional work needed on the second and third floors, and the men hired to attend to those tasks were busy laboring.

When he reached the closed doors of the drawing room, Griffin motioned for Georgie to remain outside. The child nodded in understanding and took up a position near a large potted palm.

Griffin yanked open the door, entering unannounced, and indeed discovered two strangers having tea with his wife. A middle-aged man and woman, just as Georgie had said.

At his entrance, all conversation ceased. Three sets of eyes swung his way, but Griffin's main concern was his wife.

The gray light of the rainy afternoon etched Faith's features in a soft illumination that could not conceal their tautness. She sat unnaturally rigid, her mouth set in a grim line. Yet she was still the picture of grace and nobility. Under fire?

There was certainly enough tension and undercurrents of distress in the room to suggest that might be possible.

"Good afternoon, my dear," Griffin said, going immediately to Faith's side.

He lifted the limp hand settled in her lap and kissed it in formal greeting. Her fingers were cold as ice. Griffin felt a twinge of irritation. If she was upset, she should have called for him. Or thrown these two upstarts out on their ear.

"I was unaware that we had company," the viscount continued in an even tone. "You should have summoned me."

Faith turned her head and gave him a valiant smile. "I did not wish to disturb you while you were working," she replied softly. "My cousin and his wife have surprised me with a visit. They have come from London to discuss some family matters."

"Yes, family matters," the man muttered hastily, his eyes shifting to the corner of the room.

"Family matters? Well, then, I have arrived just in time." Griffin replied smoothly, deciding he did not like Faith's cousin. "However, I am not acquainted with your relations. Would you do the honors, my dear?"

She hesitated, bit her lower lip, then inclined her head fractionally.

"This is my cousin Cyril and his wife Amelia. Upon my father's death Cyril inherited the title. He is the new Baron Aston."

Ah, now it made a bit more sense. Griffin remembered that one of the reasons Faith had been so adamant about marrying him was to keep her beloved Mayfair Manor out of her cousin's clutches.

Faith cleared her throat. "Lord Aston has expressed some concerns over the validity of our marriage. As it pertains to my father's will."

"Has he now?" It was the most congenial, restrained response Griffin could force past his clenched teeth. "Then why did he not address these concerns directly to me?"

"My solicitor advised against it," Lord Aston replied. "However, I felt it was only fair to inform Faith of our intentions to have her father's will overturned. After all, we are still family."

"How generous of you." Griffin's mouth curved up, but it really wasn't a smile. "What precisely do you find objectionable about our marriage, Lord Aston?"

"Everyone knows you aren't the right Viscount Dewhurst. Her father wanted her to marry your brother. Not you."

"Well, since my brother is not here to object to the marriage, I see no reason that you should." Griffin raised his brows with an exaggerated motion, as if a new thought had suddenly occurred to him. "Unless you are hoping to gain possession of Mayfair Manor by challenging our marriage?"

"Are you daft, man?" Lord Aston snorted in disgust. "The title is useless without the property. I have bills to pay, a family to provide for, not to mention a higher standard of living to maintain now that I am a baron. The only way I can do that is by assuming ownership of what is rightfully mine. Mayfair Manor."

"Yes, the manor is rightfully ours," Lady Aston chimed in. She moved closer to the edge of the lavender satin chair she sat upon to emphasize her point.

Griffin noted that the fabric of the chair clashed horribly with the bright yellow day gown she wore and gave her severe features a pinched, sallow look. Her mouth was set at a mulish angle, her brow wrinkled in a scowl.

Griffin immediately decided he liked her even less than her husband.

"I suppose the fact that my wife has fulfilled all the legal requirements of her father's will is to be ignored?"

"Your marriage is a sham," Lord Aston sneered. "There are servants employed at the Sign of the Dove Inn where you spent your wedding night who will swear that you didn't stay together in the same room for more than an hour."

"Idle servant gossip? Is that what you are basing your case upon?" Griffin shrugged his shoulders expressively. "It shall be laughed out of court. If it even comes to trial."

Griffin saw Faith pause, her teacup halfway to her mouth. She took a huge gulp of air, set down the cup in its saucer, then picked up the teapot. She poured a fresh cup of the brew and added one lump of sugar.

She extended the cup toward him, and he grabbed at it quickly, to hide the rattling of the china. *Devil take the baron!* Faith was obviously very upset, probably because the man had managed to uncover an unsavory bit of truth.

Griffin immediately placed his tea on the table. He

did not want his hands encumbered with delicate china if he felt the sudden need to put his hands upon Lord Aston and toss him from the room.

"There are those among the beau monde who have unusual marriages, but once the true circumstances of yours becomes known, society will be vastly amused," Lord Aston predicted in a dire tone. "I'm sure Faith would prefer to avoid the gossip and humiliation that—"

"Have a care, sir," Griffin interrupted with deadly calm, not allowing the baron to finish his sentence. "You are speaking of my wife. Anything you say about her reflects directly on me. I protect what is mine, with any means necessary."

The viscount advanced steadily on the baron as he spoke, coming close enough that he could smell the mutton and sour wine Cyril had consumed for lunch.

Aston held his gaze and shrugged his shoulders, as if this were of little concern to him, but Griffin could see the tension creep into his adversary's shoulders.

"I must say," Griffin continued in a droll tone, "that a man so enamored with the goings-on of another couple's bedchamber activities must not have much of interest occurring in his own to keep him occupied."

There was a gasp of outrage from Lady Aston. Her red-faced husband's nostrils flared as he tried to sputter a reply, but it was Faith who spoke.

"My cousin has brought a document he wishes me to sign," she said hesitantly. "Designed to save me from any sort of ridicule."

"Yes." Lord Aston gasped for a moment, fumbled in his breast-coat pocket, and pulled forth a rumpled document. "My solicitor has drawn up the papers stating that you will not oppose my suit against the will."

Griffin drew an audible breath. "If you think that

I would allow you to come into my home and bully my wife into signing over a property that is rightfully hers, then you are even more of an imbecile than I first thought," he said.

"Now, see here," Lord Aston sputtered.

But Griffin would not allow him to continue. "You should consider yourself most fortunate, sir, that I have been so excessively restrained this afternoon," Griffin declared. "When I saw how much you distressed my wife and upset my son, my first inclination was to slam several hard blows to your face."

"Such savagery!" Lady Aston admonished.

Griffin did not react to the comment. Instead, he strolled casually to the drawing-room door and placed his fingers on the polished brass handle. "I shall have my butler summon your driver immediately. Good day."

Lord Aston opened his mouth to protest, but Griffin held up a staying hand and looked from the baron to his wife with careful disdain.

"I am certain that you do not wish to push my temper beyond its limit," Griffin continued. "I can assure you, with no false modesty, that my reputation with both sword and pistol is accurate and well deserved."

Lord Aston turned a bit pale, but he puffed out his chest with a great show of bruised dignity. He held out his arm, and his pinch-faced wife attached herself to it. They stalked to the door, pausing briefly at the threshold to glare at Griffin.

"This is far from over, Dewhurst."

"Oh, but it is, Aston." Griffin looked assessingly at his opponent. "I suggest strongly that you enjoy your new title and status and content yourself knowing that it is all you shall be receiving.

"For I give you fair and clear warning, though you

hardly deserve it. If you pursue this matter in any way that upsets my wife, I shall take great delight in stripping from you all manner of luxuries you currently enjoy and do everything within my power to ensure that you are forced to live in the poverty you now claim to be experiencing."

Lord Aston's eyes widened in astonishment, and he looked as if he might burst from indignation. Yet he gave no reply and escorted his wife from the room. Quickly.

Griffin shut the door quietly when they departed, resisting mightily the urge to slam it with the full force of his anger. But he would not give Aston the satisfaction. And he did not want anything else disturbing his wife.

There was no mistaking the expression of relief that washed over Faith's face as the door shut. Something in Griffin's stomach tightened. Clearly she had been far more upset by the encounter than he'd originally thought.

"Thank you, Griffin. I was uncertain if I would ever be able to get them to leave," Faith said quietly. "I know you will find it difficult to comprehend, but the moment Cyril began speaking of our marriage my mind and tongue froze."

"Yes, it is difficult for me to imagine you at a loss for words," Griffin teased gently. But his remarks did not bring forth the desired smile from his wife's lips.

"Nevertheless, I am most grateful for your spirited intervention. I did rather enjoy watching all the bluster drain out of Cousin Cyril."

"An odious man." Griffin shook his head. "Yet I cannot help but observe that you seemed almost surprised that I would come to your aid. Have I been so lacking in character that you believe I will allow you to be insulted in my own drawing room? By such a sniveling worm as your cousin?"

"Of course I knew you would come to my defense." She said the words, but it was clear she did not entirely believe them. Griffin was unsure if he should be flattered or insulted by this revelation.

There was a lengthy silence between them as Griffin tried to formulate the words that would aptly demonstrate his feelings on this matter.

"Let me assure you, Faith, that I shall never allow anyone to set foot in my home and proceed to verbally abuse my wife."

"Really?"

"Absolutely." Griffin gave her a slow wink. "That is a privilege I retain exclusively for myself."

Only the viscount's quick reflexes saved him from being hit square in the chest with the large pillow his viscountess hurled in his direction.

Eighteen

The days of autumn slipped past. There was no further word from the odious cousin, Cyril, nor his solicitor, and gradually Faith began to relax. She no longer haunted the post each day, dreading the news that might arrive, fearful of a lawsuit or some other challenge to her ownership of her childhood home.

Apparently Griffin's forceful handling of the situation had stopped Cyril dead in his tracks. Faith was grateful to her husband for his intervention, though she felt ashamed to have needed his help. She was embarrassed that her cousin would be so greedy, yet she felt even more guilty because there had been some truth in his claim.

Her husband had come to her rescue, but knowing him as she did, Faith realized Griffin had had little choice. It was too much a part of his nature to deny anyone in need.

She was his wife, his responsibility, in essence his possession. He would not allow anyone or anything to harm her, if it were in his power to prevent it. She fully believed he would protect her with his very life if it were necessary.

Yet that did not mean he loved her. Did it?

Their relationship had improved significantly over the past few months and she was grateful. There was a level of comfort and ease between them that she cherished, a meeting of mind and spirit. It was a respectful and mature partnership, flourishing in many ways.

Yet they never spoke of love. She had revealed her heart but once to her husband and he had ignored her declaration. Completely. Faith took that to mean that he was uncomfortable with the emotions she felt for him and clearly did not wish to know about them.

So she never again spoke her feelings aloud. It almost seemed boorish and insensitive to bombard Griffin with her love when apparently it did not interest him.

Still her love grew, for she did not fight it. Faith allowed herself to be swept along with her emotions, to enjoy the novel feeling of being in love. The one concession she did make, for herself and her husband, was to never verbalize her feelings.

She did worry about becoming too dependent on Griffin, too needy and clingy. Faith treasured the friendship and affection he bestowed upon her and knew it would be difficult to forsake. She felt a constant need not to overstep herself, not to push beyond the careful boundary they had somehow wordlessly erected.

"Do you think we shall have afternoon callers today?" Elizabeth asked as the family gathered for breakfast in the sunny dining room one late fall morning.

Faith eyed the platter of eggs the butler presented to her, then spooned a heaping serving onto her plate. "I imagine the usual group will converge upon us this afternoon. Geoffrey Barton, Mr. Huxtable, Baron Harndon, Squire Jordan."

Griffin's newspaper rattled suddenly. He peered over the top, directing his hard gaze upon his younger sister. "Squire Jordan seems to be coming around fairly often. Doesn't the man have anywhere else to spend his afternoons?"

"We are all flattered that the squire chooses to come calling. He is a very likable gentleman," Faith interceded, noticing the deep blush on Elizabeth's cheeks. "I for one greatly enjoy his company."

"As do I," Harriet added.

Griffin scowled at the three female faces staring so innocently at him, snapped his paper crisply, then buried himself behind it, not emerging until his sisters had finished their meals and left the room.

"I honestly do not understand how these gentlemen can spare so much time away from their estates," Griffin grumbled to Faith. "They should be attending to business in the afternoon, not paying court to a child. Elizabeth is barely seventeen, yet Squire Jordan gazes at her like a lovesick puppy. Huxtable is usually pathetically tongue-tied whenever he draws within three feet of her. And Baron Harndon is nearly twice her age."

Faith did not look up from the hot chocolate she was pouring into her cup. "I believe Baron Harndon's interest has been captured by a more mature woman. While he is always solicitous and attentive to Elizabeth, she is not the reason he comes to call."

Griffin nearly choked on the cup of coffee he was trying to swallow. "Mature woman? Do not tell me he is coming to see you, madame?"

Faith lifted a brow and stared at her husband with perplexity. "Why would Baron Harndon wish to visit me?"

"He was most attentive toward you during the harvest ball, taking far too much interest in your lovely shoulders and the daringly low-cut bodice of your gown." Griffin carefully folded his newspaper and placed it beside his dish. "If memory serves me correctly, Harndon has been in attendance at nearly all of the social gatherings we have graced these past few weeks. To see you?"

Faith took a bite of her eggs and chewed slowly. The look of indignant suspicion on Griffin's face was even more delicious than her food, and she wanted to savor every bite.

"If you had been paying a bit more attention, you would have noticed that we always see the same people, no matter what the social occasion," Faith said with a smug grin. She skewered a piece of ham with her fork and added it to her plate. "That is the very nature of country society. One sees the same faces at every event, and more often than not, dressed in the same clothing."

Confused, Griffin frowned, then asked, "If not you, then whom does Harndon come to visit?"

Faith rolled her eyes. "Harriet, of course. I fear he is quite smitten with her."

"Harriet?" Griffin smiled softly. "Poor sod. He is no match for her high spirits and sharp tongue."

"I agree, but her invigorating personality appears to be part of the allure for Baron Harndon."

"Is she encouraging him to pay her court?"

"Not at all," Faith bristled. "She is an engaged woman."

"For all the good it has done her." Griffin frowned. He pushed away his nearly empty breakfast plate. "I would not be displeased if she began to encourage some of the local gentry. Not Harndon; he is the wrong man for her. Perhaps we can find someone better suited for her temperament?"

Faith eyed her husband in surprise. "Harriet is engaged," she repeated.

"I have no evidence of that other than my sister's word and a wistful gleam in her eye whenever she speaks of the man," Griffin snapped. "Which is not very often. That does not overly surprise me since he appears to have forgotten her existence entirely. To my knowledge she has not received one letter from her fiancé since my arrival."

"He is fighting a war. I cannot imagine there is a great deal of time to be spared for letter writing," Faith said with a certainty she was far from feeling.

"Other soldiers manage to correspond with their families."

"Well, maybe Mr. Wingate doesn't like to write letters."

The viscount did not bother to reply and Faith realized how upset he truly felt. Her husband had mentioned on several occasions his concerns over Harriet's future. Apparently it still worried him.

"Have you been able to learn anything about Harriet's fiancé?" Faith asked.

Griffin's jaw clenched. "Nothing of significance."

Faith sighed. "You are scowling Griffin, which means you are uncomfortable, which means that you are not telling me the entire truth."

His mouth twisted in a grimace. "I have received some information. Apparently Wingate can hold his liquor, has wounded one man in a duel, and when he is living in town enjoys keeping an expensive, flashy mistress."

"Griffin!"

"I told you that what I had learned about Wingate was not of significance for Harriet. He sounds as though he conducts himself like every other hot-blooded gentleman who has too much time to fritter away. Perhaps it is better that he is in the army. At least he has a profession."

"I think Harriet might find the part about Mr. Wingate's mistresses rather significant," Faith huffed, fixating on the one aspect that truly distressed her. "Do you suppose he will give up these women after they are married?"

Griffin shrugged. "If I ever meet the man I will certainly suggest it, but I hold out little hope he will comply. Based on what I have learned, I worry more that Wingate might be drawn to a life of self-gratification and carnal indulgences. Especially if he resigns his army commission. I cannot imagine Harriet flourishing in such a meaningless existence."

"I too had heard rumors, but Harriet chose him of her own free will," Faith reminded Griffin. "She is certainly old enough to know her own mind."

"Even though she is of age, I am responsible for my sister's welfare. I will not allow her to enter into an ill-suited marriage." Griffin's gray eyes grew serious. "Above all else, I want her to be happy."

Like you? Faith wanted to shout. *Are you happy? Or do you still feel regret over our marriage?*

For the first time Faith noticed the vulnerability and uncertainty in Griffin's face. Her chest tightened. Her role was to help and support him, not burden him with her own insecurities. She might have lost her heart to this man, yet she still retained some pride and reason.

It could cause the viscount even greater distress and embarrassment to be interrogated by her over the state of their marriage. Faith told herself she was sparing them both by not addressing this issue. Yet secretly she was angry with herself for lacking both the courage to ask and the fortitude to hear the answer.

They spoke no more of Harriet's fiancé in the coming weeks, but Faith knew it still troubled Griffin. She too began to watch the post for letters to Harriet that never arrived. And she also started to view the local gentlemen in a different eye—as prospective husbands for her sister-in-law.

Having lived all her life in Harrowby, Faith was used to the monotonous tenor of country living. At times she suspected her husband was restless and bored with this routine, for it was a far cry from the excitement and interest of his days as a sea captain.

But the viscount made an effort to be sociable, insisting that they host and attend various entertainments of the local gentry. They soon became a great favorite wherever they went, and no gathering was considered a success until the viscount and his bride made an appearance.

Quickly their days developed a pattern, a comfortable rhythm that brought a sense of peace, if not complete contentment, to Faith. She enjoyed their at-home evenings best, after dinner had ended and Harriet and Elizabeth had taken themselves off to bed.

Seated alone together in the drawing room, she and Griffin would discuss the events of the day or plan the activities of the remainder of the week. Occasionally Griffin would read aloud to her in a deep baritone voice that made her insides feel like a swirling cauldron of bubbling liquid.

When the clock struck eleven, Griffin would rise purposefully from his chair. With a wicked, teasing glint in his eye he would offer his arm and formally escort Faith to her bedchamber door.

Once there, the viscount would raise her hand to his lips, brush her knuckles lightly, and then bid her a pleasant good night. Faith would practically fly into her chamber, impatient with her maid to help her quickly disrobe. The moment she was clad in a sheer nightrail, she would dismiss the servant, admonishing her to attend to the cleaning and organizing of the clothes in the morning.

Then Faith would be left to wait, tense with anticipation and a slight edge of fear. Would he come to the door that connected their bedchambers and quietly knock? Or would this be the night that it all ended?

Nerves stretched taut she would listen anxiously for the tapping at the door, releasing her breath when it finally came. Then Griffin would step into her bedchamber, looking impossibly handsome, a ghost of a smile about his lips.

Faith always answered that smile with a warm, lingering kiss, pressing herself forward so they touched from breasts to hips to thighs.

"Are you feeling very tired?" Griffin would ask.

"A little," she would answer, blowing into his ear.

"Then I shall be a most considerate husband tonight and allow you to fall asleep at least an hour before dawn."

"I am honored, my lord."

He would lift her in his arms and carry her to the bed, resting her in the middle. Pausing only long enough to strip off his black satin robe, he would come down beside her, dragging her mouth to his for a ravishing kiss.

Some nights their coupling was swift and lusty, other nights it was agonizingly slow and thorough. Faith marveled that even after so many intimacies there were still new ways of touching and arousing each other.

Griffin's skilled hands and mouth seemed to read her mood, to know instinctively what she needed to achieve fulfillment. He taught her how to please him and she discovered that heightened her own pleasure.

Faith was always alone when she woke in the morning, with the lingering scent of Griffin's masculine sensuality clinging to the bed linens the only reminder of where he had spent the night. And thus the new day began.

On Sundays they attended church, sitting solemnly together in the family pew, distracted from the vicar's sermons only when Georgie became restless and started squirming in his seat. Weather permitting, they would stroll home together after the service, arm in arm, with Georgie running eagerly ahead and Elizabeth and Harriet trailing discreetly behind.

It was not, of course, a perfectly idyllic existence. They quarreled, too. About his interfering sister who still persisted in giving her opinion and advice when it was neither sought nor welcome. Over the elderly gentleman who had been hired as Georgie's tutor, when Faith had specifically requested a kindly governess.

Though in time she had to concede that the tutor, Mr. Cabot, was a patient man, who appreciated his pupil's bright mind and did not wish to break his engaging spirit.

If questioned, Faith knew she would reply that she was content. She had learned to bend and compromise without breaking, had learned to pick and choose the battles that mattered most, had come to understand that there would be highs and lows in her marriage.

The physical desire she felt for her husband still left her breathless. At times it took only a look, or the sound of his deep voice to set her body aflame. And while she was pleased and flattered that Griffin spent his nights in her bed, Faith wanted more from her marriage than physical gratification.

Yet deep in her heart she almost dared not to hope for it, fearing it would jeopardize what she had achieved.

With the passing of autumn came the days of Christmas, a holiday Faith had always enjoyed. This year it was especially joyous thanks to Georgie's presence in the household. He was enchanted by everything—the evergreen boughs draped over many of the fireplace mantels in the house, the colorful bows and ribbons, and the profusion of red-berry holly and mistletoe that lent a cheery ambience to the rooms of the manor, and the delicious smells of holiday treats wafting up from the kitchen.

On Christmas Day he even managed to sit still during the entire church service, but was too excited to do justice to the sumptuous feast of roasted goose, salmon, rabbit, turnips, parsnips, carrots, mincemeat pies, gingerbread, and candied fruits. The gaily wrapped parcels piled high on the drawing room credenza were far more enticing to a young boy than his favorite kidney pie and custard.

At long last it was time to open the gifts. Gathered around a blazing Yule log in the drawing room, the family sipped mulled wine, exchanged small tokens, and wished each other well.

Georgie had the most impressive pile of presents, as was fitting for the youngest member of the household. He exclaimed with such earnest delight as he opened each parcel that each was his favorite gift, that the adults were soon laughing before he had even unwrapped his present.

Faith was pleased with the lovely embroidered handkerchief from Elizabeth but was nearly speechless over the cashmere shawl that Harriet gave her. The true shocker of the day came when she opened the small, thin, flat box from her husband.

"Oh, Griffin, you should not have wasted the funds on this extravagant present for me," Faith protested as she lifted the stunning necklace from the satin-cushioned lining. The diamond and gold necklace sparkled gaily in the firelight.

"I suppose that is one of the hazards of letting your wife look at your account books," Griffin said with a mocking smile.

He took the necklace from Faith's trembling fingers and clasped it around her neck.

"It looks beautiful," Elizabeth said sincerely.

"Very pretty," Harriet seconded.

"Goodness." Faith touched her throat. The elegant necklace felt cool and smooth against her fingers. "I hardly know what to say."

The viscount leaned close so that only Faith could hear. "I wanted you to have something special, something memorable to mark the occasion. This is, after all, our first Christmas together as man and wife."

Faith's eyes filled with emotion. She glanced away, not wanting anyone to see the tears trickle down her cheek.

"Look! It's snowing!"

Georgie's boyish cries of excitement commanded everyone's immediate attention. They all rushed to the windows and crowded around to look outside.

"The ground is completely white," Harriet observed. "It must have been falling for some time."

"I want to go outside and touch it," Georgie exclaimed.

"Splendid idea," Griffin said. " 'Tis not yet dark. If we hurry, we can manage a sleigh ride. Is anyone interested?"

There was a deafening chorus of yeas. Everyone quickly scrambled into hats and coats and gloves and fought good-naturedly over who would get to ride first.

Georgie and Faith won that argument. They snuggled together under the thick fur lap robe while Griffin deftly drove the sleigh over the thin layer of snow that had fallen. Then they waved gaily to Harriet and Elizabeth as the women took a turn in the sleigh and watched it disappear across the meadow, the viscount once again in command of the reins.

It was serenely silent in the deserted meadow. Faith and Georgie immediately set to work trying to construct a statue made of snow. Suddenly, a strange cawing sound broke the quiet.

"What was that?" Georgie inquired.

Faith cocked her head and listened intently. "It sounds like birds. Rather noisy ones."

"Can we find them?" Georgie asked excitedly, dropping the large ball of snow he was packing. "Then we can bring them bread for their Christmas dinner."

"I suppose we could look for their nest." Faith brushed the snow off her gloves and reached for Georgie's hand. "But you must be very quiet while we search for the birds, or else they will be frightened and fly off."

Hand in hand they followed the noise, through a small clump of bushes, then to the end of the low hedges that surrounded the meadow. Faith's eyes scanned the bare branches, yet she saw nothing perched in the trees.

They stood side by side in the snow and listened, their warm breath clouding the cold air.

"I heard it again," Georgie exclaimed. "This way."

He let go of Faith's hand and raced forward.

"Wait for me," she cried, charging after him. Georgie rounded the hedge and disappeared from view. Faith quickened her gait, but it was hard to run in the ankle-deep snow wearing her thick, heavy boots.

Panting from exertion and fear, Faith finally turned past the hedge. With a gasp of pure relief she spotted Georgie. He was standing very quiet and still, staring down into a clump of low evergreens. Faith hurried to his side.

"They aren't birds, Faith."

She glanced down to where the child was pointing and saw a tangle of gray, white, and black fur. "Kittens," she declared in surprise.

Georgie's head turned sharply. "Really?"

He reached down eagerly, but Faith stopped him. "Let me do it." Gently she separated the ball of fur and discovered three very young, very noisy animals.

"Why are they making so much noise?" Georgie asked.

"They must be hungry," Faith decided. She alternatively stroked the fur of the two kittens she held while Georgie struggled to keep the adventurous feline in his arms under control.

"I don't think the kittens like the snow," Georgie decided. "We should bring them home. They could sleep in a box near my bed. It is warm in my room."

"Oh, no, we cannot move them. The mother cat will no doubt come back to care for her babies. She would be very sad if they were not here."

Georgie lowered his head dejectedly while Faith scanned the area for signs of a mother cat. It was unusual for a female to abandon such young offspring.

Faith was trying to think of the best way to persuade Georgie to leave when Griffin, Harriet, and Elizabeth arrived. The women immediately began cooing over the tiny creatures.

"Aunt Harriet can have the gray one and Faith can have the white one and I can have the black one," Georgie decided generously. He turned a winning smile toward his father. "Okay?"

"I tried to explain that we should not move them," Faith said weakly. The kitten in her arms had buried its head in her neck and was purring softly.

"But we can hardly leave them out here," Elizabeth protested. "They will freeze."

A debate ensued over the correct and proper course of action. Griffin announced that he would take one of the kittens to Higgins, the stablemaster, who had superior knowledge of all types of animals and ask his advice.

Faith reluctantly handed over her kitten. The viscount placed the animal in the sleigh and drove off, but he returned quickly.

"Higgins found the mother cat yesterday afternoon in the stable loft," Griffin whispered to Faith. "She must have been in a fight with another animal."

"That explains why she has not returned." Faith lifted the kitten from her husband's large hands and cradled it in her arms. "Is she badly hurt?"

"I'm afraid she is dead."

"Oh, no," Faith moaned. "What will happen to these poor creatures?"

"Higgins thinks it would be best to drown them."

"Oh, my!" Faith pulled the kitten closer to her breast. "What a beastly thing to suggest."

Griffin shrugged. "He thought only to prevent a prolonged suffering. They are too young to survive without a mother."

"But surely we must try to save them," Faith protested.

"I'm inclined to agree with Higgins," Griffin replied. "They will most likely die anyway."

" 'Tis Christmas Day," Faith said softly. "Could we not at least try?"

Faith knew she was asking the impossible, but it suddenly seemed very important that she try to save these helpless creatures. A very reluctant Griffin agreed to bring the orphaned animals home. It was difficult to get Georgie to bed that night and even more difficult to persuade him that the kittens would be safe and warm in the box Higgins made for them in the stable.

Faith slept fitfully that night, arising just after dawn. As was his custom, Griffin was already gone from her bed. She dressed quickly, without the help of her maid, tossed a warm cloak over her shoulders, and headed for the stable.

When she walked to the warm corner where the kittens were kept, she discovered her husband standing over the box with a grim expression.

Worry splintered through her. "What has happened?"

"The black kitten died during the night."

"Oh, Griffin," Faith's eyes filled with tears. She rushed forward and gazed at the limp body in the viscount's hand. "The poor little thing."

"I warned you, Faith." A muscle tightened in his cheek. "They were so young. Too young to survive without a mother to care for them."

"I know," Faith sniffed. "I couldn't bear the thought of letting them die, but this is far worse. Georgie's heart will be broken. And what of the remaining two kittens? I fear they will suffer the same fate."

"Most likely." The viscount's mouth went thin. "The black was the largest and strongest of the bunch. I cannot imagine how his siblings will survive when he could not."

"Can Higgins offer no advice?"

Griffin grumbled something beneath his breath. "He thinks I am crazy for not allowing him to act upon his original solution."

Faith bent her head. The two remaining animals were cuddled together in a tight little ball. They seemed so pathetic and helpless. "What are we going to do?"

Griffin did not reply. Instead he stood staring down at the box for several long moments. Then he turned, plucked a clean cloth from the rag bin in the corner, and gently wound it around the body of the dead kitten.

The click of his boot heels on the hard floor told Faith he was leaving. "Where are you going?" she called out.

"On a fool's errand," he replied as he stalked from the stable.

Faith's shoulder's slumped. She gazed dejectedly out of the grimy window and noticed a light drizzle of sleet had begun to fall. With a heavy sigh she settled herself beside the box and waited for Georgie to arrive.

It was cool in the stable, but Faith was warmly wrapped in her cloak. Her eyes drifted shut and she dozed fitfully, coming abruptly awake at the sound of a door opening. She glanced up, bracing herself to break the unhappy news to Georgie. But it was Griffin who stood in the doorway.

"How are they?" he asked.

"About the same," Faith replied. The edge of concern in his voice made her feel even worse. Thanks to her intervention the entire family was now going to witness these poor creatures' demise. Faith felt profoundly sad and guilty all in the same breath.

"Well, maybe this will help." The viscount reached under his cloak and lifted out a fat tabby.

"What is that?"

"A new mother for the kittens."

Faith scrambled to her feet. The big cat stretched out its front paws languidly. She seemed none the worse for wear after her travels beneath the viscount's coat. "Where did you find her?"

"On Squire Jordan's estate. I told Higgins to ask the tenants and neighbors if anyone had a cat who had recently had kittens. Did you have any idea how many cats there are in this area? There were several new mothers, but this poor feline lost most of her babies. Only one kitten survived. Hopefully she will consider adopting our two."

"But what happened to the kitten from her litter?"

Griffin smiled and reached into his pocket, producing an indignant meowing ball of fur.

"It's black!"

His smile broadened. "Mostly. There are white markings on the paws and chest, but hopefully we can convince Georgie that he failed to notice that yesterday. Then he need never know what dire fate befell the other black one."

" 'Tis a miracle," Faith whispered in awe.

"Perhaps. However, we have not achieved success yet, my dear. Higgins warned me that a mother cat won't always accept a stray. We have yet to see what this tabby thinks of our hungry orphans."

Gingerly the viscount placed the large cat in the box. The two orphans had awakened and were meowing noisily. Yet the moment the larger cat came close they became silent. She circled them warily, nudged them each with her nose, and then began to lick their faces.

"I believe we have found a solution," Griffin said with quiet pride.

"In the nick of time," Faith whispered. "Here is Georgie."

The little boy raced into the stable, heading straight for the box. His eyes widened in surprise when he saw the new occupant.

"Where did the big cat come from?"

"Papa brought him over from Squire Jordan's. She will be the new mother for our kittens."

Georgie reached into the box eagerly. The female cat hissed suddenly and swiped her paw at him. He pulled back in alarm. "She scratched me," he exclaimed.

"You must not scare her," Faith advised, reaching for the injured hand. She examined the cut closely, pleased to find it was only a surface welt. The cat had not even broken the skin.

"Why did she do that?" Georgie asked with great indignity.

"She is merely protecting her young," Griffin explained.

"I wasn't going to hurt them. I only wanted to play with them." Georgie made a face. "I want you to take the big cat back to Squire Jordan. She is mean."

Faith crouched beside Georgie. "We were very lucky to have found such a wonderful mother cat. The kittens need her if they are to grow big and strong."

"Well, I don't like her." Georgie crossed his arms over his chest and stared mutinously down at the big tabby. "Why do they need a new mother, anyway?"

"To feed them and clean them and teach them how to be big cats," Griffin said in a cheerful voice.

Georgie's frown deepened as he contemplated his father's words. He knelt beside the box and slowly held out his hand. The tabby sniffed, then allowed herself to be petted on the head. Gradually Georgie's expression lightened. "I guess it is like Faith."

The viscountess exchanged a puzzled glance with her husband. "Like me? What do you mean?"

"I don't have a mother anymore, so Faith takes care of me. I like that." He patted the cat one last time. Standing, he moved beside Faith and slipped his injured hand into hers. She latched on to it tightly. "I think I should call you Mama."

"That would be lovely," Faith murmured. An odd tightness rose in her chest as a single tear trickled down her cheek, but the smile she bestowed upon her little boy was filled with pure joy.

Nineteen

It was a brisk February afternoon, but the cut of the wind did not bother Faith, nor Georgie, as they journeyed into town on market day. They snuggled close together in the viscount's carriage, a large, boxy, old-fashioned conveyance with sagging springs and well-worn wheels, that bumped its way along the rutted road.

A lap robe wound tight about their knees chased away the chill, and the tufted leather squabs, though old and a bit worn, were still comfortable. Heads bent close, the two eagerly discussed the plans for the afternoon in town.

It was agreed that the first stop was to be Mr. Whitehead, the village clock maker to see if he could fix a pocket watch that had once belonged to Faith's father and was no longer keeping accurate time.

Faith had told Georgie the watch was intended as a gift for Griffin, but it was actually going to be given to Georgie. He had done well with his tutor and worked very hard in learning how to tell time, and Faith felt that the boy deserved a special reward for his efforts.

After the watchmaker, a trip to the cooper was needed so Faith could explain precisely the type of barrels she wanted made for storing household grains.

Following that was a visit to the cobbler to have Georgie's feet measured for a new pair of shoes, and the final stop of the afternoon was to be at the Rose and Thistle Tavern for hot meat pies that would be eaten in the carriage on the ride home.

Faith remembered with mouthwatering delight those flaky, tasty morsels she had eagerly consumed as a child, and was looking forward to the treat almost as much as Georgie.

It was a busy, bustling day in the village and the various errands were accomplished at a leisurely pace. Feeling well pleased with the results, Faith and Georgie strolled down the street toward their final destination, bidding a cordial greeting to several acquaintances as they went. As they rounded the corner they ran into Mrs. Hinkle.

"Have you finished all your business in town yet, my lady?" Mrs. Hinkle asked by way of greeting.

"Nearly." Faith inclined her head as Mrs. Hinkle dipped into a polite curtsy. Faith hoped she responded graciously. It was still difficult to get used to such formality from people she had known since she was a young girl. "I have promised Georgie a treat from the Rose and Thistle."

"A meat pastry?"

"What else?" Faith smiled. "Are you enjoying your afternoon? There seems to be a great number of people about, despite the coolness of the weather."

"Thankfully it is a sunny day, which makes it bearable to be out-of-doors, though my weary bones are suffering from the cold bite of the wind," Mrs. Hinkle said with an exaggerated sigh.

Faith nodded her head. Mrs. Hinkle was firmly set in middle age and had always appeared healthy and robust. Yet for some odd reason the woman seemed to enjoy portraying herself as a frail creature, suffering from every sort of ill, real or imagined.

"The sun does manage to ward off a bit of the chill," Faith replied, knowing better than to inquire about Mrs. Hinkle's health. That conversation could easily take up the rest of the afternoon. But since she lacked a good reason to hurry away, Faith felt compelled to stay and chat for a few moments.

"I heard the vicar is suffering from a particularly nasty cold," Mrs. Hinkle confided. "I sent my maid over with the ingredients for my special herb poultice to ease the tightness in his lungs since I could not visit the poor man myself."

"One cannot be too careful when dealing with illness," Faith agreed. She felt a deliberate tug on her sleeve and glanced down. Georgie gave her a silent, pleading look.

Sympathizing completely with the boy's feelings, Faith began to discreetly peruse the other individuals strolling down the street, hoping to spy someone she could draw into the conversation. Alas, there was no one.

"I see Mrs. Renford is still dressing herself in frills and flounces," Mrs. Hinkle commented as the woman in question stepped into her carriage. "An unfortunate choice of clothing for a woman of her age."

"Mmm," Faith replied in a noncommittal tone. She leaned down and whispered in Georgie's ear, "I'm glad Mrs. Renford has climbed inside her coach. That green feather perched atop her bonnet was bobbing up and down so fast, it was making me seasick."

The little boy put his hand over his mouth, trying to hold back his giggles. He was not successful. The childish mirth brought Mrs. Hinkle's full attention to the boy.

"What do you have to say for yourself, young man?"

Georgie turned uncertain eyes toward Faith. She placed a hand on his shoulder. "Georgie is hoping they have not run out of meat pies at the inn."

"A legitimate concern," Mrs Hinkle agreed. "You should send him along so he may get his pie. It is only across the street."

Faith hesitated a moment, but the look of excitement in the boy's face swayed her. She pulled a coin from her reticule and pressed it into his hand. "Bid Mrs. Hinkle a proper good day," she instructed the child.

Faith glowed with maternal pride as Georgie bent at the waist, one arm clasped to his front, the other to his back.

"My, what a courtly young gentleman," Mrs. Hinkle tittered. "I feel like a royal princess. Where did you learn such fine manners?"

"Mr. Cabot taught me," Georgie replied earnestly.

"The boy's tutor," Faith added in explanation. "I confess I was originally opposed to hiring him, preferring the gentle guidance of a female hand. But the viscount felt strongly that Mr. Cabot should be engaged instead of a governess. I never like to admit being wrong, yet I cannot deny it was a good decision."

Mrs. Hinkle nodded energetically. "Your husband was right, my lady. 'Tis a smart idea to give the child every advantage. I daresay it will stand him in good stead when he gets older, poor mite."

"Um, yes." Faith was distracted from that cryptic statement by Georgie tugging again on her sleeve.

"I'm going now, Mama," he announced. "To buy my meat pies."

"Be careful," Faith called out as the child dashed

across the street. She smiled as Georgie lifted his hand and waved, yet never once broke his stride.

Still smiling, Faith turned toward Mrs. Hinkle. "No matter how many times I tell him to watch where he is running there—Oh goodness, Mrs. Hinkle, are you all right?" Concerned, Faith reached out to steady the older woman, who had suddenly turned pale.

"He called you Mama," Mrs. Hinkle said in astonishment.

"Yes." Faith's chest puffed out with pride. "I'm so pleased. When the viscount and I were first married, Georgie didn't really call me anything, and then later he began calling me Faith. I knew his memories of his natural mother were dim, she died when he was so young, yet I felt it was intrusive to insist that he call me Mama.

"I have longed to be his mother in truth, and I'm glad I waited for Georgie to decide when the time was right. It makes it far more meaningful to me, knowing it was his choice."

"I always knew you were a progressive-thinking young woman, but frankly I am shocked." Mrs. Hinkle blinked rapidly.

"It is hardly an extraordinary occurrence," Faith replied, wondering at Mrs. Hinkle's odd behavior. Perhaps the woman had been imbibing in too many of her own home remedies and they were finally beginning to have an adverse effect on her. "I'm certain there are many children who address a stepparent in the same familiar manner."

Mrs. Hinkle's mouth dropped open. "But he is not a proper stepchild!"

"I beg your pardon?"

"He is illegitimate."

"W-what?"

"The boy is illegitimate. A bastard."

"I know perfectly well what the word means!" Faith dealt Mrs. Hinkle a glare that had sent many a servant scuffing for cover. "I am just overwhelmed that you would speak such vulgar lies in my hearing. How did you ever come up with such a mean, vicious thought? I had always believed you to be a fine Christian woman, Mrs. Hinkle. 'Tis lowering to discover that you are nothing more than a vicious gossipmonger who must fabricate outrageous stories in order to gain attention."

Faith spun on her heel and stalked away. The throbbing of her heart was matched only by the pounding in her head. She could hear the patter of Mrs. Hinkle's shoes as the woman hurried after her.

"Wait, please. Viscountess Dewhurst . . . My lady . . . Faith! Please, wait."

Faith slowed a bit and swallowed hard. She took another step forward, stopped, then wheeled about. Mrs. Hinkle, who was breathing hard, placed a tentative hand on her arm. There was sincerity and distress in the other woman's eyes. A cold shiver of fear ran down Faith's spine.

"Yes?"

"I thought you knew. Please, you must listen." Mrs. Hinkle took in several deep gulps of air. "I am not lying, nor did I fabricate this tale. My brother owns a small clipper ship that trades in the Americas. Nothing as grand as the viscount's business, but it does journey on some of the same routes. Several months ago my brother traveled to Portsmouth to help the captain hire on a new crew.

"One of the men they employed used to sail with your husband. He spoke well of the viscount and pridefully of the captain's little boy. The child that

Lord Dewhurst had recently discovered he had sired and brought to England to raise as his own."

"Recently discovered? I do not understand what you are saying."

Mrs. Hinkle flushed. "Apparently the viscount did not know the boy even existed until his nurse brought him to the ship one day. She was searching for the child's father because his mother had died."

"My husband was captain of one of his ships, traveling for long months at sea. The child was born while he was away on a voyage. Perhaps he was unaware of the pregnancy before he set sail. The viscount once told me that he did not live with Georgie's mother. But that does not make my son illegitimate," Faith retorted frostily.

Mrs. Hinkle shook her head sadly. "Lord Dewhurst did not know of the child because he was never married to the boy's mother."

" 'Tis only sailors' gossip," Faith whispered forcefully, trying to put on a brave face as her heart was twisting in anguish. *It cannot possibly be true. It cannot!*

"Has the viscount ever spoken of the boy's mother?"

"No."

"Or spoken of a prior marriage?"

Mrs. Hinkle's voice was kind, sympathetic. Faith's stomach started churning with fear.

"I am certain you are mistaken," Faith heard herself say. Her voice sounded dull and muffled, as if it came from a great distance.

Mrs. Hinkle shook her head. "I am not trying to be a moralist, though most people will agree it is lowering to be of illegitimate birth. I think it is a fine thing his lordship has done, claiming the child and taking responsibility for him. I'm sure his father's rank and influence will help the boy achieve some level of success in life and society. Perhaps there will be opportunities for him abroad. In the Americas."

Faith forced her mind to clear, to concentrate. Georgie sent off to the Americas? Living his life across the ocean where they would never see him? It was unthinkable. Oh, dear Lord, she had to get away from Mrs. Hinkle. Now.

"I cannot discuss this any more," Faith said numbly. "Good afternoon, Mrs. Hinkle."

Faith fled without a backward glance, nearly crying with relief when she saw Georgie emerge from the inn, his small hands filled with meat pies wrapped in clean linen cloths.

She bent low and snatched the boy to her chest, hugging him tightly, seeking to shield him from this horrible truth. Trying to hide him, protect him from the inevitable hurt he would experience.

"Careful, Mama," Georgie said, trying to pull himself out of her grasp. "The pies are hot."

"Hurry, now." Faith choked out. "We must hurry home."

Without waiting for an answer, Faith dragged the little boy toward the carriage, startling the coachman and footman at her unexpected, early arrival.

"Take us home," she shouted. "Immediately."

She boosted the child into the coach and jumped in after him, not bothering to wait for the footman's assistance. When she heard the door close behind her, Faith spread her hands over her hot cheeks. Then she glanced across the carriage at a very puzzled little boy.

"I brought you a pastry, too," Georgie said, hesitantly holding out the treat.

Faith's vision blurred. That sweet, innocent face. A pit of bottomless despair opened in her heart.

"Please don't cry, Mama." Georgie reached over and patted her hand awkwardly. "I saved the better pie for you. I don't mind eating the one that is squashed."

"Where is the viscount, Gregory?" Faith asked, tugging off her gloves and tossing them at the footman who stood beside the butler.

"The library, my lady," the butler replied. "Shall I escort you?"

"Don't be an idiot," Faith snapped. A slightly raised brow was the only reaction she received from the stiff-necked butler. The footman was not as well trained. His lower jaw sagged noticeably. "Is my husband alone?"

"I believe so. Would it be idiotic of me to offer to check, my lady?" the butler inquired.

Faith's forehead wrinkled. "One more insolent remark and you shall find yourself walking the streets, searching for employment without a proper reference. Is that idiotic enough for you, Gregory?"

She thrust her cloak at the butler and stalked away, not caring that the butler was now suitably shocked at her bizarre outburst. Her mood had swung from despair to grief to humiliation, settling lastly on anger. And anyone who was foolish enough to provoke her temper the merest fraction would suffer her full wrath. Including her servants.

Faith entered the library in a huff and discovered that Griffin was in fact alone. He was seated comfortably in front of the fire, reading a book.

"Back so soon, my dear?"

She reached out and slammed the door. It shut with a resounding bang. "Tell me about Georgie's mother," Faith commanded.

Griffin slowly closed his book and politely rose to his feet. The expression on his face was wary, unreadable.

"Is there a particular reason why you are suddenly so curious?" the viscount inquired.

Faith stared hard at him for a moment, then moved forward until she stood nearly toe to toe with her tall, impressive husband. "Tell me."

Griffin's eyes narrowed fractionally. "Georgie's mother was an American from South Carolina. The daughter of a successful merchant that I had business dealings with for several years."

"What was her name?"

"Rosemary."

Faith flushed a deep, furious red. "What was her *last name?* Not her family name, but her name upon her death. It was not Sainthill, I'd wager."

Griffin moved over and tried to take Faith's arm. She shrugged him off. "Sit down," he said forcefully.

Faith hesitated, then sat. But she lifted her chin defiantly and glared daggers at her husband.

"Rosemary Morton and I engaged in an intimate relationship for several months, then parted on amicable terms. Business kept me away from South Carolina for several years after our relationship ended, and when I returned I discovered that Rosemary had died."

"Were you in love with her?"

"No." Griffin's eyes were shadowed, dark with reserve. "It wasn't that sort of relationship."

"You had a child together!" Faith retorted.

His raised brow told her how foolish he thought that statement. "I did not know Rosemary was pregnant. If I had, perhaps things might have turned out differently."

"You were never married to her, were you?"

"No."

" 'Tis true, then." All the bluster drained out of Faith. "Georgie is a bastard, destined to lead a life where doors of opportunity will be slammed in his face. He will never be fully accepted in society; instead, he will be forced to exist on the fringes." The chill around Faith's heart grew colder. "My God, what will happen to him?"

"I will educate him, settle a generous yearly allowance on him when he reaches maturity, perhaps set him up in a business if he so desires. He is my son and shall always remain so, despite the circumstances of his birth."

It took a tremendous amount of inner fortitude to keep her eyes from sliding away from Griffin's pained gaze. She would *not* feel sorry for him.

"Is there nothing else we can do? Perhaps there is some way to make him legitimate?" Faith asked desperately.

Griffin sighed. "I have already consulted a solicitor. It will take some time, and money, but Georgie can be adopted. He will legally bear my name and be known as a Sainthill. However, he can never inherit my title."

Faith flinched. A tense silence settled between them. Something cold and dark started growing in her chest until it could no longer be contained.

"Damn you!" Faith swore loudly and thumped her fist down hard on the cushion of her chair. "You should have told me, Griffin. You should have trusted me enough to confide in me."

Griffin turned and walked restlessly to the window. "At first, my only thought was to protect the boy. Given the unusual circumstances of our marriage I felt it best to remain silent. I feared the truth would be revealed all too soon anyway. And so it has."

"Oh, yes, the truth is now known." Faith's eyes blazed with indignation. "And it should not matter that I was told this truth not by my husband, the child's father, but by an acquaintance, in the middle of the street, on market day. Can you even fathom how dreadful that made me feel?"

Griffin shrugged his shoulders helplessly. He met her gaze, then shifted uncomfortably. "I thought I had more time. I never dreamed that anyone would discover the truth. Harriet—"

"Harriet knows?" Faith shrieked, popping up from her chair.

"We have never spoken directly about it, but clearly she does not believe I ever had a wife while I lived abroad."

"I suppose Elizabeth is aware of the truth, too." Griffin nodded, and Faith threw up her hands in mock despair. "I guess that makes me the only gullible fool in the household."

"Faith, you are making too much of this," Griffin said. "I apologize for my lack of judgment, but I thought I was doing what was best for the child."

Faith slowly sank down into her chair. She could feel a glow of humiliation heating the back of her neck, but it did not matter. Nothing seemed to matter. How could she have been so wrong, so incredibly stupid?

The trust she had worked so hard to reclaim was a mere illusion, the dream of one day building a strong, healthy marriage a mockery to her naïveté. It had been doomed from the start, from the moment she had realized Griffin was only marrying her because he believed she had been compromised.

"You must think me a gruesome creature indeed to keep this from me for so long," she said softly.

Tears prickled so hard at the back of Faith's eyes that she had to swallow three times to hold them back. For she would not cry. This final lesson had revealed the inner core of Griffin's feelings for her, and she would not shed one more tear over him.

She rose silently to her feet. Pride kept her head held high, but her heart was weighed down with so much pain it really did not matter.

"Did Georgie also discover the truth today?" Griffin inquired anxiously.

"No, thank goodness. Though I doubt he would understand it. For him *bastard* is just another word. Yet I fear all too soon he will understand its meaning." Faith let out an ironic laugh. "He saw that I was very upset this afternoon, but he thought I was crying because the meat pies had been squashed."

Griffin managed a weak smile. "Where is he now?"

"In the stable with Higgins. He wanted to help rub down the carriage horses and then visit with the kittens. They have grown so much it takes him a while to catch them." Faith placed her palm against her forehead and discovered her hand was trembling. "I need to gather a few personal items from my room. I'll say good-bye to him out there."

"Good-bye?"

Faith swallowed, but the sick feeling in her stomach did not vanish. "I need to be away for a while. I shall return home, to Mayfair Manor."

The viscount reached out and cupped her chin, forcing her to look at him. "Is that really necessary?"

"I do not know what else to do," she whispered.

His silver eyes flashed with fire, yet his fingers

were gentle as they caressed her cheek. He abruptly released her face. "Perhaps it would be best."

Faith closed her eyes briefly as a fresh wave of pain washed over her. It suddenly seemed so real, so final.

"You will allow Georgie to visit me each day." It was not a question.

Griffin bowed his head solemnly. "I would not keep him from you."

"Thank you."

There was nothing left to say. With the politeness of strangers, the viscount escorted his wife out of the library and deposited her at the foot of the main staircase.

He gave her a low, courtly bow, so reminiscent of Georgie she had to bite her lip hard to keep from bursting into sobs. Faith watched his retreating back with blank, expressionless eyes, fighting valiantly the lump that had formed in her throat. Then she turned and slowly climbed the stairs, feeling like a woman eighty years of age.

The first few days of Faith's absence passed slowly. Griffin deliberately kept himself busy from morning till night, hoping to lose himself in his work, but it seemed that everything he came into contact with reminded him of his wife.

Her subtle scent lingered in their bedchamber; the embroidery piece she had been stitching was in the sewing basket in the sitting room. The day lilies arranged in the Chinese porcelain vase in the entrance hall were her favorite flower. The new draperies for the dining room that had been hung were her favorite shade of blue.

Even the discovery of a discrepancy for payment

of household goods by a former estate manager two years prior reminded Griffin of Faith. Would she be as passionately annoyed as when they had discovered Mr. White's duplicity? Griffin wondered. Or would she no longer care about the fate of the estate she had forsaken?

Outwardly the household did not suffer. The servants performed their duties efficiently and satisfactorily. Meals were prepared and served on time, the linens were changed and the bedding aired each Wednesday, the silver polished each Thursday.

After a long, exhausting day Griffin would sit in the drawing room with his sisters, a fire crackling cozily in the hearth. Elizabeth would play the pianoforte or Harriet would read aloud from one of her favorite books, and the three siblings would quietly pass the time.

This was no different from the way Griffin had spent many a winter's evening, and yet try as he might the viscount was unable to recapture that comfortable, restful, contented feeling he normally enjoyed.

Instead, he would lean back in his chair, sip his brandy, and try not to indulge in depressing thoughts. In these quiet, contemplative moments, a terrifying sense of loss would grip him, and Griffin was finally forced to admit that with Faith gone Hawthorne Castle was no longer a home. 'Twas merely a residence.

Initially he had arrogantly assumed she would be gone only a day or two. He understood her emotions were raw; he knew that she had been hurt, though he did not understand why she needed to be away from him to cope with her distress.

As the days passed into a week Griffin was beginning to think he had handled the situation badly. It seemed the longer his wife was gone the more she wanted to stay away.

However, true to his word, the viscount had arranged for Georgie to visit Mayfair Manor each afternoon. To his astonishment, it was his own two sisters, Harriet and Elizabeth, who volunteered to accompany the boy on the short journey.

Most days they stayed for tea, and occasionally later, arriving home as dusk settled. Worse, when the trio finally returned they never spoke of Faith, except to comment that she looked well and appeared content. Hungry for news of his errant wife, Griffin thought to corner his son and shamelessly pump the boy for information, but in the end his conscience would not allow it.

"I am home, Papa!" Georgie's eager young voice echoed through the entrance foyer.

The viscount's mouth curved wryly. Even if he had not been watching through the front parlor window he would have known of his son's return. The boy made as much noise as ten children.

Georgie made his way into the room, with Elizabeth trailing behind him. Griffin knew better than to ask about Faith, knowing he would receive the usual bland response. He grimaced. A lesser man would surely begin to think he was living amongst a nest of ungrateful traitors.

"I was wondering where you had gotten to," Griffin remarked after he hugged the child in greeting. " 'Tis nearly dark. I'll wager that Georgie's supper has grown cold waiting for him."

"I'm sorry." Elizabeth nervously twisted her fingers together. "The road was extremely muddy after last night's rain, so the coach had to proceed slowly and carefully to avoid getting stuck."

The viscount pressed his lips together, effectively squashing the urge to bark a reply. His chest tightened with a restless, unfamiliar emotion, and Griffin wondered if his sister also felt this uncustomary awkwardness between them.

"I don't care about my supper. I'm not hungry," Georgie announced. "I ate three pastries and one apple tart today. Mama's cook said she has never met a little boy who likes to eat as much as me."

"It does a father's heart proud to hear of such a boastful accomplishment," Griffin declared.

Georgie nodded proudly. Then his face took on a serious expression. "I like to visit Mama and I like to eat the treats the cook makes for me. But I liked it better when she was here all the time. Why does she stay at the other house?"

Griffin shook his head. He could think of no answer to give his son.

"Do you think she left because she was mad at me?" Georgie inquired anxiously. "For letting my kittens get in her sitting room and wet the floor? Mistletoe made a big mess."

A rash of guilt swamped the viscount as he beheld the wounded look in his son's eyes. He had not realized the full impact this quarrel was having on the boy.

"I'm sure she has forgotten all about that," Griffin said firmly.

Georgie frowned, then wrinkled his nose. "It smelled really bad."

"Mrs. Hodges cleaned the carpet thoroughly," Griffin told the child, but he could see that answer did not satisfy the little boy. "Mama loves you very much. No matter what happens, you must never forget that, Georgie."

There was a short silence. "I want her to come home."

"So do I," Griffin muttered.

"Perhaps you should visit Faith," Elizabeth suggested timidly.

Griffin looked at her sharply. "Why? So she may have a chance to turn me away? Or better still, invite me in and then ignore me?"

"Oh, I am certain she would never do that," Elizabeth replied emphatically.

Griffin immediately straightened his spine. "Has she said something to you? About me?"

"Well, er, not exactly," Elizabeth hedged.

"Mama called Papa a horse's arse," Georgie piped up in a helpful voice. "I heard her whisper that to Aunt Harriet."

Elizabeth cast a worried look in Griffin's direction. "I am sure you must have misheard, dear."

"Oh, no, that's what she said," Georgie replied earnestly.

The viscount's mouth curved in a small grin. At least he knew Faith was still angry with him. A far better state of affairs than total apathy or disinterest. Perhaps now was the right time to make a move. "I believe Aunt Elizabeth is correct. 'Tis time for me to journey to Mayfair Manor to speak with Faith."

"Will you bring her back, Papa? Please?"

Georgie's hopeful expression tempered Griffin's confidence. How humbling to realize his son's well-being involved far more than providing adequate housing, clothing, and food. The child needed a mother.

"I shall do everything possible to persuade her to come of her own accord," Griffin declared. "And if that does not work, I suppose I will have to throw her over my shoulder and carry her out by force."

He had spoken the last words jokingly, attempting to coax a smile from Georgie, and the boy did indeed giggle. However, when dealing with his stubborn, headstrong wife, Griffin was astute enough to realize that physical force might be the only way to gain his objective.

Twenty

Griffin arrived at Mayfield Manor by the light of the rising moon. He reined his horse in front of the portico, taking a brief moment to admire the simple, clean architectural lines fronting the stone entrance. Swinging down from the saddle he waited until a young footman emerged from the house.

"Good evening, sir," the young man said. "Can I be of some assistance?"

Griffin turned and realized with a start that the servant had no idea who he was. It was a rather humbling, somewhat disquieting experience. Deciding not to identify himself, the viscount tossed the fellow his reins.

"Be careful when you handle my horse," he instructed. "It usually takes him a few minutes to settle down after a hard gallop."

"Yes, sir." The young man obediently took a step back from the dancing hooves. Then he cautiously led the snorting animal off toward the stables in the rear of the manor.

Griffin waited until the servant was gone before climbing the steps leading to the front door. The last thing he wanted was an audience. It was galling enough to have to admit to himself that he had come to see his errant wife in hopes of convincing her to return home.

The maid who answered the door stared very hard at the card Griffin presented her. For a moment he thought she might be unable to read it, but the way she scampered off after telling him to please wait a moment let him know that at least she knew exactly who he was.

He cooled his heels in the entrance foyer for several long minutes, studying the painted ceiling. It was a whimsical scene of various mythical Roman gods majestically displayed against a deep blue sky. It was not difficult to identify many of them, though he found his eyes continually drawn to Venus, Cupid, and Psyche.

Griffin was beginning to think he had been forgotten when he heard muffled voices coming from the other side of the foyer. An older, stout woman emerged from behind a heavy wooden door and rushed toward him.

He recognized her as Mrs. Craig, the housekeeper, a servant who would not give him any information about Faith's whereabouts when he had followed his wife to London those many months ago.

Donning a pleasant smile, Griffin braced himself for the inevitable clash.

"Good evening, my lord." She dipped him a quick curtsy. "I regret to inform you that her ladyship is not at home."

"Not at home?" He allowed the skepticism to creep into his voice. "Are you certain?"

"Oh, yes. Quite certain." The housekeeper blushed. "I'm sorry that you have come all this way, and at this time of night, for nothing."

Griffin balled his hands into tight fists. "So she refuses to see me?" He stared at the deepening blush on the housekeeper's face. "Is she here?"

"Pardon?"

"Is my wife here, in the house, or has she gone out for the evening?"

He did not yell or scream or threaten when he spoke, though in truth he wanted to do all three. He merely asked the question. But the housekeeper took a noticeable step back from him. Her eyes lowered guiltily and she began wringing her dimpled hands.

It was all the answer he needed. "Will you show me to the drawing room, please? I believe I would like to wait in there. And do inform Lady Dewhurst that is where I shall be, long into the night if necessary."

There was a brief pause. The housekeeper heaved a shudder. She looked to the cowering maid who stood behind her, but the young girl merely shrugged.

"This way, my lord."

The housekeeper silently led the way. As they walked through the house Griffin surveyed the well cared-for furnishings, took notice of the thick Persian carpets, the valuable paintings, and expensive antiques.

For a moment he felt a brief unease. In many ways Mayfair Manor was grander than Hawthorne Castle. It was certainly better maintained. And possessed that elusive quality he so missed now that Faith was gone. Mayfair Manor felt like a true home.

The drawing room was a very formal affair, done in shades of gold. Yet it was tasteful without being opulent. He removed the coat Mrs. Craig had not offered to take from him and carelessly tossed it over a chair. Then he explored the room with interest for several moments.

The walls were covered in gold-flecked paper that matched exactly the shades on the upholstered pieces of furniture. There was an ornate marble mantel upon which a variety of porcelain figures and a dainty gold and porcelain clock rested.

Mrs. Craig had grudgingly lit a few of the candles before leaving, and they cast a merry, twinkling glow about the room. Griffin settled himself upon the gold brocade sofa, crossed his right ankle atop his left knee, and absently drummed on his leg.

He idly wondered how long Faith would keep him waiting and then realized it didn't matter. He had managed to talk his way through the front door and was now comfortably ensconced in her drawing room. It would take no less than an army of burly servants to physically remove him.

Yet despite his vow to be patient, after a full half hour of waiting Griffin was starting to grow restless. He knew all too well the timbre of his wife's stubborn streak. If she had a mind to, she would leave him there all night.

The viscount was trying to decide how much longer he would wait before beginning a room-to-room search of the manor when the drawing-room door opened.

He lifted his chin and gazed at the woman in the doorway. Faith. His heart melted at the sight of her. She was wearing a simple gown of pale ivory he had never seen before. It was high waisted and gathered beneath her breasts with a long blue ribbon. Both the style and shade of the gown highlighted the natural paleness of her skin.

Her hair was swept up off her neck, the soft brown curls piled on the crown of her head, cascading gently down her back. Her throat was bare, her neck long, graceful, and regal.

Her face looked lean and a bit tired. There were traces of darkness beneath her eyes. Not quite circles, but evidence of restless nights.

Griffin thought she looked more beautiful than he had ever seen her. His body tightened painfully, reminding him of how many recent nights he had spent alone in bed.

"Good evening." He rose to his feet, hoping he looked more confident than he felt.

She gave him a steely glare instead of returning the greeting. Griffin felt his palms begin to sweat.

"Mrs. Craig informs me that you insisted on being shown into the drawing room, even after she informed you that I was not at home. Why?"

"I wanted, nay, I needed to see you."

She looked down at her fingers. "I thought we agreed that I needed time alone. Away from you."

"I have given you that time."

"It has only been a week."

"It feels like a lifetime."

"Oh, please." She brought her hand to her hip and cast him a cynical glare. "There is certainly no need for all of *that*."

He blinked. Ever since he had stormed out of Hawthorne Castle after promising his son he would bring Faith home, Griffin had been thinking about what he would say to her and how she would react to his tender words of need. He had imagined her face going soft with emotion, her eyes brightening with delight, her arms flinging joyfully around his neck as she pressed herself closer to receive his kisses.

Never in his wildest imaginings had he expected such coldness, such indifference. Well, not precisely indifference. If given the chance, Faith appeared to be ready to fling a variety of breakable objects at his head.

Griffin paused and cleared his throat. "I want you to come home with me, Faith. Tonight."

"No." Her expression never altered. "Not tonight."

"When?" he asked, almost desperately.

"I am not certain."

Her cool composure was starting to eat away at him. She seemed so untouchable, so unattainable, so very much unlike the woman he knew her to be. When Griffin realized he would prefer to be dodging hurling objects than facing those frigid eyes, he knew he had lost complete control of the situation.

Desperate times call for desperate measures.

"I love you, Faith."

Her eyes flew open in shock. Some of the tightness left her features. With a feeling of triumph, the viscount waited for her lips to soften, her eyes to light with joy and excitement. He barely resisted the urge to open his arms wide so she could throw herself into them.

The delicate porcelain clock on the mantel ticked away. There were no other sounds in the room except the rise and fall of their breathing. Faith seemed unaware and unconcerned about the silence that was stretching longer and longer.

He moved closer, reaching for her hands. "I said I love you," Griffin repeated.

"I heard you," she said, tugging her fingers out of his grip.

He tightened his grip. She pulled harder, but he would not let go.

Her expression grew annoyed. "How dare you bully your way into my home, command that I leave, and then calmly announce that you love me? Do you think that really changes anything? Because you now suddenly claim to love me, that gives you the right to abuse me? To keep secrets from me? Secrets about our child. I think not, my lord."

Griffin abruptly dropped her hands. He had promised himself that he would not get angry, would not lose his temper, but Faith was pushing him to complete frustration with her attitude.

"I have explained my reasons for keeping the truth about Georgie from you." Griffin looked at his wife helplessly. "I have apologized. I . . . I—"

With a muttered curse, Griffin turned and stalked away. She wasn't really listening; she was still judging him. She was hurt and angry and confused. And in a most ironic twist of the absurd, Griffin understood those feelings. Hell, he even agreed that she was entitled to them. Well, some of them.

The night air felt cold and bitter. He was forced to wait on the front steps for several minutes while his mount was retrieved from the stables, but the respite helped to clear his muddled head and calm his rising ire.

The viscount swung into the saddle without assistance, forgetting to toss the young footman a coin. Once clear of the gravel drive, Griffin let the horse run hard, galloping through a shortcut in the fields.

The full, bright moon and star-filled sky lit the way back to the castle. As he rode, Griffin, no longer feeling tongue-tied, thought of all the things he should have said to his wife. How he should have been more forceful in expressing the depth of his feelings and less demanding in his expectations of her behavior.

And yet, though she did not express it, Griffin had formulated the clear impression that Faith expected him to somehow prove his love. Not just express it.

Exactly how that was to be accomplished was a true mystery. What male ever truly understood the complex workings of a female mind? Not to mention the intricate, unstable feminine emotions?

Griffin suddenly smiled. For so many years he thought himself to be a great connoisseur of women. What a joke! Faced now with the challenge of winning over his wife, he realized all he could do was to lumber along clumsily and pray that he would eventually get it right.

With a single-minded purpose, the viscount set about preparing himself to accomplish this all-important task.

Faith sat alone in the drawing room a long time after Griffin left, her emotions in complete turmoil. She had truly not expected him to come to the manor. He had made no real protest when she had left the castle, simply allowing her to leave.

He had not written, had not sent any messages with his sisters when they came each day to call. During her afternoon teas with Elizabeth and Harriet, Faith had asked only a few, vague questions about her husband, usually inquiring politely after his health.

She had been told that he was well, working as hard as usual, eating properly at meals, keeping regular hours at night. As though she had never left, or worse, had never once been a part of his life.

And then he had arrived. The moment Faith set eyes on him she couldn't decide if she wanted to cry or scream or throw her arms around his neck and never let go.

She had not wanted to see him. And when she finally did, she had wanted to look away. To turn her head and pretend he wasn't standing before her, forcing her to face the emotions she was trying so hard to tame.

She hurt so badly it was nearly impossible to maintain her composure. His declaration of love had shocked her. Never in her deepest longings had she thought to hear him speak those words aloud. And yet they had not brought the rush of joy and emotion she had always expected.

She knew Griffin believed he was being sincere, truthful. Yet she wondered at his sudden epiphany of emotions, fearing it was born out of guilt.

That was not what she wanted. She wanted his love to be born from the same burning emotions that engulfed her, wanted him to feel that same desperate need that she did, wanted him to realize they could nourish their hopes for the future and fulfill their dreams only if they were together.

So she had steeled herself to coldness, showing almost no reaction. Which had been by far the most difficult thing Faith had ever done. Because despite all that had happened Faith knew that she was utterly and hopelessly in love with her husband.

Griffin returned to Mayfair Manor two days later. He did not march up to the front doors and demand to see his wife as he had done on his previous visit. Instead he sat upon his horse and waited for nearly two hours in a grove of bare trees, knowing she would eventually emerge from the manor house.

It was Thursday, and on Thursday Faith always paid a call on the vicar and his wife. Griffin suspected that despite her temporary change of residence, his wife would adhere to her usual routine whenever possible.

So with a hopeful heart and a charming smile, Griffin intercepted her carriage the moment it rolled out of the gravel drive.

It took no effort to get the coachman to stop. By the time Faith poked her head out of the window to investigate the delay, Griffin had secured his mount to the rear of the coach.

"Good afternoon, Faith."

"Griffin!" She lifted her head so suddenly it almost hit the top of the window. "Is something wrong?"

"No." He walked to the carriage door and leaned nonchalantly against it. Her eyes widened.

"I am on my way out," she said unnecessarily.

"To see the vicar and his wife?"

She stiffened, then blinked. "How did you know that?"

Griffin's charming smile deepened. "I make it my business to know about things that concern you, my dear." He resisted the urge to tap his finger to her nose. "I should like to accompany you on your visit this afternoon. If you have no objection?"

A grim expression flashed in Faith's eyes. "I thought riding in an enclosed carriage made you ill."

"I believe I can tolerate a short journey. As long as John Coachman manages to avoid the larger ruts in the road."

"I'll do my best, my lord," the burly coachman promised.

"Faith?"

With wary resignation she inclined her head. "As you wish."

The viscount climbed into the coach and boldly took the seat next to his wife. The carriage lurched, along with his stomach, but the driver proved true to his word and skillfully avoided the larger dips and bumps.

Faith sat silently. Griffin was very much aware of her sitting beside him. He could feel his own heartbeat thumping in his chest. For several long moments the only sounds were the steady clopping of the horse's hooves and the rattling rhythm of the wheels.

Faith kept her eyes fastened on the passing landscape. He wondered briefly what could possibly be so fascinating. Had she not traveled this stretch of country road a countless number of times?

After a few minutes Griffin realized, with some surprise, that he did not mind the silence. It was not oppressive nor overwrought with tension. It was almost soothing, and preferable, if one considered the tone, direction, and results of the last few conversations he and Faith had undertaken.

Inspired, the viscount reached down and clasped her gloved hand. Faith made a sudden strangled sound deep in the back of her throat. She flexed her fingers, but did not pull away.

Griffin slid his thumb across the palm of her hand and then back again. Faith closed her eyes and shuddered.

The viscount smiled broadly.

Tea with the vicar and his wife was a pleasant, uneventful occasion. The two couples spoke of local events and mutual acquaintances, the fine weather, and the coming spring.

However, as they left, the vicar's wife beamed at them with such patent approval Griffin knew the gossip mill had been churning madly. Most of the village knew that Faith was living away from him, at Mayfair Manor.

Now they would hear that the viscount and his wife were reconciled. Griffin dared to hope that perhaps today they had taken the first step toward making that a reality.

When the coach arrived back at Mayfair, he escorted Faith up the stone steps and deposited her at the door.

"Squire Jordan has promised me first crack at his new foals," Griffin said in a casual voice. "I would be honored if you would accompany me tomorrow when I make my selections."

Faith stared at him in some surprise. "I am hardly an expert on horses. You should take Higgins along."

"I do not need assistance or advice in choosing the animals." Griffin gave her a lazy, teasing grin. "But I could use some help haggling over the prices."

Faith took a deep breath. "I shall be ready at noon."

He tipped his hat politely. And left.

It went on for six days. Trips to the village to savor the meat pies at the Rose and Thistle Tavern, strolls in the wintry garden at Mayfair Manor, even a shopping expedition on market day where he teased her for looking at nearly everything and purchasing almost nothing.

They talked, they laughed, they even argued a bit. They spoke cautiously of the past and optimistically of the future. But they continued to live in separate houses.

The seventh day dawned clear and bright and unseasonably warm. By prearrangement Griffin arrived at one to take his wife riding. She was fashionably dressed in a green velvet riding habit with a small matching bonnet that he thought made her look especially fetching.

But it was her welcoming smile that warmed the viscount's heart.

They started out at a slow trot, following a well-worn path between their properties for nearly a mile. Yet the moment they reached a clearing, Faith dug in her booted heels and made a mad dash across the field.

With a startled laugh, Griffin took up the challenge of the race. The element of surprise had given Faith a good lead and it took considerable skill to catch her.

They galloped in tandem, each straining to be the first to pull ahead. In a burst of speed, Griffin managed to nose forward. He heard Faith laugh. The sound distracted him enough that she was able to overtake him. And win the race.

Her eyes were sparkling with excitement as they walked the horses to cool them down, but she was gracious in victory and limited her gloating to a few choice words.

Soon they came upon a small dwelling.

"My goodness, I had no idea this was still standing," Faith exclaimed.

Griffin considered the whimsical structure before them, a white-columned Grecian temple, designed and constructed by one of his ancestors. He remembered fondly running between those ivy-covered columns and playing in the many alcoves as a child.

"Shall we see if any of the stone statues remain intact?" Griffin asked.

Faith nodded. He tied the horses' reins around a small tree trunk and they climbed the steps together. The interior was in decent repair considering that the temple was open on all sides and thus exposed to the seasonal elements. The tall statues of Greek gods and goddesses were still standing, but the legs of the stone bench were broken and crumbling.

They had no blanket, so Griffin removed his greatcoat and spread it on the floor.

"How gallant," Faith murmured as she settled herself primly on the edge.

" 'Tis just a small part in my grand plan." He sat beside her, focusing fully on her face. "I am certain by now that you have surmised my plan for this past week. I am trying to woo you, my dearest."

Her left eyebrow shot up in interest. "With gifts? Do you have a jewel box stuffed in your coat pocket?"

"Jewels are for men with no confidence," he scoffed.

"Flowers perhaps?"

"A rose for true love?" He shook his head. "Too trite and obvious."

"Sweets, then? You know how I enjoy my confections."

"Sweets are for boys to give to girls. I am long beyond boyhood and you are very much a woman."

She lowered her chin, but not before he saw her smile. "Far be it from me to tell you, a confirmed rake and scoundrel, how to successfully woo a woman, my lord. But I do feel compelled to point out that I am not at all impressed with your efforts this afternoon."

His face was all innocence. "I let you win our race."

She blustered with feigned indignity and he laughed. Then Griffin twisted around, placing his hands on her face. "Shall I tell you that I love you? Ah, but I have already done that and my words did not make a very good impression. So I shall tell you that you are beautiful. Now, don't scrunch up your face like that, dearest, 'tis not very flattering."

With effort, Faith lost her scowl.

"I have written you a poem," Griffin declared.

"Really?" She bit down on her bottom lip to keep from laughing.

He cleared his throat. *"Roses are red, violets are blue, my life is incomplete, without you."*

"Do not tell me you that you composed that entirely on your own?"

"I did. 'Tis a fine piece. A true gem of literary endeavor. Don't you agree?"

"It sounds as if Georgie wrote it. On a day he had a toothache or some other dreadful ailment." Her eyes twinkled brightly with amusement. "Lord Byron need never fear any competition from you."

"Then I shall dispense with the rhymes and speak from my heart."

Griffin bent his head forward, pressing soft kisses along the line of her jaw until he reached her ear. Then he carefully sank his teeth into the plump lobe.

"You are not speaking, Griffin," Faith said breathlessly. "You are nibbling."

"I am setting the mood," he replied. His hand slipped up to Faith's cheek, caressing it softly.

Then he turned and angled her head so he could gaze deeply into her eyes.

"I love you, Faith," he said in quiet seriousness. "It has taken me far too long to realize it and far too long to say it. But it is the truth. And it is too precious a gift to waste."

She swallowed and nodded, saying nothing in return. But there was a light of tenderness and understanding and acceptance in her eyes that made his heart lurch with joy.

"We did not marry for love or even affection," Griffin continued. "Through misunderstandings and your father's blasted will we suddenly found ourselves bound together as man and wife. And for a very long time I thought that was not what I wanted. I thought *you* were not want I wanted."

He paused. "But I was wrong. You are mine, Faith. Oddly, I cannot envision myself married to any other woman. 'Tis almost as if I have no control over the matter, for my heart has dictated it and I find I have no choice but to comply.

"I have discovered this past week that love is not easy. But loving you is. And I know with true certainty that I want to share my life with you, create a home with you, have children with you. Only with you."

His mouth hovered over hers. There was a moment's pause before their lips met. Softness, tenderness, gentleness. It was not a kiss of passion, but a pledge of commitment, a promise of love.

A lone tear forged a path down Faith's cheek. Her heart, nay her very soul, had recognized the difference.

"Ask me," she whispered brokenly in his ear. "Please, ask me."

Griffin drew back. There was a heartbeat of silence. "Will you come home with me? Today? And spend the next fifty or so years waking by my side each morning?"

"It would be my greatest pleasure." She searched his face and met his eyes with a loving promise. "For I find that I am very much in love with you, and try as I might I cannot imagine surviving the next fifty years without you beside me to drive me witless."

Epilogue

Hawthorne Castle
3 Months Later

"Papa! You must come at once. Mistletoe is stuck in a tree and Aunt Elizabeth won't let me climb up and get her!"

Griffin lifted his head lazily from his wife's lap. They were sprawled comfortably beneath the shade of a towering oak, with the remnants of a picnic lunch sharing a portion of the blanket they were reclining upon.

The sky was a brilliant blue, dotted with a few puffy white clouds floating on a gentle spring breeze. It was quiet, save for the chirping of insects and the occasional hum of an adventurous bee. And the boisterous antics of Georgie.

Griffin turned and saw his son circling the base of a large tree, hopping excitedly from one foot to the other, while his two aunts tried to distract him. *Fat chance.* Griffin smiled.

"The cat will come down from the tree when she has decided it is time," the viscount called out loudly.

Faith giggled. "I think that poor kitten scampers away whenever it can, trying to avoid all the attention Georgie lavishes upon her."

"Most likely." Griffin smiled.

"But she might get hurt," Georgie whined.

Griffin propped himself up on one elbow. "Then you may help Higgins bandage her up and she can sleep in a box beside your bed so you may take proper care of her."

There was a long pause. "Really? Mistletoe could sleep in my room?"

"If necessary."

"Oh, Griffin, what a thing to promise the child. Now he will constantly be imagining that poor cat is ill so he can take care of it."

The viscount sat up. "He has to catch her first. Fortunately she is a very nimble and quick animal."

Faith laughed again. "You are incorrigible," she mused affectionately.

The viscount shrugged philosophically. He lazily arched his back, enjoying the serenity and contentment of the afternoon. Placing his fingers inside one of the smaller baskets, Griffin pulled out a handful of small, red strawberries.

"Would you like one?" he asked his wife as he once again reclined on the blanket. "Or is your stomach still giving you trouble?"

"Please don't remind me," Faith bowed her head and flushed with embarrassment.

It had been a most humiliating start to the day. The nausea and queasiness had come upon Faith so suddenly this morning she had time only to throw off the bed linen, lean over the side of the bed, and grab for the chamber pot.

Since she had not eaten anything that morning there wasn't very much to expel from her stomach, but she had retched and convulsed for what felt like hours.

Between bouts of heaving, she had shouted, cried,

and pleaded with her husband to go away. But the viscount would not leave her to suffer in peace. Instead he had calmly and quite offhandedly pulled the heavy strands of damp hair off her neck, tucking them behind her ears.

Then he climbed on the bed beside her, held the chamber pot with one hand, and rubbed her back soothingly with the other. When finally the shuddering ended he had settled her upright against the pillows, disposed of the meager contents in the pot, and wiped her face and forehead with a cool, clean cloth.

By then Faith had felt too limp and drained to protest. Upon her request, Griffin had opened their bedroom window to let in some cool, fresh air and brought a glass of water so she could rinse out her mouth.

And then he had the gall to tell her, with a most sincere and tender expression, that she was the most extraordinary, remarkable, beautiful woman in the world and he loved her beyond reason.

Faith had promptly thrown her damp cloth at him.

"The post has just arrived, my lady," a dignified voice said. "Since there were several letters I thought you might like to read them out here."

Faith scrambled to an upright position and lifted the neat packet from the silver tray. "Thank you, Gregory. That was most considerate of you to walk all this way."

"It was no trouble at all." The butler bowed low, then began the considerable walk back to the castle.

Griffin popped a berry into his mouth, rolled onto his back, and gave his wife a considering look. "What exactly have you done to Gregory? He is even more stiff-backed and formal than the stuffiest town butler."

Faith smiled mysteriously, remembering the threat of sacking him without a reference. She had flung it out in the heat of emotion, but it had made a lasting impression. Ever since that incident, Gregory had been the most respectful of servants.

Faith shifted her position so she could relax against the tree trunk while reading her correspondence. With a contented sigh she stretched out her legs, crossed her ankles, and began thumbing through the pile in her lap.

"Oh, my goodness." Her breath caught in surprise. She pulled a missive out of the pile, turning it over and over in her hand. "There is a letter for Harriet!"

Faith and Griffin stared at each other for a long moment. "I'll get her." The viscount sprang from his prone position and hurried off.

"Have you finally come to get Mistletoe down from the tree, Papa?"

Faith only heard Georgie's question, not her husband's answer. She was still too amazed by the extraordinary sight before her to think of much else.

Griffin and his sister arrived posthaste. Wordlessly Faith handed Harriet the parchment. The other woman blushed furiously, then carefully broke the seal.

"It's from Julian," she announced breathlessly.

Griffin inhaled sharply. "We assumed that, Harriet. What does he say?"

There was no response. Griffin reached out and gave his sister a gentle shake. "What does he say?"

"He is coming home," she whispered in amazement. Harriet raised her chin and broke into a wide, dazzling smile. "Julian is returning to England. He should be here within the month."

"That is very good news," Faith said sincerely. "We shall all look forward to meeting him. And planning your wedding."

"My wedding." Harriet turned startled eyes toward Faith. Her voice became soft, almost shy. "Do you think we could have it here?"

"This is your home. We would be delighted to host your wedding. Isn't that right, Griffin?"

"Naturally." The viscount smiled at his sister. "Do you think I would be so foolish as to pass up an opportunity to give you away, Harriet?"

They all laughed. Then, without warning, Harriet threw herself forward and wrapped her arms so tightly around Griffin's neck she nearly choked him. "Thank you," she whispered.

He hugged her. "All I really want is for you to be happy—as happy as I am."

"I shall try." Harriet sniffed loudly. "There is so much to do. I must write back to Julian at once. He has included his new town address." She stepped out of her brother's embrace, lifted her head, straightened her shoulders, and marched toward the house.

"Well, it looks as though we are finally going to meet the elusive Mr. Wingate," Griffin mused. "I just hope I can keep a civil tongue in my head. I have not been overly impressed with how—"

Griffin abruptly ceased talking and knelt beside his wife. "My God, Faith, is everything all right? You look shocked. Are you in pain? Is it the baby?"

The sheer panic in Griffin's voice jolted Faith out of her stupor. "No, nothing is wrong with me. I'm fine." She held out the single sheet of parchment she had just finished reading. " 'Tis Merry."

Griffin snatched the letter from Faith's nerveless fingers and quickly scanned the contents. He smiled briefly. No wonder his wife was acting so oddly.

"Now I understand why you quickly lost the bloom of color in your cheeks. This is most shocking news." Griffin whistled loudly. "Our dear Lady Meredith has gotten herself married. Rather suddenly, I would say. I cannot help but wonder at the reason for such haste."

"Do you know him?" Faith asked, still trying to take it all in. Merry a wife! When she had always protested so vehemently against matrimony. It did not seem possible.

"I've never met the groom, but I am well aware of his reputation." Griffin took a deep breath. "He is certainly not the type of person I would expect her to choose."

"I never thought she would choose any man." Faith rubbed her temples vigorously. "We have received quite a parcel of news this afternoon. You must remind me never to read the mail while I am standing up or else I might injure my head as I fall into a dead faint."

Griffin continued to read the letter. "Merry has sent us her husband's London address and hopes we shall come to call on them when we arrive in town. I suppose she assumes we will be accompanying Elizabeth when she makes her coming-out this season."

"I was going to write to Merry at the end of the week and explain why we will be staying at home," Faith proclaimed with an ironic twist in her voice. "My heavens, it certainly promises to be a diverting social whirl this year. I'm almost sorry we are going to miss all the excitement."

"Don't fret, my love. There will be other seasons." With a wicked gleam in his eye the viscount reached out and lightly caressed the slight roundness of her stomach. "We have far more important matters keeping us at home."

Faith smiled. She leaned forward and gave him a warm, tender kiss. "Aren't we the clever pair?"

Griffin's arms encircled her tightly. She could feel his chest rumble as he laughed with pure joy. "Yes, we are, my love. And so very lucky, too."

ABOUT THE AUTHOR

Adrienne Basso lives with her family in New Jersey. She is the author of three Zebra historical romances and is currently working on Lady Meredith's story, *To Protect an Heiress,* which will be published in July 2002. Adrienne loves to hear from readers, and you may write to her c/o Zebra Books. Please include a self-addressed stamped envelope if you wish a response.

BOOK YOUR PLACE ON OUR WEBSITE AND MAKE THE READING CONNECTION!

We've created a customized website just for our very special readers, where you can get the inside scoop on everything that's going on with Zebra, Pinnacle and Kensington books.

When you come online, you'll have the exciting opportunity to:

- View covers of upcoming books
- Read sample chapters
- Learn about our future publishing schedule (listed by publication month *and author*)
- Find out when your favorite authors will be visiting a city near you
- Search for and order backlist books from our online catalog
- Check out author bios and background information
- Send e-mail to your favorite authors
- Meet the Kensington staff online
- Join us in weekly chats with authors, readers and other guests
- Get writing guidelines
- AND MUCH MORE!

Visit our website at http://www.zebrabooks.com